Review

Stefan Vučak presents a fascinating look at racism, discrimination and fear of 'normals' in a fresh way, which could not have arrived on the market at a better time than now. Part science fiction, part political drama, and part cultural observation, Vučak has conceptualized some truly human attitudes and ideas, and created a fascinating narrative that pops like a pressure valve as it unfurls. *Lifeliners* is an apt and excellent work, which I would highly recommend to readers of all types.

Readers' Favorite

Wow, the details in this book are simply superb! Literally from page one of the story you are drawn in by the excellent attention to detail. I would recommend this book; it was a page turner from start to finish. There are not many books that I can see myself reading multiple times, but *Lifeliners* is definitely one of them.

Literary Titan

Books by Stefan Vučak

General Fiction:
Cry of Eagles
All the Evils
Towers of Darkness
Strike for Honor
Proportional Response
Legitimate Power
Autumn Leaves
All My Sunsets
F/X-26
28th Amendment
Night Sirens
Broken Rose

Shadow Gods Saga:
In the Shadow of Death
Against the Gods of Shadow
A Whisper from Shadow
Shadow Masters
Immortal in Shadow
With Shadow and Thunder
Through the Valley of Shadow
Guardians of Shadow

Science Fiction:
Fulfillment
Lifeliners

Non-Fiction:
Writing Tips for Authors

Contact at:
www.stefanvucak.com

LIFELINERS

By

Stefan Vučak

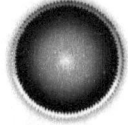

Stefan Vučak ©2018
ISBN-10: 0-9942923-4-1
ISBN-13: 978-0-9942923-4-6

Dedication

To Gloria ... with a life full of promise

Acknowledgments

The term 'dobers' used in memory of John Brunner, 1934-1995, in *The Shockwave Rider*.

Additional proofreading by Charlotte Raby.
https://charlotteraby.wordpress.com/

Cover art by Laura Shinn.
http://laurashinn.yolasite.com

Melbourne Center

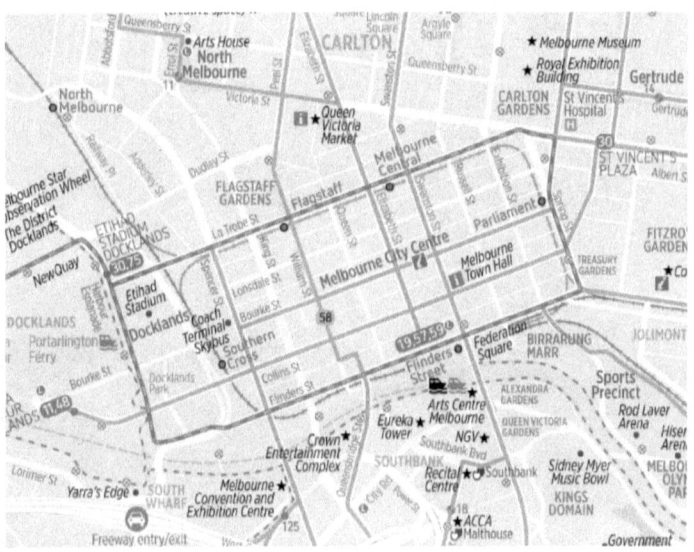

Chapter One

Dawn burst over Melbourne's jagged skyline, bathing the city's towers with gauzy golden light, and the stars fled. Lit from within, the cluster of skyscrapers made an enchanting contrast against the strips of low painted clouds. Cars meandered along St. Kilda Road, mostly heading toward the city, their red taillights sharp and the noise of engines a muffled hum. Overhead, Nash could see several skycars making their way to landing pads built on roofs of taller buildings.

He took two deep breaths to steady himself after running up the steps to the top landing of the Shrine of Remembrance, the huge stone war memorial with its towering colonnades looming before him. He turned and gazed at the city's sprawl spread before him. This early the air still had a crisp bite and his skin tingled after a brisk four-kilometer run through the Kings Domain Park. Everything felt fresh and new. Colors were bright and hard, and sounds seemed to carry forever. Later, as the sun burned its way through a layer of shredded clouds, the air would become heavy and hot, another typical summer's day.

Nash preferred to do his running in the morning before the city fully wakened, before the streets filled with indifferent, self-absorbed pedestrians oblivious to those around them, hurrying to reach their particular destination. Rivers of people clogging the city's arteries, life flowing endlessly. He often speculated on the purpose of it all, and was still to find a satisfactory answer. It could not be simply a blind march to merely further procreation, although it sometimes seemed that way.

A dark change was sweeping the world and he feared that he and others like him might not survive it. Humans as a species would not die easily.

Standing there, gazing at the city stirring from slumber, he wondered if the people down there really knew what was happening around them, or even cared? He suspected that most did not, and wouldn't, until prodded into action, turned into a mindless tide in a futile attempt to stem the change whose ripples were already being felt. He had not felt them personally, but riots, protests, and demands for action were becoming more frequent and vehement, leaving the silent majority puzzled and concerned, uncertain of a future they did not fully understand, but feared it nonetheless. That uncertainty generated dread, something easily fanned into flaming waves of retaliation, since no one knew any alternatives, especially the government. What action they had already taken was disturbing enough.

Seeing the painted clouds, the flowing red and orange streamers could be portents of things to come.

But it did not have to be.

He shook his head to dispel the angels of death. Tomorrow was a blank page still to be written…perhaps in blood.

Sweaty T-shirt cool against his skin, he exhaled softly, then ambled down the steps to the broad walkway that lead to the memorial, past the large metal bowl holding the eternal flame, and picked up his pace as he made his way across the grassed slope toward the sidewalk. The pervading stink of an occasional petrol engine exhaust made him wrinkle his nose with distaste. Two trams clanged their bells as they passed each other. A tall girl dressed in navy shorts and a blue singlet, long ponytail swaying from side to side, nodded to him in passing, then she was gone, leaving a trace of lavender in the air, her padded footfalls fading behind him.

He had seen her a number of times and pondered who she was, what she did to fill her life. Did she also question what it was all about, the strife, the struggle, the emptiness, the shallow texture of living that swept everything before it in a singular pursuit to survive, to continue? Perhaps she did, although it was unlikely he would ever find out, short of stopping her and asking.

The image made him smile.

What if he did stop her and asked? She would probably think he was nuts, hitting on her, and she could be right.

He crossed the busy Domain Road and slowed to a walk as he approached Bromby Street and his apartment block. Cleared through a link with his Personal Identification Device, the entrance lock clicked and he waited for the heavy glass panels to slide back. The security guard at his round console station gave him a brief wave and returned to reading his book. As Nash walked toward the elevators, he heard a car whisper by. These days, in cities at least, most were electric, which over the last six years had largely removed the perpetual blanket of brown smog that used to cover them. There were still plenty of petrol guzzlers around, but increased registration charges and insurance premiums were seeing them slowly weeded out. Much to the lament and angst of their owners.

After a shower, he climbed into a business suit and knotted his tie. Tuesday mornings were always hectic, reserved for Telstra sob sessions where he got to hear how his project managers were running things. Yesterday, he held an in-depth recap with his PMs of all work done to date. Fair was fair. On Fridays, Telstra held status dissections with PMs from both sides. As an IBM program manager, he didn't have to attend, and did not. He had enough progress meetings already.

He thought about dropping into his office before going to Telstra and decided against it. Snoden would probably waylay him in the corridor—the man was always there by 7:30, a high-pressure achiever type—and Nash did not want to have a mini status session with the IBM program director, especially since a formal management one would be held tomorrow anyway. He *could* have done the Telstra meeting over the holoview wall virtual presence link in the comfort of his apartment, but some things required personal attendance. Besides, a clear, warm morning deserved appreciation from the outside.

He told Sally to play a selection of Brahms' chamber melodies, and the housekeeping computer flooded the apartment with full surround music. The percolator finished its bubbling and he fixed himself some coffee. Breakfast usually light, but filling—mixed vegetable juice and homemade muesli with dried fruit, having bought the ingredients at the renovated Victoria Market, the stuff from supermarkets still containing a lot of sugar and salt. After years of pressure from the Australian Medical Association, the Food & Nutrition lobby and other organizations, Canberra finally imposed a sugar tax, refusing to bow to the powerful sugar industry group.

He also had a side dish of sliced tomato and capsicum, red or green. He alternated. This morning, he figured a shot of NutriBullet juice would be enough. Getting things sorted out around the table, he told Sally to switch on the ABC news channel. Humming to himself, he occasionally glanced at the holoview wall display showing the usual news staple: shootings, car wrecks—they still allowed manually controlled vehicles on the road despite growing protests—a hurricane building off Queensland, and latest political antics, local and international. Those were always good for a chuckle or two. He sometimes wondered why he bothered to watch, but like a junkie, he could not turn away from his morning news fix. Besides, he liked to eavesdrop on the more morbid side of human behavior. What did that say about him? Better not go there, he told himself.

He shook his head and sighed. Instead of shedding pheromones of gloom, he should be perky and elated, having secured another date with Cariana—a proper date. A Latin derivative for *beloved*, he could not think of a more perfect name. It was also a constellation in the southern sky. Fitting, he thought.

Tonight, they would be dining at the exclusive Box Seafood restaurant in Collins Street. An expensive outing, but worth it to glow in her sunny disposition and enjoy lively conversation. This would be their first night-out date and he pictured her corn colored hair piled high or left to flow across one shoulder. Her oval face appeared before him: large almond eyes, small mouth and pert nose, high cheekbones, she was enchanting. Nash liked her uninhibited personality ready to challenge established dogma and what she termed his cube opinions. When she laughed, she showed even teeth and a dimpled left cheek. A devastating woman and he willingly placed himself in striking range of her charms. Living alone had its good points, but there were also enough reasons for him to want a permanent companion and partner. A conundrum he hoped she would help him resolve, which implied that he *wanted* a major change in his life. Was he ready for another relationship? However, knowing what Cariana wanted, and women in general a game of contradictions.

She held a PhD in genetics and worked at The Alfred Hospital on a cooperative project with the CSIRO. She told him—must have been on their first lunch date—that she had an apartment in St. Kilda Road and did not socialize much, her research keeping her busy. He could relate to that. His own work often kept him chained to a desk for long hours. From their first encounter, Nash sensed a mutual attraction, but he still knew very little about her as a person. She had a page on Wikipedia, but apart from listing her academic record, publications, and professional credits, she was somewhat of a mystery, one he intended to resolve. Still, at twenty-eight, she had a broad footprint of achievements.

They met two weeks ago, also a Tuesday, at Southbank's La Asiago, an eatery Nash favored, being close to the IBM building. He came out of a tough meeting with his six project managers and needed to stretch his legs and get some fresh air. Always the same thing: budgets, resources, and schedules. He didn't have much sympathy for any of his people. After all, they were the ones who set up their program of work, including project estimates and KPIs, admittedly after some hard negotiation with Telstra and strategic massaging by Nash. They would just have to tough it out, but he made it clear he would not swallow costs or schedule overruns, unless caused by changes in client requirements. In that case, he told them to get a signed contract variation.

Clients everywhere loved to make changes to signed-off requirements, hoping IBM would absorb costs and schedule creeps with a veiled promise of future business, and Telstra were experts at this game. As far as Nash was concerned, any change regardless how innocently small affected a project. A few little things could and were regularly absorbed, but there were limits and all had to be properly costed and documented. A friendly business-based client relationship generated future revenues, not by taking on add-on freebies that might have unforeseen consequences. He fired one of his PMs before the others realized he wasn't fooling. Nash would be the one having to explain to IBM management why his program of work had blown out, which would cut into the corporate profit margin. He made sure his PMs never put him into that position. That made him a hardnosed bastard, but also earned him rueful admiration from IBM and Telstra.

He didn't push his project managers, provided they did their job. When he wore his business hat, everything they did counted. He admonished in private and fought with management for whatever they needed. After work, they shared an occasional beer or a glass of wine, but even then, he was the program manager, not a friend or drinking buddy. He wanted to be their friend, but if he crossed that line, he could no longer remain their boss.

Coffee cup in hand, memories chased each other as he remembered vividly walking out of the IBM building into a hot, but not oppressively so, day. A cooling breeze came off the Yarra River as he strode along the riverside promenade filled with restaurants and shops and people enjoying their lunch break. An occasional jogger—some girls wore very little, which only added to the interesting scenery—weaved through the throng. He could never figure out, and no one was able to explain to him, why girls could wear skimpy shorts, while guys had to saddle themselves with knee-length jobs. One of life's inexplicable fashion mysteries.

A tourist barge left a frothy trail in its wake as it made its way downriver toward the harbor. Kayaks and multi-scull boats played the brown waters. The Yarra still came in for its share of low jokes about being a sewer. Even though it looked dirty, it was quite clean and had a healthy ecology. Across the river, the city's jagged skyline reached into a hard, clear blue sky. A Virgin Air skycar drifted almost silently toward a landing pad next to the Aquarium. The airspace above the city full of them. He looked up, feeling good soaking in the UVs.

He spotted her sitting alone at a small square table in the open part of La Asiago along the promenade and the world faded around him. Dressed in cream slacks and gray business jacket, flaxen hair spilling across her left shoulder, time stopped and he stared at this captivating woman alone in her shell, surrounded by chattering people, yet unreachable. He traced the lines of her delicate face, the fall of her hair, and a small frown creasing her forehead that made her perfect.

You don't want to become involved again, old son!

Probably not, but he could not see any harm in an interesting lunchtime diversion compared to the alternative of a lonely bench beside the river, warm sunshine notwithstanding. It might do him good to seek out some distracting company and wash out the unpleasant taste of his IBM meeting.

With the exterior section of the restaurant packed and no empty seats, he took a deep breath and weaved between the tables toward her. If she didn't like his approach, she could always tell him to buzz off. It had happened before. Some women didn't want to be bothered. Peace.

"I don't mean to intrude, but you seem to have the only spare seat. May I?"

She glanced around, gave him an appraising look with eyes that cut and probed, and finally nodded.

"There are tables inside," she said softly, her clear voice sending an unexpected tingle down his spine. What the hell was going on? He reminded himself that this was only lunch—diverting as it might be—not a romantic encounter.

"Yes, but it's not the same thing, and it's too cold and

7

crowded in there," he declared as he pulled back a chair.

Her eyebrows rose. "You prefer your own company?"

"Depends on the company," he said and eased himself down. "I never take chances I don't have to."

"You're taking a chance now, aren't you?"

"Sometimes you have to." He glanced at two David Jones store shopping bags beside her, and she smiled.

"I took advantage of a nice day to pick up a few things before returning to The Alfred," she explained.

"You're a doctor?"

The babble of voices around them created a shield of intimacy and a sense that time had stopped. Even the crowd strolling along the promenade faded from his view.

"Geneticist."

"Fascinating line of work," he said, genuinely interested.

When the waiter arrived, he ordered spiced ravioli and gnocchi and half a bottle of red Chianti. Shortly afterward, her spaghetti marinara arrived. Looking at her speculatively, he lifted the bottle. She frowned and brushed back a stray lock of golden hair.

"Is this your standard gambit when picking up women?"

She had slim, delicate fingers with a subdued red nail polish that complemented without being gaudy. He imagined fondling those hands, running his fingers over her smooth skin. Could he be getting infatuated with a woman he just met? No, this was merely an interesting meeting with someone attractive and sophisticated. Still, she possessed a magnetism he could feel and his soul reached out to her, warning bells clanging in his head. He clamped a lid on them, prepared to enjoy this moment.

"I don't do casual pickups."

She inclined her head in disbelief. "And I am…"

"A fortuitous and pleasant accident. No spare tables, remember? Besides, you looked so lonely…"

She lifted a finger. "Don't push it."

He grinned at her. "A peace offering, then. A glass of wine?"

"I shouldn't—"

"It's a very light Italian red. Won't do anything to spoil your day."

She bit her lower lip, then slid her glass toward him. "Only a little."

"Great."

He poured both of them half a glass. She lowered her fork and took a cautious sip. Her eyebrows arched and she nodded.

"Interesting flavor."

"Glad you like it. By the way, I'm Nash Bannon."

"Cariana Lambert, and I still think this is a pickup routine."

Nash winced. "Now I'm hurt. I really—"

The waiter brought a bowl of steaming ravioli and gnocchi, cutting off whatever he was about to say. Nash thanked him, picked up his fork, stabbed one of the gnocchi and popped it into his mouth. It was nice and chewy the way he liked it and he relished the tangy mushroom sauce.

Cariana watched him with an amused expression. "That won't do much for your waistline," she remarked dryly.

"It's my carbs day," he explained between bites. "I usually have a mixed salad and fruit juice, but that's not always enough to keep me fueled and beat off the sharks at work."

She glanced at her bowl. "I know what you mean. Seeing you relishing your gnocchi eases my own guilt for being weak." She dabbed her lips with a napkin and took another sip of wine. "And what fills your days, Mr. Bannon?"

"Nash. I do systems integration for IBM."

"Weren't they taken over by Facebook?"

"They certainly were. The IBM culture was getting stale and needed an infusion of new methodology and ideas. I have doubts that it worked, but they run some cutting-edge projects."

"And what are you working on right now?"

"I'm currently managing a major Telstra network program where everybody is giving me a hard time."

"Poor you."

"Your sympathy is appreciated."

She turned serious. "I did not mean to tease you, and I do understand, finding myself in a similar position. Doing research would be fun if it weren't for the oversight protocols, although necessary." She finished the last of her marinara and gathered her bags. "Thank you for the wine…Nash."

Dismayed to see her about to leave, his mind raced. He could not let it end like this. "I enjoyed meeting you and I would enjoy it even more if we could do this again, taking more time."

What the hell made him say that! This was supposed to be a simple lunch without sticky romantic overtones.

She stood and laughed. "Are you always this forthright?"

"I don't go out much, and meeting someone like you is rare," he said quickly and rose, figuring his pickup line could use some updating. "What do you say?"

Frowning prettily, her eyes searching for something and apparently finding it, she dug into her purse and held out a business card. With a nod, she made her way out and disappeared into the crowd ambling along the promenade, leaving behind her a fresh spring fragrance. Bemused, he sat down and studied the card, his gnocchi momentarily forgotten. Despite inner red flags, he found that he definitely wanted to see her again. If it led to something substantial, so be it. Going over her face in his mind, he picked up his fork and dug into the ravioli.

Except for one vivid time two years ago, and the memories still burned, he never had a serious relationship with a woman, the longest lasting three months. It began as a chance meeting, shallow with no expectations from either of them, which quickly progressed into something more serious. Open and vulnerable, he allowed himself to love her unreservedly…until that fateful night when they took her from him. Some of the light went out of his life then.

Sally…

Afterward, his job kept him consumed. Before that, university studies left little room for lasting encounters. At thirty-two, he had done well to be a senior program manager and strategic consultant groomed by IBM for higher things. They were a demanding taskmaster and rewarded top performance. The alternative was turning himself into another body shop contractor. Nash liked the organization's passion and megaprojects they handled, but disliked intensely the stifling procedures and endless reporting requirements that in his view only added unnecessary overheads. Overheads in cost, manpower and time—deadly for any project. One of the things he did to get himself noticed was streamline the lifecycle process in his program of work that eliminated what he saw as bureaucratic redundancy, which incidentally saved Telstra two-and-a-half million dollars and shaved the delivery schedule by nine months. He encountered a lot of opposition from older entrenched managers when he proposed to apply those changes across all programs, but a vigorous discussion with a visiting Senior VP for Software Solutions from New York saw his procedures implemented across IBM worldwide and earned him promotion and a hefty bonus.

Professional success came at a price. He lacked personal fulfillment, someone to share his life with, be his companion and confidant. Someone with whom he could live out his hopes and dreams and overcome disappointments. He wondered if Cariana could be that someone. Could he actually share *everything* with her? Being what he was, could he do that with anyone?

Cariana…

As the news clips washed over him, he took an occasional sip of juice and his thoughts drifted to having something more substantial than a smoothie, but his body did not crave being stuffed with bacon and eggs. Even as children, he and his twin brother Mark never ate much red meat, although he did like fatty foods, preferring vegetables and fruit, shunning takeaway snacks, which set them apart from other kids and got them talked about amid snickers. These days, Nash didn't see Mark all that much, his brother's work keeping him busy in Canberra. They kept in touch with emails and cellphone/holoview calls, and Mark visited a few times, but Nash missed the sober talks they used to have while studying at Melbourne University.

His sister Natalie, three years younger, had a precocious six-year-old daughter who wound both uncles around her little finger with giggling ease. Adriana a demanding handful, but when Sandra and Kevin suddenly came along as a boy/girl package, she had to adjust, no longer the focus of the family. From what Nash could tell when he visited their tastefully renovated North Melbourne terrace house, they were a happy bunch, and Shaun Mills an attentive husband.

Shaun had a quiet, strong-willed personality and a good listener when they talked. An IT manager at the National Australia Bank, his revelations into the inner workings of international banking—his own area of expertise—made Nash sit up and blink. Shaun often said that all the major banks wanted to concentrate their business on the corporate sector. That's where the money lay. Retail business was a hindrance, having to maintain branch networks to support small business and mom and dad customers. They had to put up with it, though, as they could not get around government legislation.

Nat could eat anything and burned it off without any problems, much to the dismay and envy of her friends struggling with waistlines, and she had never taken a shine to meat either. Even now, married, she kept her fine, trim figure. Nash and Mark were also slim, both 181cm, muscular without being bulgy, light brown hair, black eyes, and always full of energy. The whole Bannon brood had a happy and carefree childhood, but when the boys turned thirteen, something happened that shattered their carefree, innocent lives. A secret only the boys and their parents knew. A secret he fervently could not reveal to anyone, one that had grown into a terrible, weary burden.

Glass of juice halfway to his mouth, he paused and stared at the holoview.

"Last night, Senator Holt Ryner, leader of the Australian Greens, with support of all Senate crossbench members, vowed to block legislation by the

federal government to introduce its controversial Personal Identification De-
vice tracking feature, which according to Ryner is designed to further erode
individual freedoms under the tired old argument to broaden protection and
safety for all citizens, but in reality is a blatant violation of human rights
and would only serve to promote unwarranted monitoring of the population
at large. The opposition leader, Macey Gardner, remains noncommittal, say-
ing the Labor Party will make its decision once it sees the legislation. Intro-
duction of a tracking feature does have merit, he claims, provided individuals
are able to deactivate the function at will. Governments do not have a man-
date to monitor an individual's movements and activities in the name of na-
tional security. Law enforcement agencies already had adequate mechanisms
to safeguard people, he added."

Nash frowned. The coverage troubled him on several fronts.
Not the enhanced PID tracking function *per se*, but its application
to monitor lifeliners, which he suspected was its real purpose. If
the authorities wanted to find someone, they can track a person's
smartphone even when switched off, and *everybody* carried a cell.
Admittedly, that only provided location of the phone, but most
of the time, it's a safe bet that locating the cell will also locate the
person carrying it. However, tracking a person's PID would be a
sure thing every time, and would reveal much more than merely
his location. Besides, there were enough face recognition cameras
plastered all over the place, the images used by authorities to
build vast surveillance databases. Another public safety measure.

The announcement may have come from the Liberal Party,
but everybody knew their far-right Australian Conservatives partner engineered the policy. It takes eighty-two seats in the federal
parliament's 160-seat Lower House to form a one-seat majority
government. The government of the day having to provide the
Speaker of the House who usually does not vote unless there is a
tie. At the 2030 election, not able to form government in their
own right even with the support of their traditional allies, the
Liberal National Party—who absorbed the Nationals and Country Liberals parties years back—the Coalition was six seats short
and left with a bitter-sweet choice: embrace the Conservatives or

sit on the opposition benches. They figured sleeping with the enemy they knew was better than allowing the Labor Party to rule, but that pragmatic decision came at a steep price. Although a strong leader, the Prime Minister had hamstrung herself with single-issue interests of her coalition partners who sidetracked much of the government's legislative agenda. The Labor Party cynically announced that they would never stoop so low as to embrace the crossbench members or the Conservatives' ten seats for the chance to govern. The pragmatic federal parliamentary wing might entertain the idea, but the Labor National Executive would run them out of the party first.

The upcoming general election will prove interesting on many fronts.

To Nash, it did not matter which party held government. The declaration to track PIDs nothing less than another step in the escalating war against lifeliners, despite a major UN statement and numerous court rulings in many countries that guaranteed their rights.

In March 2027—it took three years for them to make the announcement—the full session of the UN General Assembly finally reaffirmed that Article 2 of The Universal Declaration of Human Rights adopted in 1948 applied with equal force to lifeliners, which stated, *'Everyone is entitled to all the rights and freedoms set forth in this Declaration, without distinction of any kind, such as race, color, sex, language, religion, political or other opinion, national or social origin, property, birth or other status'.*

Unfortunately, the announcement had little effect on world opinion from an organization that had for a long time lost much of its credibility as a global policeman, the main reason for creating it. Tired of propping it up with more than a quarter of its annual budget, meaningful action too often blocked by a veto from one of the permanent Security Council members, in 2022 the U.S. dropped its contribution to a paltry five billion, which it maintained ever since. This left the bureaucratic rump with humanitarian, health, and economic programs, and the Security

Council a gentleman's club, although everybody pretended it still had relevance.

Another problem, many governments questioned the validity of the Declaration, asserting that lifeliners were not human, notwithstanding overwhelming scientific evidence to the contrary, which opened the door to witch hunts, vigilante activists, and general unrest, with people not really comprehending what went on, but not liking the growing social dislocation. When the U.S., seen as a bastion of freedom and human rights, opened internment camps and set up secret laboratories to conduct experiments on lifeliners, it was not hard to understand why the more extreme regimes carried out what amounted to open pogroms. Muslim radicals labeled them agents of Satan, and the Vatican continued to vacillate, still to release a positional papal bull, which only fueled confusion among the faithful. Everybody else pretended the problem did not even exist, hoping to wake tomorrow to a saner world.

For Nash, the problem was personal and manifestly real. Since their emergence, he wondered whether lifeliners had achieved any meaningful recognition and acceptance under laws seldom enforced. Current events pointed to a gloomy future.

"Politicians! Assholes, all of them," he muttered. "Rats!"

"Voters savaged Labor for its lack of a coherent policy on lifeliners, the latest Morgan Poll showing the Opposition slipping an additional three points behind the Liberal-led coalition, 32 to 48. Some in the Labor Caucus are questioning Mr. Gardner's leadership, troubled by this slip in confidence and the effect it could have on the October election.

"The Prime Minister, Atarah Readman, dismissed concerns raised by Senator Ryner, saying that provision of a tracking function is merely a by-product of an integrated PID system already in place as outlined by Neil Travers, Minister for the Department of Human Services, and has nothing to do with invading personal privacy, access subject to strict legislation. Asked if the federal government recognized lifeliners having the same rights and privileges as ordinary citizens, the Prime Minister failed to provide a coherent

response, saying that emergence of lifeliners represented a major social challenge facing governments around the world, and Australia needed to deal with the issue responsibly for the welfare of all its citizens, which suggests that the Coalition government, particularly its Australian Conservatives partner, does not consider lifeliners to be citizens, something the Prime Minister nimbly sidestepped.

"Much to public consternation, the police released without charge several People First Party far-right extremists arrested during a march in Canberra last Sunday where they demanded that all lifeliners be interned permanently, sterilized and their citizenship revoked. The march coincided with picketing of the Lifeliner Party headquarters in Carlton Place, Melbourne, and the firebombing of Sydney's North Shore Lifeliner Help Center. Outraged civil liberty groups are urging the federal Director of Public Prosecutions to intervene and indict the perpetrators.

"In Berlin, a twenty-two-year-old man, allegedly a lifeliner, was badly beaten by three neo-Nazis as he walked out of a popular nightclub. Police arrested the assailants and the victim taken to a hospital with non-life-threatening injuries."

Nash ground his teeth in disgust, alarmed at the growing trend of lifeliner persecutions and apparent unwillingness by politicians of all persuasions to address the matter. Forceful sterilization already used by some totalitarian regimes and, according to rumors, even in the United States and Europe. The suggestion that Australia should adopt such a vile practice as a solution, he found particularly disturbing. Didn't governments realize that simply entertaining this option could tear democracies apart? After an uneasy truce over the last five years, civil unrest was growing, and extremists were becoming more vocal, emboldened by lack of firm action from lawmakers and the courts. Instead of addressing the lifeliner issue in a meaningful way, the government appeared more interested in milking the politics angle.

Last Wednesday night, a gang of four youths attacked a seventeen-year-old teenager outside the Flinders Street train station, claiming he was a lifeliner. The kid lost an eye, suffered a broken arm and numerous lacerations. By the time the dobers arrived, the youths had fled…and nobody saw a thing. The irony? Tests, primitive as they were, showed the kid wasn't even a lifeliner. Disturbingly, such incidents were becoming more common everywhere. Reaction to such attacks generated a natural and predictable response. Lifeliner teenagers tended to group for mutual protection, which inevitably led to clashes and vandalism, creating a vicious cycle that defied sanity.

New Zealanders seemed to have escaped this cancerous madness, accepting lifeliners without fear or prejudice. When lifeliners emerged, they were simply another group in the multicultural mix. Sociologists talked learnedly about seamless integration of indigenous Maori and Asians into the social fabric, but a clear explanation why the country remained so stable eluded them. If their cousins across the Tasman could make the adjustment without violence, Nash wondered why Aussies, who had an even more diverse population mix, couldn't do the same. The Kiwis were simply different, he decided.

"Last night, the Senate failed to pass the controversial Superannuation amendment bill for the second time, giving the government a double dissolution trigger for an early election. Given the current polling numbers, it is doubtful the Prime Minister would risk facing the voters before she had to. The bill is intended to change how the Consumer Price Index is calculated, which would have helped recipients of government benefits, including pensioners. Commentators criticized Labor's failure to support a worthwhile social initiative.

"In partnership with Blue Origin, an aerospace company set up by Jeff Bezos, chairman of Amazon, SpaceX successfully launched a third unmanned supply mission from their Texas Boca Chica facility aimed at the northern rim of Peary crater, close to the Lunar north pole. SpaceX claims that its manned mission in August will finally establish a semi-permanent Moon base. Elon Musk, the founder of Space Exploration Technologies Corp. stated that private industry can operate profitably in space without reliance on a bureaucracy-hampered government."

That's what he should do…emigrate to the Moon, Nash told himself.

"Sally…"

"Yes, Nash?" the house computer queried in pleasant contralto.

"Switch off…one a moment."

"Beijing announced the final phase of its withdrawal from the Democratic People's Republic of Korea, to be completed by June this year after its occupation of the rogue state in 2020 following the U.S. bombing of the Mansundae Assembly Hall in Pyongyang, which killed Kim Jong-un and most of the Supreme People's Assembly, effectively neutralizing the nuclear threat to the region and the free world. The attack ordered by a former president after North Korea launched an advanced ballistic missile armed with a thermonuclear warhead that detonated at an altitude of 200 kilometers off the Oregon coast. The White House Press Secretary said that President Elliott Mackay welcomed the announcement and looked forward to the upcoming meeting with the Chinese president Cheng Hung in May, to discuss normalization of the Korean peninsula and a common approach to resolve the lifeliner problem. You can see a special ABC Four Corners *coverage of events leading to the U.S. strike and analysis of its impact next Monday at 8:30 pm.*

"You are watching ABC Breakfast *on Tuesday, January 20, 2032. Recapping our other headlines…Prime Minister Atarah Readman continues to push for a referendum to extend the federal term for both Houses to a fixed four years—"*

Not interested in other headlines, he told Sally to kill the holoview, took the glass carafe of coffee to the balcony table and pulled back a wooden chair. South Korea won't mind seeing the Chinese withdraw from the peninsula, and neither will the North Koreans. The United States had left only a token force in ROK after a popular pullout in 2026, which freed badly needed billions to repair a fractured U.S. deficit. The pullout didn't catch anyone by surprise, especially when in 2023 the U.S. reduced its NATO role to observer status, part of a layered policy to untangle itself from its role as the global policeman whom nobody wanted. Understandably, the Europeans were not overly impressed, having to shoulder their own defense budget for a change, which left American voters unmoved. It takes troops to hold conquered ground, but Russia wasn't the red menace of old. Awash with natural resources, economy growing steadily, they did not have a tactical or strategic reason to contemplate invading NATO countries, particularly after Turkey pulled out of the alliance in 2021 and aligned itself with Russia, which gave it unrestricted access into the Mediterranean.

Nash gazed absently at the broad St. Kilda Road thoroughfare three floors down and sipped the fragrant brew, not paying any real attention to the building traffic noise and pedestrians striding purposefully to catch a tram into the city and vanish in one of its towers, the day absorbed with work. Tomorrow, everyone would wearily repeat it all again. Endless days of seemingly endless labor. It did not surprise him that many teenagers found the prospect of such a life repellant. Repellant or not, that was the price society demanded for the benefits and privileges it delivered.

Delivered for some, he reminded himself.

Nevertheless, the social contract had many holes through which people could fall, and life on the edges cold and dark. Nash had never experienced the harsher side of life, although he had seen it revealed in the bleak, vacant faces of the unemployed sleeping in streets and alleyways, their jobs taken over by robots or AI systems. As automation increased in absence of political will to integrate technology with people's needs, a social dilemma seemingly beyond resolution.

What did *he* want out of the social contract? To leave something behind other than memories did not seem to be enough.

Breakfast done, he cleaned up, told Sally to set security, and walked briskly out of the apartment.

* * *

As the tram stopped, Nash pursed his lips when he saw the standing room only crush inside. The double doors sighed open and he stepped in, those inside reluctantly making way for new passengers clambering onboard.

"Stepped on," his PID vocalized to him as he grabbed a polished steel stanchion for support.

The doors closed and with a clang from the bell, the tram lurched forward. The passengers around him were the usual mix of office workers and students from RMIT and Melbourne University, most of them engaged in animated conversation or voice texting, absorbed in their smartphones that had become a virtual PID extension. A starched executive type in a dark gray pinstripe suit, having snagged a seat when he got on, stared intently at his tablet. Nash admired the man's misguided dedication. Didn't he have a life other than being an office slave?

Past the Arts Center, the tram slowed as it approached the Federation Square stop. It chimed its bell madly, probably at people scrambling across the tracks to catch one of the trams going up St. Kilda Road. The doors snapped open and there was a rush to get out, those outside barely containing their impatience to board. Nash could not understand this frenzied eagerness. There was always another tram, especially during the rush period, but getting this one seemed to constitute a small moral victory. There were a few empty seats now, but he preferred to stand.

A skinny little girl, perhaps twelve, short light brown hair almost blond, in rats, hopped in and grabbed the stanchion below his hand. She wore dirty green corduroy slacks torn at the knees, red sandals, and a stained violet short-sleeved shirt. Her round face might have been cute if it had a wash. She lifted her head and large, impenetrable dark eyes momentarily locked with his. Nash figured her to be a street kid, running away from whatever demons haunted her days, her trust in fellow human beings forever shattered. There weren't many of them around as dobers— that's what a lot of people called the cops these days—usually hauled them in on sight. By the look of her, she could use a good bath and several solid meals. Sad to see children in such a state, but it wasn't any of his business and he couldn't do anything for her.

The tram surged forward and clattered across tracks running

along Flinders Street. He felt a warm touch as the kid slid her hand up the stanchion, thinking nothing of it. He used the same technique when he jammed. He wasn't sure why they called it jamming and nobody had taken time to explain it to him. The idea was to touch a donor without being obvious and allow the life-force, as he called it, to seep into him. Feeling the energy suffuse through him akin to having pulsing waves of pins and needles ripple through his body, but extremely pleasurable. However, not so pleasurable that it could become an addiction. Simply something his body craved as any other food…almost. He usually did it in a crowded tram either in the morning or when going home, the press of people disguising the accidental touch.

He didn't *have* to feed regularly, as ordinary food sustained him adequately enough, but a period of strenuous physical or mental exertion, or when feeling unwell, which was very rare, triggered an impulse deep in his belly that demanded fulfillment. He often went for a week without jamming, but when the impulse came, he could not ignore it. As little boys, he and his brother Mark would ride the trams practicing the touch, learning how much to take before the donor became disturbed. Drain too much and the donor could faint, which would cause unwelcomed attention, something to be avoided at all costs. In extreme circumstances, a lifeliner could kill when all the life-force drained out of the victim, but he suspected this was only street talk, as he never heard of that happening. The idea was to take a little from two or three donors until he charged fully. His initial attempts were clumsy affairs that almost got him caught more than once. Nash remembered the scolding they received from their mother after one escapade, accompanied by stimulation with a large wooden spoon, when one of their donors fainted. Still, they played a good game. Those were happy, innocent times, and seemingly such a long time ago. Little innocence left in the world these days.

Could this little child just into puberty when the ability first manifested itself, be one? Nash felt a faint tingling sensation race up his arm. No, surely not. Masking his surprise, he glanced down, but the girl appeared to stare vacantly at shop fronts along Swanston Street without realizing whom she touched. That recognition takes time and practice to develop. He allowed her to feed for a few more seconds, then pulled away his hand.

She was a lifeliner!

It would explain her bedraggled appearance. Like other runaways, she may have fled from home when her parents found out what she was and threatened to hand her over to the authorities as the law required. Regrettably, realizing they had a lifeliner child, some couples who initially chose to keep this hidden could not handle the daunting prospect of a lifetime of secrecy suddenly thrust on them. A curtain of secrecy from family, friends, and most importantly the government, which they could never break. The trauma left shattered lives in its wake, particularly for the child concerned who could not comprehend what was happening or why.

Nash knew intimately how it felt to be a lifeliner.

He remembered as though it were happening now, one evening after dinner, Dad talked to him and Mark about lifeliners. At fourteen, they were experiencing the numerous signs of puberty, and not sure how to deal with them, especially the hunger deep in their belly that occasionally overcame them. Expecting the usual embarrassing father/son talk about girls, Nash glanced at Mark, figuring how to save their father from making a fool of himself. They were familiar with the facts of life, but the facts of life Dad laid out left them sober and more than a little frightened. He knew his parents suspected for a long time that their boys were lifeliners, but their sister Natalie wasn't, which created yet another awkward problem. Nash recalled a set of medical tests two years earlier he and Mark had at a clinic in East Melbourne when they turned twelve. Afterward, Mom and Dad were very quiet for about a week, giving the boys an occasional odd look, but they never stopped caring for them. It wasn't until Dad's talk that they learned the reason for those tests, and their parents' wariness.

There he was, a boy of fourteen, his future bright, only to find the world to be a much darker and sinister place than he believed. Something they only saw in holoview news reports had suddenly become very real.

One thing Dad could not tell them why they had to jam. The drive clearly satisfied some unknown physiological need, but despite many learned papers on the subject, no one really knew or understood the need. When the urge came, he had a few days to give into it. Simple as that.

What Nash found infinitely comforting, his parents kept loving their odd boys as though nothing had changed, and never played favorites. They were breaking the law by not reporting them, but Dad was wise not to have done so.

For the little girl beside him, that appeared not have been the case. Could he help her in some way?

When the tram stopped at the Bourke Street pedestrian mall, he reached for the girl's wrist. An atavistic impulse, as he had no real idea what to do or say to her. He wanted to let her know that he was someone who knew and understood what she was going through. Her head jerked and she looked at him in astonishment, small mouth open, even teeth white against her smudged face, the expression immediately turning into panic.

"Hey! What's with you? Let go!"

Her reaction caused heads to turn. Someone bumped his shoulder on the way out and Nash lost his grip. The girl jerked back her hand, jumped out and disappeared into the crowd. Staring after her, he wondered who she was, knowing he would probably never see her again. A leaf fluttering in the wind.

He tried to figure out why he reached out to her, but a clear reason eluded him. He sighed, shook his head and tried to forget it, knowing he couldn't.

The tram slowly clanked forward.

* * *

At seven o'clock sharp, Nash linked with the apartment's security system and waited. He hadn't done the dating thing in a while and wished the little butterflies of anxiety would stop fluttering about. After all, it is not as though this was their *first* date! Still, in a way it was. They were going out, which had not happened before. The other times they met were merely lunchtime encounters. Diverting, but not intimate, and he desperately sought to make a good impression. If this evening turned into a flop, it would be strike one and out. Something about her captivated him, stirred feelings he had not experienced for some time…since Sally. Feelings deeper than mere physical attraction.

After two years, time to put the past behind him.

He heard muffled footsteps and exhaled fully as the lock clicked. Cariana stood there; hair piled high, dense violet dress hugging her knees, shoulders bare, black pumps adorning shapely legs. She smiled faintly at his goggling expression. Her red lips glowed and a touch of blue shadow accentuated her dark eyes, complemented by rose pearl earrings and matching necklace.

She tilted her head slightly. "I expect to be admired, but you're ogling, Mr. Bannon."

He grinned broadly and spread his hands. "I couldn't help it. You look lovely."

"Thank you. You don't look bad yourself."

Wearing a tailored cream silk shirt open at the collar, navy dark worsted slacks, and Gucci loafers, he thought himself presentable. He liked wearing casual gear, but it had to be elegant.

"It'll do. Shall we?"

She stepped out, closed the door behind her, and they made their way to the elevator in thoughtful silence. Very conscious of her standing beside him, Nash linked his PID with the elevator and waited. After a minute, a soft *ting* and the polished steel double doors opened. He extended his arm and waited for her to get in.

"This apartment…nice location," he remarked as the elevator dropped.

"It's within easy walking distance from The Alfred and close to the city by tram. When I need to stretch my legs or go for a run, Fawkner Park is right behind me. I have a house in Woodend I use as my weekend retreat. I only live here during the week."

"How…I mean—"

"How can I afford two places? Actually, I can't. Not on my salary, and the body corporate fees are a drain."

"I dodged that one by setting myself up as a limited liability company," he told her. "As a freelance consultant, I work from home a lot, which makes most of my apartment costs tax deductible."

"Ah, wish I could do that."

"You can. Form a company or trust and sell your apartment to it, then lease the apartment."

She searched his face. "I can do that?"

"Definitely. I'd recommend getting professional advice, though. It's a tricky area of law as the Taxation Office may look on it as a tax dodge, which it is in a way."

"Mmm, something to consider, thanks. What about you? Didn't IBM mind you going freelance? I would have thought that would be a career stopper."

He shook his head. "Not really. Going freelance saves them a lot of administrative overheads. Being a contractor can be risky, but the kind of work I do gives me a measure of employment security and pays far better. You were telling me how you got your apartment."

"My father did well after the 2023 crash and got me the apartment as an investment. The house in Woodend is mortgaged. I should get rid of it, but it's quiet and allows me to readjust and clear my head."

"Funny you should say that, about the crash. In 2022, my old man also had a feeling from financial indicators he collected that things were about to melt down," Nash said.

The elevator sighed to a stop and the doors opened. He escorted Cariana through the thick glass main entrance and they were immediately assaulted by noises of evening traffic, clanging trams, and strolling pedestrians. Still high in the sky, the sun no longer burned, making the evening pleasantly warm. When they slid into the waiting fully autonomous driverless taxi, it surged away from the curb and eased into St. Kilda Road traffic. Under the toughened plastic bubble that served as roof and windows, they had an excellent view of their surrounds.

"He told everybody the world is due for a crunch. Not from the U.S. this time, but the highly leveraged Chinese shadow banking system. Nobody believed him. He sold his shares portfolio and two investment properties, much to everybody's consternation, and converted his retirement superannuation into cash."

"My dad did the same thing!" Cariana said brightly and flashed him a dimpled smile.

"Then it hit, two days after my birthday, would you believe it?"

It hit, all right—February 2023. Worried about their exposure, the shadow banks started calling in loans from overextended municipality and provincial leaders. Although the People's Bank of China held over five trillion dollars in currency reserves, it could not prevent the tsunami of foreclosures that swept through the economy, which sent the yuan plummeting and dragged down the world's stock exchanges with it.

Australia avoided a major economic shock when the Labor government of the day withdrew $160 billion from the Future Fund to pay down some of its debt liability, which in turn reduced the interest repayments burden and improved the budget fiscal position. Initially intended as a guarantee to meet superannuation payouts for federal public servants, the Future Fund expanded its role to support national infrastructure projects, health, education, and disability care, but with over $280 billion in reserves, the government did not see any significant economic or political fallout by making that withdrawal. Given the circumstances, a risk worth taking. In a rare moment of bipartisan cooperation, the Coalition opposition approved the move despite considerable negative commentary from chair pundits.

"I was only twenty-three at the time and working on my MBA—"

"Where did you do your bachelor's?"

"Melbourne University. Since IBM sponsored my MBA, I figured, why not go for it? It didn't harm my career. Anyway, as you know, the Australian property market was also due for another correction and took a major hit. A lot of apartments suddenly came on the market from owners who had leveraged themselves into bankruptcy, and property managers found themselves holding assets they could not offload. Cash rich, my old man raked it in, picking up prime stocks that had lost more than half their value.

"He bought a rundown place in South Yarra on the other side of Fawkner Park. Tore it down and built himself an ultra-modern double-story house. Probably worth a couple of million at least right now. He still had some spare cash and one evening, he shows up at my Prahran studio pad with a bulky envelope. You can imagine my surprise when I found myself owner of a two-bedroom St. Kilda Road apartment."

"Where?"

"Directly after Bromby Street at 401. At first, I didn't know what to do with all that space."

She grinned at him. "I'm sure you managed. It looks like we both had sharp parents."

The cab slowed as it neared the Arts Center bottleneck. Although heavy, the traffic had moved reasonably well. Harsh booming came from a car behind them, the driver oblivious to the crashing decibels.

Turning her head, Cariana looked at him. "A downtown rendezvous?"

"A seafood place in Collins Street."

Her eyes sparkled. "I love seafood."

"I thought you would."

"But…"

"I had an alternate in case you didn't."

She laughed, a merry, carefree sound, and her left cheek dimpled. "Do you plan everything?"

"Everything."

"Mmm."

"Don't worry. Meeting you wasn't planned. As I said, a fortuitous and pleasant accident."

She searched his face. "Your exact words."

"I have an eidetic memory, which is very useful, but it can be a nuisance."

"In what way? I imagine something like that would give you a tremendous advantage."

"It does and helped me get my MBA at twenty-four. Acquiring knowledge and information does not automatically translate into understanding."

"That's a useful insight," she said soberly. "Do you remember everything you see and experience?"

The cab stopped at the Swanston Street intersection and waited for the lights to change.

"Pretty much. I also have an excellent infantile memory. Clutter, mostly."

"Do you remember your dreams?"

"I do, and some are journeys into weird stuff. A mind bender's paradise. You must have a good memory yourself."

"Why do you say that?"

"Getting a PhD in a specialty like genetics requires a lot of information. You worked at the Monash Medical Center for two years after getting your degree and you spent the last two at The Alfred Hospital, which means you also got your PhD at twenty-four. That takes smarts."

"You've been checking up on me?" she demanded accusingly, but her eyes shone.

"Your Wikipedia page."

She snorted. "CSIRO did that despite my objections."

"It's an impressive record. If you don't mind me asking, how did you and CSIRO get together?"

"They're running a federal project on lifeliners."

A cold ripple ran down Nash's spine. Another clandestine eradication scheme? Seeing what's happening around the world, it's easy to be suspicious.

"I haven't heard. Interesting."

"My thesis on gene switches must have caught somebody's attention and I was seconded."

The cab dropped them off at the Swanston Street mall. Nash authorized his PID to pay the transaction, then slid out, walked to the other side and opened the door for Cariana. She nodded and stepped out. They strolled slowly up the street, the mall filled with pedestrians taking advantage of a warm evening. Traffic was forbidden all the way to Bourke Street, opening the city center. When initially proposed some ten years ago, businesses ran a protest campaign, saying the move would stifle the center. As it turned out, it energized the street. The shops and restaurants thrived.

After taking a right at Collins Street, it was a few meters to the Box Seafood Restaurant next to the Regent Theater. Small groups clustered on the sidewalk waiting to get in. A driverless tram clattered across the Swanston Street tracks. Bell clanking, it sped up the slope toward Parliament.

Inside the restaurant, a pleasant young woman wearing a white blouse and red skirt escorted them to a corner table past others already occupied by guests. An intimate buzz of conversation filled the narrow room. She waited for them to sit, handed them a menu, and lit a candle in a blue glass jar.

Looking around, Cariana pursed her lips and lifted an eyebrow. "Not bad. Kind of rustic."

"It doesn't have the flashy look of Realto's Vue de Monde restaurant, a place I hope to take you next time, but the Box serves some of the finest seafood in town," Nash explained, taking a breadstick out of a tall glass.

She lifted her eyes from the menu and gave him a sidewise

glance. "You've been here before?"

"A few times." Seeing her frown as she wrestled with the array of selections, he put his hand on the menu and pushed it down. Her large eyes probed him. "Unless you are fixated on something special, let's make this easy and go for a hot platter."

She turned the menu page and gasped. "I couldn't possibly eat all that!"

"Have only what you want."

"Well…" She pouted, glanced at the menu, then looked up. "Okay, but I'll probably end up with indigestion."

"No fear. Besides, seafood is supposed to be good for you." Nash lifted his arm and raised a finger. A moment later, their hostess arrived.

"You want to order?" she inquired warmly.

"A hot platter for both of us."

"Excellent choice. Something to drink first?"

Nash looked at Cariana. "Do you fancy anything in particular?"

"I'm not much into wines—"

"Leave it to me, then," he said and turned to their hostess. "We'll start with Jonsz Cuvee, and for the meal, a bottle of Artus chardonnay."

"Very good. Anything on the side?"

"A mixed salad with Italian dressing."

She nodded, collected the menus, and ambled off.

Nash sat back and crunched on the breadstick.

"I like a man who takes charge," Cariana said with a whimsical grin, and brushed back a wayward lock of hair. "What if I don't want Jonsz Cuvee, whatever that is?"

"It's a Tasmanian sparkling wine," Nash said confidently. "Better than some French champagnes. Often, you're paying for the name, pretending you're enjoying the sour brew. Try it. If you don't like it, we'll get something else."

Cariana laughed. "You're a cube," she declared and he relaxed.

He took a risk ordering the wine without consulting her, but it seemed to have paid off. Not a wine connoisseur, he sampled enough of them to know what he liked.

"Tell me about your research, if you don't mind talking shop," he asked.

"As a scientist, there is nothing more exciting than unraveling the lifeliner genome switches."

"I thought they had the lifeliner genome mapped out."

"The genome, but not the noncoding parts, which some dag early on in the DNA saga named junk, a term I hate. About three percent of DNA controls how protein-coding genes work, and protein synthesis is everything. Some noncoding parts produce regulatory RNA, among other things, but there are regions that at first didn't seem to be doing anything. They turned out to be the real treasure in the genome study, a switchboard that regulates every function. Researchers around the world are scrambling to identify gene switches that have been turned on or off in lifeliners. Not only turned on, but understand why."

"You believe they're a new species? *Homo renata?*"

Cariana fondled her cloth napkin and absently began to fold it.

"Some are calling them that, newborns I mean. Not a new species, but definitely a step in adaptive evolution." She leaned forward, her eyes alive with excitement, clearly passionate about the subject. "What is worse, we may have done this to ourselves, causing those switches to turn on. You know that birthrates have been falling steadily for decades in every advanced Western country, and it is accelerating. In places like Japan, Germany, France, and the U.S., it is negative, which means growing male and female sterility, while in non-urban areas of less developed countries there is no measurable decline. The social implications of that are daunting. Before you raise the point, I am aware of the correlation between lifeliner emergence and high-density cities. Technology and industrialization has given us our modern standard of living, but that lifestyle appears to be slowly killing us. I'm oversimplifying, of course, as there are other factors to be considered."

"You're saying that lifeliners are nature's defense mechanism to preserve the species in our highly artificial environment?"

"It's an ongoing debate. Analyzing the incidence of diabetes, obesity, asthma, and food allergies with countries where they are most prevalent. Those same countries also have falling birthrates, infertility, and the highest population of lifeliners."

"That would imply lifeliners are a mutation caused by social and environmental dynamics."

Cariana shrugged, working on her napkin. "The weight of evidence seems to support that hypothesis. What we don't know is why emergence of lifeliners mirrors sterility in the general population."

"I would have thought the answer was obvious. One species dies to make room for another."

"If it were only that simple. One thing we do know. The process seems to be accelerating."

Their hostess arrived rolling an ice bucket. She filled their glasses with white bubbly, smiled, and sauntered off. Nash picked up his glass and waited for Cariana to do the same. Grinning at each other, they clicked them.

"To enchanting company," he said with feeling.

Cariana nodded, took a sip and raised an eyebrow. "This is good. Delicate and not overly dry."

Nash took a sip and put down his glass. "I'm glad you like it."

She regarded him over the rim of her glass. "You seem well informed about lifeliners."

"I've studied," he said truthfully, a rueful grin hovering at the corner of his mouth.

"And clearly not happy with what you found."

"What do you think? Scratch the veneer of civilization, man is still very much a savage. I think Alexander Pope in his *Essay on Man* was right when he said, *'Our nature is a sharp accuser, but a helpless friend!'* All our philosophical writings on morality and ethics urges people to be cooperative and selfless, but our behavior is an antithesis. We have become so competitive, selfish, and aggressive, that life has become all but unbearable for some, which cannot be explained in terms of evolutionary genetic bias alone. Man has a thinking mind able to override his primitive inner self, but we choose to be cruel to one another."

The repressive laws enacted prior to 2027 effectively made lifeliners second-class citizens. It took the 2029 Curtis Sands case for the High Court to strike them down. In America, influenced by far-right evangelical groups, the Administration simply ignored the courts, which polarized the country and caused widespread civil unrest. Control of both Houses by the Republicans avoided a full-blown constitutional crisis, for now. Sooner or later, there would be a reckoning.

Her face turned hard. "No one can excuse what has been done to lifeliners, but social consciousness is changing."

She was saying the words, but her rigid posture told him something else.

"I don't believe that and neither do you. There is still active discrimination and persecution. They're human beings like everyone else."

"They're not and you know it!" she retorted hotly.

Her vehemence startled him, forcing him to look at her in new light. As a geneticist, she could not possibly have that view. He accepted her drive and commitment to break the lifeliner genome, but locked in a lab, such commitment can easily shut out the ugliness of history and, potentially, ugliness that might still come. Were lifeliners for her merely subjects of objective study? What happened in her life to make her hold such a clouded view? He did not want to open that door, not right now, reluctant to spoil their evening, but her outburst shook him. If she truly believed what she said, he could never reveal himself to her, which would be intolerable, and an end to any relationship he hoped to have.

"Perhaps."

"I cannot expect you to know," she said stiffly and took a sip of wine.

He folded his arms over the table and leaned forward. "I want to. Humor me. What makes them different?"

She brushed back a strand of hair to collect herself. "Apart from their ability to tap into someone's bioelectromagnetic field to draw energy? Don't ask me why they do that. It doesn't appear to be a survival trait…what's the matter?"

"Something occurred to me, and I'm surprised I haven't thought of it before. Do you know if lifeliners can also discharge energy?"

Since the first officially recognized existence of a lifeliner reported in the July 18, 2024 Paris *Le Monde* daily—they didn't call them that then. A wit in the September 13, 2025 issue of *The New York Times* coined the phrase—no one had suggested this obvious possibility.

Cariana looked thoughtful. "You mean, feed energy into a biological system? I haven't seen any papers on it. What function would such an ability fulfill?" She picked up her glass and took a long pull. "An evolutionary change must have some long-term survival value. It wouldn't be much use as a defense mechanism. Too energy costly. An interesting concept, though."

"Just a thought. Anyway, you were telling me why lifeliners are different," he prompted.

"Energy management," she said promptly. "Humans metabolize twenty amino acids, of which eight cannot be manufactured by the body. They're called essential amino acids naturally enough and must be obtained externally from food, but I suppose you knew that."

"Actually, I did."

"Cube! Then you also know that amino acids are used to synthesize proteins and act as oxidizers that generate energy in cells. The genetic changes that created lifeliners gave them the ability to manufacture two of those essential amino acids, leucine, and valine. Very interesting it is too. In normal humans, the liver has lost the complex enzyme pathway to synthesize pyruvate into leucine and valine. Somewhere along our evolutionary path, nature figured it easier to obtain these amino acids through food than make them."

"And how is that significant?"

She arched her eyebrows. "You mean, you don't know?"

"Cariana..."

She flashed him a smile. "Sorry, I couldn't help it." Noting his scrutiny, she frowned. "Why are you looking at me like that?"

"I like the sound of your voice," he said gently, fascinated by her enthusiasm and vitality, allowing himself to be smothered by her personality.

He wondered what his previous girlfriends would think if they saw him right now, eyes dreamy and vacant. They probably wouldn't believe it. The hardboiled Nash Bannon gone all soft and gooey? Cariana had touched some hidden part he thought locked, immune to rejection, hurt, and loss. Apart from obvious physical attraction, Cariana had some extra quality that made him want to connect with her on a more intimate and personal level. He hoped she shared that connection in some small way.

Her almond eyes did not avoid his scrutiny. "And you're nice when you're not teasing."

"You were telling me about those amino acids," he said, not wishing to be sidetracked, which could happen easily if he allowed it. "I'm genuinely interested."

"Okay, but I still think you were teasing." From a very attractive woman, she turned into a serious scientist, her napkin forgotten. "Remember what I said about energy management? Well, these two amino acids play a crucial role. Among other things, leucine directly stimulates muscle protein synthesis and slows degradation of tissue, which makes lifeliners stronger and gives them more stamina. It decreases food intake and body weight, making them slimmer. Valine has a stimulant effect and is needed for muscle metabolism, tissue repair, prevents tissue breakdown, and is an energy source during physical activity. It is important for optimum operation of the nervous system, cognitive functions, and regulation of the immune system. I wouldn't be surprised if they have longer lifespans, but that's yet to be proven. Lifeliners are also incredibly resistant to disease."

Nash stared at her. It was true. He and Mark had never been ill. They both caught an occasional sniffle and had an occasional stomach ache, but it only lasted a day or two at most. The few lifeliners he knew were also robustly healthy.

He took a sip of wine. "That's it? All that because lifeliners can break down pyruvate?"

"No, that's not it. Lifeliners are able to synthesize vitamin C. Unlike primates, which includes humans, almost all vertebrates can produce their own vitamin C. We still have the gene, but somewhere along the line, it was switched off."

Nash raised an eyebrow. "That's a new one for me. Given our low fruit and vegetable diet, I can see how this could be useful."

"Look at our modern diseases: general lassitude, neurological dysfunction, defects in blood vessels, and loss of bone integrity. They all point to a poor intake of vitamin C. Lifeliners also have more brain mass. On the order of five percent, especially the prefrontal lobe and the hippocampus, which helps explain their eidetic memory…like yours. This is significant, as those parts of the brain control all higher functions such as planning, judgment, emotional expression, creativity, and comprehension. Lifeliners have larger livers that can store more carbs and they're able to expel excess sugar from food rather than converting it to fatty deposits. These are major evolutionary changes from a regimen of fat accumulation when food was scarce."

"Energy management," he murmured, fascinated by her explanation. Such a profound impact from a seemingly small change in the body's biochemistry. All the research he did missed those connections.

"Exactly! Evolution has given lifeliners immunity against our Western lifestyle where food is cheap and abundant, and part of my job is to find the genes responsible."

"When you do find them, what then?"

Before Cariana could answer, their hostess walked up carrying a large tray piled high with steaming seafood, the enticing smell making Nash rub his hands in anticipation.

"Now we're cooking!" he hooted.

Cariana rolled her eyes and shook her head.

"I shall bring the Artus chardonnay directly," the hostess said with a grin.

Staring at the loaded tray, Cariana winced. "You have to be kidding me. No normal person could possibly eat all that."

"Forget what's normal. Just dig in."

Mouth set in concentration, she filled her plate with shell crab, scallops, king prawns and two spring rolls. Nash helped himself to some oysters, a half lobster, calamari, and scallops. Their hostess filled fresh glasses with icy chardonnay and left them to it. Silence reigned for a few minutes as food occupied their attention.

Cariana dipped her fingers into a bowl of lemon water, wiped them on her napkin, and sighed with satisfaction.

"This is wonderful." She took a sip of wine and nodded. "So is the chardonnay."

"It's not bad," Nash agreed and waved at the loaded tray. "Don't give up now."

"I won't, but I have to let things settle down first. You haven't told me much about yourself."

"You mean, talking about my work doesn't exactly cut it?"

"I have enough problems—"

"Without listening to mine."

"Cube! I didn't mean—"

"Never mind. I know. Nothing much to tell. Mark and I— he's my twin brother—raised the usual hell boys do while keeping our parents from finding out what we were up to."

"Is he in Melbourne?"

"Canberra, working as a weapons procurement consultant for

the Defense Department."

"That's a pretty responsible position."

"For someone so young? It is. He worked at the South Australian naval shipyards for a couple of years streamlining tendering procedures, which enabled the government to undercut a French and American bid for coastal patrol boats Indonesia was interested in. That got him moved to Canberra."

"He also has an eidetic memory?"

"He does."

"Must have been hard on your parents, coping with twins, I mean."

"We didn't make it easy for them," Nash admitted. "I remember how we used to pretend that we were the other twin. It raised hell at home and school, but Mom could almost always tell us apart. We fooled Dad all the time. I don't know about our sister Natalie, she's a geophysicist at BHP. I think she could work out who was who, but never said, preferring to enjoy the confusion. Being older, Mark and I gave her a hard time sometimes."

"Boys!" Cariana sighed in exasperation. "I had an older brother—"

"Had?"

Her eyes changed and something terrible flashed in their depths.

"He and his wife were killed by a drunk lifeliner a year ago running a red light." She chewed her lower lip. "He pleaded momentary mental incapacity, lost his license for two years and got off with a twelve-month jail sentence."

Nash sat back, uncertain how to handle this. He reached for her hand and squeezed.

"That sucks."

She brushed back a lock of stray hair. "One of life's bad deals. Anyway, what I wanted to say, my brother was just as mean. And your parents?"

"Dad is an exec at QANTAS and Mom is a graphic designer with a home office."

"Talented family."

"Genes," Nash quipped, and Cariana laughed.

"*Touché.*" She picked up another spring roll and nibbled at it. Eyeing the tray, she began filling her plate.

Pleased to see her enjoying herself, Nash did the same.

After a time, she patted her stomach, exhaled loudly and leaned back.

"That's it. I'm done."

"There is still that crab, king prawns and a lobster tail."

"Help yourself. I don't think I'll eat anything for a week."

"Until breakfast tomorrow. Seafood doesn't stick to the ribs."

"The seafood might not, but all those sauces…"

"The sacrifices we make…" Nash agreed and topped up their glasses.

She looked at him speculatively. "Never married or anything?"

"There has been an occasional 'anything', but nothing serious. Not recently anyway."

Right now, he did not want to rake over Sally's scabs. Part of the problem with casual dating lay with him, of course. He never enjoyed dancing, going to discos or rowdy gatherings, which clearly made him an outsider. The stylized gyrating and waving of arms were to him absurd and primitive expressions of ritualized courtship. He genuinely could not understand the fun in it.

Perhaps he was a cube as Cariana suggested.

He looked deep into her eyes. "It might not be too late, though."

She grinned mischievously and took a sip. "I still think you were picking me up when we first met."

"At the La Asiago? I told you, an accident."

"Mmm."

He pointed a finger at her. "Any room left in there for dessert?"

"Not a chance." Regarding him, she worried her lower lip. "Why the interest in lifeliners?"

He shrugged. "Pure curiosity. They *are* the most significant thing that has happened to the human race, which by the way could turn our society on its head, and in some ways, it already has, but I'm not fixated on them. I am fascinated by lots of other things."

"Such as?"

"Oh, politics, sociology, economics, cosmology, the looming water wars."

"Water wars?"

"India is building canals to join all its major river systems, channeling water into its parched central plains. This is already causing major problems in Bangladesh. In the meantime, China has started to syphon water from Tibet, which incidentally is the source of all the rivers running into India. Picture it. Two nuclear powers facing each other off over water, with prickly Pakistan ready to start lobbing nukes at both. Meanwhile, Egypt and Sudan are facing a crisis as countries upstream of the Nile are draining more water from the White and Blue Nile and Lake Victoria. With growing populations and increased industrialization in the region, the need for a secure water supply has become a strategic consideration."

"Worth going to war over," Cariana murmured.

"Mexico is experiencing severe shortages as the United States holds more water upstream of the Colorado River for its own use. It is not in a position to do much militarily, but there are other ways to get attention."

"Terrorism?"

"Blowing up Hoover Dam would get them attention. Given the American administration's protectionist policies, it might happen. There are other places around the world where one country controls a water source needed by its neighbor, and all of them are potential flashpoints." He lifted a bread stick from the tall glass and nibbled. "I'm also interested in the history and application of PIDs."

Cariana took a stick herself and crunched on it. "I would have thought it pretty much clear cut. Developed by DARPA—"

"The U.S. Defense Advanced Research Projects Agency. I know."

"You would. Cube. As I was saying, developed in early 2020s for the U.S. military as neural interfaces with ship, aircraft, and smart weapons systems, it did not take the American administration long to realize the potential for civilian applications. I remember watching the August 2025 UN General Assembly session, which passed a resolution to implement a constantly variable encryption key, unique to every individual, that prevented monitoring and hacking of personal data."

"Not without some reluctance from the U.S., China, and Russia," Nash added. "To name a few. They claimed that withholding the master key would reduce the capacity of their intelligence and law enforcement agencies to protect their citizens. Developers maintain the personal key could be broken by a quantum computer, but not within a timeframe to make the information useful."

"Yet they signed up for it."

"Too many economic and social advantages for them not to, and the networks are virtually secure. Predictably, though, civil liberty groups raised a ruckus about government Big Brother surveillance and control of people's minds, but Americans welcomed the technology that eliminated most card-based systems and made it easier to interact with growing social technology. It also gave rise to a raft of multiplier industries scrambling to build plugin neural interfaces into every imaginable product, which incidentally made Intel billions."

"Talking to my fridge or stove is progress?"

"A point of view. PIDs don't work in countries without total network coverage, but I give them another five years at most. The variable key made personal PIDs possible, but my worry is what governments the world over are doing to get around it. Including ours."

"What do you mean?"

"Don't you see? In the past, NSA and organizations like it, routinely intercepted most data that traveled across the world's communication networks. PIDs introduced an impenetrable wall, and it went against the grain. Thwarted by their inability to spy on their citizens and each other, they turned to subtler mechanisms to subvert an individual's data security. You heard the announcement by Canberra to introduce a tracking feature?"

Cariana scrunched her nose. "I remember seeing something about it in the holoview."

"A textbook example of a government attempting to circumvent our privacy. The classic being when in 2029 they allowed the Australian Signals Directorate to record the content of all electronic communication, which implies they can break personal encryption keys. It's scary."

"You're into this security thing in a big way."

"Regardless of its unquestionable social benefits, I sometimes wondered whether PID technology should have remained purely a military application."

"I *can* see situations where tracking someone's PID could be useful," she countered.

"So can I, provided I control the function. It's indiscriminate access that worries me."

"Point taken," Cariana said. "Nobody thought the watchmaking industry would take such a hit, though."

She was right. With PIDs providing accurate time with a mental command, wristwatches were relegated to memory drawers. People continued to wear designer watches as fashion statements, and wall clocks had a niche market, but many prestige brands disappeared.

"Innovate or perish," Nash said.

Cariana shook her head. "You can be a hard man, Nash Bannon. Talking about politics, which way do you lean, if you don't mind saying?"

He shrugged. "I don't like Atarah Readman much. Disappointment really. When she became Prime Minister, I thought

Australia finally found a strong leader with visionary policies to lead this country into a technological and social renaissance. Her failure to articulate the Liberal Party's position on lifeliners cost her seats at the 2030 election. Then she compounded her error by embracing the Australian Conservatives to form government, a poisonous union if there ever was one. I shouldn't be disillusioned, knowing how party machines operate, but I expected more character from her."

"You think the Coalition will lose in October?"

"They will unless Readman announces policies relevant to the current social climate, which is fast deteriorating, by the way. What about you? Do you follow any party?"

"Me? I'm interested in what's going on, but like most of the ambivalent majority, I don't pay much attention to the Canberra gaggle, although I realize I should. I've got more pressing issues to deal with."

"That's the problem, Cariana. The silent majority is permitting gradual degradation of ethical and responsible behavior from our politicians. I hate to say it, but if we're not careful, we could end up controlled by the fanatical far-right. By the time people realize what has happened, we'll be in a virtual autocracy that will invariably lead to a messy civil war. Economies that never recovered from the 2023 crash, Italy, Spain and Greece, have already gone down that road, abandoning the euro and the European Union."

"You have a wide-ranging mind."

"I have a low boredom threshold."

"And your eidetic memory helps you retain what you learn. Not only that, you can integrate what you learn." She fiddled with her glass, studying him. "It must be terrible sometimes not being able to forget."

Images and memories cascaded before him, vivid and real as the moment when they were implanted. Not all of them were clothed in light, and shadows lurked there.

"I learned early that I could not hide myself in the dark corridors of my mind and create other realities with happy endings that erased the truth. It forced me to become rational at a time when other boys still fantasized."

"You never created imaginary worlds or lives?"

"Worlds and lives out of time. I have a powerful imagination and my dreams are particularly intense. Having an eidetic memory is a penetrating light that shines on everything I do and feel. That light does not allow room for self-deception or casting judgment."

"You must be extremely well-adjusted."

"It helps me cope with the demons." Nash leaned forward and gazed into her magical eyes. "What fills your empty hours when you're not consumed by work?"

"Consumed…an interesting way of putting it, and you're right. My work does consume me. It gives direction, a purpose and goals to strive for. However, I do have other interests."

"Mind sharing?"

Her eyes glittered. "I love American classical poets: Eliot, Poe, Emerson, and Dickinson, among others. I also indulge in origami."

Nash inclined his head at the cloth napkin she'd been twisting into odd shapes. "I noticed."

She flushed slightly, but did not look away.

"Do you ever write any poetry yourself?" he asked gently, sensitive to her feelings.

"I've written a few pieces."

"I wouldn't mind reading them sometime."

"We'll see." Cariana smoothed down her skirt and sat up. "As much as I'd like to stay, and I do want to talk more—you're a good listener—we should be leaving. I enjoyed myself immensely, Nash, but tomorrow is a working day."

"And the fantasy must end," he added with genuine regret, wishing this moment would never stop. He loved listening to her, loved the crisp sound of her lyrical voice, the energetic sparkle in her eyes, and the subconscious little mannerisms that combined to make a complex, vibrant personality. Could he build on what they shared tonight? Would she want to?

One step at a time, old son, but be careful what you're getting into.

Outside, warm dusk had fallen and the city blazed with light. Colors were sharp and the noises louder. Pedestrians crowded the sidewalks, ambling, hurrying, vanishing in the flowing streams of people. A full tram clanked down Collins Street and stopped past the Swanston Street intersection. Passengers spilled out and others pushed in, afraid to lose a slice of time out of their lives having to wait for another tram. Somewhere a police siren momentarily intruded into the ambient noise, their cars rarely seen in the city after drones were introduced as surveillance vehicles of choice. Nash wondered how a drone issued an infringement ticket to a driverless car. He thought about getting one, an electric Tesla Viper with a range of 1,200 kilometers that recharged in fifteen minutes. When they come down in price, he told himself. Until then, he would put up with his old level 3 Toyota Corolla hybrid.

Nash flagged down a taxi with his PID. Inside, he found himself in a cocoon of relative silence and peace. He turned to Cariana.

"Anything special lined up for tomorrow?"

"I'm monitoring four juveniles who are in puberty transition, which generates an obvious dilemma for me and other researchers. By the time the subject is identified as a lifeliner, most of the gene activity has already taken place."

"Where do you get the kids?"

"Grade school volunteers. To avoid potential social stigma, they're told it's general genetic research, which it is," she added. "Yesterday, we received some interesting data from a lab in the States and I need to compare the findings with my own experiments. Organic chemistry is complicated. I also need to look deeper into what you said—"

"About lifeliners able to infuse energy?"

"Somebody must have written something on it."

He searched her face. "I want to see you again, Cariana."

"Well, you haven't been too obnoxious. Friday night? I cannot get away any earlier."

"Lunch somewhere before then?"

She frowned and shook her head. "Afraid not. I'll be at the CSIRO Parkville labs most of the week. That's where we do all the human life sciences stuff." Seeing his downcast expression, she laughed. "Don't pine, Nash. We have time."

"Was I that obvious?"

The touch of her smooth fingers against his cheek sent an electrifying tingle through his body. Right then, he had a powerful urge to send her a jolt of energy to see if he could. An irrational impulse triggered by her presence and a need to draw her close to him, to join with him as two spirits, the feeling not at all sexual.

"Eager," she said. "Many men want only one thing from a woman, but I think you're not one of them. I can tell, which makes you special and I treasure that. You have a strange, captivating depth I want to explore, and you have given me enough to think about. Let's not rush it."

Traffic along St. Kilda Road flowed smoothly, the predominantly electric cars almost silent, and the drive enveloped them in comfortable, intimate calm. Cariana's fragrant perfume drifted around him and Nash wanted to bury his head in her golden hair and breathe deeply of it. He hoped it wasn't a simple atavistic drive to possess her. Both had opened a window a little, allowing a glimpse into each other. Enough for now.

The cab stopped outside The Fawkner Residences building and Nash escorted Cariana up the steps to the main entrance.

"Thank you for tonight," he whispered.

She smiled faintly. "Good night, Nash."

He took her hand and squeezed, taking his time over it, then leaned over her and gave her a peck on the cheek. She shivered and he let go. There will be other days and nights where more would be said and done.

She waited for the security system to open the glass doors and strode into the foyer. Nash watched her disappear into the elevator alcove, exhaled loudly and walked slowly down the steps, considering options for Friday night.

He climbed back into the waiting cab and gave its computer instructions. As the taxi pulled away from the curb, he turned and gazed at the flow of cars along the broad boulevard, allowing his mind to drift. Cab and car rental companies, supermarket chains and long-distance freight haulers, were the first to adopt level 5 autonomous vehicles and trucks when they became commercially viable in the mid-2020s. The transition brutal on owner-operators who could not adjust, but the conversion also dramatically reduced the annual toll of injuries and human lives lost due to driver error. Progress always seemed to demand a social price.

After a refreshing shower, dressed in a purple silk kimono, he took a tumbler of Canadian Crown Royal whiskey to the balcony. Sipping the fine liquor, he listened thoughtfully to the haunting strands of Ravel's *Bolero* coming from the lounge, reflecting on the evening's pleasant memories, recalling every moment, every detail, every line of Cariana's face, and nuance of her voice. He replayed it all like watching a holoview. He wanted to push back the darker shadows of their conversation, but there was nowhere to hide. If they were to go on, she would have to overcome her irrational hatred of lifeliners.

History had been harsh on lifeliners and, in his view, harsher on mankind in general. He firmly believed that civilized behavior was merely a veneer to keep the inner savage in check. Without laws and social institutions to enforce them, people would readily revert to sectarian tribalism. In many respects, mankind still firmly clung to entrenched tribalism. Wasn't each country a socioeconomic tribe, proclaiming its sovereignty to others with trumpets and a flutter of flags, backed by guns, which effectively said 'no trespassing'? Threaten that sovereignty in any way and the tribe would vent its wrath on the aggressor.

And the perceived threat facing national tribes today? Lifeliners, of course.

Nash sighed and took another sip, hardly noticing cars whispering along St. Kilda Road.

Since the first 2024 reporting in France, treated as a curiosity by the scientific community, completely ignored by politicians and people in general, unease replaced complacency as documented reports of lifeliners started to appear all over the world. Predominantly from large integrated cities with complex infrastructures and sophisticated populations, which mostly meant Western-type cities. With absence of widespread incidence in less developed countries, it did not take the learned community long to start connecting some of the dots, which in turn stirred political interest.

Eminent universities such as Harvard and Oxford initiated research programs to study lifeliners and called for volunteers. Pure research and, at first, utterly innocent. In November 2026, an article in the *American Journal of Medicine* changed everything. Professor Richard Friedman at the Baltimore Johns Hopkins University School of Medicine produced the first definitive profile on lifeliners. The damaging part of the paper were graphs of falling birthrates and growing sterility, correlated with geographical distributions of lifeliner emergence. The next day, *The Washington Post* headline read: *Lifeliners, doom of the human race!*

Not accurate or true, the article triggered very preventable public hysteria and demands for governments to act. To do what? Kill lifeliners on sight? The civilized West turned out not to be so civilized after all. Other parts of the world did not even pretend. It would take centuries, perhaps millennia, before lifeliners replaced *homo sapiens* as a species, but the specter of helplessness, that people's lives no longer mattered and they had no future, nature denying them children, worked at an emotional level that could not be reasoned with. Governments used that fear to push through punitive programs against lifeliners, which at the same time severely restricted personal rights and freedoms for everybody. Deliberately or incidentally, many Western countries were turning themselves into totalitarian regimes.

The problem everybody faced, how to find a lifeliner?

In those early days, unless one revealed himself, it was impossible.

The new millennium heralded a dark horizon. Neighbor spied on neighbor, and families disintegrated when a child was discovered to be a lifeliner after onset of puberty. Self-styled puritans hounded identified lifeliners. In 2026, following a vitriolic sermon by a Christian Brotherhood evangelist in Georgia, claiming that lifeliners were an abomination and walking evil, an outraged mob killed a fifteen-year-old girl following denunciation by an irate relative with a grievance against her family. Those responsible were charged with murder and convicted. However, the incident set a pattern of suspicion and retribution that spread to engulf the world.

Two months later the U.S. Congress passed the infamous Lifeliner Act, requiring registration of all lifeliners. Official identification documents such as Social Security and driver's license cards bore a prominent 'L', and PIDs broadcast lifeliner identities. Civil rights organizations mounted a joint action against the government in the Supreme Court, citing the Act violated several articles of the Constitution. The government lost the case in a pivotal sitting of the full bench and the Act struck down. Nevertheless, prevailing public opinion enabled the Administration and Congress to enact subtler punitive regulations. Lifeliners and parents of lifeliners who failed to identify themselves faced loss of employment, confiscation of property, indefinite incarceration, and active discrimination. Mounting a court challenge takes time and considerable financial resources, which individuals and most civil rights organizations did not have, and governments became bolstered.

Several European countries followed suit despite challenges to the European Court of Justice. Germany, France, Italy, and Spain claimed that lifeliners were not human and therefore were outside the court's jurisdiction. It took the 2027 proclamation by the UN to settle the issue, but it was interesting to see the right-wing U.S. Republican government and protectionist Europe oppose recognition of lifeliners and voted against the declaration.

Australia did not remain immune to hysteria and paranoia, as the Curtis Sands case vividly demonstrated. At thirty-four, Sands was the Agriculture Minister in the Victorian Legislative Assembly and a rising Labor Party star, seen as a potential premier. In 2029, a routine DNA test revealed that Sands was a lifeliner. Following an internal party furrow and public backlash, they forced him to resign and expelled him from the Party. He became an independent and took his case to the Victorian Supreme Court, citing wrongful dismissal and violation of his basic rights. After three months, the court delivered its landmark decision, viewed with interest around the world. Lifeliners were human beings under common law and enjoyed the same rights and privileges as any other person. The Victorian government appealed to the High Court and lost. All state and federal laws and regulations that limited lifeliner rights, including keeping lifeliner registers, were repealed. Sands refused reinstatement in the Labor Party, preferring to remain an independent, his career permanently blighted, and became an activist, supporter of the Lifeliner Help Center, and founder of the Lifeliner Party. Riding a wave of popular unrest, federal and state governments introduced new legislation to track and harass lifeliners. It also emboldened extremists, who physically molested and attacked anyone suspected of being a lifeliner.

Bolero's finale crescendo reverberating in his mind, Nash walked into the lounge. He told Sally to switch off the entertainment system, washed the tumbler, and sauntered into the bedroom. He slowly lowered himself to the floor and assumed the lotus position. Like a butterfly landing on a flower, he closed his eyes and allowed his spiritual awareness to expand and encompass his perception of the mind and self. Chi, his *sensei* said, embodied all the training in the physical side of Tai Chi, the Quan. Time flowed and he allowed himself to flow with it.

Totally relaxed and at peace, he went to bed. Comfortable under black satin sheets, sleep eluded him and he locked his fingers behind his head, Cariana's perfect face haunting him.

He wanted to run a finger along her soft cheek, brush her lips, and see her whimsical dimpled smile. She had a probing, incisive mind he wanted to explore. Debating her would be lively, challenging her views and beliefs. She would not give in easily, yielding only in the face of overwhelming and indisputable evidence. He would not want it any other way.

It took a while before he closed his eyes and warm darkness cradled him in its embrace.

Chapter Two

He found it easy to walk in the past because it always walked with him. For ordinary people the past could be ignored, changed or forgotten. Nash could do none of those things. He achieved a measure of inner peace, but it was akin to an armed truce and came at a demanding price—unfailing inner honesty. Everyone tells lies, some little, some dark, in the course of dealing with those they came into contact or lived with. The lies protect them, their feelings, relationships, and they protected him. Lies are a film of oil that lubricates social interaction. A totally honest person would be someone who pours sand into community machinery, a dangerous irritant to be eliminated.

Nash was such an irritant, but he learned early to coat his words with oil.

The tram slid to a stop and the doors snapped open. He stepped in and automatically scanned the other passengers. Bright sunshine streamed into the cool interior, the air-conditioning a background whisper. Watching the morning news, the weatherman said it would be thirty-four Celsius today with a possible afternoon change, and twenty-eight on Saturday. Gusty northerlies were expected to continue until then, which meant kiln heat from Australia's red center. He took it in stride. Hot, cold, windy or wet, all were variables of nature he could not influence. Nothing to get worked up about.

He reached for a stanchion as the doors clicked shut and the tram lurched forward. Dressed in a dark blue suit, white silk shirt, and a subdued striped yellow cashmere tie, he blended in with other office workers around him without attracting more than a casual glance and an occasional appreciative look from interested females. As the tram neared the Arts Center, a balding middle-aged executive type, slim brown briefcase at his side, rose and grasped the steel pole below Nash's hand. He figured the guy probably prepared to get off at the Federation Square stop. With the adjacent Flinders Street suburban rail hub across the street, a popular transit point.

Casually, Nash allowed his hand to slip a couple of centimeters down the pole until he barely felt skin contact. The man beside him did not react to the touch. Nash felt the aura of energy emanating from his intended donor and allowed the life-force to link with him. A tingle raced up his arm and defused through his upper torso in a pleasurable inner glow. He closed his eyes and jammed, slowly counting the seconds. At forty, he broke contact as the tram clanked to a stop. Unaware of what had happened, the man stepped off and ambled with the crowd toward the railway station. By end of the day, his body would regenerate and replenish the lost energy.

As the surge of boarding passengers came through the doors, Nash glanced around and picked an empty seat. His vision appeared sharper and his hearing became more acute. Intensely aware of everything around him, attuned to the flow of emotions and personalities jostling through the tram, his body tingled with energy. It may have been purely a psychosomatic reaction, but the charge of wellbeing had given his day extra zest.

His PID told him it was 8:05. Plenty of time for the impromptu meeting at nine with Amanda Fuller, his Telstra counterpart. He should have insisted doing this over the holoview virtual presence link, but the fine morning found him restless, wanting to be outside. Besides, a major contract variation demanded this level of personal communication. Nash didn't mind these sessions too much, and Amanda was a reasonable lady, although lacking in any sense of humor. Then again, working for Telstra, an understandable attitude. Meeting or not, nothing would spoil his evening with Cariana, and he missed her. He felt a connection that transcended mere physical beauty. Could he be falling for her after only a few encounters? Why not? He lived alone long enough and the empty days and solitary nights were getting weary. Being with her had added a spark to his life, and happy slumber filled his nights.

Time for a change, old son, but watch out for reefs.

As the tram moved away from the stop, his thoughts turned further inward.

Cariana was right when she said he was well-adjusted, a by-product of his memory. As children, he and Mark played games, recalling what happened a week or month ago, or what their parents said during dinner the other night, checking for bloopers. They had fun recalling pranks they pulled on Natalie until the hurt Nash saw in her eyes one day no longer made it amusing. As far as they were concerned, sister or not, she was a readily accessible girl they could taunt and annoy. Feelings? Girls didn't have feelings, always whining to Mother, complaining tearfully what bad boys they were.

Nash remembered a sunny January outing to Daylesford in 2015. They just finished a picnic lunch beside the placid waters of Jubilee Lake. Mom and Dad were talking, a beer can in his hand. A white gum arched its branches over their wooden bench in protection. Around them, children shrieked chasing each other, playing ball games, splashing in the lake, and shouted at by adults. He and Mark always did things together, happy in each other's company, independent without the need for anyone else. They had friends, but none knew what Nash and Mark were. A secret revealed could someday be a weapon of betrayal when a friend became an enemy.

They had a rented canoe pulled up dry to prevent it from drifting off. Nash vividly recalled Mark pushing it into the water and jumping in, waving at him to hurry up. Grabbing a plastic paddle, Nash was about to step in when Natalie slowly walked up. Wearing calf-length cream jeans and a pale pink T-shirt, hair tied in a ponytail, she looked at him with huge dark olive eyes and smiled shyly.

"Can I join you?"

Worrying her lower lip, small and vulnerable, she clearly wanted to be with them. The last thing Nash needed right then was having this twelve-year-old brat tag along. She would probably fall out in the middle of the lake and spoil their fun.

"Nat! Leave the boys alone!" Mom called out.

"Beat it, Nat! Go play with your dolls," Mark growled. "Come *on*, Nash!"

About to climb into the canoe, he saw Natalie's eyes mist as she pursed her lips to stop them quivering with disappointment. They hardly ever allowed her to do anything with them. After all, she was only a girl, and girls had odd ideas about fun. She stood there looking at him without saying anything, alone and rejected. Confused by sudden emotions of concern coursing through him, for the first time in his life, Nash realized she was someone he liked, not exactly sure why, although an irritating little kid always underfoot.

Not certain what made him do it, he reached for her small hand.

"Sure thing, Nat. Get in."

The light of joy that sparkled in her eyes transformed her, making her face radiant. Not daring to believe, she hesitated, expecting another prank.

"Truly?"

"No foolin'."

"Hey! This is our canoe!" Mark shouted in outrage. "Let her get her own."

"She's coming," Nash said harshly, which made his brother shut up, causing him to shake his head in resignation.

Recalling the blissful day, the three of them did have fun. Even Mark grudgingly admitted they had fun, which was something.

From that day, they stopped taunting Natalie and started doing things together. A few things only. She was still a pest and a nuisance.

Much later, Nash came to realize that he had taken his first step in understanding empathy. Sometimes hurting someone meant hurting himself even more. It took a few years to learn that. It also took a while to learn that pointing out inconsistencies in their parents' conversations wasn't a clever display of his infallible memory, but a source of pain and argument, which occasionally ended with him sent to his room without dinner. At first, he did not understand why they had a problem. He told the truth. Later, he came to realize the terrible power of truth and the need to ameliorate its effects with a few little lies, or keep his mouth shut.

Natalie's radiant eyes when he told her she could come with them held an important place in the tapestry of his memories, as did the warm looks she used to give him from time to time afterward.

He mastered the art of omitting all or some of the truth without the need to tell an outright lie. At other times, though, a lie was the only way to resolve a situation, although it never worked on him. He could shade the truth and lie to others, tell when someone lied, but he could not lie to himself. The truth imbedded in his memories forbade self-deception and did not allow him to forget.

Yes, he was well-adjusted, all right.

He pursed his mouth. Introspection wasn't getting him anywhere.

Ah, rats!

Coming to the Bourke Street mall, Nash was startled to see the scrawny little street kid he'd met on Tuesday. She stood at the corner watching people walk around her, a little red backpack with a white swan design hanging on her right shoulder. She wore the same green corduroy pants and red sandals, but now had a purple T-shirt, her short pale brown hair still in rats. When she turned her head, her face looked lost, haunted, awash with helplessness. It reminded him of Natalie's tragic look and he felt a stir of compassion for this little street urchin.

Not certain what he would do or why, he pushed his way off

the tram, keeping out of her line of sight.

"Stepping off," his PID announced, ensuring a correct charge for the trip.

Seeing her about to cross Bourke Street, he hurried toward her. Sensing his approach, she turned and gaped, recognition contorting her smudged features. Before she could make a run for it, he grabbed her arm.

"Hey! Let go of me!" She kicked him in the shin, but he held her fast.

He drew her close and leaned over her. "Make this easy on yourself, kid. I'm not a dober, and I want to help you."

"You can help me by minding your own damn business," she hissed, eyes flashing.

Right then, Nash found himself morally stranded. He could let her evaporate out of his life, perhaps a wiser thing to do. She represented trouble of the worst kind, something he did not need at any time. Her arm tugged at him, ready to flee, and his every instinct screamed to let her go. Her eyes stopped him. They were old eyes that had seen life not meant for a child about to bloom into young womanhood. They should be happy eyes filled with curiosity and excitement, welcoming each day as a promise of a wonderful future. She had no future, and her days were a promise of uncertainty, rejection, and flight. Unwanted, hating all humanity, drifting between stolen moments of quiet and peace, she would end up raped and drugged, another unaccounted body in the Yarra.

There were state programs to keep the homeless off the streets. Not for lifeliners, though, except for the Help Center, a private organization. They were supposed to report every lifeliner who entered their door, but Nash knew the Center maintained strict client confidentiality, something the authorities did not appreciate. This got the Center into legal trouble a number of times, but the Curtis Sands precedent always bailed them out. That did not stop the authorities from harassing them.

The dilemma he faced, he could do very little to free her from her miserable existence. She had to do that herself, which would be tough at the best of times. She had to make that choice, though. He figured at her age, managing to survive another day was a triumph and didn't leave much room for philosophizing or making long-term plans.

Without saying anything, he straightened, released her arm and stepped back.

"Go. I won't stop you."

People walked around them, a morass she could sink into and vanish, but he did not see or hear them. Her eyes probed and cut into him, looking for angles, a trick, treachery. Some spark faded in them and her shoulders sagged.

"I'm so hungry," she whispered dejectedly.

"To jam?"

Her eyes filled and she nodded. "It's been..."

He gently took her small hand and squeezed. "Go on. It's all right. Feed."

She licked her lips with the tip of her pointed tongue and her eyes turned misty. He felt a mild jolt as they connected and his life-force drained. Almost imperceptibly, her face began to shine with inner light and well-being.

"That's enough," he told her after one minute and broke contact.

At the rate she sucked, she must have been badly depleted, with few opportunities to charge. Given her appearance, not many people would allow her to get close, let alone touch them. Trams and trains were crowded during morning and afternoon peaks, and good places to catch a donor, but risky for someone like her with dobers always on patrol. He glanced at a nearby restaurant, one of many in upper Swanston Street, and inclined his head.

"When was the last time you had a proper breakfast?"

She followed his gaze and broke into a sunny smile that melted his heart. Why did people do these things to their littlest ones? She wasn't responsible for being what she was. She should be loved and cared for, not hunted.

"It's been a while," she said, suddenly unsure of herself. "I, ah, usually lift things at the Vic Market…You won't dob me in?"

"Cross my heart," he said with a straight face and tugged her hand toward the restaurant. "How long have you been alone?"

"I ran away two months ago when my parents called the dobers. I've been in trouble before, you know. Hooky from school, stealing, hanging around with what you would call wrong kids, stuff like that. Anyway, school sucks." Her expression turned dark. "When I first told my parents I needed to jam, they called the dobers, but I ran off before they came to the house. They've been looking for me ever since, but I'm never going back. Never!" Her large eyes searched his face. "You sure you won't dob me in?"

"Promise. What's your name?" he asked as he opened the restaurant door and waited for her to enter.

"Aleya."

"That's a pretty name."

There were enough customers inside to avoid being conspicuous and Nash made toward an empty table at the back. A young waitress dressed in a gray form-fitting uniform sauntered toward them, holding a pen and pad. She glanced at Aleya's disheveled appearance, frowned suspiciously, then turned to Nash.

"Yes?"

"I'll have a long black with milk on the side." He glanced at Aleya. "And you?"

Lips pressed in concentration, she studied the menu display board that hung above the counter. "Can I have a blueberry muffin and a vegetable smoothie?" She glanced at him. "If that's all right with you?"

He nodded. "Fine. Nothing else? Eggs, veggie patties, pancakes?"

She hit him with her sunny smile. "After the muffin."

Grinning, he nodded to the waitress.

"Won't be long," she said and walked off.

Nash sat back and studied his new charge. "So, where do you live?"

She shrugged. "Where it's convenient. Lots of empty houses around, old factories and stuff. I'm with a bunch who take care of me and teach me things. They're not lifeliners and don't know that I'm one."

"Keep it that way."

Looking at her, he could hardly imagine how she coped, but her life didn't have a future. Sooner or later, the dobers would catch up with her.

"Aren't you afraid of being mugged, or worse?"

"It's been tried once or twice, but I can look after myself," she declared, not appreciating the dangers she faced every day. At her age, getting hurt or dying was something one read about or saw in the holoview. The old died, not kids.

He wondered if she understood what it meant to be a lifeliner, with everyone around her seeking to report her to the authorities or capture her for the reward. Having taken her under his wing, what next? Allow her back to her scavenging existence, not knowing if she would see tomorrow? But what could he do? The ramifications of becoming involved and the scope of that obligation daunted him. He had enough problems in his life right now and didn't need to add another major one to the list. All very well, but he had become involved and now, he could not let her loose, cast her off, wipe her from his mind. Not if he wanted to live with himself.

"Tell me. How did you find out that you were a lifeliner?"

She wiped her nose with the back of her hand. "I had these urges for a while, like I was hungry even though I had already eaten. I knew something wasn't right. The Social Studies teacher told us about lifeliners, how they sucked energy from someone by touching them and why governments were interested in them because normal people were dying. The local library had books and I read up. Lots of stuff on the Internet too.

"At school once, I made Angela faint. She and her two friends picked on me because I'm smart and got top marks in tests. She's rich and always dressed posh. Anyway, one lunchtime, she took an apple out of my lunchbox and I shoved her off the seat. Her friends gaped, not believing I would dare fight back. It was funny. Angela grabbed my hair and slapped me. I caught her hand and felt a tingle run up my arm. It made me strong and I shoved her down. We struggled for a while, then she rolled her eyes and fainted. I let go and ran off. She must have dobed on me, because the Principal hauled me in and I had detention." Aleya wriggled in her seat. "It was worth it. Angela and her stuck-up prissies left me alone after that."

"Didn't you talk to your parents?"

"I tried, but they didn't understand, especially my dad. I heard them arguing once. Dad said if anyone found out what I was, he would be ruined and probably jailed for not reporting me. I knew governments did bad things to lifeliners, but I didn't know what to do. All I knew, my parents didn't love me anymore." Her eyes examined his face. "I wasn't changed. I'm still me. Why didn't they love me? I hate them!"

"It's complicated, Aleya," Nash said and gently stroked her hand. "I'll explain it to you one day."

She sniffed and wiped her nose.

"After dinner one night, Mom and Dad had a terrible row and, later, I heard him talking to the dobers on the holoview. Mom threatened to leave him if he did that, but he ignored her. I rushed upstairs to my room and grabbed my little backpack where I stashed some stuff. I pulled on a windcheater and made a break for it through the window. There is an old white gum at the back of the house and one of its branches hangs over the roof. I used it lots of times to sneak out to play with my friends at the local football ground.

"I wandered around the Doncaster shopping center for a couple of days before I took a train into the city, certain that no one could find me there. They never did. I was afraid if I called any of my friends, they'd dob me in. I heard that cops could track my phone and PID, so I chucked the cell and switched off my PID. At the Melbourne Central one morning, this old geezer who'd been living on the streets for a while, took me in and showed me the ropes. I've been living like that ever since."

Listening to her tragic story, Nash wanted to hug her and tell her she was safe now and could stop running. He felt irrepressible anger at what governments were doing to lifeliners. They weren't to blame for being different. Looking at her dirty face, he badly wanted to help her, but didn't know exactly how. This was summer and the nights warm. When winter came, survival would become problematic for a lone kid. Tempted to put her up at his apartment, not entirely comfortable with the idea, or the prospect that she would invite some of her wayward friends over and they'd trash the place.

"Do you want to get off the street?"

"Where would I go?"

"I know someone who can help you. You cannot live in some derelict warehouse all your life. You need to be somewhere safe."

She stared at him. "What's it to you? I do all right. Besides, all people are mean."

"I just—"

"You into little girls or something?"

Nash drew back, stung by her coarse remark. "Have your muffin and smoothie and you can go. But as I said, you need to learn how to recognize another lifeliner before you jam. He might not offer you a muffin."

He learned that one the hard way. Simply because someone was a lifeliner did not make him virtuous or honest. He pushed back his chair and made to stand up. She shot out her hand and grabbed his wrist.

"I'm sorry. It's…well, it's been a while since anybody did something nice for me."

Undecided, his instincts telling him to walk away, he took a deep breath and sat down.

"Think about what I said."

"Okay. Is there a toilet around here?" she demanded, craning her head. He pointed at an alcove and she grinned. "Back in a sec."

You sure you know what you're doing, old son?

No, he didn't know what he was doing.

Aleya came back as the waitress brought a loaded tray and walked off. Aleya reached for the smoothie and slurped noisily through the straw. Giving him a sheepish smile, she took a large bite out of the muffin. He shook his head, stirred milk into his coffee and poured in a sugar stick. Taking a sip, he leaned back.

"What's your name," she asked, finishing the last of her muffin.

"Nash."

"Nash…nice."

He grinned. "My girlfriend, at least I hope she'll be my girlfriend, said the same thing."

She arched her eyebrows and her eyes became mischievous. "You have a girlfriend?"

"She's a doctor, a geneticist."

"That's somebody who scrambles your brain, right?"

Nash laughed. "She's not that kind of doctor. Now, what do I do with you?"

"Those lifeliners…they'd look after me?"

"Find you a home, get you back to school—"

"School? Yuck!" Aleya made a face.

"It's not that bad," he said, holding back a grin. "These days, to survive, you need a good education. It will help you avoid the dobers."

"They haven't caught me yet."

"Be real, Aleya. You must know they'll get you one day by tracking your PID."

She shook her head. "No way. I switched it off."

"Yes, but they'll know you switched it off, and there are surveillance cameras all over the city."

"These people…they're all lifeliners?"

"Most of them."

She snorted. "Can't trust any of 'em. I met one on a tram once. She wanted to hand me in."

"You can trust me," he said softly.

Her face took on a dark look. "I don't trust no one."

Looking at her, she had to be strong to keep the ghosts that haunted her nights at bay. Still only a kid, she was someone who should grow up with loving parents. He could hardly imagine how she made out this long. It won't last, though. Skulking through the city, the heavy hand of a dober would clamp her shoulder one day and…he wasn't sure what would happen then. Did the federal government still run secret labs? Not sure about that either, but wouldn't be surprised if they did.

She slurped the last of her smoothie. "I'll think about what you said." She rose and slid the backpack onto her right shoulder. "Thanks for the muffin. I'll see you around…Nash."

"Anytime you have a craving for another one…" A wry smile tugged the corner of his mouth.

She nodded and walked briskly toward the door. Watching her disappear into the crowd, he picked up his cup and held it between both hands, savoring its subtle warmth. If she wanted his help, he'll hand her to the Lifeliner Help Center and they can deal with her. What would he do with a kid running around his apartment? Sending her to a regular school would mean questions, filling out forms, government entanglements…

He gave a long sigh and sipped his coffee.

A kid, alone *and* a lifeliner, she'd be better off dead.

Life sucks, he decided.

* * *

"This is elegant, Nash," Cariana said, giving his apartment a feminine scrutiny. "Sparse and masculine. It suits you."

His other girlfriends had said the same thing. "I'm not much into extraneous clutter."

Clean, simple, functional, that was how he liked things. The two oil paintings in the living room, one showing a subdued evening seascape with the sun painting the clouds in orange hues, and an alien world with two large moons hugging the horizon against a backdrop of thick stars, summed up his spectrum of artistic interest, and in many respects, his roaming mind.

"The layout looks very similar to my place," she added.

"All apartments these days seem to have the same design."

When he proposed that they have dinner at his place, he felt some reservation. Would she feel threatened at his place, uncertain of his intentions, relying on him to pick her up and bring her home? He could see doubts flash in her eyes before she agreed, and he was determined not to do anything that might shatter her trust.

He took her light alpaca cardigan and draped it across the lounge sofa.

She regarded him with a quizzical look that made her eyes shine and her left cheek dimple. "Dining out in a man's bachelor pad is something I haven't done in a while."

He laughed. "Prepare yourself, then. You're in for a treat. Come…"

"I know I said it before, but thanks for picking me up."

"My pleasure."

He led her to the balcony and pulled out a chair for her. Below, cars flowed in both directions, interrupted by an occasional tram. Somehow, every Friday, the number of cars seemed to multiply, and this evening was no exception. Fluffy clouds had drifted in from Port Phillip Bay, but the sun still broke through the cover to cast black shadows. As predicted, the change had cooled the air somewhat, taking out most of its bite. A light breeze stirred the leaves of golden elms lining the boulevard.

"This is pleasant," Cariana said dreamily as she sat down, lost somewhere in the vastness of her mind. "I miss having a balcony at my place. When I'm in Woodend, I sometimes sit outside and simply soak things in, not wanting anything or expecting anything, just to forget for a little while."

Leaning against the back of a chair, Nash nodded. "I like it out here, especially when the wind is blowing and the rain is cold and hard."

She raised an eyebrow and her eyes sparkled. "Wow. You have an odd idea what's fun."

He chuckled. "So I've been told. People reveal themselves when things are stormy. When it's nice and cozy, a mask falls into place. My personal observation on life," he announced solemnly, and she laughed.

He waved at the spread on the table: a pitcher of iced margarita, a tray of four assorted dips and crackers. He poured for them and raised his glass.

"To the successful end of another week," he declared gravely.

"To weekends," she replied with restrained levity. "There should be more of them."

They clinked glasses and sipped. Cariana nodded in appreciation, took a larger swallow and crossed her legs.

"This didn't come out of a bottle."

"My unique concoction," he assured her and reached for a cracker. He scooped a dollop of spiced red capsicum dip and popped it into his mouth. "These, I'm afraid, came out of a packet. Blame the manufacturer if they don't measure up."

She grinned and helped herself to a hummus dip.

"Business finished at Parkville?" he prompted.

"Hardly. If anything, things are getting more confusing."

"Confusing, how?"

"You would think that after six years of intensive study, we would have cracked the DNA changes that make lifeliners different. We identified some of the activated gene switches, but not the causal factors. I hoped data from the American lab would corroborate a hypothesis I'm pursuing, but it only left me with more questions."

He sat back and took another sip of margarita. "Cariana, I understand your need to neatly catalog lifeliners and file them away, but how does that address the social problems, including significant suicide rates among teenage lifeliners?"

She frowned and her forehead wrinkled. "It doesn't, I suppose. The CSIRO project I mentioned, they're working on that in cooperation with think tanks around the world."

"Any conclusions worth sharing?"

"It's the same one we've had all along. Over time, *homo sapiens* will become extinct, replaced by lifeliners."

"That's not what I asked."

"I' a geneticist, not a sociologist."

"A nice evade."

"What do you want me to say? Lifeliners may be the next step in our evolution, but right now, they're a disease, an infection."

"And you're working on a vaccine, is that it?"

"For God's sake, Nash! You're making it sound like we're trying to exterminate them."

Nash was torn. He wanted to build on what they had, and develop a meaningful relationship, but was he being honest with himself? Would she want to if he revealed himself to her? Perhaps he rushed things, seeing more between them than actually was. For her, he might be an interesting diversion. He also felt constrained, reluctant to pursue an argument that might drive her away, but an argument he would have to face sometime. Not tonight, though, which might be a sign of his insecurity. Was he that desperate?

He reached for her hand and she tensed. "I'm sorry, Cariana. I did not mean to drag you into discussing identity politics, but I am genuinely interested in your views and research on lifeliners."

After a moment, she relaxed and flashed him a small smile. "I get carried away from time to time. There are days when I don't enjoy my work. CSIRO is supposed to be an independent entity, free from government interference, but that's never been true. Especially now. People are scared, Nash. Couples are finding that they're infertile, and when they do have children, they're lifeliners more often than not, which they find out when the kids reach puberty. Instant family chaos. Add to this an increasingly intrusive government, and technology that is marginalizing even those with skills, and you have a very dark future. Is it any wonder that people out there see lifeliners as the cause of all their troubles?"

"They're human, like everybody else."

"They spell the end of mankind as we know it, and people won't roll over and die. Eventually they will, but only after a lot of bloodshed."

Bloodshed…he had to agree with her on that. Would humans be the ones shedding it, though? There were billions of them and only hundreds of thousands of lifeliners. He didn't know how many. No one did. They did not advertise themselves, and who could blame them.

She brushed back a strand of hair. "Enough of gloom and doom. Speaking of work, how was your day?"

"Had a meeting this morning with my Telstra counterpart. She wanted to add a major addition to the work program. When I explained how this would significantly delay introduction of business-critical systems, she reluctantly agreed to handle it as a separate project. She still thought I was mean for rejecting the change."

"She has my sympathies, and you *are* mean, and a cube."

"Nope. Realistic. If things went belly up, she would be the first to drive in the knife to save her own scalp."

Cariana helped herself to another dip. Nash picked up the pitcher and his glass and got up.

"Let's go inside. It's treat time."

A polished walnut table acted as a divider between the kitchen and living room. Plates, cutlery, condiments, and two sauces were already in place. He pointed at a padded wooden chair and invited her to sit. He closed the sliding door to the balcony and drew the heavy, dark green drapes. He checked the oven, nodded and extracted a large pan, then placed it on a cork pad in the center of the table. The smell of baked crepes made his mouth water.

Cariana leaned forward and examined the rolled crepes with their topping of sour cream. Nash went to the refrigerator and took out a bowl of mixed salad. Sitting down, he canted his head slightly.

"Sally, seascape four."

Instantly, the lounge dissolved into a glistening, flowing beach with waves crashing in foamy surf against dark cliffs. Behind them, the last hints of a flaming sunset hovered above a molten sea.

Cariana gasped and her hand shot to her mouth. "This is amazing. Must have cost you a small fortune."

"I know someone in the virtual reality entertainment business and he got me a package deal, including the house computer."

"Sally?"

He shrugged and grinned. "A memory."

"Must be a special memory to anthropomorphize your house computer after her."

Two years and her presence still haunted him. They had something important, a future that held a promise of fulfillment. A chance meeting on a train, both attempting to jam off each other, followed by startled recognition that over time led to something more intimate. In a callous act of revenge, her previous boyfriend denounced her on Facebook. One night, three placard-waving Humans Only League activists murdered her in front of her apartment. All three were convicted, but as the judge handed down life sentences, they held up their fisted right arms and proclaimed death to all lifeliners.

"I've been meaning to change the name. Not good dwelling in the past." He grabbed two wooden spatulas and hovered them over the steaming pan of crepes. "May I?"

"What are they?"

"Savories, my own recipe variant." He scooped out two long crepes and placed them on her plate, then filled his own. "Help yourself to the salad. The bowls contain sweet chilly and Worcestershire sauce. Add to taste."

Frowning, she cut off a morsel, blew on it and gingerly took a bite. Her eyebrows arched as she chewed.

"Say, this is great. What's inside?"

"Nothing unusual. Some onions, bacon, potatoes, eggs, and some cheese."

"You made the crepes?"

"With my very own hands."

She took a sip of margarita. "Where did you learn to cook?"

"I picked up a few things from Mom and cookery books, but it's been mostly trial and error. As you can see, my culinary experiments haven't managed to kill me."

"Yet," she added.

They put in some serious time eating. Watching her, Nash felt a glow of satisfaction, happy to see her enjoying herself. He resisted an impulse to touch her, stroke her hand, feel the smoothness of her skin, hold her in his arms, never letting go. He took the pitcher of margarita to the fridge and brought out a bottle of red burgundy. He filled fresh glasses and took a pull of the delicious wine.

Cariana finished her crepes, pursed her lips, and helped herself to two more after giving him a guilty grin.

"If it's worth doing, it's worth overdoing," he assured her, taking two himself. "I read that somewhere."

She laughed and slapped his hand. "That's terrible."

After taking one more crepe, she sighed and drained her burgundy. "That was excellent, Nash. Thank you."

"Ah, we're not done yet, but I'll let this stuff settle first." Leaning back, glass of wine in hand, he tilted his head slightly. "Going to your Woodend retreat this weekend?"

She nodded. "There is always stuff to do around the house, and with the hot weather we've been having, I need to check up on my garden. The watering system is automated, but…"

"If you need help with some things…"

She waved her hand. "Thanks, but I don't mind the chores. It lets me forget about my job."

"I know what you mean. I drive out occasionally to get away from things, stop at a little restaurant somewhere, and watch the locals. I think people in bush towns have a better lifestyle. They seem to have density and texture missing in impersonal cities."

"You're looking for simplicity," Cariana said softly.

"I guess. Cities are pressure cookers and humans have not learned to cope. It is no wonder that most social problems are generated in cities."

After a silent moment, he slapped his knee and stood. "Time for the finale. Sally, end session." The seascape vanished and they were again in the real world.

"Magical," Cariana whispered, her eyes soft, lost in the hologram.

He cleared the table and laid out fresh plates and cutlery, then brought out a large glass bowl of biscuit and honey ice cream laced with sour cherries. Next came a smaller bowl of purple sauce and a shaker of caster sugar. Humming a tune, he strode to the microwave and pressed a sensor pad. After two minutes, he extracted a wooden plate piled high with steaming crepes.

Cariana shook her head. "Oh no. More crepes?"

"This, my dear, is where you do things yourself. You take a crepe, load it with ice cream and fold it. Sprinkle on some sugar and help things along with a generous dollop of my genuine homemade blueberry/strawberry sauce. Let me show you."

She smirked and rolled her eyes.

He proceeded to make himself an ice cream crepe and dug in. A second later, he raised a finger. "Forgot the margarita!" He retrieved the pitcher and refilled their glasses.

Folding herself a crepe, Cariana dabbed a morsel into the fruit sauce and forked it into her mouth.

"Oh my."

"Not bad, eh?"

"This is incredible. You could be very useful around the house, you know."

"I even do my own dishes…with occasional help from my dishwasher."

"Of course," she deadpanned. "Cube."

He feigned outrage. "I don't think you believe me!"

Her left cheek dimpled. "I'm trying to picture you with an apron hovering over a sink."

"Oh ye of little faith…" he murmured and gave a weary sigh.

After two more crepes and another glass of margarita, she settled back and patted her stomach.

"I'm full. If I gain a kilo, it'll be your fault."

"Hey! That's not fair. I wasn't the one stuffing it in."

"I wouldn't have if it hadn't been so good. So, it's your fault."

He threw up his hands and laughed. "Okay, guilty."

She nodded. "Next time, it's on me. Sunday at seven, okay? I've got to warn you, though. I'm not much around the kitchen. Never was."

"Anything, as long as I'm with you."

Turning serious, her almond eyes probed him. "Nash, I don't want to rush into anything. You've been sweet, but…"

"I know. One day at a time."

"Thank you. I knew you'd understand."

He did understand, not wanting to rush things either. Was he afraid to let go, content to keep replaying Sally's stale memories? To commit, opening himself again, also meant acceptance, sharing, having a new beginning. What the hell. He lived in a world where tomorrow might never come, and making plans merely an illusion to shield himself from a dark reality.

Very well. He would allow a little bit of Cariana's light to shine in and dispel the shadows of his memories. Besides, after finding her, he did not want to lose her because of a lingering past love he ought to relegate to the archives where it belonged. However, Cariana's attitude about lifeliners a shadow he needed to cast some light on.

"Coffee or something to top things off?"

"I better not. It's been a long day and I have to prepare for my drive to Woodend." She pushed back her chair. "It's been lovely, Nash."

Reluctant to see her go, he understood that she had to be comfortable with how fast this relationship would develop.

She frowned, sensing his pensiveness. "Why the gloomy face?"

A fleeting grin played at the corner of his mouth. "Nothing. My yesterdays catching up with me and they haunt me some-times."

Her eyes studied him with lively interest. "I don't know if I could cope, not able to forget, I mean. How do you do it?"

He shrugged. "I compartment and avoid opening certain doors. I am also well-adjusted, remember?"

Cariana snorted. "With a unique pickup routine." She lifted a hand. "I know, an accident. Never mind. I had a fine time and your apartment reflects your personality, but I must be going." She stood and smoothed down her white slacks.

Cloaked in comfortable, intimate silence as he drove up St. Kilda Road, Nash did not attempt to strike up a conversation. He pulled up at The Fawkner Residences driveway and stopped in front of the steps. Without waiting, Cariana opened the door, got out, and waited for him.

She brushed his cheek with soft, fleeting fingers. "Thank you for tonight."

He wanted to gather her in his arms and hold her against him, crush her lips with his, but he hesitated. She had said that she liked a man who takes charge, but this was something else. He did not want to do anything she wasn't ready for. On the other hand, he didn't want to appear timid.

He leaned slightly toward her, waiting for any sign of rejection. Seeing she appeared willing, he kissed her, a gentle, tender touch. If she wanted more, she had to choose to walk this path.

"You have the most mysterious eyes I have ever seen in anyone," he whispered, and she smiled.

"Good night, Nash."

With a flutter of fingers, she hurried up the steps. Darkness swallowed the spot where she had stood.

* * *

Bright sunshine greeted Nash as he walked out of the Telstra building. Cars crowded the broad Exhibition Street, and leafy elms along the central divide provided shade and relief from the heat. Pedestrians clogged the sidewalks, flouting their casual attire among more conservatively dressed office slaves. Noise, whispering cars, people everywhere, a bubble of anonymity. Virgin Air and Uber skycars crisscrossed the air above the city. It looked peaceful, but that bubble was straining, ready to burst into unrestrained violence. He hoped it wouldn't happen, but he feared it was only a matter of time, and the sands were running out.

It did not have to be, though. It didn't, but who was going to stop it?

Time perhaps for another golf game and a serious chat with Garrett Bartlett from Grange, Strand and Bartlett. Nash tried to play at least once a week, but work commitments did not always permit such luxury. He could hash over his concerns with Dad, and it's been some time since his last somber *tete-a-tete*, but he didn't want to wait until the weekend. Besides, some things were better tossed around with a friend, and he trusted Garrett with his life.

Nash first met the lawyer when starting out as a consultant with IBM, an introduction made by his father. G.S. & B. was an old Melbourne law firm with a reputation for taking on tough industrial cases, representing labor unions and corporations alike, and they only handled referrals. They were also the ones who defended Curtis Sands in his case. Clearly, they had no qualms about taking on the government. How his old man got to know the firm and the dealings they had remained their business. His father simply said that he would need somebody good to handle his investments and field legal problems. No need to explain the kind of problems Nash and Mark were likely to have.

The lawyer, of course, knew what Nash was and welcomed getting the raw facts on lifeliners firsthand, often playing the prosecutor in their spirited discussions, which made Nash suspect the old codger knew more than he let on. Garrett turned down an appointment to the High Court bench, preferring to execute law at ground level. It gave him a better feel for justice, the older man confided over one golf game. Nash won that one by two strokes. Garrett compensated for his lack of physical strength with a superior short game technique and finesse to sink some unbelievable putts, whereas Nash tended to rely on flare and phenomenal tee drives.

As he walked casually along the sidewalk, he told himself he'd call Garrett after his meeting with Snoden; no need to spoil his morning with dark thoughts.

He stripped off his jacket, flung it across his right shoulder, and wandered toward Bourke Street, pleased with the morning's meeting. Amanda Fuller grudgingly acknowledged satisfactory progress, which made Nash grin. The program of work running below budget and slightly ahead of schedule. She had nothing to gripe about. She did raise several non-critical issues, which he would email his project managers for discussion and action. All minor stuff.

Telstra, eat glass.

He hoped Snoden had cleared funds for additional server hardware, or his happy morning would quickly turn gray. The IBM program director could be a pain, but he delivered…usually. Nash expected to find out quickly enough when he presented his summary to the bean counter, leaving him free to clean up his administrative chores. He *could* do that from his apartment, but his position demanded an occasional face-to-face appearance at the office, or somebody might start to wonder if they needed him at all.

Buoyed by bright sunshine and warm air, he refused to be dejected by portents of looming social unrest. Even the missed date with Cariana on Sunday did not dampen his spirits. Unexpected data from the States meant a long day at Parkville, weekend notwithstanding. By the time she got home, she only wanted to sack out. Nash knew how these things happened; he'd had more than a few long days at work himself and did not hold this temporary setback against her. She promised to make it up to him tomorrow night, and that suited him fine.

What did get him down a little was yesterday's announcement by Raines Latham that the government has passed legislation giving police officers power to interrogate a person's PID to establish identity without having to obtain prior court permission. The Victorian state Premier explained smoothly on Channel Nine's morning breakfast talk show that this was merely another positive step by a responsible administration to combat terrorism and crime and increase public protection. The sting in the tail came when he said that blocking or turning off the PID would become an offense, subject to a $500 spot fine. The declaration had immediately set off clanging alarms with Liberty Victoria, supported by the Australian Privacy Foundation—something Nash found gratifying—promptly lodged an action in the Supreme Court citing unwarranted violation of individual freedoms.

Over the years, he became finely tuned to government maneuverings to identify and track lifeliners, and this development made him sit up and take notice. Everybody's PID held a lot of personal and biometric information, undeniably useful in emergency conditions. What the device did not hold, the issue still before the courts, was a DNA print. Eminently worthwhile in a medical situation, it nevertheless spelled potential doom for life-liners in particular.

Accelerated deprivation of civil liberties started in 2006 after emergence of ISIS in Iraq, which led to increased terrorism activities, predominantly in Europe and England. In Australia, federal governments of both persuasions exaggerated isolated lone-wolf criminal acts, labeling them terrorist attacks that threatened the country, then used them as a pretext to enact draconian laws that seriously undermined individual rights because it made the government appear proactive. The public and the media had a field day last September ridiculing the NSW police for calling an armed robbery of a Sydney's petrol station an act of terrorism.

Nash remembered vividly a remark made by Daniel Andrews, the then Victorian Premier, on October 4, 2017, although as a teenager, he did not quite understand what it meant:

"The luxury that no political leader in Australia has is to say 'no' to law enforcement. No, we won't give you what you say you need, we won't give you the technology that you need to keep us safe..."

To keep us in control...

The comment raised an inevitable storm of indignant commentary from civil liberty groups, which achieved nothing. Voter apathy killed the protests, and the Labor government quietly gave the police more invasive powers. Admittedly, Andrews made that comment fifteen years ago, but it reflected, and still reflects, a pattern of increasingly autocratic behavior by all levels of government.

As far as Nash was concerned, liberty was not a luxury to be sacrificed on the altar of public security, but a fundamental pillar of democracy. Chip away at that pillar and it would eventually crumble, toppling the social institutions that provided checks against a regime's grab for control over its citizens and their actions.

He admired Latham's sneakiness. Unable to contravene the 2029 High Court ruling that prohibited tracking and maintaining lifeliner registers, the Premier—probably with federal government encouragement and the decision by President Elliott Mackay to reinstate the infamous U.S. Lifeliner Act by executive order in defiance of the Supreme Court ruling—neatly sidestepped the problem by disguising the move as another link in the public safety chain. After all, if lifeliners enjoyed the same rights and privileges as ordinary humans, interrogating PIDs merely an extension of social services, something to be welcomed. However dirty and underhanded, Nash did not object to the announcement *per se*, provided a person could block access to his PID and biometric data at will as suggested by the federal Labor Party opposition leader Macey Gardner, something the Premier had now nimbly circumvented. Giving law enforcement agencies power to bypass such a block effectively removed all protection lifeliners had against identification and open persecution.

What he had to remember, civil liberty groups did not launch actions to protect lifeliners, regardless of any benefit lifeliners might garner from such actions. Lifeliners needed to take up the fight themselves to stem the tide of discrimination and prejudice, using the same political tools employed against them. So far, those efforts had been marginally successful at best. The fledgling Lifeliner Party held two seats in the Victorian Upper House, and one in NSW; not enough to block punitive legislation, but enough to provide a voice of reason. Preselection for the October federal election had already begun, the party hoping to secure at least one Senate seat to guarantee national exposure. All laudable goals, but being a parliamentarian and an identified lifeliner wasn't always comfortable in an increasingly acerbic social climate, as Curtis Sands found out. Of course, to get elected, a lifeliner did not *need* to identify himself. Nash wondered how many state and federal representatives operated inside the Liberal and Labor party machines, pushing Lifeliner Party policies. He felt certain the federal government probably wondered the same thing and had undoubtedly taken steps to find out.

Such as inserting special instructions into PID software updates? He could not avoid updates, and there were legitimate reasons to accept them. What worried him was lack of mechanisms to ascertain the underlying purpose of those updates. Paranoia setting in? He wouldn't be the first person thinking about this, and as the guy said, just because you are paranoid did not mean they weren't after you.

Life had gotten tougher and his comfortable existence might not last very long. If Canberra followed the U.S. and decided to ignore the High Court, it would be a nightmare come true.

A lesser nightmare had already come true, not political, but moral. Vatican finally announced a positional papal bull on lifeliners that shook all Christian denominations. Pope Conon II declared that although lifeliners were human, they lacked a soul made in God's image. Adam, he maintains, did not have the ability to suck life out of another person. Most religious commentators agreed that the ultraconservative Greek pontiff who succeeded Pope Francis had alienated many followers and accelerated the drift from Christian churches. Instead of providing a healing middle ground to dampen bigotry and discrimination, the declaration served to fuel extremism. The word Conon, Nash recalled, meant 'raise the dust', and the pope had certainly managed to do that for the faithful.

At the intersection of Bourke and Swanston, he walked past a bedraggled figure sitting on the sidewalk next to a newspaper stand, a cardboard sign proclaiming his tale of woe. He never dropped a coin even if he had one, having gone totally electronic when PIDs were introduced in 2026 and banks started phasing out hard currency. Facilities existed to help such people without the need to beg. Truthfully, he didn't feel any empathy for them, especially for those who smoked. The cost of a pack of cigarettes could easily support an individual for a day.

He glanced at the colorful magazines and stacked tabloids crowding newsstand shelves, and reflected on the resurgence of print. In early 2020s, most publications were struggling to survive the Internet surge, everything going online. By the middle of the decade, print slowly came back into vogue. No one denied the convenience of online news, but people remembered and liked the tactile feel of a magazine or newspaper paper provided.

He was startled to see Aleya standing at the corner, apparently waiting for him. Hair stringy, clothing badly needing a wash, as did her smudged face, she nevertheless held herself with poise and dignity, not looking at all like a haunted street urchin.

He stopped before her and inclined his head.

Her mouth curved up in a mischievous smile. "Took you long enough to show up."

"I'll have a stern talk with my social secretary," he deadpanned, and she giggled. "So, what's up?"

"The dobers ran us out and I'm looking for a new place to stash out."

"Us?"

"Hard luck cases." She wrinkled her nose. "Like that guy over there. You wouldn't approve of 'em."

"Then why hang out with them?" he demanded, fascinated by her capacity to cope and apparently thrive in an environment hostile at so many levels.

She shrugged. "They understand the local setup. The old geezer I told you about? He's a bit older than you—"

Vastly amused, Nash laughed, generating several puzzled glances from passing pedestrians.

"You consider me an old geezer?"

"To me, anyone over thirty is pushing it," she declared with unshakeable authority. "Anyway, he's been nice to me and taught me things."

"Like stealing?"

Her expression darkened. "Nobody's ever given me a break. To survive, I do what I have to."

"I'm sorry, Aleya. I didn't mean—"

"We should walk. People are starting to stare."

He nodded and took her hand. "Hungry? You look like you've been on a diet."

"Well, I *could* swallow some orange juice."

"I don't doubt it." He paused, searching her face. "Have you jammed?"

"On a tram. Don't worry, I'm good at it and the mark never twitched."

Torn with conflicting emotions, Nash reminded himself that picking up a stray kitten meant taking on a level of responsibility he felt uncertain he could handle. Managing a rebellious young teenager wary of all authority wasn't his first choice, and triggered some uncomfortable images. Yet, he could not allow her to sink back into anonymity without making some effort.

Rat crap. He was making excuses and knew it. Content in his safe cocoon, allowing someone else into his life meant disruption and definite problems. Problems he did not need.

Nash, old son, stick your cocoon up your ass.

Ever since losing Sally, he rejected intimacy, togetherness, and sharing, preferring not to become involved, choosing safety over the pain people would otherwise inflict on him. Even with Cariana, did he unconsciously look for reasons not to become involved, using his lifeliner identity as a convenient pretext, believing he would be inflicting pain on *her*? All this time, he might have been living a lie, believing he could not find fulfillment in a world that would surely reject him if it knew him for what he was. Alone, comfortable, he thought himself superior gazing at the mindless multitude struggling to survive through their days. Yet, what made him were people he chose to surround himself with, allowing them to touch him, regardless of the superficiality of that touch. Without their touch, he was barren, a dust mote drifting in the wind, and just as insignificant. He wondered why it took him this long to realize it, and he supposedly couldn't lie to himself.

Cariana's antipathy against lifeliners not exactly conducive to an open relationship either, and something he would need to resolve if they were to go any further.

Staring at this little lost vagrant, the walls of his protective shell crumbling around him, he recognized that he could not walk away from her, not if he wanted to live with himself.

Ah, rats!

"Aleya, move in with me. At least until I find you something permanent."

Her eyes grew round. "You'd do that for me?"

"You need a place to stay and I have a spare bedroom."

"Clean and sterilized, no doubt?" she remarked and made a face, clearly not enamored with the idea.

He was tickled by her expression of scorn for things neat and tidy. Given her current lifestyle, a reasonable attitude.

"A bath and some new clothes would change your mind."

"I suppose you'd want me to go to school and stuff?"

"Eventually."

"School sucks. It's boring and the teachers don't actually know much. I finished year seven in three months and stared at walls the rest of the time, which got me into trouble, by the way," she added with a cheeky grin.

"I don't doubt it. You remember everything you see and read?"

"Just about. My Social Studies teacher called me a Miss Know-It-All, but he was a jerk. At end of the second term, I quit going, preferring the Library—"

"Library?"

"You know, the State Library opposite the Melbourne Central station. They've got hundreds and hundreds of books! The dobers told on me and I had a terrific row with my dad over it." Her face turned moody. "It wasn't long after that I ran away."

Looking at her, Nash found it remarkable that she survived at all. He crouched and held her small hands.

"You can't live like this, Aleya. You must know that."

She pouted and scuffed the sidewalk with her shoe. "I guess, and it's not as though I have many choices."

He sighed and shook his head. She didn't trust him and he could hardly fault her for that. Life had handed this little girl some hard kicks and it takes time for the bruises to heal.

"Why were you waiting for me?"

"I was on my way to collect my stuff when I saw you. Trent— that's the old geezer I mentioned—knows a place in St. Kilda where we can hang out if I don't find something."

"Move in with me and you won't have to worry about dobers…ever."

She tilted her head and looked at him with a speculative gaze. "Sounds nice, but the idea of going to school…I don't know."

"Have you heard of the Lifeliner Help Center?"

"I know what they do. What about it?"

"They can get you off the street, help you sort yourself out, perhaps even reconcile you with your family, although from what you told me, that might take a bit of doing."

"They'd only turn me in," she declared with scorn. "No thanks."

"They don't work like that, Aleya."

The smell of fresh coffee, buns, and fried eggs coming from a restaurant made Aleya pause. Grinning, Nash steered her inside.

Watching her tuck into two fried vegetable patties—she turned up her nose at the offer of fried eggs—dabbing them with a bun, tall glass of pineapple juice at her side, he marveled at her ability to enjoy the moment, apparently unconcerned what the day might bring. She told him she did not trust anyone, yet she sought him out. That had to count for something. She could also be using him, hiding behind a façade of girlish innocence. He acknowledged the possibility, but did not mind. In her position, he might have done the same thing.

Aleya downed the last of her juice, sighed with contentment, and sat back.

"Thanks, Nash. I needed that."

"Obviously. Tell me. Why were you waiting for me? The truth."

She blushed and lowered her head. "You've been nice to me and I thought…I've got no right to ask…but…"

"What is it?"

"I need to get some things…"

"And you don't have any money."

She lifted her head. "A few dollars. That's all I need, and I'll pay you back, honestly!" Chewing her lower lip, uncertain what he would do, she tensed, ready to flee.

Without saying anything, Nash nodded. "Activate your PID."

She nodded and he authorized a transfer. "If you need more…"

She gaped when she checked her PID. "Wow, that's more than—"

"Take it," he assured her, "and you don't have to pay me back."

A look of puzzled bewilderment crossed her face as though undecided about something.

"I…thank you," she whispered. Her penetrating eyes cut into him. "You're a lifeliner, aren't you?"

"What made you say that?" He did not want to pretend or lie to her, but revealing himself to anyone not a wise thing to do at the best of times. Particularly to a little girl who could inadvertently blurt out the truth and land them both in serious trouble.

She digested that for a moment. "I don't know. The way you helped me. I thought…I guess there are nice people after all."

"There really are." He reached across the table and squeezed her tiny hand. "Aleya, I don't want to rush you into anything, but think about staying at my place. You can leave anytime and rejoin your…friends. And I won't make you go to school."

She flashed him a smile.

"We could go shopping for new clothes," he added. "Washed—I've got a spa bath—"

"A real spa?"

"You can swim in it," he assured her. "Properly dressed, you would look pretty."

Her eyes turned misty as she cleared her throat. "It's been a long time since anyone said I was pretty. Living in old warehouses or squatting in derelict homes don't give me many opportunities to look nice."

He extended his hand. "Deal?"

She bit her lip, exhaled and slowly grasped his hand. "Deal," she said solemnly. "Me in new clothes. Trent won't recognize me."

"Let's go, then."

They caught a tram going up St. Kilda Road and got off at Bromby Street. A short walk later, Nash waited to be cleared by the building's security system. After giving Aleya a curious look, the guard at the security desk nodded to him. Aleya looked awed as she craned her head at the luxurious surrounds inside the lobby. The elevator stopped at the third floor and he led her to his apartment.

"Cool," she remarked, giving the place close scrutiny. Her eyes lit when she saw his library and immediately walked to the shelves and examined the books. She paused and pointed at one.

"Buddhism?"

"A very profound spiritual philosophy."

"And you read them all?"

"Every one of them," he told her as he strode into the kitchen and dug out a ribbon tape. "You can look at them later. We're going shopping, remember?"

"Nash, if you don't mind, can I take that spa bath now? I can't go with you, not in my gear. They'd throw me out."

He took in her ragged appearance. "I see what you mean. Tell you what. I'll get some black jeans for you, a white blouse and new runners. With those on, you won't be thrown out. What do you say?"

"Well, okay."

"Good, but I need to get you measured."

She dropped her backpack to the floor and waited with restrained patience as he took her statistics.

"Done! Let me show you the bathroom."

Aleya paused when Nash opened the door and her eyes grew as she took in the gleaming tiles, large mirror, and triangular spa tucked into a corner beside the shower cubicle.

"Wow, I could get used to this."

He retrieved a soft towel from the linen cabinet and dropped it on the vanity bench.

"Take your time and have fun. I should be back in an hour or so."

She turned and looked up at him. "Nash, there is something…"

"What is it?" he asked gently.

"I…" Eyes filling with emotion, she spread her arms and hugged him.

He returned the hug, holding her tight, and stroked her bony back. "You won't have to be afraid of anything anymore, Aleya," he whispered fiercely and swallowed hard.

"Thanks for everything, Nash," she murmured into his chest.

This little stray kitten had broken through his defenses with absurd ease when he thought them impregnable. His emotional barriers never stood a chance.

He straightened and brushed her cheek. "I won't be long," he said gruffly, then turned and hurried out.

Outside, gray clouds were bunching, drifting in from the bay. He walked to the tram stop and waited. An involuntary shiver ran through him as a cool gust rolled a plastic cup along the tracks.

You're walking into something dangerous, old son.

Perhaps, but he had no choice. He made himself responsible for a child he knew nothing about, but how far did that responsibility extend? Certainly further than the altruistic act of getting her some clothing. She would have to reenter the social mainstream, but as soon as she started using her PID and became known to the authorities, she might be in grave danger. More so if her parents reported her as a missing lifeliner, almost a certainty. His involvement would be questioned, followed by exposure. End of a bright career and his comfortable lifestyle.

That's what happens when you allow emotions to control your actions.

He did not know how to handle his problem, but Adam would. Adam was his shadowy Help Center contact. He didn't know much about him and did not pry. He recalled a holoview article in the 2030 November 14 edition of *The Age*. It had a picture of Neale Wilkie, the newly appointed Victorian state treasurer. In the background stood his chief of staff. Having an eidetic memory came in handy when linking odd bits of information. There *were* ordinary people who did not proscribe to the notion that lifeliners should be hounded or exterminated, and willing to help. It didn't matter. They met three times over the last two years, Adam avoided personal meetings to safeguard his identity, and Nash had warmed to the sophisticated man at once. Adam never said what he did for a living, apart from being covertly involved with the Help Center, and Nash didn't have to ask. Whatever reasons Adam had for becoming involved, it gave him the ability to help lifeliners navigate through the tortuous maze of often hostile state and federal bureaucracies. He admitted cheerfully that one day the dobers would expose him and the underground network he helped run. After all, what he did not illegal exactly, but if they wanted to, the authorities could make life very difficult for his friend, and probably end his political career.

He will hand Aleya to the Center and they would take care of her better than he ever could. Either way, it meant an end to the precarious life she now led roaming the streets.

Before taking any decisive action affecting her life, he would have to talk it over with her. What he thought might be best for her did not necessarily imply her automatic agreement.

Loaded with two shopping bags, humming a tune he picked up from the radio, Nash waited for the elevator doors to open. He bought a few more articles than intended, but he did not think

Aleya would throw them out.

"I'm back!" he shouted as he strode into his apartment, to be greeted by silence.

Sensing he was alone, he tilted his head. "Sally, identify occupants."

"Nash Bannon."

Placing the bags on the dining table, he saw the note, written in precise, flowing letters.

Dear Nash,
Thank you for the bath. It was grand. I like the idea of staying with you, but I must talk this over with Trent, and I have to collect my stuff.
Aleya

Staring at the note, the words burned and he felt a stab of disappointment. In his eagerness to help her, did he rush her into something she wasn't ready for?

He checked the bathroom. She clearly used the spa, but wiped it clean, and the towel left neatly folded on the edge. Nothing else looked disturbed.

Coffee cup beside him, Nash told Sally to activate the holoview wall in computer mode. Might as well do some office business while he was here, and he needed to see Snoden.

Looking at the screen, Aleya's elfin face stared back at him.

Chapter Three

Nash ran up the steps two at a time to the top landing of the Shrine of Remembrance, turned and raised his arms, making like Rocky Balboa from an old movie he'd seen. The city's jagged towers clawed toward the sky bathed in morning's golden light. This was his kingdom and he its lord. The crisp air made his skin tingle and he breathed deeply, feeling invigorated, pleased with his four-kilometer dash through the park.

As he jogged up St. Kilda Road, he spotted a familiar figure loping easily toward him. This time, she wore a purple singlet above the same navy shorts. Long ponytail swaying, she smiled faintly when he nodded to her in passing. They should stop meeting like this. Then she was gone, their lives on different tracks.

Slowing to a brisk walk as he approached Domain Road to cool down, his thoughts wandered. He did not sleep well last night, waking up several times to brood as he stared at a dark ceiling. Until a few days ago, his life had direction, certainty, and a level of stability. He lived comfortably, enjoyed it, and expected things to continue in the same predictable pattern, for a little while anyway. Except they hadn't. It wasn't difficult to identify the disturbance.

Cariana…

She was…exciting, vibrant, and fresh. Not at all like his previous encounters, relationships of mutual convenience with no pretense to be anything else. With Cariana, Nash decided he wanted more. He wanted permanence, time to explore the depths of her mind, enjoy her laughter, challenge her ideas, debate his. Not since Sally did he feel such hunger, a yearning to have someone close. Was it real love or merely physical desire? It didn't matter, but to realize his dream, he would have to remove a wall that stood between them. Could he dare hope for something lasting, being what he was? Would she accept him, knowing it meant a radical change to her life, especially if his identity became generally known, which seemed increasingly likely?

He recalled her vehement reaction when he claimed that lifeliners were also human. He saw something hard lurk in those captivating eyes, almost hatred. He remembered her saying a lifeliner killed her brother. A connection definitely, and he needed to pry open this door into her soul and find out what lay beyond if there was to be something lasting between them.

Would she feel the same way about him once he revealed himself? And he needed to tell her…soon. Better a clean break now than allow her to commit herself, only to find out the terrible truth later. Of course, he did not have to tell her anything, continue living a lie. Sooner or later, though, it would come out, which would destroy both their lives. He could not do that to her, or himself.

They had a date this evening at Vue de Monde. Not an ideal setting to reveal a dark secret, if there was such a thing as an ideal setting for something like that. He frowned and bit his lip, not looking forward to what could be an end of many things, least of all his growing longing for her. The alternative, living a lie not an option, no matter what the consequences.

Close to his apartment block, his frown deepened as he considered another shadow that had fallen across his life.

Aleya…

It bothered him how easily the little street urchin had managed to worm her way into his heart. The hardened Nash Bannon, armed against anything this stinking world could throw at him, felled by a dirty-faced little girl. His friends would never believe it.

Because you are a sentimental slob, old son.

Evidently, and ironic to be smitten by two females who were poles apart.

As he watched the morning news, he felt unsettled, dismayed

and frustrated. People First Party and Humans Only League activists had set up camp on Canberra's parliament grounds, demanding closure to the lifeliner problem. Their solution was simple: permanently intern all known lifeliners, strip them of all rights, and confiscate their property. They wanted the federal government to follow Victoria's lead and give every law enforcement agency authority to interrogate people's PIDs.

Fringe groups everywhere were quick to promote one-liner solutions, ignoring the rule of law when those laws did not support their position. The insidious nature of these organizations, they fed on public apathy, proclaiming support that did not actually exist. Worse still, fearing perceived voter backlash if something wasn't done, political parties had allowed their legislative agenda to be undermined under the dubious pretext of increasing public safety. With an ineffective Prime Minister, erosion of the rule of law could very quickly turn into a landslide of growing lawlessness.

All governments evolved into authoritarian regimes with the consent of the silent majority, and Nash was witnessing a vivid demonstration of this principle across the world's so-called democracies. Such regimes invariably failed, but not after years of turmoil and bloodshed. He had good reason to fear the gathering clouds.

It had not been the best start to his day.

He walked up the driveway to his apartment block and stopped. Aleya's face split into a broad grin as she scrambled to her feet, an abused navy blue duffel beside her, red backpack on top of it. He shook his head, walked up to her and opened his arms. She ran toward him and embraced him, her short arms barely managing to go around his torso as he held the warm bundle. Clearing his throat, he crouched and studied her.

She pulled back and looked at him with penetrating frankness. "I hope you're not mad at me for leaving you yesterday."

"Not mad. Worried."

"Were you really? Why? I told you I can take care of myself."

How to explain a tangled, complex world to someone who lived from hand to mouth, her biggest problem avoiding the dobers. It wouldn't mean a thing.

"Forget it." He picked up her duffel. "Come on."

Aleya gasped with delight when he showed her the new clothes. She lifted an orange-striped cardigan and crunched her face.

"This one's not for me. It's too cube."

Startled, he stared at her as she picked over the clothing. Cariana had used the same phrase. Coincidence, that was all.

"Take what you want. You can change in there," he said and pointed at the spare bedroom. "Your old stuff, and I mean everything, keep it in the duffel. We're getting rid of it and you're in for some serious shopping."

Hugging a light white sweater to her chest, her eyes rounded in alarm.

"Everything?"

"Save your toiletries, but the rest goes. You won't need it."

"Well…"

"Did you have breakfast?"

She shook her head.

"I'll whip something up while you're changing. Now beat it. I need to confirm a reservation for tonight. I've got a date."

"A date?" She made a face. "You'll be kissing and doing other stuff?"

Nash laughed. "I hope there will be some kissing, but I'm not sure about the *other* stuff."

He told Sally to confirm his booking at Vue de Monde and got busy around the kitchen. Some ten minutes later, looking smart in black slacks and white shirt, Aleya walked out of the bedroom, regal in her new outfit. Pitcher of juice in hand, he paused.

"Looking good."

She curtsied and beamed. "Thank you."

Washed, dressed tastefully, he found it difficult picturing her in a ragged outfit, face smudged, eyes lost and wary. She had so much potential, wasted prowling the streets. She should have had the world at her feet. Regrettably, once she stepped out of his apartment, that world would be closed to her.

"What's wrong?" she demanded, pulling back a chair.

He poured juice for her. "Oh, thinking." He swept a hand at the loaded table. "Fresh capsicum, tomatoes, rolls, and my specialty: deep fried veggie patties. Way better than what you'd get at a restaurant."

She reached for the juice, eyeing the spread. "Nice," she declared and proceeded to load her plate. Studying her patty, she cut off a piece and gingerly bit into it. Her eyebrows climbed and she proceeded to make serious inroads into it.

"This is great. What is it?"

"Grated zucchini, cheese, flour, and eggs."

She forked a piece of red capsicum. "Tastes good. I'll have to get…"

"What?"

"Never mind."

Nash laid down his fork. "Aleya, we need to talk about something."

A frown clouded her face. "Rules. I knew it."

He grinned. "No rules while you're with me. Well, one or two perhaps. We need to discuss your PID."

"Don't worry about it. I got it fixed."

"Fixed? How?"

"Yesterday, Trent told me about the new law allowing dobers to talk to your PID. I knew I'd be in trouble, being a runaway, so he fixed it for me."

"He planted a new ID?"

"I don't know what he did. He connected it to his tablet, and after a few minutes said I won't be bothered by the dobers."

To help her avoid unpleasant entanglements with the law, Nash needed to find out what Trent did to her PID. Setting up a new identity profile could be done, but not something he expected a homeless hobo to know.

"Aleya, what do you know about Trent?"

Her eyes lost focus as she chased down memories. "Not all that much. I met him outside the Melbourne Central station. He sat on the sidewalk reading a book, waiting for people to transfer him some money. I remember the title: *Quantum Mechanics and the Speed of Light*. I was curious that he read such stuff and I got a book from the State Library to find out about quantum mechanics."

Nash felt a tingle of alarm. Supposedly down on his luck, Trent did not fit a character who would study something so esoteric.

"He also talks posh, like you," she added with a grin.

"Perhaps we should see him and find out how he talks," he said, returning the grin. "Have you given any thought about getting help from the Lifeliner Center?"

"I thought you were going to help me. Looking to get rid of me already?"

"You can stay with me for as long as you want, and I'm not looking to get rid of you. I'll take care of you, but there are things we must do if you are to have any kind of future. You must know that, don't you?"

She worried her lower lip and hung her head. "I guess." After a moment, she looked up. "But I can stay with you for a little while? Can I? I won't be any trouble."

"For as long as you want," he told her.

She hit him with a sunny smile. "Thanks, Nash."

"It will all work out, you'll see."

"I wish I could have you as my dad," she murmured shyly.

He didn't say anything, his emotions chasing each other. "I'll take care of you, Aleya. Whatever it takes."

"Promise?"

"Promise."

She lowered her eyes. "Nash, I've got to tell you something."

"What is it?"

"I…I'm not…" She bit her lip. "Never mind. It's not important."

He stood and started gathering the dishes. "Finish your breakfast and we're off to the big city. We've got some shopping to do, remember? Afterward, you want to go somewhere? See something different?"

"Can we go to Luna Park?" Her eyes looked hopeful.

"Sure. Anywhere."

"Don't you have to go to work or something?"

"I'm my own boss."

"That's cool."

Shopping with Aleya, the inseparable red backpack on her shoulder, an experience Nash did not look forward to repeating often, not prepared for the whirlwind the little girl managed to create in two hours. Moving deliberately from boutique to boutique, Aleya's discerning eye picked only the best, which surprisingly were not always name brands. She clearly had sophisticated taste acquired before she took to the streets, her parents teaching her well. He was happy to share Aleya's joy buying new jeans or a pleated skirt. Like a professional, she would hold up a garment and check it for flaws, cut, and quality of material. With a nod, she would glance at Nash and smile.

His PID approved a lot of purchases that morning.

Satiated, Aleya did not resist when he suggested a refreshment stop. Bundling bags and packages into a driverless cab for delivery to his apartment, they sauntered toward the Melbourne Central shopping complex. Along the way, she gave him a running commentary on street life, the funny, the sad, and the dangerous, a world totally alien to him and most people who only saw opulence and glitter the city provided.

Some of the glitter wore off when a mob of chanting, placard-waving Humans Only League activists dressed in paramilitary gear blocked trams along the Bourke Street mall. Their incantations and palpable hatred froze bystanders who stopped to gawk at the procession.

"What do we want?"

"Down with lifeliners!"

"When do we want it?"

"Now!"

What disturbed Nash was seeing several young men peel off from the crowd to join the protesters, taking up their chant with vigor. A heavy police presence prevented rioting, but the silent onlookers were not in any mood to offer trouble, preferring not to get involved. Reporters mingled among the crowd, taking shots of everything, soliciting statements for the evening news. Most people declined to comment when confronted by a reporter, unwilling to commit themselves, but some stood their ground.

Not enough, though.

Governments wouldn't destroy lifeliners, he decided. It would be public indifference, allowing the radical fringe to dictate policy. Not being prepared to protest against a growing tide of injustice against lifeliners, the silent majority apparently accepting the nibbling away of personal freedoms for everybody, which only served to embolden mainstream political parties to enact further repressive legislation. His thoughts flashed to the Premier's newscast, not liking any of it.

As he watched the inflamed radicals ready to unleash violence at any opposition to their views, Nash felt a wave of shame. Where was *his* voice of protest? Like other onlookers around him, he too remained silent, unwilling to be noticed, not prepared to have the comfortable cocoon he weaved around himself disturbed. The realization hit him hard and gave him much to think about.

What did Thomas Jefferson say when he and fifty-five others signed the U.S. Declaration of Independence? To stand up, identify himself, and add his voice for the preservation of rights and liberty, Nash had to accept the harsh reality that he too must be prepared to sacrifice his life, fortune, and honor. Perhaps not honor. Without honor, he would be no better than those he fought against, for such people knew no honor. A noble goal, but was he prepared to become a focus of hatred, bigotry, religious intolerance, and the perceived cause of everyone's ills, however irrational?

Edmund Burke rightly said, *'The only thing necessary for the triumph of evil is for good men to do nothing.'*

Nash wondered if lifeliners were doing enough to help their own cause…and he was a lifeliner.

Aleya clutched his hand and cast furtive glances at the unsettled crowd as the marchers made their way up the street toward the state Parliament. Looking pale, she did not relax until the two of them parked themselves at an open restaurant under the glass ceiling of the old Shot Factory. Noisy, crowded, busy, the place had an air of anonymity. Yet the atmosphere wasn't impersonal, broken by occasional bursts of laughter and animated conversation. Not a place Nash usually frequented, but judging by Aleya's recovered bubbling spirits, she liked it. One of her favorite haunts, she said.

After a long slurp of a mixed fruit smoothie, a half-eaten muffin at her side, she gave him a guilty glance and dabbed her lips with a paper napkin.

"Sorry. I shouldn't neglect my manners, especially since I am now all posh and prim."

Nash smiled as he held a warm cup of excellent coffee between his hands, savoring the aroma, trying to push back images of fanatical protesters and his failure to make a stand.

"We'll have to work on that. What next?"

She crunched her face in concentration. "Luna Park? Then the beach maybe?"

"We could have some real gelato there," he suggested, and her face lit up.

"Cool!" She took a more ladylike slurp of her smoothie. "I've been thinking about what you said, going to the Help Center, I mean. I guess I'll have to, won't I?"

"You don't have to do anything, Aleya," he said gently. "But if you want something better than living on the street, and that might be hard for you to understand now, you should use your real identity and get a court to appoint a guardian if you don't want to live with your parents. The Center will be able to help you with that. Whatever Trent did to your PID may work for a while, but the dobers will be on you sooner or later. Once you're in their hands, there is no telling what might happen to you."

Her eyes opened wide. "You could be my guardian, couldn't you?"

His heart melted. With a surge of emotion, he wanted to promise that everything would be all right. He wanted to tell her he would protect her and take care of her, that life would be bright and her days filled with carefree laughter. Unfortunately, it would be a lie.

In reality, a minefield of government legislation and bureaucratic procedures to become someone's guardian. As a lifeliner, those procedures would be doubly onerous, if not impossible to overcome. It would not be without considerable risk to him, his parents, Nat and Mark. If it were only his life on the line, he would not hesitate for a moment. Not a decision he could make without talking it over with them.

Seeing the thoughtful expression on his face, Aleya pouted. "You don't want to, do you?"

"Aleya—"

"I get it. What am I to you anyway? A stray kid you felt sorry for."

He sat back and sighed. "That's not true. I wouldn't mind being your guardian, seeing you safe and happy, but it's not that simple."

"If they caught me, the dobers would hand me back to my parents, wouldn't they?"

"Probably."

"More likely, I'd end up sterilized at a government lab."

He gaped at her. "You don't believe that, do you?"

Her eyes flashed in defiance. "Why not? That's what Trent said they do to lifeliners."

Ah, Trent again. Who was this enigmatic character who roamed the streets, but could doctor a PID?

"Your friend is confused. Tell you what. I'll talk to someone I know at the Center, okay? This is not something you and I can settle in ten minutes. What do you say?"

"In the meantime, I can stay with you?"

"I told you. For as long as you like."

"I won't be any trouble, and I can be useful around the house."

"It's settled. I'll hire you as a permanent maid."

"At what rate? I don't come cheap."

Nash snorted. "Yes, I found that out this morning."

"You're not regretting this, are you?"

"I wouldn't have done it if I had second thoughts."

She looked over his shoulder and tensed. "Dobers."

Thinking quickly, ignoring his churning stomach, he leaned forward. "Deactivate your PID. If they ask for your name, it's Gladia Gorman. Don't say anything else, okay?"

Looking more composed than he felt, she nodded and slurped her smoothie. He raised his cup and took a sip.

"What are they doing?"

"Walking between tables…they're coming."

Two uniformed cops, guns holstered, slowly walked past them. Both had a double-lens 3D bar camera above the left breast pocket and wore Virtual Reality glasses connected to their PID. The senior constable, his Aboriginal brown face grim under his cap, paused and glanced at his chunky partner. He scowled, took off his glasses, and stared hard at Aleya, then shifted his dark eyes to Nash.

"Mr. Bannon, your little girl's PID is switched off. Since she's underage, you are liable for an on-the-spot fine."

Nash waved his hand in dismissal. "She's been having trouble with it. We're on our way to Centrelink to have it checked out."

"Mmm. According to your PID, you're not married. So, who is she?"

"I'm doing a favor for a colleague, Wayne Gorman."

The cop's expression took on a vacant look as he consulted his PID. After a moment, he cleared his throat and glanced at Aleya, who hit him with a broad grin. He slowly turned to Nash.

"Okay, he checks out, as does his daughter, but a word of advice, Mr. Bannon. Don't linger having her PID fixed."

"I appreciated that, officer."

"Mr. Bannon. Why have you blocked your PID?"

Nash glared at him. "I allowed you to verify my identity as the law dictates. You have no justifiable reason or right to interrogate my biometric data or anything else."

"Pursuant to investigating a possible crime—"

The cop's chunky partner raised his VR glasses. "Selby, the kid's profile matches a runaway we've been after, Aleya Sommers. She's supposedly carrying a red backpack with a white swan design, same as this kid. There's also an L tag against her name."

"A lifeliner, eh?" Selby scowled and his hand slid to his revolver. "Well, well. How about we take a ride to headquarters and sort this out. Larry, call for a car."

"You got it."

Nash stared at the two officers in disbelief as something cold slithered down his back. Despite the High Court ruling, the Victorian government and, by extension, other states, still maintained lifeliner registers. He should not have been surprised, but the revelation nevertheless came as a shock. Deep down, he hoped…for what? Law, order, justice, and rights for everybody? Depressed, he reluctantly accepted that the world was in fact more rotten than he thought.

Several bystanders, curious to find out what was going on, stopped and waited to see what would happen. It did not take long to form a small crowd. When they heard the word 'lifeliner', it generated an excited ripple of whispers. Selby turned on them and glowered.

"Go about your business!" he grated, and the group quickly melted. Those sitting around nearby tables suddenly had reasons to be elsewhere.

Not liking the developing situation, Nash slowly got to his feet. "Are you arresting us? If so, on what charge?"

"You're not under arrest, Mr. Bannon. We only want to clear up your girl's identity. If she's a runaway, you'll have some hard explaining to do. If her PID is damaged as you claim, we have facilities to fix it." He allowed himself a small smile. "It'll save you a trip to Centrelink. If you want to make this difficult, consider yourself under arrest for obstruction of justice. Let's go."

"How can I be obstructing justice when I'm sitting here peacefully drinking my coffee?"

Selby gave Nash a sour grin. "How about kidnaping of a minor, harboring a runaway, not reporting a lifeliner, aiding and abetting, and refusing to cooperate with a police investigation. Now, we to do this the easy way or do I cuff you?"

Nash turned to collect Aleya, but her seat was empty and her backpack gone. Startled, he looked up, seeing her melt into the crowd.

"After her!" Selby bellowed. Larry set his mouth and pushed his way through the milling people. It didn't take long for him to return, his glum expression saying everything.

"She's gone. There are a dozen ways out of here."

The senior constable snarled in disgust and fixed his eyes on Nash. "Okay, Mister. Let's go. We're not done with you yet."

Nash insisted on paying his bill first, then walked casually toward the Swanston Street exit, pleased that Aleya had managed to slip away. The dobers would be after her with renewed vigor, but he felt confident in her ability to evade them. Would he ever see her again, or was she a shooting star that had momentarily intruded into his life, leaving only a searing memory, but for how long?

Outside, flanked by the two police officers, he pondered his own immediate future. City noises enveloped him in a protective shell: cars whispering along the thoroughfare, pedestrians hurrying to reach their particular destination, absorbed in their private world, pigeons fluttering on the sidewalk looking for crumbs, the scene familiar and comforting. He allowed part of himself to sink into that soothing anonymity. The watchful sentinel part evaluated the seriousness of his predicament. Apart from concealing Aleya's identity, the cops had nothing. With her gone, they had even less. Associating with a lifeliner was not a crime—yet. Selby thought it was, though.

Nash wondered how long he would be able to enjoy his contented carefree existence before everything descended into rampaging chaos. The soothing obscurity within which he lived might be developing cracks faster than he believed possible. Perhaps he simply preferred not to see them, as the current situation suggested.

A black unmarked BMW sedan pulled up at the curb and Selby opened the rear door. Nash slid onto the back seat without waiting for an invitation. Selby squirmed in his bulk and slammed the door shut. From the sidewalk, Larry watched the car pull away.

The police car turned right onto Flinders Street past the railway station hub and followed traffic going west toward Spencer Street. Seeing the looming brown IBM tower on the other side of the Yarra reminded Nash that he still had a job and needed to check up on his project managers. The modern police headquarters complex on the corner of Flinders and Spencer loomed large and he bit his lip.

The driver parked on the second underground level. Selby immediately got out and waited for Nash. The three of them strode briskly toward a bank of elevators, mingling with uniformed and plainclothes officers. There were enough cars coming and going from the sprawling parking lot not to feel gloomy. A ride to the second floor and they bundled Nash into a small, white painted room whose only decoration was a rectangular wooden table surround by four metal chairs. It did not inspire cheerfulness.

"Have a seat, *Mr.* Bannon. This won't take long," Selby said with a smirk. He waited for Nash to pull out a chair and sit down, then walked out, closing the door after him.

Nash heard the lock click and smiled. If the dobers wanted to play, he would need a heavy bat. He dug out his cell and told the PID to connect with G.S. & B. It only took two rings to get an answer.

"Good morning. Grange, Strand and Bartlett." In the hologram image projected above the phone, the firm's logo dissolved to show an elfin face framed by long chestnut hair that spilled across her shoulders. "Kathleen speaking. How may I…oh, it's you, Mr. Bannon. Nice to see you again."

"Thanks, Kathleen. Can I speak to Mr. Bartlett please?"

"One moment. I'll see if he's available. Please hold."

Stern, formidable, and extremely efficient, she could freeze a caller with her large granite eyes, or floor him with a beaming smile. A glutton for candied cherries, but otherwise watched her weight. That was Garrett's description of the firm's principal receptionist and secretary. Nash wouldn't know. Kathleen had always been warm and welcoming to him.

The screen changed into swirling color patterns accompanied by soothing music, then melted.

"Nash, how are you, my boy? Haven't heard from you for a while, which might be good. When are we going to have that golf game you promised? I want a chance to whip your butt again."

Nash grinned at Garrett's hearty chuckle. Face craggy, silver hair slicked back, in his mid-fifties, the highly accomplished barrister looked relaxed. Life appeared to be treating him well, better than Nash experienced right now.

A genuine and valuable friend he badly needed right now.

"Get Kathleen to book us a Saturday at the Metropolitan and we'll have it out."

"You're on!" Bartlett hooted. "Since this is Wednesday, my guess is that you're not calling about golf."

"Afraid not. I need your help, Garrett. Can you come down

to the Spencer Street police headquarters?"

"What have you done?" the older man demanded briskly, using his courtroom tone.

Without going into details, Nash told him about Aleya.

"Mmm. Telling the senior constable she was Wayne Gorman's kid wasn't exactly smart, but being dumb is not against the law. The most they can do is slap you with that spot fine when your friend switched off her PID, but I doubt they'll do that. The way I see it, nobody has committed a crime or misdemeanor. The fact that she's a runaway isn't your problem. As for blocking access to your bio data, you were perfectly within your rights."

"They're clearly not seeing it that way."

"Immaterial. They are bound by the limits of the law."

"Talking about law, the officers revealed they have a record that Aleya is a lifeliner."

Bartlett gave a long sigh. "I've known about it, and it's being looked into. The problem we're facing is that authorities can claim the information is held on a case-by-case basis and only accessible on a need-to-know."

"A case-by-case basis means all lifeliners!"

"Like I said, it's being looked into."

"Garrett, I don't like what's happening out there."

"I saw the coverage of the Bourke Street rally, and it's going to get worse. This has been building up for some time and we're reaching a tipping point. We should get together and talk. Right now, though, we need to sort out your immediate situation."

The lock clicked and the door opened. A young man in a smart gray suit, dark red tie, and white shirt, paused in the doorway then walked in.

"Who are you calling?" he demanded with intimidating softness.

Nash directed the PID to activate the cell speaker and placed the smartphone on the table. "Garrett Bartlett from Grange, Strand and Bartlett."

The cop stared at Bartlett and pursed his mouth, clearly aware of the law firm and their reputation. He sat down and cleared his throat.

"For the record, this room is monitored. Now—"

"Please identify yourself," Bartlett demanded in his best courtroom voice.

"My name is Acting Inspector Charles Worsley, and I am interviewing Mr. Nash Bannon in relation to a runaway minor and a lifeliner. The time is…11:32 on Wednesday, January 28, 2032. Mr. Bannon, I have a few questions regarding your relationship with Aleya Sommers. I hope you will cooperate with my investigation."

"Before you go any further, Inspector. Is Mr. Bannon charged with anything?"

"He misrepresented and aided a known lifeliner—"

"Being a lifeliner is not a crime, Inspector."

"Perhaps not, but under law, he is required to report one."

"Have you established that Mr. Bannon was aware of her alleged identity?"

Worsley scowled. "Ah, no. However, harboring a minor and a runaway—"

"Is trying to help someone an offense now?"

"He misidentified her—"

"We already covered that, Inspector. You have detained my client without due cause, exposing the senior constable who arrested him and the police department to legal action. Action which he would win."

Two red spots appeared on Worsley's cheeks and he bit his lower lip. "Aleya Sommers is a runaway. We have to find her and return her to her parents, and Mr. Bannon's cooperation could contribute to her apprehension."

Bartlett gave a sour chuckle. "Arresting my client on a technicality is not the best way to gain his cooperation."

"He also blocked his PID!"

"He only prevented unauthorized intrusion into his privacy as a citizen, allowed by law. I believe Mr. Bannon deserves an apology."

Face white with anger, Worsley rose. "Your client deliberately falsified the kid's identity! That's a criminal offense."

"According to the arresting officer. Moreover, you have circumstantial proof at best the child was Aleya Sommers."

"Enough proof to probe into the matter more fully."

"Without evidence of criminal intent or action, you have no grounds to hold my client, Inspector."

Worsley glared at Nash. "You're free to go, Mr. Bannon, but this is not the end of it," he snarled and stomped out.

Nash picked up the cell. "Thanks, Garrett. I owe you. That clown was about to grill me, and I couldn't allow that."

"Understandable. Are you free tomorrow afternoon? Say around four? We need to have that talk sooner than expected."

"I've been meaning to call you anyway."

"Good. Worsley doesn't sound like a forgiving character, and I need to know more about this Sommers kid and how you came to be involved. I also want to discuss something else with you."

"Discuss what?"

"Not over the phone."

"Okay, four o'clock it is," Nash confirmed.

"See you then. In the meantime, stay out of trouble," Bartlett said, cut contact, and his image faded.

Nash stared at his cell, pocketed it and walked out. He believed Worsley when he said this was not the end of it…and he made a new enemy who was also a senior police officer.

More cracks…

Outside, the world seemed the same…almost. Clouds were gathering in the west. Appropriate, he thought. Clouds were gathering, all right, and not only in the sky.

He flagged down a cab with his PID and told it to take him home, the morning's events replaying in his mind. Garrett was right. They needed to talk. He'd been lucky this time, but the hunters were loose now and he had to be doubly wary. Would he crawl back into his comfortable hole, hoping not to be noticed? How long would that last? The image of chanting activists along the Bourke Street mall changed in his mind to a river of protesters picketing the Parliament, the scene multiplied in Canberra and other capital cities.

How does one fight species cleansing when the ordinary man on the street believed in the righteousness of genocide? Particularly when official propaganda said this was necessary.

Cars moved around him in whispering streams, but he did not see them, his mind elsewhere.

The hole he made for himself was not deep enough to protect him and other lifeliners from the gathering clouds. He knew what he had to do, but doubted the courage of his convictions to act, realizing he faced professional and personal obliteration once exposed. No, his comfortable hole wasn't deep enough.

Time to be counted, Nash old son.

His day wasn't totally ruined. He still had a date tonight with Cariana.

He paid off the cab and walked up the driveway to his apartment block. Sitting on the steps, Aleya sprang to her feet, her fingers twisting the front of her shirt.

"I didn't know where else to go," she whispered brokenly.

"Come," he said and scooped up her inseparable backpack.

He linked his PID with the security system and the lock clicked. They rode the elevator up in silence. Inside his apartment, Aleya glanced at the shopping bags and boxes left in the middle of the lounge, her fingers worrying her shirt.

"Stop twisting that thing," Nash commanded. "You'll wear it out."

Her arms immediately dropped to her sides. "You're not mad at me, are you? Coming here, I mean."

He reached out and brushed her head. "Not mad. Concerned."

"About me?"

"About you. You need to go to the Help Center. It's no longer safe for you on the streets after what happened this morning. The dobers won't rest until they get you."

"Are you in trouble because of it?"

"I can handle it. You can't."

"Does this mean I won't be able to stay with you?"

He crouched before her and took her hands. "You can stay with me for as long as you want, but we need to sort out your legal status first. Otherwise, the authorities and your parents will keep after you until they get you. They must miss you."

She hung her head. "I guess."

He stood and dug out his cell. "Let me make a call." He told the PID to select a private number and establish contact. After only two rings, the projected image showed a strong Mediterranean face with a full head of thick black hair and a high forehead. Chestnut eyes looked at him with penetrating frankness. Tall bookshelves framed the background of his office.

"Hi, Nash. It's been a while."

"Apologies for not getting back to you sooner, Adam—"

"I know about you busy executive types. Forgetting who your friends are."

Nash felt bad. "You don't have to rub it in."

His friend laughed. "Just yanking your chain, buddy. What can I do for you?"

"I have a little girl who needs your kind of expertise."

"Oh? The dobers are after her?"

"And her parents."

"We're talking about a minor? She'll need protection and a safe place to stay until her situation is sorted out."

"Can you handle this for her? I'm asking a lot, I know."

"A minor, a runaway, *and* a lifeliner…that's the business I'm in, Nash. When can you bring her in?"

"It's better if this is done right away."

"Agreed, but not to the Center. The feds have it under surveillance and could apprehend her as she tries to get in. Mmm. I don't ordinarily do this myself, but seeing it's you, I'll meet you.

Footscray Market entrance on Barkly Street. Half an hour. Suits?"

"Thanks, Adam. You don't know how much this means to me. She is something unique."

"They all are. Pay me with a beer and we'll be even."

Nash laughed. "Deal!" He cut contact and looked at Aleya. "You heard? Are you all right with this?"

Her shoulders sagged and she sighed. "Since there is no other way…"

"There isn't."

"Can I go to the bathroom first?"

"Sure thing." He glanced at their shopping. "I'll keep your stuff here in case you're able to stay with me."

She flashed him a broad grin, picked up her backpack and walked toward the bathroom.

Nash gave a long sigh when the door closed after her. Life had been so much simpler a week ago, but it was also time to tie up a loose end with Cariana. A flutter of apprehension tightened his stomach. Tonight, he would tell her everything, which would force her to make a simple binary decision. Perhaps not so simple. No, it *was* simple! She had to know that he cared for her, and his affection would not be any stronger if he were an ordinary human. Perhaps he should have told her sooner, allowing her to make a choice before committing herself. In that respect, he mislead her, which might not be fair, but he did not want to end what had grown into something important. Of course, she might not see it that way at all.

If she walked away, he could always call Adam to arrange a date with a lifeliner woman. He wondered how they coped with exposure and rejection. Probably not well, haunted by the same demons.

Aleya came out and Nash told Sally to secure the apartment.

Backpack slung on her right shoulder, they waited for their cab. Knowing what women lugged with them, Nash was mildly curious what Aleya had in there. The yellow driverless City Cabs sedan pulled up and the two of them piled onto the back seat.

With a quiet surge of electric power, the car sped off.

She tugged his elbow. "Nash, what will happen when we get there?"

"Adam, a very nice man, will meet us. You'll be going with him."

She thought about that for a moment. "Does that mean I won't see you again?"

He brushed her cheek. "It will only be for a little while, honey, then you can be with me if you want. Besides, you can always call me."

"Cube! No phone."

"Adam will get one for you."

She squeezed his hand. "Thanks for everything, Nash."

The drive down Kings Way spent in silence. Nash had a few things on his mind and, judging by her thoughtful expression, so did Aleya. Did she regret her decision? Life on the streets may have been tough, but at least she understood the setup. Too late now for second thoughts.

Heavy traffic going both ways slowed the cab to a crawl as they approached the Maribyrnong River Bridge and Nash feared they would be late. He couldn't do anything about the swarm of vehicles, and Adam would have to wait. Unless, of course, he also ran late. Cars were a convenience and a curse. Improved public transport accounted for most of the intra-city traffic, but many people were prepared to pay hefty tolls for the privilege of point-to-point travel. More people meant more cars, which meant more traffic and gridlocks. No satisfactory solution to the problem had been found anywhere in the world.

The cab crossed the bridge and stopped in a line of cars that weren't going anywhere. Tired of waiting, Nash authorized payment through his PID and they walked the two hundred meters to the Footscray Market, not believing the crush of pedestrians, mostly Asian; the suburb practically taken over by the Vietnamese community. What the hell were all these people doing here?

Nash pushed through the crowd and saw Adam waving,

standing in front of a butcher shop.

"Sorry for the delay. Traffic," he explained as they shook hands.

"Don't worry about it. I just got here myself." Adam turned and looked at Aleya with an engaging smile. "So, this is the source of all your troubles."

"I'm afraid she isn't," a familiar voice said behind Nash and he felt a hot flush of consternation ripple down his body. "I am."

Four men clad in severe dark suits emerged out of a black Ford Falcon parked at the curb, blocking any attempt at escape.

Aleya beamed with delight and embraced the slim woman. "I caught a big one this time, Aunty!"

"You certainly did, sweetheart," Cariana said, her almond eyes challenging Nash. "Two big ones."

* * *

Frozen in shock, Nash seemed to have an eternity of time as many things he believed in slowly crumbled around him, turning to bitter ash as they fell. Something tore deep inside him, leaving him broken and cold. Regret, betrayal, and loss, they slowly oozed into the gaping hollow. He felt the rapid change that now colored his view on life and relationships, and waited for anger to blossom. It didn't. He only felt enormous disillusionment.

Cariana stared boldly at him, but he thought he also saw sadness lurk in her eyes. Perhaps he wished for something not there at all, unable to believe what she had done. The woman he wanted to make his own, share everything with and trust had ripped him open, robbing him of a future and a measure of happiness. Swayed by a simple juvenile hormonal reaction generated by their first encounter, which overwhelmed cool self-interest, he allowed himself to love her, allowed her to reach him through his guard. Looking back, he walked into this openly, permitting the promise of intimacy with a non-lifeliner to snare him. Knowing it was a doomed love, he could have stopped it and walked away, but he didn't. He would not repeat this mistake ever again.

Time to wall himself in once more.

He slowly turned his head.

Aleya…she must be the daughter of Cariana's late brother! It all made sense…almost.

She had lost her jovial air and stood silent beside her aunty. Did she comprehend the shattering effect of her mischief? He reached out to her, permitting himself to care, when all along, she used him to play an elaborate game. They both used him. Obviously intelligent, possessing an eidetic memory, evidently well trained, Aleya had executed a masterful performance. There were two instances when she tried to tell him something, reveal her deception? Perhaps, but playing her game clearly overcame any thought of remorse. Besides, what would a kid barely into adolescence know about remorse? It takes a lifetime of emotional cuts and bruises to appreciate tragedy and anguish.

What he could not understand, why the elaborate snare to catch lifeliners using kids? He did not believe she was the only one doing this. A covert operation to ferret out lifeliner networks? Possible, and something he could see the government doing. On the other hand, mixing it with other street kids and the homeless, she might very well pick up information not obtainable any other way. She could also be used to identify likely experimental test subjects, a much more plausible explanation. Nobody would care if another street bum disappeared, one who happened to be a lifeliner…grist for Cariana's mill.

Nash swallowed hard, feeling old, tired, and worn.

Cariana grinned broadly at Adam. "Well, well. Mr. Gatt, the Treasurer's Chief of Staff himself." She patted Aleya's shoulder. "You have indeed caught a big one, darling. Well done."

"What about Nash, Aunty?"

"Our Mr. Bannon? I don't know, my dear. We'll have to check him out."

Aleya looked at Nash and had the grace to blush. "I'm sorry. I tried to tell you…"

Seeing his frosty stare, she blanched and shrank back. She had to have *some* understanding of the terrible thing she had done.

Adam stepped toward Cariana and the four men around them tensed.

"Who are you, and what is your authority to detain us?"

A trim man, silver showing at the temples, emerged out of the Falcon saloon and tugged down his jacket. Not tall, but command presence sat on him like a visible cloak, filling all the space around him.

"Dr. Lambert doesn't have the authority, but I do," he said smoothly.

"And you are?" Adam demanded.

The man opened his jacket to reveal a silver Australian Federal Police badge clipped to his belt.

"Commander Lyle Sutton."

"You cannot detain us unless we're charged with an offense," Adam remarked. "As far as I know, we haven't committed any offense."

"Dealing with lifeliners, I don't have to charge you with anything. However, if you want to be pedantic, you and your friend are held in preventative detention under the Criminal Code Act 1995 for the duration of our investigation. Which means I can hold you for up to fourteen days and do whatever I want with you."

"Mr. Sutton, the Preventative Detention Orders amendment had a sunset clause. It expired in 2028."

"Extended when lifeliners were identified as a security threat."

"What threat? And who said we're lifeliners?"

"That's what we need to find out, Mr. Gatt."

"It is not against the law to be a lifeliner."

"No, but it is if you pose a security threat, which your activities certainly do." Sutton extended his hand at the Falcon. "Shall we?"

Mouth set in a tight line, Adam glanced at Nash and walked toward the car. Pedestrians crowding the sidewalk barely gave them a glance. Some were interested to know what was going on, but nobody stopped to gawk, probably preferring not to get involved.

The fragile moment of peace shattered when something smashed through a large plate glass display that scattered shards over meat trays, salami, and sausages stacked inside the butcher shop. A piercing scream followed the loud crash and a tinkle of glass.

"Lifeliner!"

A young teenager pushed through the stunned crowd, apparently the culprit of the incident.

"Stop him! Lifeliner!"

From people minding their own business, the crowd turned into a frenzied mob, tearing after the youngster, terror contorting his face. As the youth rounded the corner, a uniformed police officer lunged and tackled him to the ground. Another dober appeared and they hustled the youngster away.

"More of them here!" somebody bellowed, and Nash found himself the center of unwelcome attention by angry onlookers ready to explode into violence.

Sutton glowered and raised his arms. "Federal police! Go about your business."

"We want the lifeliner!" a bull voice shouted and the crowd pressed in.

Cariana and Aleya were gone, swallowed by the throng. Sutton glanced at his men, and they unceremoniously bundled Nash into the Falcon. The cop got onto the front seat and the car lurched forward, blocked by what had now become an unruly rabble pounding on the hood and sides. The four dark suited men valiantly held most of them back, which gave the driver time to ease the car into the crawling traffic. He activated his siren and the sedan sped along the tram tracks, drivers and autonomous oncoming cars obediently giving way. Something struck the back part of the dome, which created a small pattern of fractures. The self-healing mechanism kicked in and the fractures disappeared.

Shaken by the raw power of the mob out of control, Nash looked at Adam who did not appear totally composed himself.

Sutton turned, still wearing a scowl. "Dangerous out there, especially for a lifeliner."

Putting the pieces together, Nash stared at the dober with contempt.

"You engineered that little incident. Why?"

About to say something, Sutton paused. "What gave me away?"

"Too convenient. Why would someone smash a display window in broad daylight with witnesses all around, and then run off? Random vandalism? And the two cops suddenly on the scene to bundle him away? The man yelling lifeliner? How would he know? You set up the whole thing to put me and Mr. Gatt on a spot, then 'rescue' us. Why?"

"You're pretty sharp, Mr. Bannon. Perhaps too sharp for your own good."

"You mean, your good."

"It cuts both ways. The answer to your question is simple. I wanted to demonstrate the power of raw emotion channeled into violence. You saw what happened back there. To an individual sitting at home watching a holoview program about lifeliners, it would never occur to him to pick up a two-by-four and attack one. Place him in a mob primed against lifeliners, though, he becomes a mindless weapon. He might be behind on his mortgage payments, maybe he lost his job to a robot, his wife walked out on him, or he simply found it a grind just to cope. It doesn't matter. Seeing a lifeliner, it all becomes simple. There is the cause of all his problems personified, regardless how illogical. Remove that object and everything will be all right again. Lifeliners are a threat to national security, Mr. Bannon. A clear and present danger to society, and the government intends to remove that danger using any and all means."

Sutton's rant made Nash recall a striking similarity with the incident that occurred in Pakistan in the late 1990s. During his term as chief of the army, General Pervez Musharraf used the notorious Interservice Intelligence Directorate to create the Taliban as a mechanism to curb the growing power of Afghani tribal warlords. In an ironic twist of fate, his creation overcame him and the Taliban now ruled Pakistan.

He pointed a finger at Sutton. "Is the AFP behind the Humans Only League?"

"Whatever gave you such a silly notion?"

"Any and all means, and the demonstration we witnessed."

The dober's eyes turned frosty. "You have a very active imagination, Mister. Active and unhealthy."

Perhaps, but the rise in Humans Only League activities suggested they were approaching critical mass beyond anyone's power to control. Perhaps the government didn't want them controlled, happy to use them as an instrument of intimidation, prepared to ignore the basic fact that all such organizations attracted extremists and the malcontents.

"This is harassment and violation of my rights," Nash grated.

Sutton laughed, genuinely amused. He wiped his eyes and shook his head. "Harassment? Didn't I tell you that we're at war? The rule of law is the first thing that gets cast aside when the social fabric itself is threatened. What is more, people out there give it up willingly, as you just witnessed. A smart man like you should have known that."

"What kind of society does the government want to make where there is no rule of law? Another United States where autocratic dictatorship now holds sway?"

Sutton's face suddenly looked ugly. "The government exists to maintain order, and lifeliners threaten to destroy that order and everything humanity has worked for. Now, muzzle it or I'll shut it for you."

Turning right at Ballarat Road, past the Flemington Racecourse, Nash knew where they were going—CSIRO's life sciences labs in Parkville…where Cariana worked. Would he be another experimental subject? He dug out the cellphone and told his PID to contact G. S. & B.

"No calls!" Sutton snarled. Nash ignored him.

"Grange, Strand and Bartlett...Mr. Bannon! What—"

"Kathleen—"

"I said no calls!" Sutton reached for the cell, but Nash sat back out of reach.

"I need to speak to Mr. Bartlett. It's urgent!"

"One moment, sir."

Sutton pulled out a revolver and cocked the trigger. "The phone. Give it to me."

"Hi, Nash. What's—"

"Garrett! The AFP is taking me to the CSIRO Parkville—"

He got no further as pain exploded across his knuckles and the cell clattered against the dome, landing on the floor between his feet. Sutton, his eyes devoid of emotion, clearly prepared to use his weapon.

"Reach for it and I pull the trigger," he said softly, daring Nash to do just that. "Your phone, Mr. Gatt," he growled without moving his head.

Taking extra care, Adam slowly reached into his jacket, extracted the smartphone and held it out. Sutton pocketed it and his eyes flickered to the floor. "Hand it over."

Glaring at the cop, Nash groped for the cell. Still on and his call live. He terminated the connection, hoping Garrett heard everything. He held the phone to Sutton and the dober glowered.

"You don't do or say anything without my permission. Is that clear?"

"You made a huge mistake by taking us."

"You think calling your lawyer will get you out of this? Let me tell you something, Mr. Bannon. You are nothing. I can make you disappear and nobody will give a shit. Now, shut your mouth before you say something else I won't like."

Nash massaged his bruised knuckles, figuring it wouldn't be wise right now to push the envelope. Not with a hardcase like Sutton who seemed to take particular relish stomping on people.

In any organization, those who set policy and manage, dictate its behavior. If Sutton was a typical example of government policy, things were grimmer for lifeliners than Nash thought. Grimmer for everybody.

For a few moments, he allowed himself to be distracted by the picturesque tree-lined Royal Parade boulevard, then turned to Adam. His friend shook his head and raised a forefinger to his lips, which left Nash wrestling with some disturbing thoughts.

Cariana…

Okay, he suffered a rather painful and extended burn to his ego, but he would live through it, having learned a valuable lesson—don't open yourself to anyone. Time to look at the bigger picture, Edmund Burke's words echoing in his mind.

All his life, he tried to blend into the amorphous sea of humanity, become one of the unseen, pretend to be one of them. So far, it had worked, attested by the success of his career and material wealth. All along, though, he had been deceiving himself, and deep down, he knew it. To maintain his anonymous lifestyle, he sacrificed part of his integrity and self-respect, compartmentalizing the truth.

He could not be like the others because he wasn't, and time to accept and act on that fact. Governments the world over were acknowledging the evolutionary change that would eventually eradicate *homo sapiens* as a species, making way for *homo renata*, and were determined to stop it, or at least slow it down. He understood the instinctive triggering of the self-preservation response. He refused to believe and concede the savage nature of that response. He thought people were better than that, although he always knew he would be disappointed, but he pushed that into a memory hole in the mistaken belief that sanity would eventually prevail, all evidence to the contrary.

An image of a drowning man dragging down his rescuer, dooming both, seemed apt at this moment. Well, he would not allow the doomed masses to drag him down. Time to test mankind's moral and ethical code to destruction. Time to speak up and fight for his rights. Perhaps others would also pick up his cry, lifeliners and normals. He could *not* accept that Sutton represented a social mirror, because if he did, disorder and chaos were already here.

Unless he found a platform to voice his words and mobilize a resistance, all he had were noble sentiments. There *was* a platform he could use—the Lifeliner Party. Not very effective or vocal, but there. Since he was purging himself of all self-deception, the reason for their lack of effectiveness painfully obvious. Lifeliners like everybody else preferred the comforts that social integration delivered to the alternative of dangerous public exposure. Not that he could exactly blame them. They had careers, families, children to nurture and protect. Waving a lifeliner flag on the street ran counter to that instinct.

He did not have children to worry about, but he did have a family. He could not blindly drag them along his path of martyrdom. Idealism was always firmly anchored by the reality of simple survival. Yet, what sort of life would his parents, Mark and Natalie, have in the years to come if the Suttons of this world took over? Survival reduced to mere existence? It wouldn't be worth the price.

He knew with unshakeable certainty that he reached a turning point in his life, and possibly the lives of many other lifeliners. If they did not stand up for themselves now when the situation was at least marginally tractable, lifeliners everywhere would be slowly stripped of their rights, enslaved, and exterminated.

Before doing anything, Nash would talk to his father and Mark…and Nat would finally need to know what her brothers were, although he suspected she already knew. His sister was *very* smart. First, he needed to extricate himself out of his present difficulty, and he had no idea how.

The car slowed and turned left into a driveway running alongside a gray-rendered six-story building. They parked in a reserved spot and Sutton got out, followed by the driver, his eyes wary. Nash slid out and waited for Adam, figuring his chances to jump

Sutton. He kept himself fit and he'd had more than fifteen years of Tai Chi and taekwondo, all of it in a dojo in stylized practice. He used his skills only once against four rowdy kids prowling along Swanston Street late one evening, an encounter they were not likely to forget. As his *sensei* often said, martial arts was as much a discipline for the mind as a tool of aggression. You win not by pushing, not by tensing and gritting your teeth, but by relaxing and persevering over time. However, when immediate action was called for, don't hesitate. Use it with devastating effect. Studying the two police officers, Nash did not feel inclined to test his training, not knowing Adam's abilities. He would persevere and survive.

Still, a tempting notion. All he had to do was disable one of them, drain enough life-force from the other to induce unconsciousness, and walk away free…with every dober in the country after him on legitimate criminal charges. Not a great beginning to his career as a reformist. He would keep that option in mind if his situation became desperate.

Sutton stared hard at him. "Even if you are not lifeliners, if you and Mr. Gatt attempt to touch either of us, you'll be shot. Are we clear? Let's go."

Well, that was that…for now.

They walked toward the back entrance. The place looked deserted, but the number of cars in the parking lot told a different story. A dour individual suspiciously eyed the approaching group and nodded to Sutton. The lock clicked on the solid black door and the cop palmed it open. They marched toward the single elevator in silence. On the third floor, Nash and Adam were bundled into a spacious meeting room well-lit by tall windows. On the other side of the boulevard, white gums filled a small park. Sutton waved his arm at comfortable chairs that surrounded a large oval wooden table.

"Make yourselves at home. Believe me, this will go much easier if you cooperate."

"Cooperate with what?" Adam demanded. "You are holding

us without charge or legitimate justification."

"Didn't I make it clear? You're held in preventative detention."

"Without cause."

Sutton raised both eyebrows, feigning surprise. "Cause? I'll give you cause, Mr. Gatt. We've been monitoring your clandestine activities with Lifeliner Help Centers all over the country for some time. Apart from being subversive—"

"Who said they are subversive?"

"—a closer look revealed that many of those activities were also illegal, like harboring unregistered lifeliners, for openers. As long as your group confined its operation to Victoria, you were a minor irritant. When you decided to expand your network nationally, we had to act. Even as we speak, federal officers are arresting principal cell leaders in all states. The Lifeliner Party and your Help Centers could not operate without high-level support. And that's where I became involved.

"My taskforce is responsible for ferreting out your faceless backers, whether in government or industry. You would be surprised at what we found. Then again, perhaps not. Your boss...the Honorable Neale Wilkie...the Victorian state Treasurer? Why would a senior minister soil his hands with a grubby operation that helps lifeliners? Could it be because he is also a lifeliner? If he is, the government intends to find out how far the rot has spread and cut it out. We're pruning branches to make sure the tree lives."

"You can't get away with this, Commander. What you are doing contravenes the 2027 UN declaration and the 2029 Curtis Sands High Court ruling. Lifeliners are citizens in every respect and enjoy all the rights and privileges of human beings everywhere, because they *are* human, like you," Adam retorted hotly, then snorted. "Well, maybe not like you."

"Cute, but misguided, and you have forgotten a few important points. For one, the United Nations is in New York, and its ambassadors are cushy chair warmers out of touch with reality. As for the 2029 Curtis Sands case, it doesn't apply. I'm not holding you and Mr. Bannon because you're lifeliners, which is still to be determined. You are held to assist in my investigation into illegal activities conducted by Lifeliner Help Centers. That is all the authority I need to detain you."

"You won't get away with this," Nash grated, wanting to smash his face in.

"I am through playing games and explaining myself. Both of you will cooperate, willingly or otherwise. The first thing we need to do, of course, is establish what you are. Don't worry. It won't take long to get your DNA profiles. Afterward, we'll talk. And you know what? I doubt that I'll need fourteen days to get everything I need out of you. However, if I should have cause to dislike you, which won't take much, you'll be charged—I'll think of something—and your visit with me will be extended. That, gentlemen, could be for quite some time. If that happens, I can tell you right now, you won't like it, regardless of any pleasure your company might give me. Oh, I almost forgot. If either of you turns out to be a lifeliner, he'll be sterilized. See? I can be nice when I want to."

Nash gaped at the repulsive man, never having come across someone so predatory and scheming. He thought IBM and Telstra executives were unscrupulous manipulators without morals. Compared to Sutton, they were amateurs. Intellectually, he knew the government was conducting covert operations against lifeliners, but something detached, removed from his everyday reality, happening to somebody else. Having his face rubbed in it, he definitely did not like the stink.

"You can't do that!" he blurted, not believing what he heard.

"We're at war, Mr. Bannon, and in war, you use whatever weapons you have to win."

A knock on the door and the dour individual who met them at the parking lot peered in.

"All set, sir."

"Good work, Harris." Sutton got up and rubbed his hands.

"Time, gentlemen." He glanced at the driver and nodded. "Mason…"

The man immediately drew his revolver and allowed his arm to hang loose, his intention clear.

Nash and Adam were marched down the corridor and led to a small examination room that smelled like a medicine cabinet. A nurse in a white lab coat finished sorting her needles and looked up.

"You first," Sutton told Nash and pointed at a chair.

"You don't have my consent to take a blood sample," Nash declared.

"I thought you were aware of your position, Mr. Bannon. I don't need your consent, because I'm not gathering evidence for a court case. I am after information for direct action."

Sutton shoved him into a chair and gave the nurse a sharp look. She positioned a tray containing a needle and a small glass specimen vial on a cabinet next to the chair.

"Take off your jacket and roll up your sleeve," she told him pleasantly.

Nash did not blame her for this as he stripped down. She did what she was told, not fussed about legalities. If she held any concerns, she didn't show it.

She pulled on rubber gloves, swabbed the inside of his elbow with alcohol, then extracted four cc's of dark blood and stuck a Band Aid on the puncture. She labeled the vial and executed Adam's procedure with equal impersonal efficiency.

"You will have the results in fifteen minutes," she told Sutton and walked out with the vials.

The AFP commander nodded and glanced at Mason. "Take them back to the meeting room and stand guard outside."

The driver waited for Nash to put on his jacket, then shoved him roughly through the open doorway. It hadn't been a great day for Nash at many levels, and being manhandled, treated like a murderer, released something he wanted to do for a while. He spun and slammed an open palm under Mason's chin, snapping back his head. The man staggered and fell with a crash, arms flailing.

Sutton crouched and whipped out his gun.

Nash scowled at him. "If anyone touches me again, I'll break his neck." Ignoring the gun, he turned and walked down the corridor, not caring if he was shot. He had as much pushing around as he was prepared to accept.

He kept walking, but no shot came, and he allowed himself a small exhale of relief. Inside the meeting room, he kicked back a chair and slumped into its embrace. His moment of bravado had bolstered his ego, but he still had no idea how to extricate himself from here. Worse still, his act of rebellion was not going to endear him to Sutton, not that he would lose much sleep over it.

Adam ambled in and Harris smirked as he closed the door. Adam sat down and shook his head.

"I applaud what you did, however misguided."

"Like I give a shit right now," Nash growled, his spirits badly needing another boost.

"I gathered that." Adam dug out a small smartphone from his jacket and held it up triumphantly. "I knew they would leave us alone sometime. In my position, having a spare has been useful more than once. Good thing we weren't searched."

Nash slapped his friend on the shoulder. "You're a genius!"

"If I were a genius, we wouldn't be here, but this makes up for it a little. I've been recording everything that's been said since we met in Footscray, and my PID sent the file to my office and the Attorney-General."

"Wow. Sutton is dead."

"This will help bury him, all right."

"Can you send it to a couple of networks?"

"Mmm. Should have thought of that myself...done." Adam scowled and stared hard at Nash. "We were targeted. You know that, don't you? And your little friend Aleya played a key part."

"Yeah, and I'm sorry as hell to have dragged you into this mess."

"The woman with Aleya—"

"My girlfriend," Nash grated. "Former girlfriend."

The door burst open and Harris stood there, his gun leveled. Seeing the smartphone, his gun wavered.

"You couldn't leave well enough alone, could you?"

Adam glanced at Nash and threw the cellphone at the dober. Startled, the cop instinctively reached for it. That brief moment of distraction was enough. Nash dove and tackled him, and the large man crashed to the floor. Adam leaped for the gun hand and pinned down the arm. Anger, frustration, and hate, all surged through Nash in a wave of heat as he slammed his elbow into the cop's chin. Harris twitched and lay still.

Breathing heavily, Nash knelt and slowly looked at Adam. Without saying anything, his friend exhaled loudly and rolled the body. He glanced at the gun still in Harris' hand and stood.

"He tripped…in case anyone asks," Adam said briskly. "Right now, it's more important than ever that I call someone to help us get out of here before we're interrupted again. We probably don't have much time."

"Neale Wilkie?"

"He shouldn't be involved, not now anyway."

"Because he's a lifeliner?"

"Despite being a politician, he is simply a decent human being and I don't want to embroil him in a mess that might threaten him in any way. Getting myself apprehended by the federal police will be damaging enough, but it is something I can mitigate. No, the man we need is the Attorney-General."

Nash shook his head. "When this comes out, there will be mud splattered everywhere. Calling him could place him in a precarious position with the Premier. From what I know, they don't exactly like each other."

"Mmm. You're right. Raines Latham is a weasel, and he *would* go after the AG. Nevertheless, the AG is the highest law officer in this state. Who do you have in mind instead?"

"Bartlett."

"As in Grange, Strand and Bartlett, *et al*? The man you tried to contact in the car?"

"The same. By the way, it might be an idea to send the recording to them as well."

Adam nodded. "You're right…done," he said and handed over the cell.

"How the hell did the driver know you were transmitting?"

"Must have been monitoring our PIDs."

"But—"

"I know. They're not supposed to have that ability. 'Curiouser and curiouser', as Alice would say," Adam mused. "Make that call."

A PID consists of two modules: a neural interface implanted above the left ear that enabled nanobot tendrils to connect with the Broca's area responsible for language processing and various cognitive tasks, which also powers the PID, and a communications interface to link with any wireless comms network. For Harris to listen in meant he could circumvent Nash's personal encryption key. The implication made him shudder.

"Bastards." He told his PID to make the connection and Kathleen immediately put him through.

"Where are you, my boy?" Garrett demanded briskly, his face a mixture of relief and concern.

"At the CSIRO Parkville facility. Adam Gatt, the Treasurer's—"

"I know who he is."

Garrett knows? Also curiouser…

"We were taken into custody by the AFP, a Commander Lyle Sutton—"

"I saw that part of the altercation."

"He's holding us under the Preventative Detention Orders Act. He's fishing, Garrett, and we're bait."

"A PDO? That's it?"

"That's what he said. They've also taken blood samples for a DNA profile without our consent."

"Hang in there, Nash. When I saw what was going on, I took steps."

"Thanks, Garrett. By the way, Adam sent an audio file to your office. It will fill you in."

"He managed to record the events in question? It won't be admissible unless Commander Sutton provided prior consent."

"We didn't consent being dragged here either!"

"We'll talk later," Garrett said and cut contact.

Adam snorted. "Legal weenies are the same everywhere, worried about points of law than their client. Let me have the phone."

Nash handed it over. Adam pocketed it, then immediately walked to the open doorway and peered up and down the corridor.

"Help!"

"What are you doing?" Nash demanded in dismay.

"Like I said, the man tripped, and we don't want anyone suspecting that we helped him trip."

"When he wakes up—"

"He'll dob on us, I know. Hopefully, Mr. Bartlett will be here to bail out our asses before that happens. If not, we'll think of something."

Nash sat down and tried to look relaxed and unconcerned. Nevertheless, his stomach churned as he gazed at the sprawled body on the floor, not feeling relaxed at all. Odd as it seemed, he was also excited. Not only that Adam managed to outwit the AFP with his recording, which would cause the government some severe embarrassment when it came out, regardless how momentary, Nash was also relieved to find that he was not found wanting when he had to act…a physical coward. The tree huggers and pacifists claimed that violence never settled anything, blindly ignoring history, an odyssey of unremitting violence. Sometimes one must do rather than merely talk. By doing, of course, one can also get mashed by a superior force. Those were the breaks.

Footsteps pounded in the corridor and Sutton slid to a stop

in the doorway, gun in hand. Recovered from his fall, Mason gave Nash a sour look, knelt beside his colleague and retrieved the gun.

"What happened?" Sutton grated.

"He barged in and tripped," Adam said airily.

"Tripped, eh? Why the drawn gun?"

"We're not mind readers, Commander."

Sutton bit his lower lip, glanced at Mason and nodded at the prone Harris. "The gun, then get him out of here."

In minutes, two men appeared pushing a gurney and carried off the cop.

"Stay here and watch them," Sutton told Mason and stomped out, slamming the door shut after him.

Having a suspicious AFP cop standing guard did not make for a conducive atmosphere. Nash crossed his arms and stared at the trees across the boulevard. Traffic noises intruded into his wandering thoughts.

He slowly turned his head and glanced at Adam. His friend shrugged. Nothing they could do now except wait. Raking over worst-case scenarios would not help their situation and would merely drain their energy. Nash shifted in his chair, feeling the urge to jam and pushed it to the back of his mind. Must be the excitement, as he jammed two days ago. He'd be okay for a few days or so. A thought struck him, surprising him that it hadn't occurred to him before.

What happens to a lifeliner who is unable to jam? Someone totally isolated, out of reach of another human. He pictured several situations where that could happen: trekking alone in the wilderness, in prison under solitary confinement, in a hospital bed. What would he feel when the urge came and he couldn't satisfy it? Day after day, the urge would gnaw at him, as would frustration and helplessness to satisfy it. Would the urge slowly fade, or would it become stronger, demanding fulfillment, refusing to be placated? Could he jam off an animal, or even a tree? It too was a biological system. It had to be more complicated than that.

Nash had read volumes of scientific literature on lifeliners, but he could not recall seeing an article on life-force deprivation. Over the years, some lab somewhere must have investigated this and kept the results buried. Would Cariana know? Her face appeared in his mind and he blotted the image. He did not want to think about her, not now, not with the wound still raw and weeping. He sighed and slumped back against the chair.

Rats!

The door flew open and banged against the stop. Sutton, face tight with anger, cheeks flushed, walked in and stared at Adam. He raised his arm and gave a little wave with the cellphone in his hand.

"I'll ask this only once. Where is the audio file?"

"What audio file, Commander?"

"The one you sent to ABC and Channel Nine. They've been calling you."

"I get a lot of calls from the networks about many things."

Sutton's eyes flickered at Mason. "Frisk him!"

The driver grinned and motioned Adam to stand up. He quickly patted him down, paused, then opened Adam's jacket and extracted the small cell. He shook his head and handed the phone to Sutton, who dropped it to the floor and stomped on it with his heel. Glass crunched and the smartphone was a twisted bit of metal and plastic.

"That was a 650-dollar cell," Adam remarked quietly, looking unconcerned.

"Bill me!" Sutton snarled.

"He will do more than that, Commander," a gruff voice said from the doorway. Garrett Bartlett walked in accompanied by two uniformed Victoria police officers and a neatly dressed, white-haired man who looked like he wanted to be someplace else. Garrett glanced at Nash. "How are you?"

Nash grinned broadly and stood. "Much better now that you're here."

Garrett nodded, turned to Sutton and held out a folded piece

129

of paper. "This is a Supreme Court order demanding the immediate release of my clients, Mr. Nash Bannon and Mr. Adam Gatt. It also requires the return of any personal property seized during their confinement." He turned to the white-haired man. "I think you two have met, Dr. Connell, director of this facility."

"And you are?" Sutton grated.

"Garrett Bartlett, from Grange, Strand and Bartlett."

"I see. Well, Mr. Bartlett, that piece of paper doesn't mean anything. I am acting under federal jurisdiction, which supersedes any state authority."

"Only if you have laid down a proper groundwork with the Attorney-General, which has not been done in this case."

"I'm handling a multijurisdictional taskforce into clandestine lifeliner activities. Your clients were detained on suspicion of involvement in those activities as permitted by the Preventative Detention Orders Act. Which means, Mr. Bartlett, you can blow."

The barrister gave an indulgent smile. "The Act, Mr. Sutton, states *verifiable* suspicion. You cannot hold my clients without some basis in fact. Have you established such a foundation, apart from claiming that my clients are lifeliners, which in itself is not against the law?"

"I shall have that proof shortly."

"The blood tests? Inadmissible, as they were carried out without my clients' consent or prior establishment for cause. National police and security forces are meant to uphold and protect citizen's rights, not trample them when you find them inconvenient to your clandestine operations."

The nurse who took the blood sample walked into the room, looking flustered and uncertain when she saw the two uniformed officers. She cleared her throat, glanced at Dr. Connell and held out a piece of paper to Sutton, who made a grab for it. Bartlett plucked the paper from her hand, folded it, and slid it into his pocket.

"That's federal evidence!" Sutton roared.

Bartlett shook his head. "No consent, remember?" He turned to the nurse. "I have served Commander Sutton a court order to release my clients and return all personal belongings. That includes their blood samples. Under pain of contempt of court, you will hand over the samples and destroy all records, computer and paper, of the tests. Understood?"

She blanched and looked at Dr. Connell for help, who gave a curt nod and the nurse swallowed. "Yes, sir."

Bartlett turned to one of the uniformed dobers. "Go with her and see that she complies."

"Sir!"

Bartlett held out his hand. "Dr. Connell, I appreciated your cooperation."

The director glanced at the livid Sutton, unable to do anything. "My pleasure, sir," he said as they shook hands, even if it was not.

Bartlett turned to Sutton. "The smartphones, Commander."

Teeth clenched, Sutton dug into his pocket and held out two phones. Bartlett slid them into his jacket.

"Nash, Adam, I think we're done here."

Sutton stepped up to Bartlett and prodded him in the chest with his forefinger. "Have your moment of victory, Mister, but you haven't heard the last of this."

"I assure you, neither have you." Bartlett's eyes turned icy. "By the way, if you touch me again, I shall have you charged with assault. Clear?"

On the way out, Adam scooped up his broken cell, scowled at Sutton, and strode through the door.

Outside, Nash had another surprise, which he wasn't sure he welcomed. After receiving the audio file, Channel Nine and ABC crews knew they had a blockbuster story on their hands and had not wasted any time getting here. Several passersby stopped to watch the developments. Two police cars parked at the curb flanking a driverless black BMW sedan added a touch of intrigue to the scene.

Julia Candice, Nine's prominent exposé reporter, stepped in front of Garrett.

"Mr. Bartlett, is it true that the Australian Federal Police are running a sterilization program against lifeliners?"

The provocative comment generated a predictable ripple of incredulous gasps from the gathered onlookers, which Nash figured was the reaction Candice sought. Controversial news made headlines and bolstered careers.

Bartlett gave the reporter a stern look. "No comment at this time, Miss Candice."

Nash had seen the straight-shooting reporter in action and her persistence at pursuing a story legendary. Not tall, jet black hair cut short that framed a delicate Asian face, she had a reputation for uncovering and airing dirty political laundry. Her objects of attention rarely enjoyed their interviews.

"Are your clients lifeliners?"

"Talk to my office and I'll arrange a statement," Bartlett retorted briskly and strode toward his BMW, a uniformed dober at his side.

"I'll make a comment, Miss Candice," Adam said softly. Bartlett turned in alarm and Adam raised a hand. "It's okay."

"Mr. Gatt, why are you involved with Lifeliner Help Centers?" Candice jumped right in. "Is it because you're a lifeliner yourself? Or is it that Neale Wilkie, the state Treasurer, your boss, is a lifeliner?"

"Mr. Wilkie is not a lifeliner, but I am," Adam replied in a ringing, confident voice. "Lifeliner rights, and the rights of every citizen, are being trampled by all levels of government in defiance of common law. We are persecuted for not being like you, which is apartheid in its most insidious form. We're no longer prepared to sit back and watch a segment of our society eradicated under the misguided notion that somehow we're a security threat or the cause of perceived personal and economic problems. It is time to raise our voices in protest. What the federal police tried to do today was clearly illegal, but that did not stop Commander Sutton, which means his actions were sanctioned by the Department of Home Affairs."

"You're suggesting that Gibbs Gilmore, the Home Affairs minister, is conducting a sterilization campaign against lifeliners?"

"All I am saying, Julia, the AFP falls under the jurisdiction of his department."

"How did you happen to get caught up in what looks like an elaborate entrapment plot?"

"That's something I hope Mr. Sutton will explain to proper authorities."

The ABC *7.30 Report* anchor lifted her finger at Nash. "Mr. Bannon, you seem to have been involved in the same entrapment yourself. One that apparently involves the CSIRO. Can you elaborate?"

Nash took a deep breath and exhaled slowly to steady himself. He watched the program regularly and admired the slim reporter, her hard pale blue eyes having seen things beyond her years. Wearing a dark business jacket and skirt, chestnut hair also cut short, to her, he was probably just another story.

"I honestly don't know, Miss Russell. I suggest that Director Connell, who is in charge of this facility, will be in a better position to comment."

"Are *you* a lifeliner?"

This produced another ripple of murmuring.

Nash pursed his lips. This was it. He had reached his cusp. If he wanted to make his stand, he could do it now or crawl back into his safe lifestyle and continue living a lie as the world crumbled around him.

Garrett stepped toward him. "Don't—"

"I am a lifeliner," Nash said calmly and felt a wave of relief wash over him. A weight of thirty-two years rolled off his back. A weight of having to hide, pretend, and look over his shoulder waiting for that tap from a dober. "I didn't choose to be one, and

I cannot change what I am, but I am a person like you."

A young man in a tan suit pushed through the crowd, his face contorted with anger.

"You're not like me at all! I had a wife, house, and a good job. All I have left now is my job. We tried to have children, and found that we were both sterile. She got herself treated, but they couldn't do anything for me, so she left me." He cleared his throat and glared. "You call yourself human? You're an abomination!"

A can of Coke slammed into Nash and brown liquid splattered across his jacket. He winced at the pain that radiated from his chest, physical and emotional.

The two uniformed cops immediately stepped forward and the onlookers fell back.

Garrett nodded to Adam, grabbed Nash and dragged him toward his car, then got onto the front seat. He waited for his passengers to buckle in and told the car to take them to his office. The BMW immediately sped off. Something clanged off its side, the crowd behind them evidently not in a reasoning mood, but it would make great footage for the evening news.

Garrett rotated the seat and glared. "Idiot!"

Nash winced. "I just—"

"Next time you want to bare your soul, check with me first! Talking to reporters takes skill to get your message across. Blurting out stuff gets you a can in the face, or worse." Disgusted, he turned to Adam. "And you, shooting off your mouth like that!"

"Better to have come from me than a distorted press release," Adam replied, not at all apologetic, and held out a wad of tissues.

Confused, disheartened, Nash dabbed at his jacket, then sat back and stared at houses and apartment blocks sliding by. He only wanted…what? Bare his soul like Garrett said? Apologize for being a lifeliner? *Don't blame me for your troubles, I'm like everybody else…almost.* He might be like them in most ways, but that small 'almost' made all the difference needed for them to hate.

He did not consider himself brilliant, but was way above average and knew it, sophisticated and worldly-wise, able to handle everything that came his way. That's what he always thought, but what he handled up to now had been within a narrow set of parameters. Contemplating the mess politicians made of everything, he formulated his homemade 'if only' solutions, smug in the knowledge the world out there couldn't touch him. Today, that world had not only reached out and grabbed him, it made him feel insignificant, an irritant to be disposed of.

Ideals, the rule of law, justice, social order, belief in human kindness, all had turned out to be illusions, a façade to placate the masses behind which those in power manipulated events to maintain their power, obeying the don't get caught law, or ignored it altogether. So, he wanted to stand up and fight for his rights and the rights of other lifeliners? Revealing himself to a cynical reporter hoping for sympathy clearly hadn't cut it.

It hurt to admit it, but he was incompetent in the only arena of change that mattered—politics. Dirty politics at that, but he had known that all along. A righteous man standing in a pack of hungry wolves will invariably end up as lunch. Time to turn himself into an even hungrier wolf?

"I blew it, didn't I?" Nash said contritely, the admission costing him a lot of pride.

Garrett didn't say anything, his displeasure evident. Finally, he sighed.

"You've thrown it all away in a grand gesture of self-immolation and probably ruined yourself professionally. Not only that, you may have destroyed your family as well. Young fool!"

Chagrined, Nash accepted the unpalatable tongue lashing. In his moment of hubris, he had forgotten about his parents, Mark and Nat…and he was supposed to be the one with perfect memory.

"You're right, Garrett, and I'm sorry."

"You'll be much sorrier when this unwinds. I still cannot believe you did it!" Garrett exhaled softly and shook his head. "It's my fault in a way. I should have warned you when I saw the reporters. Right now, we need to mitigate the damage. I'll call your father—"

"I should—"

"Apologize, is that it? What I have to say will be far more useful. I won't tell you not to worry, but your father and I have discussed this possibility. Besides, it was bound to happen sooner or later, and it will take a few days before the media gets around to your family. Right now, you're the one in the firing line. When we get to my office, we'll consider your options."

"What about you?" The awful consequences of what Nash had done crashed on him with brutal force. "I may have put you in hot water. You could lose your partnership!"

Garrett looked amused. "It won't come to that, and you're not the only lifeliner on our books."

Nash could almost hear the pieces clicking into place. "Like the Help Center?"

The barrister lifted an eyebrow. "You figured that how?"

"When you confronted Sutton, you talked as though you knew him. That was only possible if you had prior knowledge of his taskforce." Nash turned to Adam. "And you can drop your cloak of innocence."

Both men laughed and Garrett slapped Nash on the knee. "Exceptional reasoning. Given Adam's activities, he had occasions to call on our services. What neither of us anticipated was your damn idiotic stunt."

Nettled, Nash flared. "I said I was sorry, didn't I?" Too many things had piled up and he needed time to sort them out. Calming down, he lifted his hand, palm up. "I apologize, Garrett. I was thinking about myself—again—instead of working the problem." He turned to Adam. "Sutton said he is rounding up your network—"

"When the recording of our conversation hits the channels, he and his taskforce will be out of business and we won't be bothered. Not for a while anyway, enough time for us to regroup.

If they arrested anybody, I doubt they'll be held for long. Sutton has become toxic and the government will want to sterilize *him* to contain any damage."

"They will slap a suppression order—"

"I doubt it. The story is already out and I hope President Ngarra boots the Coalition out of office. Imagine the reaction when people learn that lifeliners are being subjected to forced sterilization."

"The right-wing extremists like the Humans Only League and the People First Party will love it."

"They might, but not the ordinary guy on the street, which is what matters. If the government can do this to lifeliners, they can do it to some other minority group they happen to dislike. The Coalition is facing an October election. What the federal police have done will substantially cut their lead in the polls. It's a gift for the Labor opposition…and the Lifeliner Party. Believe me, the Prime Minister will be the first in a long line to disavow Mr. Sutton's taskforce and the extremists."

"What if the Labor Party were supporting her?"

"We're looking into that possibility," Garrett said. "If Macey Gardner is involved, Labor will be scrambling to deny everything. Atarah Readman will argue that this was a bipartisan policy to deflect the fallout that's about to descend on her, but we'll run our campaign on the premise that both parties were in on it."

Nash stared hard at the lawyer. "By 'we', you mean the Lifeliner Party."

"My partners and I are members of the organizational committee," Garrett said simply.

"Why are you telling me all this?"

Bartlett and Gatt looked at each other and something passed between them.

"That's obvious," Adam said, wearing a broad smile. "We want you on the Senate ticket."

Chapter Four

Traffic flowed smoothly as the MBW turned before reaching the Elizabeth Street mall, and the city's towers rose around it. Pedestrians crowded one of the busiest streets in the CBD. Coming, going, wandering, no one could tell.

Nash stared at Adam in shock, fantastic images running through his mind of him in the hallowed Canberra chamber, then burst into laughter. Adam and Garrett exchanged tolerant glances. Nash wiped his eyes.

"Me? Run for the Senate? You guys are cracked. I'm not a politician."

"Nobody is born a politician, my boy," Garrett said indulgently. "They're made, groomed into the position and managed."

"Somebody should look at the recipe, then. The idea of mixing it with those ego tripping basket cases makes me want to bomb the place."

"Those ego trippers you so colorfully denigrate govern this country," Adam pointed out mildly.

Nash looked hard at his friend, no longer amused. "And I don't like what they've done with it."

"Then stop bitching," Garrett snapped. "Step up and do something about it. Politics is something on which everybody has an opinion, whether passionate or indifferent, but few are prepared to take up the challenge and make a change, make a difference. It's easy to pontificate from a comfortable lounge seat how *you* would fix things. Well, we're giving you that chance."

Adam leaned toward him. "Nash, I don't have to tell you how rampant electoral apathy has allowed successive federal governments to erode our democratic rights under the guise of protecting them, which has shifted our political landscape toward a virtual autocracy. You've seen it working this afternoon. Do you want the Suttons of this world dispensing justice?"

"I'm not totally naïve, Adam. I understand the mechanics of state and federal politics."

"I know you do. That's why we're making this offer. When I see the Prime Minister in the holoview spouting her inane platitudes, it leaves me wondering about her sanity, not believing she has the responsibility to run this country and manage its international affairs. Macey Gardner and his Labor opposition aren't any better, torn by factional squabbles within the National Executive, hampered from making visionary national policies by the increasingly protectionist left-wing National Conference delegates who are seeing their cushy union positions threatened by declining memberships. People are right when they say the Labor Party's federal wing is a retirement village for union bosses."

"But you're working for that same Labor Party," Nash said.

"That's right, I am. Despite their misguided ideology, they act as an important social counterweight to rampant *laissez-faire* exploitation, but the party machine needs to be reminded of that from time to time. Latham is a political opportunist and a manipulator, interested in personal power, but not everybody in the state parliament is like him."

"Your boss, Neale Wilkie?"

"Come the November state election, the backroom numbers men will see to it that he is the next Premier, but Latham's center-left faction won't go down easily, though."

"What happened today won't enhance Wilkie's prospects."

"Revealing myself as a lifeliner was something that had to be done sooner or later, and Sutton provided a perfect moment. Better to ride out the publicity storm now rather than have it blown into a scandal by the Liberals during an election campaign. Besides, it's high time Labor declared a firm policy on lifeliners, and I'm not the only lifeliner in the party."

"Are you sure Labor doesn't have a policy to deal with lifeliners?" Nash asked softly.

"You mean, are they working with the Coalition to promote the sterilization program? It's possible, but I haven't heard anything."

"Or people in the know aren't talking." Nash bit his lip. "Adam, I've known for a while that you were Wilkie's Chief of Staff. What I cannot figure out, why aren't you working for Chad Everett? As the senior Lifeliner Party state representative, I would have thought he would be your natural focus."

Adam gave a lopsided grin. "I *am* working for Chad…in a roundabout way, as are others. Lifeliners are intimately involved in organizational machines of all parties, state and federal, but that's not enough. We badly need elected representatives to influence policies and shape public opinion. Unfortunately, finding someone who is prepared to face exposure has hampered our cause."

Nash smiled wryly. "And this afternoon, I made my stand."

Garrett gave him a fond grin. "Reckless and misguided, you did make a stand, and Sutton pushed you into making it. You saw a social system badly fractured and you tried to voice your protest. Never mind it was ineffective and will ruin your career, you stood up, it created the tipping point in your life you were looking for…and the quality we were looking for. You want to make a substantive protest and enact meaningful change? We're offering you an opportunity to prosecute your fight. All you have to do is accept the challenge."

"I don't know anything about running a campaign!"

"Nobody does. That's why political parties have organizational machines. We'll teach you what you need to know."

"Look, Garrett. All this sounds enticing, and I want to see things change, the alternative is to crawl into a cave and slam the door, but I never even read the Lifeliner Party policy manifesto."

"You should. Not only our manifesto, but platform policies

of all parties, and the new Constitution that turned us into a republic. You'll be interviewed and you must be prepared. You cannot afford to make a gaffe because you were too lazy to bone up on something. With your eidetic memory and smarts, you already hold a major advantage over your competition."

"It sounds daunting, I know," Adam said. "It did to me when Garrett got me involved, but you and other Lifeliner Party candidates will be stepping into a receptive political climate. We have a sinister government who may have sponsored an extremist organization like the Humans Only League—"

Nash raised a finger. "A supposition only."

"One worth pursuing."

"Elections aren't fought on facts, although they're a component," Garrett said. "You run on emotion by exposing people's fears and concerns, regardless how irrational, and blame it on the other guy."

"And if necessary, you create that fear," Nash added with a wry smile.

"Whatever it takes. This isn't a kid's game, my boy."

Adam cleared his throat. "We'll parade you as evidence of everything Readman's administration is doing. Young, responsible, successful, your life destroyed simply because you're a lifeliner. People will rally around you. Trust me. The voters are ready to be swayed by a properly coordinated publicity campaign. Not necessarily because you're a lifeliner, but they don't like growing government arrogance and authoritarianism, which both major parties have embraced."

Nash pointed a finger at Adam. "Since you know how this game is played, why aren't *you* running for the Senate?"

"I'll be contesting an Upper House seat in the state election. If we can build a balance of power, we'll be making a significant difference how politics is run in Victoria. Canberra isn't everything."

It still sounded crazy to Nash and he sighed. "Do you think it's possible to change the Canberra mindset by electing a lifeliner senator?"

"It won't happen at all if we don't make a start," Garrett growled.

"I still think the whole idea is ridiculous and you two ought to be certified," Nash told them. "Besides, I already have a job."

Adam frowned. "Do you?"

Nash looked at Garrett. "You think I'll get canned?"

"You'll find out tomorrow. You know why Australian voters rarely give an absolute majority in both Houses to a single party?" Garrett demanded.

"Of course," Nash said. "The Senate acts as a check against rampant government legislation not always in the public or national interest. This makes passing some legislation through the Senate difficult, as the government of the day has to scramble for support from minor parties and the crossbench, given that Oppositions seldom side with the government purely on partisan grounds."

"And the October election is unlikely to improve the Coalition's position," Garrett added. "Provided they win the Lower House and are returned to government, by no means a sure thing. Even if Labor wins office, they will face a similar problem, as the Coalition will challenge anything Labor wants to legislate. This uncertainty has opened the door for the Lifeliner Party, and we intend to take full advantage of a singular opportunity to gain seats. Any seat we hold will be a bargaining chip the government will have to play with. That means exercising real power to secure concessions, if some of the crossbench and minor party senators are prepared to side with us, not a given. A Senate seat also gives lifeliners an important public voice. Without one, we have nothing. Holding state seats is important, but to influence national policy, it is imperative for the party to secure federal representation."

"They could call a double dissolution election," Nash pointed out. "They have the trigger."

"The Superannuation Act? Why would they bother? And the

political landscape might improve by October."

"Potentially, we have another more serious problem, which most people aren't even aware of," Adam said softly. "You heard about the proposed referendum?"

Nash nodded. "The Coalition wants to amend the Constitution to introduce a fixed four-year term for the federal parliament. They tried in 2025 when we declared ourselves a republic, but the voters had little stomach for more changes. Nevertheless, I think it should be done. The current three-year flexible election cycle gives a government barely eighteen months to formulate and execute its legislative program before they swing into election mode again. It's a wonder that anything gets done."

"Ordinarily, I'd agree with you, but I suspect they have an ulterior, darker motive. Think about it. A fixed four-year term gives the government unrestrained power to act against lifeliners and further undermine democracy in this country, with nothing to stop them."

"We have the courts to keep them in check."

"What happens if it ignores them, as has happened in the States?" Garrett pointed out.

Nash studied his friend, grim scenarios running through his head.

"Patterns of behavior, Nash. Imagine what they could do with unlimited power over four years."

"On an assumption that Labor and the Coalition would work in unison to nullify the Senate."

"Against lifeliners, I believe they would. I also believe they already have."

"If you're right, what's the point in opposing the referendum?"

"Don't forget that power is addictive. Why stop with three chancy years when you can have certainty with four?"

"You have a morbid way of looking at things, Garrett."

"Given the current political and social climate not only here, but around the world, I'd say realistic."

"The Lifeliner Party will campaign against the amendment?"

"As will the Greens and most of the Senate crossbench. We need to shift public opinion from the superficial advantages pushed by Readman and highlight genuine dangers for everybody inherent in the proposal."

"Emotion and fear," Nash murmured. "The major parties presumably know all this and will run their own disinformation campaigns."

"Time we paid them back with their own coin. We need you in the Senate, my boy."

"Senator Nash Bannon…I still say it sounds ridiculous."

Garrett snorted. "This is serious business with more at stake than the future of lifeliners. We're talking about pivotal social change."

"Will the Lifeliner Party run candidates for the House of Representatives?"

"We'd like to, but the party doesn't have the resources to do it. Even if we managed to get someone elected, his or her voice wouldn't count for much unless there is a hung parliament."

Nash nodded. It made sense. The Coalition and the Labor Party always carved up the lower House between them, and the party that manages to win 81 seats forms the government. With the exception of the Australian Greens who manage to win three to five seats, the independents are usually never heard from.

"I'll need to know much more before I commit myself, Garrett, but I'll consider your offer."

"Don't take too much time. The party must finalize all candidates we want to contest and prepare submissions for the Electoral Office. Then there are eligibility checks to be done under Section 44 of the Constitution."

Nash recalled the fiasco in 2017-18 when a number of Labor and Coalition parliamentarians were found ineligible to hold a seat because they were dual citizens of another country. It caused severe embarrassment all around and generated a lot of public hilarity and shaking of heads.

"We also have to orchestrate a campaign for every state and secure organizational volunteers. A lot of work to be done, my boy, and the sooner you're on board the better."

* * *

Strands of *Tales From the Vienna Woods* drifted to the balcony. It created a bubble of calm and sanity where Nash could shelter from the storm of his turbulent thoughts. Afternoon traffic had thickened as city workers escaped their places of employment, anxious to get home and snatch a few hours of rest before having to do it all again tomorrow. Still high in the sky, the sun shone down with biting warmth, ready to crisp exposed skin. Sally automatically adjusted the balcony slats, keeping him in shade. A tumbler of Chivas Regal at his side, brow knitted in thought, he replayed the day's cascade of events, none pleasant.

On the way home from Garrett's office, he called Snoden and apologized for not coming to the office, and would see him first thing in the morning. His boss waved off the apology and told him not to worry about it. Did any of his project managers need him? Apparently not, or they would have called or emailed. Nash did not look forward to tomorrow. Snoden's congeniality probably won't survive the evening news. Nothing Nash could do except face whatever happens. Garrett told him what he might expect, not mincing his blunt words. It had not improved his mood.

Cariana called twice on his cell, but he instructed his PID to block her. She was the last person he wanted to talk to.

With business out of the way, he gritted his teeth and called Dad. He expected another stern lecture and a deserved dressing down, but his dad managed to surprise him again. Instead of getting skinned for being so stupid, his father showed unexpected understanding and sympathy, more concerned how this would affect his son. They had always gotten along, even when Nash and Mark rebelled against what they saw as unreasonable rules and overbearing parental authority. Like all teenagers, they wanted to fly free, ignorant of dangers that lay out there, or at best dismissive. His dad's words of support stirred a gush of affection for his father he had not felt for a while, and lifted some of the burden off his soul. Tomorrow night, dinner at his place, Dad ordered. Natalie would also be there. Time to reveal everything. His father would talk to Mark and see if he could come down from Canberra.

Having taken time to think things through, the appalling consequences of his misguided revelation on the rest of his family had finally sunk in. Nash castigated himself for being so dumb, giving into an impulse.

When he called Mark, he only got a 'leave a message' from his phone. He wondered how his brother would react when he sees Nash's public catharsis on every channel. Probably not as favorably as Dad's calm acceptance, and Nash would not blame him at all. Would his brother have a job and a future tomorrow? Would he?

If Mark chose to punch him on the nose, Nesh felt he had it coming.

He'll find out tomorrow if he still had a family.

Garrett was probably right when he said the government would likely batten down and go into damage control. Given the Sutton stink, firing Mark because he was Nash's brother and a lifeliner might not be a very astute political move, but they could do it out of spite. They may not fire him, but Mark's career was probably irretrievably tainted. The People First Party and the Humans Only League would certainly be clamoring for his dismissal. More shattered hopes, dreams, and expectations, and Nash would have to carry the guilt for it. And Natalie? She wasn't a lifeliner, but associating with siblings who were could still tar her.

He took a sip of whiskey as the last track finished and the enchanting *Blue Danube* calmed his thoughts. He allowed the music to fill his mind and transport him to Austria's forested hills, craggy mountains, and placid valleys. He would not mind being there right now, sitting in lush grass on a sloping meadow beneath an alpine backdrop, cow bells clanking from the pasture around him, butterflies fluttering among wild flowers…

There were no flowers in this concrete meadow, only a city that pressed on him, stifling his spirit.

He took another sip, realizing he allowed himself to slide into morbid introspection.

Run for the Senate?

He could not believe that Adam had suggested such an absurd idea. Nash closely followed the machinations of state and national politics, and watched the ebb and flow of all parties with interest. Occasionally, he viewed House Question Time on ABC, and the experience always left him shaking his head, bemused. He could not believe that people who behaved like squabbling children were supposedly mature, responsible adults. What comforted and alarmed him, politicians the world over weren't any better. However, those same people would decide the future for all lifeliners.

Then again, as someone said, people deserve the politicians they got. Which only reaffirmed for him the effect of rampant electoral apathy. As Garrett observed, politics was something on which everybody had an opinion, but few were prepared to step forward and make a difference. He was right. Easy to pontificate from a soft lounge seat.

That, Nash admitted sourly, included him.

Did he have the internal strength needed to accept the challenge?

Senator Nash Bannon…It still sounded ridiculous.

"Nash, Dr. Cariana Lambert is requesting entry to the building," Sally announced quietly, and he almost spilled his drink.

What the hell did *she* want! Rub it in and gloat over his misery?

"Deny access," he snapped.

Stung by the gush of raw loathing, he slammed down the tumbler, which caused the whiskey inside to jump and dance.

Damn her. Hadn't she done enough to him?

He rose and strode to the balcony rail. Traffic, people, build-ings, trees, it all looked the same, yet different somehow. Some spark was missing, but he couldn't define what took it away.

You *had taken it away!*

Whatever this moment wrought, he must remain true to him-self. No lies, deceptions or pretense. If he lost that anchor, his transformation into that hungry wolf would be complete. What would distinguish him then from the rest of the savage pack? If he ran for the Senate, the process might turn him into one of the wolves simply to survive. It took a certain character type to run for public office. He wondered if he could abandon his principles to get elected and continue to live with himself.

If he did get elected, could he remain true to his principles in Canberra's factional cauldron of murky deals, backstabbing, and outright deceit?

Nash didn't know how much time passed as he gazed absently at the boulevard below without really seeing anything. Probably only a few minutes, but it felt like a lifetime. An eternity of cosmic time where the world he knew had stopped turning, and he did not know the world he found himself in now.

"Nash, Dr. Lambert is requesting entry," Sally's soft voice brought him down hard from his reverie.

What possible good would it do to see her? She savaged him enough. Yet, deep down inside, her spark still flickered gamely. He wanted to snuff it out, and it would only take a dark thought, but he hesitated. To his dismay, he couldn't do it, finding that he still cared for her. Wasn't that a crock?

He snorted and shook his head.

"Permit access," he growled in resignation, his feelings on a slow roast. He walked into the lounge, clasped his hands behind his back and waited.

A few minutes later, enough time for the elevator to come up, Sally announced she was at the door.

"Let her in."

The lock clicked and the door opened. Cariana hesitated, then slowly walked in. Sally closed the door after her. She looked good in a cream business jacket and black trousers, a small brown leather bag on her shoulder, hair tied in a piled-up bun, her almond eyes glistening with emotion as though she had cried. Over him? He didn't believe it. He didn't want to believe it. She probably came to rage at him for disrupting her cushy research program. Well, it also gave him a chance to rage at her. They were supposed to be dining out tonight at the Vue de Monde, but that wasn't going to happen now. Perhaps never.

He waited.

She bit her lip. "Sutton...he took Aleya." She sniffed, but made no move to wipe away the tear that slid down her cheek. "He's got her, Nash. I didn't know what to do..."

A jolt of alarm raced through him, but he forced himself to stand still and pretend indifference, the little girl's betrayal also poignant and raw.

"When you left Parkville, he made some calls and went berserk. I didn't see it, but Hardy...Dr. Connell, told me later. Sutton ordered his men to take two lifeliners I had at the facility to his car, then he took her. I tried calling you...Nash, say something or I'll go mad."

"You called the authorities?"

"Hardy...I'm sorry, Nash...I'm sorry. I should have told you everything last night when I could have stopped it, but I was confused and afraid of Sutton."

"You played me...used me."

She stepped toward him, eyes pleading. "I didn't want to! What we had, maybe not anymore, was real. At least it was for me."

"Aleya—"

"It was Sutton's idea. He trained her to find information about lifeliners. She wasn't the only one. Adults often talk in front of children thinking they didn't understand. Playing a homeless street kid was an elaborate game and a way to make some pocket money. They didn't know what they were doing, not really, and I got my test subjects. Who would miss a bum lifeliner? That wasn't our only source. The Ravenhall Correctional Center and the Youth Justice Center in Parkville supplied many CSIRO inmates."

"You told me you had grade school volunteers."

"We do, but they weren't the only ones."

"That's all lifeliners were to you, test subjects," Nash hissed, his voice dripping with scorn.

Her eyes flared in defiance. "That's right! We didn't hurt them, although I wanted to, just as they hurt me. When my brother was killed…Hate me if you want, but Sutton gave me a chance to do some groundbreaking research and a shot at the Nobel Prize for the one who cracked the lifeliner DNA. He knew about my brother and used that to get me on his taskforce. I told you there were days when I didn't enjoy my work, but that came later. Too late, as it turned out, and I couldn't back out." Her shoulders sagged.

"When he found out I was Aleya's guardian, he convinced me that she could help in a substantive way. She wouldn't be in any danger. He would have agents disguised as hobos looking after the kids. If I didn't cooperate, he said I would never work again. My research meant everything to me and I was afraid what he might do to Aleya if I didn't agree. But I didn't know about you! Aleya told me how you two met, but she never mentioned your name. It was only last night when she said how you took her to your apartment that I realized she was talking about you. You can imagine my shock. I immediately called Sutton and told him I didn't want her involved anymore. He threatened me with imprisonment for harboring a lifeliner if I didn't cooperate. You have no idea what he's capable of."

"This morning at the Footscray Market, you didn't look threatened. You looked like you were enjoying your moment of triumph."

She clenched her fists. "Don't you understand? He was watching. I had to go through with it because of Aleya."

"How did you know Adam and I would be at the Market?"

"Aleya keeps a smartphone in her backpack. Before you left your apartment, she called somebody. Probably one of Sutton's men. Then she called me and I told her what to say when you got there. I hated what he made me do, but I was in it too deep. I don't expect you to forgive me…"

Nash nodded, remembering how Aleya asked to go to the bathroom.

"And the scene in front of the butcher shop?"

"Staged. You must have guessed that."

His rampaging emotions were ripping him apart and he didn't know what to do. This could also be a staged performance on her part, but why would she bother? She had done her job. She couldn't ruin him any further.

You did that to yourself, old son.

Perhaps, but could he pass judgment on her with what he knew?

"What do you want from me, Cariana? Absolution?"

"I…I thought…" Eyes glistening, her resolve crumbled. She buried her face in her hands and sobbed.

"I think you'd better leave." He was being nasty as only a man betrayed can be.

His words shook her and she flinched. She didn't look arrogant, indifferent to the misery her work inflicted on lifeliners, thinking only about personal glory and professional recognition, but she damned herself with her own words. She allowed herself to be seduced by an image of success, a little naïve perhaps, but she had known what she was doing.

Watching her standing there, he wanted to be cold and uncaring. Better to walk away, safe again in his cocoon, not feeling, untouched. That's what he did after Sally was gone, and thought himself emotionally secure. He allowed Cariana to slip through his guard, not that he tried to keep her away, prepared to treat her as merely another transitory amour. Wanting to have someone close again, he ignored the warning signs. She *told* him of her

151

hate for lifeliners.

In it too deep, she said. If she had real feelings for him, she could have warned him, but she didn't. That was the telling point.

He saw her searching for something in his unyielding face, but he could not give her what he did not have. She clamped her mouth and strode toward the door. She paused, gave him a last look, hoping for acceptance, then slowly walked out. He could hear her hurried footsteps as the door gently closed after her. Something broke deep inside him and burned.

His thoughts mixed as he ambled toward the balcony table, he picked up his whiskey tumbler and made his way to the railing. He sipped and felt the liquor sear his throat as it went down, tasting bitter…cinders of disappointment, regrets, disillusionment, of innocence lost. Perhaps if reality had caught up with him sooner, he would have been better prepared, but he thought he was safe, untouchable despite all evidence to the contrary.

That's what happens when you live in denial, old son.

He looked down at a lone figure crossing the inner road lane, maybe just as lost and disillusioned. A tram clattered by heading downtown. Cars whispered along the boulevard—unknown faces, unknown destinations, dreams fading in the distance.

Cariana reached the tram stop and stood under the curved glass shelter; alone and rejected. He wondered what she was thinking. A future lost, haunted by demons? Possibly, and then again, perhaps not, because those were his thoughts. Given what she was, her career, her goals, he could hardly imagine what images crowded her mind. Dark images of dark tomorrows.

A tram came up heading out, stopped and she got in, which meant she was going home. He could see the doors close, shutting her from view. It clanked its bell and, with a whine of power, vanished from view. He took another sip of whiskey, but the amber liquid had lost its appeal. Below him, pedestrians ambled along the sidewalk, sheltered beneath golden elms. Across the road, more people, more mysterious lives, destinations and lost thoughts, never intersecting. Silent shells impervious to those around them, possibly preferring it that way.

That is what he had been most of his life, a shell with a one-way view—out. Unreachable and untouched, and he liked it that way. Sifting through a cascade of memories, he realized that even with Sally, he hadn't had the expected fulfillment of having another person close, a part of him. It might have been, but he would never know. They took her from him before he could find out.

He turned his head and gazed up the street where the tram had gone.

Sally was taken from him, but he pushed Cariana away. Why did she come to him today? It couldn't be because of Aleya…another problem to resolve. To help find her? His day hadn't turned out well, but Cariana's day also walked in shadows. Did she want someone to lean on, comfort her, be there for her? Apologize and explain a whole lifetime of emotional baggage that could not be explained or apologized away? She sought his forgiveness and he turned her away because of bruised pride.

In the sky, the sun shone bright, indifferent to the fragile beings touched by its light.

Staring at nothing, Nash came to understand something terrible. He had been deliberately unmoved and uncaring. Easy to make excuses and dredge up reasons for his indifference, for pushing her away. It appeased his wounded ego, but did nothing to resolve his raging emotions.

He could not escape or hide from what he felt for Cariana even now. Was it love? Did he even know what real love was? Was it possible to love someone he did not truly know? He'd read enough philosophy and had one meaningful relationship, but that wealth of knowledge had not prepared him when confronted with the real thing. Love is a tenuous, fleeting thing that brushes an individual with passion, longing, joining…a million things with a million shapes and guises unique for everyone. So he had read. Love had touched him in the shape of a wondrous woman and she betrayed him. Or had she?

Looking at events objectively, she hadn't *exactly* betrayed him. She merely omitted to warn him about Sutton, forced into inaction by her need to protect Aleya. That was the crucial difference. Did he make excuses for her?

Time moved, but he did not feel its passing. He recalled every sweet moment they had together, from the first chance encounter at the Southbank eatery, the lunches they shared, their first date, the crepes evening at his place, and added everything up. It came to quite a tally of experiences, satisfying emotional rewards, and a glimmer of a possible fulfilling future.

And he pushed her away.

He pulled back a chair and sat beside the balcony table, the city noises a comforting blanket for his thoughts as he coldly examined his emotional responses. She figuratively stabbed him in the back—and it might as well have been for real—but she had not done it deliberately, entangled in circumstances that culminated at the Footscray Market. Her irrational hate for lifeliners merely demonstrated an understandable reaction to her brother's death, which simply made her like everybody else, prone to failure, prone to making mistakes. Highly educated, she probably understood the basis for her neurosis, but powerless or unwilling to do anything about it. That only made her human.

The thought forced a wry grin from him. Human…

Replaying every event in his mind, he eventually accepted the harsh truth why he pushed her away.

Wounded pride, a major drag.

Ah, rats!

Perhaps he could still wind back some things and make a fresh start. Would she want to? Only one way to find out. There were crumbled bridges to repair between them, and things would never be bright and innocent as before, but an occasional rainstorm also cleaned the air, making things new again.

He banged the whiskey tumbler against the table and walked with determined strides toward the door. Fists clenched, mouth set in a tight line, he waited impatiently for the elevator to come up. He rode it to the basement and marched to his car. The driver's door unlocked and the running lights came on as his PID linked with the onboard computer. The engine started at his command and the tires squealed as the car surged toward the exit.

He half expected to be mobbed by reporters, but the driveway was empty. This moment of peace probably won't last. They would get around to him once the story of his detention broke everywhere.

He stuck to the inner lane as he drove up St. Kilda Road, thankful not to be jammed in the afternoon crush. The Fawkner Residences building loomed ahead and he slowed down. He parked in a rare free spot and scrambled out, his heart picking up a few beats. At the wide glass entrance, he connected his PID with the building's security system and requested to see Dr. Cariana Lambert.

Would she want to see him? Perhaps not, but he was prepared to wait until she did see him. She had to come out eventually. Then again, she might call the dobers to remove a stalker. On top of everything else, that would make an interesting twist to his day. She might also play the same childish game he played with her and make him wait. He winced at the memory.

He cursed the crawling seconds, but the entrance doors did not move. About to repeat his request, his breath caught when he saw her emerge out of the elevator alcove. She stopped and waited for the entrance doors to slide back. Her eyes were red from crying, but standing there, he saw determination and resolve etched on her face. She walked through and her cold look stabbed at him. He could sense the protective shield she erected around her.

"What do you want?" she said in a tight, brittle voice.

He walked toward her, stopped and stared into her swollen eyes. He badly wanted to take away her pain, make her whole again, make her laugh. It would also melt the cold around his own heart.

"Can you forgive me, Cariana...for everything, for being a

jerk? Is there a chance that we can start over?"

He felt his heart flutter and swallowed hard, waiting for some reaction. Her eyes glistened and he saw them soften. The wall she erected finally cracked. Her arms went around his neck and she melted against him.

"Oh, Nash…Nash."

"I blamed you for betraying me and robbing me of something that was becoming important between us. I crawled back behind my wall and pretended that nothing had happened. But it did happen and I couldn't ignore it."

She stood there, tense, her eyes searching.

"When I thought it through, I realized you didn't betray me at all. You were simply protecting Aleya, and I was too blind to see it." He stroked her cheek. "I wanted to unload that and dispel any lingering ghosts between us."

Her body trembled as he held her. He stroked her back and buried his head in her hair. If she meant to burn him again, a few more scars wouldn't make any difference now. He was being cynical, but it will take time to clear the emotional rubble between them and regain trust.

He pulled back and brushed her cheek. "I love you and I want you with me for all time," he whispered gently.

She looked at him and broke into a radiant smile that made her cheek dimple. "Cube! I waited so long for you to tell me that, you lug."

Then she kissed him hard. A sweet moment later, she pulled back and sniffed back tears.

"When I found out you were a lifeliner, I hated you. I fell for you, and you turned out to be something I despised. I also hated myself for feeling that way, blaming all lifeliners for an act of one drunkard. It wasn't rational, I know, but I couldn't help myself. It gave me strength to push on with my research. Then Sutton took Aleya and I realized how twisted I was. All this time, I refused to accept that she too was a lifeliner." She choked back a sob.

"You must have been very close to your brother," he said.

"He was strong and kind, and always had time for me. I adored him. Then he was gone, and I had this black hole inside me..." She dabbed at her eyes. "How do I get Aleya back, Nash?"

"Do you know where he's holding her?"

"I'm not sure. Probably at the Youth Justice Center, but it could be anywhere. I'm afraid what he might do to her, and the others. Hardy won't do anything, scared they'll shut down the facility, and Canberra is already asking some hard questions."

"Well, we won't get her by going there and pounding on the door."

Cariana dropped her arms and stepped back. "After what I have done to you, what she has done, you're still—"

"Crazy, I know. Crazy about you," he said lightly and steered her toward the entrance.

Arm around her waist, feeling content in her company, they waited for the elevator. In her apartment, she smiled shyly.

"I won't be a moment. I need to freshen up."

When she disappeared into the bathroom, he looked around at the neat layout with the added feminine touches: flowers, table runner, a crystal bowl filled with bright pebbles, scented herbs, and tasteful gauzy curtains. Next to the holoview wall, a plain crayon drawing of a man leaning over a woman added a surreal touch. He liked it, but the décor and color combinations would never have occurred to him. He pulled back a chair from the dining table and grunted as he sat down. Getting involved with Cariana again, the package also included Aleya. He hadn't planned it this way, but since both his feet were in it, he would have to handle whatever came.

Cariana emerged looking composed, her face washed and hair back in place.

"You want something to drink?" she asked.

"Something strong. I could use it."

She got a bottle of whiskey from the bar and poured two fingers for him into a crystal tumbler and a more restrained amount for herself. She handed him the glass and sat opposite him.

"You said that Sutton might not have taken Aleya to the Youth Justice Center," he prompted. "She must have talked to you about what she did, where she stayed, her training, anything."

Cariana took a sip and worried her lower lip. "Mostly, she stayed with me, and we usually spent our weekends in Woodend, but not always. Sutton wanted her to work during weekends, but I put my foot down. She was still a child learning to be a teenager and deserved to have a little fun with friends over the summer break. Sometimes, she would sleep at one of their safe houses. She never said where. I suppose her trainers told her not to. Part of the intrigue, and I didn't pry too hard. When she stayed with me, I'd help her with her working outfit, as she called those dreadful clothes, and she would catch a tram into the city."

"Didn't this interfere with her schoolwork?"

"She only started after school closed for summer, but she's been training since September."

"Did she talk about the safe house, the other kids with her, or the people looking after her?"

"They did part of their training together, she said, but they worked alone. There was one man who ran the safe house and acted as a contact, but Aleya didn't talk about him."

"Do you know his name?"

She frowned. "She mentioned him once. It sounded like tram."

"Trent!" The enigmatic beggar; not so enigmatic now. "Can I use your holoview to call someone?"

"Of course." She tilted back her head slightly. "Computer, open phone."

"Ready."

Nash raised an eyebrow. "Computer?"

Cariana smiled and shrugged.

"Computer, personal for Garrett Bartlett at Grange, Strand and Bartlett."

The holoview wall rippled in random colors and cleared.

"Nash, what can I do for you? In trouble again?"

"Not exactly. Garrett, may I introduce Dr. Cariana Lambert."

"Ah, the source of your problems. One of them anyway. A pleasure, Dr. Lambert."

Bemused, Cariana nodded. "Mr. Bartlett."

Nash cleared his throat. "It's Aleya, Garrett. Cariana thinks Commander Sutton may have her at the Youth Justice Center, and she's concerned what he might do to her and other lifeliner inmates."

"Why there?"

"Because that's where I obtained some of my juvenile test subjects," Cariana replied in a tight voice.

"I see. You could be in serious trouble, young lady, as could Dr. Connell, but we'll get to that later. If Sutton is holding your niece, that would constitute kidnapping, detention of a minor without cause, and deprivation of liberty. The courts take a dim view of such things. However, Sutton's activities fall under federal jurisdiction, which means we need a heavy lever."

"How do we get her out, Garrett?" Nash snapped, not giving a damn about levers.

"You've alerted the police?" Bartlett demanded and Cariana nodded.

"The man we need is Van Ross."

"The federal Attorney-General?" Nash was impressed.

"We were classmates at Melbourne University."

"Isn't the Prime Minister trying to get rid of him?"

"Trying, but she won't. Van Ross is impartial and the back-benchers love him, as does the Opposition. I'll talk to Van and see what can be done. By the way, have you seen Channel Nine's afternoon news?"

"I was there, remember?"

"Watch it. Miss Candice did a nice job for you, which probably hasn't done Commander Sutton or the government much good."

"Like I care right now. Something else, Garrett. Aleya spoke to Cariana about a safe house Sutton used for his operations."

"That would be the first place he would sanitize."

"He may have taken her someplace else, a second safe house."

"The thought had occurred to me, my boy."

"The cops could find her by tracking her cell or PID."

"Mmm. Sutton has probably dumped her cell, and tracking a PID shouldn't be possible."

"An incident this afternoon leads me to believe otherwise."

"We'll try to locate her phone first and I'll look into the other possibility. We can only hope he hasn't disposed of it, but he is a professional and knows all the evasion techniques. Before you mention it, we'll follow the same procedure to find him. I'll put out a state-wide apprehension order against him, but it might be a while before they get him. Leave it with me," Garrett said and switched off.

Nash locked eyes with Cariana, reached for her hand and squeezed.

"What now?" she whispered.

"We wait. Nothing much else we *can* do."

She regarded him with a quizzical smile. "A second safe house? Track her cell?"

"That's what happens when you read all those detective books," he quipped. "You get ideas."

She laughed and punched him lightly on the shoulder. "Cube!" For a moment, her face transformed into something radiant.

He loved the way she lit up when she was gay. Her glow made everything around her brighter. His urge to take her, make her pant with passion, coursed through him, palpable as heat. He recognized it for what it was, a primordial compulsion to mate, but naming it did not lessen its force. Right now, though, both of them walked on fragile ground, and he would be doing himself irreparable harm if he pushed her into doing something when she was emotionally vulnerable. She might regret it later and resent him when she started thinking objectively. He did not want her

for only one moment. He wanted her for all time, a willing partner.

"I appreciate that you thought you could come to me," he said
softly.

"I almost didn't. The nurse who took your blood sample, she's
one of my assistants. We talked sometimes, girl talk. She knew I
was going out with you and she deliberately broke protocol to tell
me that you were a lifeliner." She took a sip and held the tumbler
between her hands.

"Every woman dreams of meeting the right man, her prince
on a white charger who would take her to his castle and make her
a princess. A silly fantasy, I know, but after that dinner at your
place, I began to wonder if you could be that right one. I sensed
you wanted me, and I appreciated that you didn't try to force
yourself on me, revealing yourself to be another chauvinistic
brute. I've seen them in operation and never liked it."

Her eyes were bright and he wanted to say that he understood.
In the end, he said nothing. Uncertain, moody, she had to work
through her feelings and put the past behind her—as he needed
to.

"At first, I didn't believe her. She had to be wrong. Then the
realization hit me and I felt the tears run. She tried to hug me,
but I waved her away. I hated you for shattering my fantasy. I
hated you for not telling me, and I hated all men. You never said
or did anything to give yourself away, but I've been working with
lifeliners for more than two years and I saw the little things. Your
physical characteristics, eidetic memory, a twin brother, intelligence, it was all there.

"When Hardy told me that Sutton had Aleya, I fell apart. I
didn't know what to do or where to turn. You want to know the
silly part? I called you, not believing I did that. When you didn't
answer, I took a cab to see you. Not to cry on your shoulder. I
wanted to vent my fury and hatred on you for ruining my life.
You took away my dream, and you took Aleya. As I waited downstairs for you to let me in—I wasn't even sure you were home—

I realized how wrong I've been about everything." Eyes swimming, she blinked. "Then you sent me away…" She chocked back a sob.

He stood, walked around the table and gathered her in his arms.

"I would have told you tonight I was a lifeliner and taken my chances," he murmured into her hair.

She lifted her face and brushed his mouth with soft lips. Holding her tight, he returned the kiss, not forcing her, but showing that she could trust him. Her velvety tongue touched him and he felt a pleasurable jolt similar to jamming. She moaned and clung to him, demanding more. After a timeless moment, out of breath, he pulled away and cupped her captivating face between his hands.

"Maybe I don't know what real love is, but it has to be more than mere physical desire. I want you, Cariana. Not for a day or a night, but for always. I want to make you happy, but I won't blame you if you walk away. It was stupid to reveal myself this afternoon, and I have probably ruined my family. The shining knight you hoped for has turned into a hounded villain. If you stay with me, they will hound you, and I cannot allow that."

"Shouldn't that be my decision?"

"This is serious. We cannot let ourselves be carried away by adolescent emotion."

"You want to send me away…again?"

"That's the last thing I want, Cariana, but you need to understand what being with me will mean for you, your career and your future."

"Everything you said will probably happen, but the future is not set. I would be lying if I said it doesn't frighten me a little, and I'm not sure I am ready to commit to a relationship right now. Too many things are going on and I need time to work them out in my own way. The Nobel Prize I was so desperate to get doesn't seem so very important right now. To think it warped my judgment about everything…" Her soft fingers stroked his cheek and she rose. "My shining knight, I should get back to Parkville. Things are in chaos and the authorities probably want to question me. About our date tonight…"

Nash smiled. "I already canceled. If CSIRO or the dobers give you a hard time, call me. Better still, call Garrett."

"A powerful friend to have in your corner."

"And I might need him. We both might."

He stood and made his way toward the door.

"Want to come with me in a cab? I'm going past your place anyway," she offered and he shook his head.

"I drove up. I'll call you if Garrett has anything."

At the door, she paused and looked at him. "Thank you, Nash…for coming back."

He pecked her cheek. "Thank you for letting me back," he said.

A new beginning? He hoped so, but there were still shadows to clear.

* * *

Twenty minutes of hard calisthenics and Tai Chi moves, followed by a brisk run, toned up the muscles and prepared Nash for a hearty breakfast. This morning, he decided to go all out. In addition to his usual vegetable/fruit smoothie, he added two hardboiled eggs to last night's salmon salad. A carafe of freshly brewed coffee on the lounge table, he sat down to enjoy himself.

"Sally, ABC news."

The holoview wall cleared to show a serious news presenter and his equally serious lady partner.

"*—the Home Affairs Minister, Gibbs Gilmore, nor the Prime Minister were available for comment. The PM's office said a statement will be provided later today. While the government is trying to weather a disastrous negative poll as a result of clandestine Australian Federal Police activities against lifeliners, and the allegation that it created the Humans Only League, the opposition leader, Macey Gardner, has distanced himself from any suggestion* *that the Labor Party condoned in any way a program of forced sterilization against Australian citizens."*

Marina Lennon smoothly picked up the narrative.

"The startling revelation that Mr. Adam Gatt, the Victorian state Treasurer's Chief of Staff, is a lifeliner caused a stir in the state Labor Party. Neal Wilkie denied knowledge that his aide was a lifeliner, extoling Mr. Gatt's performance and character, scoffing at the notion that Mr. Gatt would be dismissed or expelled from the party. He expressed surprise that such a notion has even been entertained.

"At two o'clock this morning, a group of People First Party protesters accosted two men outside the King Street Three Cats *nightclub frequented by lifeliners. There are reports of injuries from the ensuing scuffle, and police made a number of arrests. A similar altercation occurred inside Sydney's Kings Cross* Paladin *bar. Two patrons and one protester required hospitalization."*

The alarming rise of attacks across the country against anyone suspected of being a lifeliner reflected a dark social mood. If allowed to continue, Nash would not be surprised to see People First agitators standing on intersections demanding proof from passersby that they were not lifeliners.

"Mr. Nash Bannon, a 32-year-old IBM program manager, arrested with Mr. Gatt on suspicion of subversive activities, was allegedly threatened with forced sterilization by Lyle Sutton, a senior AFP officer, because Mr. Bannon is a lifeliner. Here is an excerpt of yesterday's interrupted interview."

Disgusted, Nash told Sally to switch off. He had seen it all last night. By now, the whole world must know he was a lifeliner. The rest of his breakfast lost some of its appeal and he decided to go to the office. He picked a light black worsted suit, a pale blue shirt, and a navy tie. The silver cufflinks added a nice touch without being gaudy. IBM allowed its employees a lot of leeway and did not have a formal dress code, but executives were expected to project a professional image, especially to clients. A business presentation did not carry much weight given by someone wearing an unbuttoned shirt and rolled up sleeves.

Nash did not mind a little formality, understanding the psychological warfare waged with clients, and every gambit counted. Inside the IBM building, he did not insist that his project managers wear a suit and tie, except when seeing a client, personally or through a virtual presence link. One of his bright PMs quoted HR guidelines and refused to comply. Nash didn't get mad, but simply told him, 'Those who insist on being right, sometimes get left'. The PM got the unstated message that unwritten rules often carried more weight and were ignored at one's peril.

As Nash knotted his tie, he thought the quote rather apt in his present situation—a possibility that he too might get left. He checked himself in the wall mirror and decided he was presentable. Eyeing the slim Gucci calf leather briefcase, he decided not to bother with it. The paperless office *had* slowly become paperless.

About to walk out, he heard muffled chanting. He unlocked the balcony door and peered down the railing. A small crowd of about a dozen men clustered before the entrance, their vigorous voices had attracted passersby along the street who stopped to gawk. A Channel Seven reporter was making running commentary, the 3D camera pinned above her breast transmitting everything to the studio via her PID. Two police paddy wagons stood in the driveway ready to bundle away the unruly.

"We want the lifeliner!"

"When do we want him?"

"Now!"

Nash pulled back in dismay.

How the hell did they know where he lived?

"Sally, Channel Seven news and record."

"—*activists are demanding the arrest of Mr. Nash Bannon, a self-confessed lifeliner arrested yesterday by the federal police on suspicion of terrorism. The spokesman for the Humans Only League claims they have proof that Mr. Bannon and a group of lifeliners he is associated with, planned an attack on the Flinders Street station—*"

"Sally, switch off!"

Shaken, Nash could not believe the nonsense he heard, designed to further inflame and polarize people's attitudes. It hadn't taken long to sensationalize the story, the blame for yesterday's events laid at his feet. If people accepted this propaganda as fact, he could expect more marches and protests everywhere, including his apartment.

"Sally, forward the clip to Mr. Bartlett, C/O Grange, Strand and Bartlett. Personal message to follow."

"Very well...executed."

Mouth set tight, he walked slowly toward the elevator, not relishing a possibly ugly confrontation. The guard at the security desk gave him a polite greeting as Nash strode through the lobby.

"I wouldn't go out there right now, Mr. Bannon."

"I'm not looking to pick a fight, Eden."

"That might be so, but I doubt the mob out there will care."

"What am I supposed to do? Crawl back into my bedroom and hide? Screw them!"

The entrance glass panels slid aside and he walked through.

"There he is!"

"Stinking lifeliner!"

Alert, mentally ready to defend himself, Nash walked steadily down the steps. One of the chanters stepped in front of him.

"I don't like lifeliners, and I don't like you."

The guy was a bruiser. Heavyset, unshaven, black leather jacket with rows of studs along the seams, his type relied on size to intimidate victims. Nash topped him by five centimeters.

"We all have problems," he said easily and made to push past even as he expanded his awareness to see every part of the man, because an attack could come from anywhere.

The guy smirked and clenched his fist. "And you are one problem I'll take care of right now," the bruiser hissed and took a swing without any windup.

Nash made a small sidewise step toward the attacker, blocked the clumsy punch, and simultaneously slammed his fist against the guy's solar plexus. The bruiser gasped, went pale and crumpled, clutching his chest. Normally, Nash would follow through with a strike against the man's larynx to disable him, but that would leave him in a kneeling position, which was not advisable when facing what might be more than one aggressor. With his man down, he did not step back, which would invite attack. The others glared, ready to close on him. All it needed was somebody to move. Nash knew he couldn't take them all, but he would break bones before they took him down.

A sharp whistle broke the tense moment as four dobers pushed their way through the mob.

"Enough! Break it up!"

"Another time, lifeliner. We'll be seeing you," one of the protesters snarled as he helped the bruiser to his feet. After more sidelong looks, the group took up their chant down the street, followed by one of the cop wagons. Happy with her footage, the reporter climbed into her car and sped off.

A cop wearing sergeant stripes walked up to him and shook his head. "That wasn't a smart thing to do, coming out. We might not be around next time."

"I'll take my chances, Sergeant, but I won't be intimidated by anybody."

"I can see that. Under the circumstances, it might be better if we gave you a lift. That mob might decide to come back."

Nash eyed him, not detecting any hostility, and relaxed slightly. "Thank you, officer. I would appreciate that."

"Where do you want to go?"

"The Arts Center."

"Right. Get in."

He got onto the back seat with two cops up front and the wagon followed the driveway toward the exit.

Heavy traffic along St. Kilda Road moved steadily toward the CBD. Not in the mood to chat, Nash wondered if this protest was the beginning of a smear campaign against him. He would talk to Garrett about it. One thing bothered him. How did the thugs and the news crew know where he lived? A tipoff?

He winced at the conversation he had with Mark last night, his brother predictably not in a very forgiving mood. Fool and idiot were the kindest expletives he used. Nash deserved a brick in the face, and he would give it to him tonight at the family get-together. Nash couldn't argue with his brother, not that he tried, because his twin was right.

Maybe they could swap places like they used to when kids.

Stuck in a crush of cars next to the National Gallery, Nash thanked the sergeant and walked the rest of the way to CIS. A warm breeze stirred the golden elms along the boulevard, promising another hot day. Instead of its usual clear blue, the sky had a brown tinge, probably fine dust carried from the interior.

The weather pattern had gradually changed over the last ten years or so, with hotter summers and very cold winters. The doomsayers paraded this as evidence of climate failure caused by man's uncontrolled pollution. Pumping gunk into the atmosphere definitely didn't help things, but Nash noted that climatologists were strangely silent when it came to incorporating increased activity from more than a hundred active volcanoes around the world and the Pacific Ring of Fire in particular into their models, which annually released millions of tonnes of toxic gases and particulates. Earth was also emerging from a prolonged ice age twelve thousand years ago, returning to a more normal warmer cycle. The doomsayers were silent about that too.

Nash walked into the IBM tower with other employees and headed for the elevators. He got off at the twenty-second floor and made straight for his office. Several of his project managers were already in their open plan cubicles. One of them waved at him as he walked past, the others stared as though he had grown a second head. He got similar looks when he got himself coffee from the small kitchenette. They all knew. Well, no bricks were flying, which was good.

He directed his PID to log on into the holoview wall and checked Outlook for emails, not expecting any. An hour at the computer last night had taken care of the immediate backlog. No scheduled meetings on Thursdays, but unexpected things always came up, either from one of his PMs, Telstra, or Snoden. There was also Amanda Fuller's list of non-critical issues to check on. Well, that was why he wore the worry hat and got the big bucks.

Outlook had two CC messages and a reminder that his time-sheet was due tomorrow. It also meant he had to complete his end-of- month status report. Using a preformatted document template and his eidetic memory, he would fill in the thing to-morrow afternoon and email it off. He opened the first message and began to read when the phone icon beeped and Snoden's thin features cleared in the bottom right corner of the wall display. Bald, skin pale from too much time indoors, the program director looked decidedly uncomfortable.

"Nash, I'm glad you're in early. I need to see you right away."

"What's up?" He suspected he knew what was up, but the charade had to be played out to its grim conclusion. Then again, it could be something perfectly innocent and he fretted about nothing.

"I'll explain when you come up," Snoden said and cut contact.

Normally, Snoden would come down when he wanted something. Whenever he asked Nash to go up, it meant a budget snag, schedule slippage, or a resource issue. Right now, he didn't have any of those red lights, not enough to worry about anyway. A major beef with Telstra? He slipped on his jacket and strode to-ward the elevators, his footfalls soundless on the hard gray car-pet. Hard as some looks cast his way.

The twenty-ninth floor reflected the subdued atmosphere af-fected by high-level executives. Tall potted plants surrounded a spacious open lounge around which personal secretaries held court over their powerful masters locked in sumptuous offices. Prisons as far as he was concerned. The Facebook takeover hadn't changed the IBM culture much as they themselves evolved into a procedure-ridden bureaucracy.

He walked past Jaye's desk, gave her a brief nod, and knocked on Snoden's ceiling-high oak-veneered door. He walked in after hearing a muffled 'Come in' from inside.

Snoden looked up and waved at a visitor chair. "Ah, Nash. Sit down, please."

Directly before Nash a smart glass window formed an entire wall and gave a spectacular view of the city's skyline. On his right, the director sat behind a large executive desk that held a tablet, papers, and a keyboard. Nash hardly ever used a keyboard, preferring the voice interface, but his boss was somewhat old-fashioned. On his left, a holoview wall cycled through random colors.

He sank into the padded chair and crossed his legs.

Snoden pursed his lips and exhaled softly, clearly not relishing the moment. A development guru with Facebook, he made a swap to IBM as part of the takeover package. A hard driver, he was nevertheless fair and allowed his program managers a lot of leeway, provided they delivered. If they didn't, he had them for lunch.

"There is no easy way to say this, Nash, so I'll lay it out for you. IBM has decided to terminate your services. You will be paid the outstanding seven months of your contract, including a full year's bonus. You will also receive an additional two years' payment as penalty for not having your contract renewed which we committed to doing. I am sorry to be the bearer of bad news, but this comes from upstairs."

Nash had expected a reaction from CIS, senior managers would have seen last night's news, but this was nasty.

"Because I am a lifeliner?"

"Officially, your program of work has been suspended by Telstra, caused by major changes to their network requirements, and we don't have an immediate project into which you can be slotted. As a contractor, you're on call notice."

"That's a copout, Ted, and you know it."

Snoden winced. "You must understand CIS's position, Nash. To maintain our client base and attract new work, we must project a certain corporate image. Like it or not, and I personally don't, that image does not include lifeliners. It stinks, but that's the harsh reality right now."

"IBM is supposed to be an equal opportunity employer," Nash pointed out, surprised at his clam. Actually, he had a lid clamped on his roiling emotions. He expected this to happen, but Snoden's cold dismissal still came as a shock.

"It is."

"But not for lifeliners." Nash allowed a touch of bitterness to creep into his voice. "What about the millions I saved IBM for streamlining tender and compliance procedures? The unpaid hours I worked? The goodwill I generated for your clients and Telstra? That never happened?"

"That's why you're being paid the extra two years."

"Your thirty pieces of silver," Nash said and Snoden scowled. "I'll take this to the Human Rights and Equal Opportunity Commission."

His boss sighed. "You will win and IBM will be awarded a hefty damages bill, but you will never work as an integration consultant again, not for some time at least. I'm sorry, Nash. I wish it were otherwise, as you were one of our star performers, but this wasn't up to me." He cleared his throat and straightened. "As of this moment, your security clearance has been revoked. You are to clean out your desk and vacate the building within the hour. You're also required to turn over any material in your possession that relates to your program of work. Termination documents and severance pay slips will be emailed to you."

"IBM already has all the relevant project material."

Snoden shook his head. "No, it doesn't. I know you have a private server at home and you keep a lot of work data on it. We want that material."

"Whatever I have is private, and of no relevance to my work."

"I hope this doesn't become an issue, as it might prejudice your bonus." Snoden stood and extended his hand. "I didn't want this."

"See you in court," he told his boss without shaking hands,

and walked out. *Bastards!*

He wanted to tell Snoden a lot more, but there was no point. Snoden was a mouthpiece for the faceless men on the thirtieth floor. He probably had not relished being the news bearer, but nevertheless happy to grease his own nest. It wasn't his butt on the line. Dollars and cents, that was all that mattered. Everything else was HR bullshit for the gullible. He knew IBM was a soulless corporation, but his clinical dismissal left him outraged, disappointed, and even more cynical. He understood CIS's motivation and their lack of ethical fortitude to maintain a position of principle. Do the right thing *for* the company, but don't expect them to return the favor when things got sticky.

In his case, maybe they have returned the favor, if only a little. Their thirty pieces of silver would turn out to be a very neat pile. He charged $1,500 per day for his services, which was about $300 less than the normal market rate for a top-flight program manager, but IBM had always been tight when it came to paying people. His payout of seven months, plus the additional two years and bonus, would net him over $400,000 after taxes. Not nearly enough to set himself up for life, but with some sound investments, it would give him time to get himself on his feet again—if possible.

Snoden could be right when he said he would never work as a consultant again. News of his dismissal would circulate through the industry grapevine in a flash. Nash did not want to believe that he'd be hung out to dry simply to maintain a PR image. Things *couldn't* be that screwed up where a lifeliner never dared reveal himself and risk total personal and professional ruin. Seeing what happened to him, apparently things were that screwed up.

Ah, rats!

He had nothing to clean out of his office. The holoview wall displayed the normal blue IBM logo, but when he told his PID to log in, he was not surprised when access was blocked. He told

Snoden the truth when he said IBM already had all relevant project material, but his personal server held valuable spreadsheets that helped him run his program of work. IBM had no claim on the tools he used to supplement official compliance documentation. They may yet regret their hasty decision to can him.

He wasn't an ordinary systems analyst who could be dismissed with minor fallout. He ran a program of work worth over forty million, executed by six project managers, all very senior. That level of work required planning, organization, and monitoring, which he provided. Yanking him out of the loop meant a rapid slowdown until they appointed someone else, something Amanda Fuller was not likely to appreciate or sympathize with. He did not believe for one moment that Telstra had suspended their project. They might retaliate with penalties, but it would be a Pyrrhic victory. Telstra faced significant disruption to an important part of its network, with a corresponding impact on business processes and loss of revenue. He doubted that Payne Ogelvy, Telstra's integration manager, would be impressed.

His court action might not be the only one IBM would face.

Nash cast a last look around his office and strode out, feeling better than he thought he would, given the circumstances. He did not bother saying goodbye to anybody. At work, he maintained a friendly relationship, but he wasn't anyone's buddy. He rode the elevator down, feelings mixed. It had been nice while it lasted. Outside, the sun shone high and warm. He paused at the steps, turned and gave the brown tower the finger, which earned him several curious looks. The taxi rank had three cars and he walked briskly to the first in line. He slid onto the back seat and told the car to take him home. The plastic self-cleaning dome polarized, keeping those outside from looking in.

Losing his job was one thing, but it had not penetrated that he suddenly had a lot of time on his hands, and he had a low boredom threshold. He would work the problem in due course. No hurry now.

He dug out his cell and told the PID to connect with Bartlett.

"IBM gave me the chop, Garrett, just as you predicted they would," Nash said evenly when the image formed.

"I'm sorry to hear that, my boy."

"Like you said, I did it to myself. No regrets."

"Did they pay you out?"

"Generously, but I want to launch an action against them for wrongful dismissal. I also want to take defamation action against Channel Seven with VCAT for a live news piece they took this morning outside my apartment."

The Victorian Civil and Administrative Tribunal arbitration system would deliver a quick verdict and much cheaper than dragging the case through the clogged court system.

"What happened?" Garrett demanded.

"They stated I was arrested yesterday on suspicion of terrorism to bomb the Flinders Street station. I sent your office the clip."

"I haven't seen it, but Kathleen probably has it somewhere. Never mind, I'll get things moving on both fronts. Are you prepared to settle if either party makes an offer?"

"If the offer hurts them enough. Channel Seven must make a public retraction, though."

Garrett nodded. "That goes without saying."

"One more thing. Leak to the media that I'm taking these actions."

"You want to make them suffer?"

"I do."

"Okay, my boy. You know, of course, your career as a strategic consultant is pretty much trashed."

"Yeah. That's what IBM said. I guess, I'll have to find something else to do."

"You don't have to look far."

"Run for the Senate? I'm still thinking about it."

"Then think quickly, and I'm being serious. By the way, they've got Sutton."

"They did?"

"He was apprehended when in company with two other men, he tried to board a charter flight out of Essendon Airport."

"How did they come to nab him so quickly?"

Garrett shrugged. "They didn't say. Perhaps the Signals Directorate has capabilities not usually advertised."

Nash felt a prickle of excitement as he experienced an epiphany moment.

"What if they *could* track a PID that's been switched off?" he asked softly.

"I was only making a flippant remark, my boy."

"I wasn't. When a PID is implanted, the neural interface uses nanobot tendrils to connect with the brain to establish a permanent electrical pathway. When you switch off your PID, you only switch off the communications module. The interface is always active."

Garrett frowned. "An interesting notion. If true, it means the legislation introduced by Neil Travers would merely serve to legitimize an existing capability. It might be worth looking into. In the meantime, there is more bad news, I'm afraid. On a tipoff from the AFP, the local police stormed a safe house in Richmond and found two girls, three boys, and two Ravenhall inmates. They were all unconscious. Search of a dumpster outside found syringes and vials which the paramedics on the scene identified as chemosterilants."

Nash felt something cold slither down his back. "Aleya…"

"She wasn't among them, but Sutton is still to be debriefed. It's likely he used more than the five kids the police found. They could all have been sterilized."

"I hope to see *him* sterilized!"

"Dr. Lambert doesn't know this, and I see no reason why you should tell her, but Dr. Connell claims that all Sutton's trainees were lifeliners. He thinks Sutton used that fact to pressure parents to let him use their kids in his program, or they would face criminal charges and imprisonment. His actions had no basis in law, but I doubt the parents involved would know that."

"I'd love to get my hands on that guy," Nash hissed. "Just five minutes."

"Whatever terms of reference he operated under, it is clear he exceeded his authority. I'll see you this afternoon."

"You still want to have that talk?"

"Now more than ever, and you should realize why."

Nash sighed. "I guess."

"Don't be late," Garrett said and cut contact.

When the cab reached the Shrine of Remembrance, Nash decided to walk the rest of the way. Jacket draped over his shoulder, tie loosened, he genuinely felt good. He thrived under pressure, lucky to work from home when he chose, but the pressure never ended, from Telstra or IBM. He hadn't had a decent vacation in three years, and he figured he deserved some time off at a deserted beach with swaying palms...crystal waters lapping against white sands, a Piña colada in hand...

A day or two perhaps, and then he would probably go out of his mind. He needed a level of stress in his life to keep himself stimulated, but he wanted to control that pressure and not be controlled by it. Unfortunately, there weren't any jobs like that. Even if there were, he doubted he'd be offered one now regardless of his experience and qualifications. Walking slowly, ignoring everything around him, he wondered how things could have degenerated this far. He did not have to test mankind's moral and ethical code, because he had his answer. One less dilemma to resolve, and another still to be resolved.

Time to decide what you really want, old son.

He didn't have to. He already knew—to leave something behind other than memories. That, of course, required some clarification to be meaningful.

Sutton used blackmail to get his kids...Nash found it difficult to understand such a mind. He also found it difficult to understand the minds of people who authorized his taskforce. Lifeliners did not represent a social or political threat. It was only a threat because of unfounded hysteria, fanned by intolerance and opportunistic political expediency.

He turned into the driveway at 401 St. Kilda Road and picked up his pace, not relishing the prospect of being the attention of another crazed mob. As he approached the entrance, he saw a familiar figure sitting on the steps and jerked to a stop.

Face cast in a frown, ready to run, Aleya got to her feet and waited, red backpack beside her. Her worldly possessions. Nash stared at her, his emotions warring with each other. He wanted to shift the blame for everything that happened on her. She played him like Cariana played him. It would be easy to turn away from this mussed child, reject her as she rejected him. His bruised ego would approve and his manliness restored. Yesterday afternoon, he would have done it.

Her large eyes waited, needing…needing him.

What a crock.

He dropped his jacket, crouched, and opened his arms. Uncertain, fearing a trap, Aleya didn't move.

"Come. I won't bite. Promise," he said gently.

She gave a strangled sob and ran to him. Her arms went around his neck and her little body tried to burrow into him.

"I'm sorry, Nash. I didn't know. They told us we weren't going to hurt anybody. It was a game! I didn't know it would be this awful."

"Shh. It's all right."

"I must be a huge disappointment to you—"

"Don't worry about it."

"I can't help it. I feel so bad about everything."

He stroked her hair. "It's over now. Besides, we still have that trip to Luna Park, and gelato at the beach, remember?"

Tears ran down her face. "I wish I could have you as my dad."

She cried and he held her tight. It did not matter what she had done. It did not matter what Cariana had done. Sooner or later, he would have been exposed and in the shits. Too bad it had to happen the way it did. He will work it out and the scars would heal. The only thing that mattered, Aleya was safe.

He untangled her arms and pulled back.

"How did you get away?"

She sniffed and wiped her eyes. "That frightful AFP man? He took me and two guys to a safe house in Richmond. There were others. I trained with some, but I didn't know them all. Trent had his men running around cleaning out everything—he isn't actually a beggar."

"I know."

"You do? Well, in the confusion, I slipped away. They chased me, but I gave them the dodge." She flashed him a mischievous smile. "They trained me well."

He nodded, having experienced her training firsthand.

"Lots of places to hide in the city, and I know them all. I didn't dare go home, to Aunty, I mean, figuring the dobers would be waiting for me. I stayed away from you for the same reason and because I knew you were mad at me. You aren't, are you?"

"I was, but not anymore, truly. Where did you spend the night?"

"A place I know in St. Kilda. Not the one Trent told me about. That was another one of his safe houses." Her face clouded and her lips trembled. "It's the first time I've ever been alone at night and I was scared. I didn't get much sleep, worried what might happen to me. I'm also worried what they did to the others."

Nash was tempted to tell her, but he could not see what good it would do, and probably some harm. She didn't need more nightmares than she already had.

"I can only imagine, but you're safe now," he said softly.

"This morning, I went to Aunty's place, but there were strange men hanging around. I didn't know who they were, but I was afraid it was Trent and he would do bad things to me if he caught me. So I came here. The guard inside told me that you were out and he didn't know when you'd get back. That awful man I mentioned? He took my cell and I couldn't call Aunty or you, so I waited. I knew you'd come eventually."

"Weren't you afraid they would look for you here?"

"They did, but the guard inside hid me. He was nice and gave me some tea and a cookie. He wanted me to stay with him, but I preferred being outside. It's not that I didn't trust Eden, but—"

"I understand."

Nash grabbed his jacket, rose and headed for the entrance. Aleya clutched his hand and held it tight, perhaps afraid she would lose him? She picked up her backpack and he linked with the building's security system. Inside, he strode toward the guard who watched them approach.

"Thanks for what you did, Eden. I won't forget."

"I have a kid like her, Mr. Bannon. Terrible what's happening out there, sir."

"Yeah."

In his apartment, he told Aleya to wash and change. Her new clothes were still in the spare bedroom.

"Hungry? Want me to whip up something?" He lifted his hand. "Don't tell me. You haven't eaten since yesterday."

She dropped her backpack and gave a sheepish smile. "I could swallow something."

"Right." He got a pitcher of his homemade fruit juice out of the almost empty fridge and poured her a glass. "This will keep you alive until I whip up breakfast."

She gulped it down and held out the glass for more. The second one went more slowly.

Nash cocked his head. "Sally, we're down on some food-stuffs."

"I placed an order with Woolworths. Delivery will be made this afternoon."

"Thank you."

Aleya squinted at him. "Sally?"

"Someone I used to know."

"Wait till I tell Aunty that you're running around with another woman."

He smiled at her mischievous expression. "That was some time ago, long ears."

"So, Aunty is your girlfriend now?"

"She is. Why are you looking at me like that?"

"Like what?"

"Like I'm in trouble or something." He opened the fridge and took out two eggs.

"You'll find out."

"Spill it!" he commanded sternly.

"Oh, nothing really. It's only that her boyfriends don't last very long."

"Why not?"

"They can't keep up, but you're different. You might make the cut."

"That's comforting to know," Nash said dryly and filled himself a glass. "How many boyfriends did she have?"

"I'm not a snitch," Aleya declared, then snickered. "Been doing kissing and other stuff?"

"Haven't had a chance, if you must know…snoopy nose. Now, finish your drink and get changed."

She gave a knowing grin and ambled toward the spare bedroom.

Nash told Sally to connect with Cariana.

"Aleya is okay. She's at my place," he said when the holoview wall cleared. Cariana tried hard to maintain her composure, then her features broke and she wept.

"Thanks…for letting me know," she managed to gasp between sobs. "I was going out of my mind. I kept calling the police, but they had nothing. How did you find her?"

"She was waiting for me outside the building. She was at your place last night, but there were men outside—"

"I know. I saw them prowling about."

"She thought they might be Sutton's and didn't dare show herself."

"She's smart and can look after herself, but still, it must have been horrible for her, not knowing whom to trust."

"I've been there myself."

She winced. "What happened to you yesterday…my work on lifeliners…I wouldn't blame you if you thought I was a monster. Perhaps I was."

"You don't have to explain."

"That's just it, I do. I'm still carrying emotional baggage from my brother's senseless death. It could have been anyone, but I couldn't get it out of my mind that he was killed by a lifeliner." She sighed and hung her head.

"We'll talk it through. I'm a good listener," Nash told her.

Her face cleared. "You are, and I'll take advantage of that…later. Can I talk to Aleya?"

"She's in the bedroom, changing."

"Don't let her out of your sight. I'll be right over."

"By the way, how did it go yesterday, at work I mean?"

"Hard to say. Dr. Connell could be in some trouble, though. So could I. Too early to tell."

When the connection broke, he stared at the pooling colors and sighed. One more thing to do.

"Sally, connect with Bartlett, personal."

The wall cleared and Kathleen's elfin face smiled at him. "Mr. Bartlett is not available right now, Mr. Bannon. Can I take a message?"

Was *she* a lifeliner?

"Please tell him Aleya is with me. He'll know what that means."

"Very good, sir. Anything else? No? Enjoy your day," she quipped and cut contact.

Enjoy his day, right. He already had a hell of a start.

When he thought about it, losing his job had not been altogether unexpected, and he did have all night to accept the possibility and adjust emotionally. It still pissed him off, but he was also relieved that it happened. With everybody knowing what he was, could he have remained effective in his job? The idea of being treated as though he wore a square head and everyone pretending not to notice would have been intolerable. Better a clean break and a fresh start…doing what? There were options, weren't there? Before worrying about it, he had real issues to handle first…groveling tonight before his family while they carved him for the main course.

"Nash, Miss Rowena Russell from the ABC *7.30 Report* program wishes to connect," Sally announced.

He raised an eyebrow. Apparently, the vultures were already circling. From the newscasts he'd seen, the government had received a roasting over yesterday's events. He did not believe the networks did it out of any sympathy for lifeliners. They simply had a good story and everybody was gathering ammunition for the upcoming election. The Prime Minister was yet to officially announce a date, but everyone knew it would be sometime in October, which meant the unofficial campaign had already begun.

People did not like Atarah Readman much. Nash didn't either, or the Liberal Party's preparedness to embrace the Australian Conservatives as a coalition partner to keep Labor from forming government. Forget the noble sounding election policy slogans. What mattered was retaining power at any cost. If that meant abandoning policies and breaking promises, than that is what was done, and Readman did it. However, as more than one government found, the electorate had little stomach for such short-sighted shenanigans and usually tossed out the responsible party. Sutton's antics were literally manna from heaven for Labor, provided they could convince the electorate they had nothing to do with the sterilization policy. Perception was sometimes more powerful than truth.

So, was Russell interested in a human angle story, or did she want to use him to further embarrass the government, giving the Opposition a few free markers? Probably both. Regardless of her motive, she offered him a platform to voice his case. An opportunity he could not dismiss lightly.

"Connect and record," he told Sally.

The holoview wall cleared and the *7.30 Report* anchor smiled pleasantly at him.

"Thank you for agreeing to talk to me, Mr. Bannon."

"A pleasure, Miss Russell. What can I do for you?"

"I would like an interview. We were interrupted yesterday and I want to hear your side of the story. Mr. Adam Gatt has already agreed to appear on my program."

"I'm not available tonight."

"We can have it prerecorded. You're hot news, Mr. Bannon, and your personal story may help other lifeliners, but you need to tell it now while it's fresh in people's minds. Tomorrow, another scandal could grab the headlines, and tomorrow is Friday, not very good for ratings. Too many people go out on Friday night."

Nash recalled Garrett's stinging words regarding interviews, which made him wary of committing another *faux pas*, but he did want to have his say, and he had more information now. She could be right about another headline potentially marginalizing his case, but he suspected this was more a pressure tactic for him to accept. Nevertheless, he had to prosecute his position while he had the public's attention. Russell was right about that. This, though, needed handling with some finesse, and he would need to bone up a little on how to handle holoview interviews.

"What will be the length of the final cut?"

"Ten minutes, but it'll be up to the producer."

"I accept, and thank you for the invitation."

"My pleasure, I assure you," she said with a broad grin.

"We can have the interview at Grange, Strand and Bartlett's offices at 3:30 this afternoon, but send me your questions first, Rowena." He'll want Garrett to see them and get his input. "One more thing. I'll want to see the story before you air it and veto any segment I don't like."

The reporter's eyes sparkled with amusement. "Agreed. You'll get the questions within the hour." She nodded and cut contact.

Nash frowned and pulled at his chin, not sure he had done the right thing. "Sally, connect with Grange, Strand & Bartlett."

Kathleen's eyes widened when the holoview cleared. "Mr. Bannon, I'm afraid—"

"I have another message for Mr. Bartlett."

"Of course."

"Please tell him the ABC will be interviewing me at 3:30 this afternoon at your premises and I'll be there at three."

"Not a problem, Mr. Bannon. I'll have the meeting room ready." She nodded and the wall resumed its color pooling.

"Sally, Miss Russell will be sending me a file. Let me know when it arrives and forward a copy personal to Mr. Bartlett at G.S. & B."

"Acknowledged."

Muffled chanting from the street made him turn his head and frown. He walked to the balcony window and slid back the panel. Traffic noises immediately swamped his senses. Below, men and women waving People First Party banners and placards picketed the apartment block.

"Down with lifeliners!"

"Death to abominations!"

"Keep humans pure!"

Channel Ten and SBS reporters mingled among them, taking statements.

Well, that didn't take long. What disturbed him, there weren't any police out there. A potential riot wasn't worth keeping an eye on? Technically, the mob violated the High Court ruling that prohibited lifeliner discrimination, but it appeared the dobers didn't see it that way. Should he call them anyway? No need yet, as he wasn't going out of his apartment anytime soon. The crowd might disperse by the time he had to go for his interview.

Nash scowled and closed the balcony panel, cutting out the madness outside. What the hell was going on with the world? Tempted to go down and have it out with them, he suppressed the irrational impulse. A bloody fight was the least he could expect.

The growing number of marches across Europe and America

targeting lifeliners shown on SBS evening news made good pop-
ulist viewing, but they filled him with foreboding chills. Not the
marches themselves, tacitly condoned and perhaps even encouraged by governments, but the social environment that seemed to
accept the bellicose propaganda.

Garrett was right. Things were getting worse.

Safe in his private world, the news images had disturbed him
intellectually, but they failed to convey the emotional impact he
felt now, touched personally by the tide of hatred against lifeliners. A cold ripple slithered down his back and he shivered.

His comfortable cocoon had turned into a prison.

A soft footfall behind him made him look up. Aleya stood
there, smart in white shorts and cream T-shirt, hair neatly
combed.

"I had a quick shower. Hope that was all right."

"I expect you needed one. Come, let's start breakfast."

"What were you looking at outside?"

"Nothing you need to worry about."

"Can I have a bit more to drink, please? I'm still thirsty."

There wasn't much left in the pitcher and Nash decided to
make her one of his smoothies. Aleya parked herself on a high
stool beside the workbench and watched with lively interest as he
dug out several fruits, a carrot, and a celery stick, and had the
NutriBullet work it over into a green mess. To top it off, he added
two dollops of honey and some nuts and poured her a tall glass.

Eyeing the mixture, she took a cautious sip and her eyebrows
rose.

"This is very nice."

"Your approval is appreciated," he acknowledged with a grin
and proceeded to beat the egg and yellow corn flour mixture into
a froth. He heated a pan on the induction plate, added olive oil
and poured in the mixture. A light sprinkle of grated cheese and
parsley finished the omelet.

Aleya licked her lips as he put the plate before her and dug in
with relish. Nash drained the last of the juice and watched her

eat. Satisfied, she pushed away her plate, sat up and sighed.

"I needed that."

"Glad you liked it. More?"

She shook her head. "No thanks. You could be useful around the house, you know."

"Cariana said the same thing."

"What else did she say?"

"That she isn't much into cooking."

"She isn't. I do some of it, particularly during the school holidays, although she can cook when she's in the mood. I try to get something ready when she gets home from work, which can be pretty late sometimes."

"Yeah, I know how that works. What do you do when she's not around?"

"Oh, hang out with friends. We go to the movies sometimes, but we mostly stay at my place or at a girlfriend's. Why pay good money to go to the cinema when I can stream most anything off the holoview, and it's also 3D and VR."

"Tell me, if you don't mind me asking. How on earth did you end up with Sutton?"

She frowned. "It was Aunty. She came home late once, early August, I think, and told me about a project CSIRO ran to study lifeliners. They needed kids to dress up as runaways and mingle among the homeless. The idea was to find lifeliners and help them get into shelters. Nobody was going to hurt them. A government unit would train me and others, and we'd have grownups looking after us to make sure we wouldn't get into trouble. It sounded like fun and I'd get paid to do it."

"Sutton, did he know you were a lifeliner?"

"Not at first, but he did later. He came to a training session once before the school year ended. He said we were ready to go out on the street and he expected us to find lots of lifeliners. I remember him and Trent talking and giving me looks when they thought I wouldn't notice. From then on, I went out three or four times, always during the week, as Aunty didn't want me working over weekends. It was amusing pretending to be a runaway and wearing all those raggedy clothes."

Nash gave a rueful smile. "They certainly trained you well. The story you gave me about your pretend parents fooled me completely."

"Guys were easy to fool. You didn't exactly say you weren't a lifeliner, but I knew. They told me how to spot one." She looked down and twisted the bottom of her T-shirt. "You were different from the others, though. Mostly, they would feed me and give me money, but you tried to help me, and you weren't a hobo. I didn't think Trent would be interested in you, but he insisted that I keep tabs on you. All of us had to tell him what we did every time we went out. I didn't know why he was interested in you, but I felt something was wrong, especially after I came to like you.

"I wanted to talk it over with Aunty, but I was told never to discuss what I and the others were doing." She looked at him, eyes pleading. "I *tried* to tell you, but I was afraid what Trent would do to me if he found out."

He nodded and patted her hand. "It's all right, Aleya. Forget it."

"That's it. I can't forget it. I never will."

"The lifeliners you identified. What happened to them?"

She shrugged. "I don't know. Sutton's men took them away and I never saw them again. I know that Aunty started to get worried about me, and I heard her arguing with Sutton one night when she thought I wasn't listening. She wanted me to stop working, but I think she was afraid of him for some reason. She was upset when I told her about us, and how you brought me here, but I never connected that she was your girlfriend.

"Yesterday, when you said we were going to the Footscray Market, I went to the bathroom, remember? I called Trent, then I called Aunty. She tried to sound calm, but I knew she was worried. I could tell. Anyway, she coached me what to say and pretend to be happy that I managed to catch two lifeliners." Aleya reached out and clutched his hand. "I didn't know Sutton was after you, Nash, or I'd never have told them anything about you. You've got to believe me." Her eyes misted and her lips trembled.

He walked around the bench and gathered her in his arms. "It's over now."

She clung to him and cried. "If I knew Trent and Sutton would hurt the lifeliners we found, I would have quit. Honest. Nobody was supposed to get hurt."

"I know. It's all right."

She sniffed and looked at him, her large eyes glistening. "I miss Mom and Dad, and I thought that you…but after what I've done, what Aunty did…"

He squeezed her against him and stroked her hair. "It might work out. We'll see. Even if I can't be your dad, we can still be friends."

"I guess," she murmured into his shoulder, then pulled back. "Can I stay with you, if you'll let me?"

"I'll arrange something with Cariana, but not today. I've got things to take care of."

"You have to go to work?"

"Not anymore. I've been fired."

Her eyes rounded in shock. "Because of me?"

"Excuse me, Nash," Sally interrupted. "Dr. Lambert is requesting permission to enter."

"Granted, and let her in when she gets to the door."

"Will do."

Aleya climbed off her stool. "Aunty is here?"

"Be up in a minute."

"Nash, ah, all those clothes you bought for me—"

"Take them with you. They're yours."

"I couldn't possibly. If she found out—"

"Don't worry. I'll sort it out with her."

Aleya didn't look happy. "I'm gonna be in trouble," she declared.

"I told you not to worry about it."

Her face brightened. "I could leave them here."

"And if you want to wear something, how would you explain it?"

"Mmm. It's just that I haven't had many opportunities to shop. Not that Aunty doesn't take care of me," she added hastily, "but she never took me shopping as you did." She pouted and her shoulders sagged. "I'm gonna be in trouble."

Nash laughed and patted her shoulder. "Anytime you want to go shopping, call."

She looked at him. "Really?"

"Truly."

The door opened and Cariana walked in. When she saw Aleya, she dropped her purse and opened her arms.

"My sweet. I was worried to death about you."

Aleya allowed herself to be hugged with suffering patience, giving Nash a conspiratorial shrug.

"Nash took care of me."

"I can see that," Cariana said and looked at him. "Thank you."

He nodded. "I loved every minute."

"There is a crowd out there—"

Nash shook his head and inclined his head at Aleya, not wanting to alarm the kid.

Cariana put on a smiling face. "I didn't expect you to be home."

"He got fired," Aleya said brightly, and Cariana went pale.

"Because of yesterday?"

"Because I'm a lifeliner, but don't worry. IBM will come to regret it. Anyway, I've got another offer, but I'm not sure if I should take it. It's complicated."

"What offer?"

"Run for the Senate."

She gaped at him. "The Senate? You didn't."

"It wasn't entirely my idea. Garrett sort of talked me into it."

"I think it's marvelous."

"Does that mean you're going to Canberra?" Aleya demanded, clearly not liking the idea. "I won't see you again."

"If I get elected, which is not certain, I'll have to be away sometimes, but I won't be leaving you."

"Promise?"

"Promise."

"Nash, I'd love to talk more, but I'm in a hurry. The federal police are on my case and I've got to get back to Parkville."

"We could talk over dinner," he suggested. "You owe me one."

She bit her lip. "I do, don't I. Saturday at seven, if you don't mind coming to my Woodend retreat? I've got chores to do."

"I don't mind."

"Don't expect much—"

"But I am. Aleya told me you were a sharp cook."

Cariana frowned and glared at her niece. "You ratted on me?"

Unabashed, Aleya grinned. "You *can* cook…with my help."

"Little terror. Come on, I've got an Uber skycab waiting outside."

Aleya bit her lip and glanced at Nash, eyes pleading.

"She has a few things I got for her," he explained. "For her undercover work."

Cariana gave Aleya a stern look. "You talked him into taking you shopping?"

"It wasn't her idea," Nash added hastily. "It was something I wanted to do. Don't give her a hard time over it, okay? If you do, I'll find out—"

"I'll tell," Aleya said mischievously.

"—and I won't like it."

Cariana placed both hands on her hips and scowled, then shrugged.

"Okay, I give up."

"Cool." Aleya flashed them a sunny smile. "I'll get my stuff while you two make cow eyes at each other."

Nash turned to Cariana. "I can drive you guys to Parkville."

"I've got a cab outside. Besides, it's a crush out there, but thanks anyway. We could meet for lunch tomorrow if you like. I'm at The Alfred all afternoon and Aleya will be at a friend's place getting set for a weekend slumber party."

"They know about her?"

Cariana nodded. "A nice couple who have twin daughters of their own. Both are lifeliners, but the kids at school don't know."

Nash understood. Children can be very cruel to one another. "I'll make a booking at La Asiago for one o'clock, okay? We'll meet at the foot of Princess Bridge ten minutes earlier." He studied her. "If the dobers give you a hard time at work—"

"I know. Call Mr. Bartlett. It hasn't come to that yet." Suddenly, her face clouded. "What's going on outside?" she whispered.

"Nothing good, and I'm concerned. We'll talk about it later."

She stepped up to him and kissed him lightly on the mouth. "Thank you for looking after her."

He gathered her in his arms. "Until tomorrow," he said softly and heard Aleya clear her throat.

"Do you guys have to do that stuff?" she demanded in disgust.

Nash looked at Cariana and they both laughed.

Chapter Five

His dad said that dinner tonight would be lamb roast, but Nash suspected he would be the one roasted. Ordinarily, he enjoyed the rare family get-togethers—all of them led busy lives—but he did not look forward to the deserved pasting he was likely to receive. He didn't expect much sympathy either if he said he got carried away by the moment. How could he have forgotten all his life's lessons?

At least the ABC interview with Rowena Russell went well. Despite studying how to handle himself and Garrett's coaching, he admitted feeling nervous. Making presentations to corporate brass was much easier. A professional, she put him at ease with several introductory questions while the technicians fiddled with microphones and lighting. Afterward, she showed him the raw clips, and Garrett requested that some not be aired, but Nash looked forward to seeing the final cut.

This particular evening at his parents' place might not be as enjoyable.

He gritted his teeth and sent a ping with his PID to the underground parking lot security door. Nothing he could do about it but suck it up and take it on the chin. The door rolled up slowly as he drove up the ramp. He squinted as bright sunshine stabbed from a clear sky. He turned left into the driveway and three men dressed in blue jeans and black leather jackets stepped across his path. They all held short truncheons and smirks of anticipation. He braked and chewed his lip. One of the men was the bruiser who attacked him this morning. Apparently not happy being made a fool of in front of his gang, he was here to even the score. Not liking any of this, Nash removed his shades, told the car to switch off, and stepped out.

The bruiser smiled broadly and tapped the club against his palm.

"Well, lifeliner. I've been looking forward to seeing you again, and you know what's nice? No dobers to interrupt us. Right, boys?"

"You got it, Cliff," the other two chorused.

"You don't want to do this," Nash told him softly, his body relaxed, watching each of them closely for any tensing that would signal an attack. He expected Cliff to make the first move, but they might decide to flank him first. Difficult to do as his left side was protected by the car.

"That's where you're wrong, lifeliner. I do want to do this, and I'm gonna enjoy it more than you. You got lucky this morning, but you'll need more than luck now."

Nash did not underestimate the seriousness of his situation. Contrary to what the movies showed, even a trained fighter was likely to come off second best when faced with multiple opponents—particularly if they are trained and can fight as a team. These three were uncoordinated street thugs who relied on intimidation and brute force to carry the argument. Still, if they rushed him, he'd be in some shitty trouble.

Stay calm and keep focused.

As his *sensei* explained, a group unconsciously always takes its cue from the leader; disable the leader and the others might not be so eager. Also, fight to incapacitate and remove an opponent using whatever means necessary. Elegance never played a part in a brawl. One thing Nash could not allow is to be encircled. Above everything else, he had to maintain situational awareness. His instincts and training urged him to attack before they moved in on him. If he did, they could later claim that he attacked them. By waiting for one of them to make the first move, he could be overwhelmed.

Senses heightened to sharp clarity, he saw Cliff lift his club a fraction and his eyes flickered at the sidekick on his left, perhaps a signal. In that moment the two of them lost situational awareness. Time for contemplation was over. Nash skipped toward him and jabbed stiff fingers into his throat. Cliff gagged, dropped his truncheon and staggered back, which distracted the other two for a vital split second.

A weapon would be useful to inflict serious damage, but Nash never considered retrieving the club. By the time he got hold of it, the other two would have regrouped. Still moving forward, he lashed out with his leg at the knee of his nearest opponent. Cartilage crunched and the thug howled as his leg collapsed under him.

Nash saw the third man swing his cudgel and ducked, but it still managed to give him a glancing blow on his left shoulder. He grunted as pain exploded in his arm even as he followed through with an open palm against the thug's nose. Blood spurted across the thug's chin and he brought both hands to his face. Nash let him have a knee in the groin and the man crumpled to the ground, clutching himself. It hadn't been an elegant display of skill, but he got his opponents down, and that was all that mattered.

With all three having lost interest in the fight, Nash stepped back, took two deep breaths and massaged his shoulder. The security guard rushed down the steps, skidded to a stop and gaped at the carnage.

"I called the cops as soon as I saw the men, Mr. Bannon, figuring you'd need help, but I guess they're the ones needing help. I'll ring for an ambulance."

"Thanks, Eden."

"Never saw anyone fight like you before, and I know something about close-in fighting. Three men and you took them out in seconds. For sure, I figured you for a goner."

"It was touch and go."

"Didn't look that way to me."

Now that it was over, Nash slowed his breathing and considered the likely ramifications. It all depended on how the dobers would view the situation. Either way, he hoped he would not be late for dinner. Nobody enjoyed eating cold roast. The absurdity of that thought forced a wry grin.

The sound of an approaching siren made both of them turn their heads. The sharp wailing stopped as a police cruiser with a blue checker pattern along its side pulled into the driveway and squealed to a stop. Two uniformed officers ran toward Nash, then stopped when they saw the writhing men on the ground. One of the cops was the sergeant who gave Nash a lift this morning. He was relieved to see the cop, assured of getting a sympathetic hearing.

"Well, Mr. Bannon, you persist at attracting trouble around you."

"Just protecting myself, Sergeant."

"It was self-defense, officer!" Eden explained. "Our security footage will corroborate everything."

The sergeant turned to his companion. "Call an ambulance."

The man nodded and hurried toward the squad car.

Eyeing the three men, the sergeant bit his lip and looked at Nash.

"What happened? By the way, all this is being recorded."

"Nothing much to tell. I drove out of the garage and these men confronted me. About to be attacked, I disabled them."

"Like that, eh? They started the attack?"

"The bruiser I knocked out this morning lifted his club and I went for his throat. I didn't wait for the other two to truncheon me."

The sergeant turned to Eden. "I'll want a copy of the security footage."

"You can link into our system and download it."

"Mr. Bannon, pending investigation of this building's security footage, and given the guard's testimony, I have no reason to detain you, but you will be called to make an official statement. As for the three persons who allegedly attacked you, we'll check them out."

Nash was about to ask why they haven't been checked this morning, but he did not want to complicate an already a messy situation.

"Thank you, Sergeant."

The cop gave him a hard look. "It's a good thing that none of them is dead, self-defense or not. There'll be shit to pay as it is, you know that."

"I never intended to kill," Nash said coldly.

"Perhaps, but sometimes you cannot control what happens. You took down three men. That took skill. Next time, you could be in a hurry and a life is lost. Regardless of any circumstances, the way the system works right now, you'd lose, and I might not be around to bail out your sorry ass."

Nash managed a slow grin. "I'll try to see that there is no next time."

The sergeant nodded. "That would be good," he said and extended his hand.

Nash hesitated, then clasped the proffered hand, comforted that not everyone hated lifeliners. There had to be others, which gave him a glimmer of hope that things *could* change—provided they were also prepared to extend their hand.

He climbed into his car and merged with the St. Kilda Road traffic, the attack fresh in his mind. Given the sergeant's gesture of friendship, he may have judged humanity too harshly. Golden elms on either side provided flickering shade. Surrounded by cars, no one knew him. No one knew what he was, and no one cared. That was the key…no one cared.

The tires whispered to him.

On reflection, the silent masses out there might not care now, but they will once the lifeliner transfiguration touched them personally and they find they were irreversibly sterile, or their teen offspring showed themselves to be lifeliners. Neighbor watching neighbor, kids muttering to one another at school, wondering if everyone they didn't like was a lifeliner and how to dob on them.

Worse still, wondering if a friend was one. If a kid revealed himself at the onset of puberty, those closest to him may be the first to turn on him and his family. What then? Uproot and find a fresh life somewhere where no one knew what they were? Never able to stand tall and say, 'I too am human'.

How would those silent masses react as more and more couples gave birth to lifeliners in accelerated progression? With no future and a turbulent past to look back on, Nash knew how they would react. He'd had a taste of it a few minutes ago. He could not help those who were sterile, a personal tragedy hardly imaginable, but humanity wasn't doomed. It would live on in the shape of its children…lifeliner children. Instead of persecuting them, the emerging generation should be embraced as something wonderful. Something that would endure and strive for the stars.

You're a hopeless romantic, old son.

His inner voice might sneer at his noble vision, and with some justification, but he believed it was possible to usher in change and rise above darkness. However daunting the journey, it begins with the first step.

He slowed as he approached the Commercial Road intersection.

Nash, you're full of shit, he told himself, and turned left as the lights changed.

Nature demonstrated every day the harsh process of survival—claws and teeth without possibility of remission. Did it have to be like that? People *can* fight the Suttons of this world. All they had to do was say 'No'.

That's what those silent lifeliners before him should have done from the beginning when the situation was more manageable. Then again, they were only a few voices among millions whose only thought was to exterminate them, but it was not like that at first. Politicians and the mainstream religions started to promote hate. No single neat solution existed, Nash realized, but individual jigsaw pieces that made up what could be a workable whole, acceptable to everybody. Inevitably, some existing pieces would be discarded and those trapped in them doomed. They wouldn't go down easily.

There was no other way, or everybody faced the possibility of total obliteration.

He could ponder philosophy and man's future, but he had to survive an encounter with his own family first. By no means a certain thing.

Against the leafy background of Fawkner Park, he turned left onto Punt Road. A few streets later, he turned right into Nicholson Street filled with a mixture of old weatherboard houses, newer dwellings, and tenement blocks. Nestled between two stately brick residences whose sides crawled with creepers, number thirty made him sit up and take notice every time he saw the unusual structure. Lots of glass, walls giving the impression of height, a protruding platform that separated the upper level, everything bathed in discrete lighting, the building showed elegance without being stark. Made to look like steel cladding, the roof solar collector provided almost all the house power needs.

He parked under the garage overhang and strode across the paved front yard toward the entrance. Natalie's blue Subaru Impreza electric already there. On his left, a Japanese pebble garden and small pond with a miniature burbling waterfall instilled an impression of tranquility. Colored fish darted in its depths. The raked white stones broken with brown streaks, the kidney-shaped pool, Mom's hand evident in the layout. He stopped before the solid white gum door and announced himself with his PID.

Hard footsteps came from inside and the door opened, and Nash looked at himself. Mark had not changed at all since he last saw him at the New Year's dinner, not that he expected he would. Wearing gray slacks and a black T-shirt, his twin scowled at him.

"Well, if it isn't my asshole brother," Mark grated and clenched his fists.

Nash winced and waited for the punch that would surely knock him out. Instead, Mark broke into a grin. His arms went around Nash and squeezed.

"Good to see you again, twin," he said fiercely, untangled himself, and patted Nash on the back.

"It's good to see *you*," Nash said uncertainly, still unsure if his twin would throw that punch. "What about all those mean things you called me over the phone yesterday?"

Mark laughed. "That was yesterday, and you deserved it. Chill out, brother. Tonight, we celebrate a family asshole. Well-meaning perhaps, but still an asshole."

"With a welcome like that, how can I refuse?"

"Come." Mark dragged him in by the arm and closed the door.

They walked through the open plan lounge/entertainment area into the dining/kitchen space. Natalie and Dad looked up, pushed back their chairs and rose. Nash walked up to his dad and they shook hands. His old man had a firm grip and a broad grin. He looked like an older version of Mark, hair still dark and face without worry lines.

A warm smile lit Nat's face as she stepped into his arms. "You've been neglecting me and my brood, Nash. Sandra and Kevin keep asking why their uncle doesn't come around much, and Adriana simply pouts."

After an embrace and a kiss, Nash stroked her cheek. "I'll make an effort, Nat."

"Shaun sends his apologies for not being able to come. Work."

Nash would have liked seeing Nat's husband, but he understood.

"Give him my regards," he said and turned to his father.

"Good to see you, son." His dad slapped him on the back, which made Nash wince with pain, his left shoulder still somewhat tender. His father saw the reaction and immediately looked concerned.

"What's the matter?"

"A little encounter with some guys who didn't like lifeliners," he growled, then blanched at having made another blooper. It simply wasn't his day. Nat smiled and gave him a reassuring nod.

"Don't sweat it, big brother. I've known about you and Mark for years."

He stared at her. "Why didn't you say something?"

"I didn't want you guys to worry. Besides, it was fun watching you two tiptoe around the subject. Payback for all those horrid things you did to me as kids."

Nash glanced at Mark. "Hear that?"

His mother wiped her hands on a small towel and hurried out of the kitchen. Trim and still looking radiant, she took life in stride and never fussed over the small things. She gave him a quick hug and planted a quick kiss on his cheek.

"You weren't hurt?"

"Only a bruised shoulder. The dobers hauled them away," he said and held her at arm's length. "Looking lovelier every day, Mom."

She gave him a playful slap on the chest. "Keep it for your girlfriend. Have you got one yet?"

"Well, there is someone—"

Mark hooted with delight. "My hard-bitten brother finally felled."

"It's complicated and not a done deal, twin," Nash said. "Tell you later."

"It's about time you crawled out of your shell," his dad muttered. "Drag up a chair. You still into bourbon?"

"A couple of fingers, Dad. I've got to drive."

"Piffle. You can sack out here or take a cab."

Nash sat down and quickly looked over his family. Nobody seemed mad at him, and all appeared genuinely glad to see him. Nat's comment about not seeing her and her kids a throwaway. She said it all the time. Her black jeans and black shirt highlighted a strikingly beautiful face. Long hazel hair fell in silky waves across her left shoulder and her large olive eyes regarded him with amusement. Wearing black gear had somehow become a family symbol.

Mark looked fit as always, ready to wade in and get it done, whatever it took. In some respects, he was more successful, moving in high government circles. Nash did not shy away from his penetrating gaze.

"Mark—"

"It was bound to come out sooner or later. Don't worry about it."

"I may have cost you your job."

"I doubt it. What happened to you yesterday has given the Prime Minister more pressing problems than taking any satisfaction by firing me. It still might happen, but I've got some powerful friends in my corner. What about you?"

"IBM canned me."

His mother gaped. "They didn't! Oh, Nash."

"It's all right. They gave me a substantial payout, but I'm still taking action against them."

"With G.S. & B?" his father demanded, and Nash nodded.

"I hope Garrett creams them. And you, Dad?"

"Don't know. QANTAS is probably waiting to see which way the wind will blow. I doubt they'll do anything, though. I'm a pretty senior exec and they would have to show cause other than being a parent to a lifeliner before moving against me. Like you, they know I would take action and win. The courts at least still believe in the rule of law, even if our politicians don't."

"No pickets on the streets?"

"Nothing yet, but I did get some calls from the networks wanting an interview. What about you?"

Nash shrugged. "Predictable reaction from the far-right nut groups."

"You can expect more."

"What about your neighbors? Anything?"

"The ones we know well either rang or came over," Nash's mother said. "All are on our side. As for the others, they don't matter, dear."

Nash exhaled loudly. "I'm sorry for everything. It was stupid to reveal myself, but standing out there after Sutton worked me over, I realized I'd had enough. In my moment of self-indulgence, I forgot about all of you."

His mother patted his shoulder. "I'm proud of you, Nash. It took courage to do what you did, and it's time you stood up to be counted."

"But at what cost to you?"

"Cost? Nonsense. We'll handle it."

His father gave him a quizzical look. "Garrett tells me he wants you to run for the Senate. Are you going to?"

Nat gaped at her dad. "He didn't!"

"He shouldn't have mentioned that," Nash said, "and it was just talk."

Nat spread her arms. "Friends, Romans, countrymen, lend me your ears."

"Cut it out, sis," Mark snapped, and Nash grinned at the reference to the famous line from the play *Julius Caesar*.

"Senator Nash Bannon. Has a nice ring to it, don't you think?" she insisted.

"We were only talking," Nash protested. "Besides, it's a crazy idea."

"Perhaps not," his dad mused. "The October election offers the Lifeliner Party a singular chance to gain representation, if the party machine plays its cards right." He pushed a tumbler across the table. "Let's drink to it."

Nash gave a wan smile and took a sip.

"Seriously, twin. You should consider it," Mark said. "Especially now that you don't have a job. The way the world wags these days, I doubt you'll be working anytime soon."

"You could be right, but going into politics is way out of my comfort zone. Still, the last two days have shaken my indulgent lifestyle and made me reflect on many things. I don't like what's happening out there—"

"None of us do," Mark added quietly.

"—and something needs to be done soon, or we're all going

down the pipe, and I don't mean lifeliners. I don't know if I'm up to it."

"Enough of this pessimistic feeling sorry for yourself crap, son!" his dad snapped. "When you spoke to that ABC reporter, you had something to say. Now finish what you started. A Bannon doesn't walk away from a challenge."

"I didn't walk away, and ABC has given me my ten minutes."

"What are you talking about?"

"They'll air an interview I taped this afternoon at G.S. & B on the *7.30 Report* tonight, and Garrett made sure I didn't put my foot in it."

"I'll have to see that!" Nat said brightly, her eyes sparkling.

"We'll all see it," Mom declared. "But first, dinner. Nat, dear, help me lay out the table."

"Okay, Mom. Keep talking, Nash. I want to hear about your girlfriend."

Dad shot her a warning look and cleared his throat. "From what I saw in the holoview, this Sutton character is some piece of work."

"He is, and Cariana—"

"Your girlfriend?" Nat butted in, a stack of plates in her hands.

"Her work got me into Sutton's clutches. She and I met at Southbank about a month ago. She's a geneticist at The Alfred, but what she does for the CSIRO at Parkville is what got me into trouble."

"She dobed you in?" Natalie looked incredulous.

"Cool it, sis," Mark told her sternly, and she promptly stuck out her tongue at him.

"We dated a couple of times and I was drawn to her. She's exciting, Dad, and you'll like her, Nat. I thought that after Sally, here was someone I could get serious with, but I had one problem."

"She wasn't a lifeliner," Mark said.

"And you didn't tell her you were one," his dad added.

Natalie quietly started laying out the dishes, cutlery, and wine glasses.

"It all developed so quickly. I wanted to, but—"

"You were afraid she'd walk away," Nat said.

"That's about it."

She snorted. "Men! If she loved you, which I gather she did—"

"She did, still does."

"—she would have accepted what you are. To a woman, looks may get you to first base, but we want more. Right, Mom?"

"Depends on the woman, dear, but you're right. Admittedly, getting involved with a lifeliner is a bit different. Ask your father."

"I was going to tell her," Nash said, "but something else entered the picture. Her niece Aleya."

"Niece?" Mark raised an eyebrow.

"A drunken lifeliner killed Cariana's brother and his wife in a car accident, and she's been taking care of his daughter."

His father nodded slowly. "Hence your reluctance to reveal yourself to her. She may have been carrying a chip."

"She was. I met the kid on a tram. She looked like a tramp and I figured her for a runaway. When she tried to jam off me, I knew she was a lifeliner. Something about her made me want to help her and, of course, I didn't know who she was then. Anyway, we ran into each other a couple of times and I offered to take her to the Help Center. The dobers would get her for sure if she stayed on the street. I arranged to meet Adam Gatt at the Footscray Market, and he would take it from there. That's when Cariana sprung her trap. She and Sutton's men were waiting."

Color drained from Nat's face. "She betrayed you?"

"Not exactly, but you can imagine how I felt. What's more, Aleya worked with Sutton in an undercover project to track down lifeliners. That's how she got us. Cariana used some of them for her research."

"Bitch!" Mark hissed.

"That's what I thought initially. It was then that I found out

Aleya was her niece. For the kid, nothing but an elaborate game with no consequences. Sutton ran a gene analysis on Adam and me and promised to have us sterilized if the tests showed we were lifeliners."

His dad stared at him. "You mean, the government is actually running a sterilization program? I saw the news, but I could hardly believe it."

"They certainly appear to be, and Sutton wouldn't be doing it without high-level approval."

"What happened then?" Nat demanded.

"Before he could get the test results, Garrett showed up with a court order to have us released."

"I am sure there is much more to this than you've said," Mark mused, "but we'll get into that later."

"How did you make up with Cariana?" Nat asked.

"With his operation blown, Sutton took Aleya and some other lifeliners to a safe house. Cariana was beside herself and came to me for help. Right then, she was the last person I wanted to see. She told me that Sutton threatened her when he found out Aleya was a lifeliner, but she was in it too deep to back out. I threw her out of my apartment."

"You didn't!" Mark chortled.

"When I calmed down and started to think straight, I realized I'd been a jerk."

"You're right there," Nat said with a scowl.

"I drove to her place and asked her to forgive me," Nash said. "Then I told her I loved her."

Nat sighed, her eyes dreamy. "Oh, that's so romantic. You must bring her over. I think we could be sisters."

"Guys, it's almost seven," Mom admonished them. "I don't want the roast getting cold."

"I'll give you a hand," Mark said and strode into the kitchen after her.

"I must say, son, you've had a hell of a ride, but as Mark said, there is much more to this than your girlfriend."

205

"There is, Dad. I think the Department of Home Affairs sponsored the Humans Only League to agitate against lifeliners."

"Mmm. Possibly. It's their sterilization program that makes my hair stand on end. Behavioral trends, Nash. They want to introduce a PID tracking feature and record all personal communication. Premier Latham allows cops to interrogate PIDs—"

"They're also keeping lifeliner registers, Dad."

"Which is against the law. If something isn't done, we're going to end up in an autocracy."

"That's why you've got to run for the Senate, Nash," Mark said as he placed a bowl of mixed salad on the table.

"Garrett gave me the same argument."

"And he's right. This is more than just about lifeliners. What is worse, it's happening in other countries too."

"Enough of this gloomy talk," Mom declared. She hefted a large baking plate onto the table and beamed. "Roast lamb and vegetables. Dig in before the mice get at it." She turned to her husband. "The wine, dear."

Nash did not have roast all that often, but lamb was light and this was a special occasion. Mom knew her boys weren't much into meat, but having it once in a while did no harm. Besides, it was good for them. Sticks to the ribs, she would say. Anyway, he didn't want more stuff sticking to his ribs. He had enough there already.

His dad took it on himself to do the carving and everybody helped themselves in a scramble to heap roasted vegetables and potatoes, steamed greens and salad, on their plate, getting in each other's way.

"Hey! I wanted that." Natalie shot Mark a wounded look when he forked a piece of cauliflower.

"First come, sis," Mark countered genially as he snagged more lamb.

"There is enough for everybody, children," Mom admonished soothingly, which made no difference to ongoing banter and elbow jostling.

Nash secured a generous helping of everything. He smothered the lamb with thick gravy and dug in. Dad filled Mom's glass and held the bottle to Mark. He in turn filled Nat's before topping up his own. Nash had to fill his own glass. Meals at the Bannon residence were always noisy, fun affairs, and no one stood on formality or protocol. It had been like that as far back as he could remember, which meant always. Apart from observing basic table manners, Mom insisted that meals were social occasions, not just a necessity.

Dad always kept a firm hand on everything and acted as judge when a dispute broke out between the siblings, his rulings absolute. Mother soothed the sting of his punishments, mostly additional chores, her justice being more direct and painful for the bottom end. In their teens and rebellious, the wooden spoon replaced with psychological counseling and restriction of privileges, which Nash and Mark often resented, not understanding what they had done wrong. Understanding came later.

Regarding the boisterous table antics, he had much to be thankful for having such parents. Without their love and support during the first few years when they came to terms being lifeliners, he and Mark might very well have ended up on the street, hated and hunted by everybody, their vision of the world forever dark.

Nash tried the wine and raised an eyebrow. "Not a bad shiraz, Dad."

"Something I picked up at Dan Murphy's from a boutique winery in the Barossa."

Nat creased her nose. "You men and your wines. Nash, I want to hear more about Aleya. What happened to her?"

"She's with Cariana, safe. The other kids she trained were less fortunate."

Fork held before him, Mark stared. "Sutton had them sterilized?"

Mom pressed her hand against her mouth. "Oh my God."

"Some of them may have gotten away, I don't know. According to Garrett, the police are rounding up everybody associated with his taskforce."

"How horrible," Nat said clearly upset. "Somebody in the government had to know what he was doing."

Nash nodded. "Somebody had to. There'll be more head chopping in Canberra, I'm sure. At least I hope so."

"The Coalition is going to get smashed in the polls over this," Mark added sagely.

"Not necessarily. They'll put a favorable spin on it and ride it out," Dad said softly. "It's a long time to October."

For the next few minutes, everyone was quiet, concentrating on the food. The only sound was the working of cutlery, but some of the fun had gone out of the meal, and Nash blamed himself for injecting that moment of doom. It was said and he couldn't take it back.

"Still working on the David Jones project, Mom?" Nash asked after taking a sip.

"Just about finished with that, dear. It's some of the best graphics work I've done. Having seen samples of my previous work, Myer wants me to do something similar for their stores promotion campaign. It keeps me busy."

"What about you, Nat? Anything new at BHP?"

"I finished a geological survey of what could be a substantial new oilfield in Bass Strait. It might be the largest found yet."

Mark looked up. "I thought Bass Strait was explored to death."

Natalie shook her head. "In the Central Deep zone, yes, but I've been running a new survey on the Southern Platform that others have pretty much written off. Everybody's been concentrating on the Northern Terrace for new fields, but looking at past surveys, I knew that oil-bearing beds had to extend farther south, and I was right. It took some time to convince the higher-ups, but they finally allowed me to do some test drilling."

"That's nice going, Nat," Nash told her warmly and she

smiled at him with something a little extra. She had never forgotten his act of kindness at Jubilee Lake when they were kids.

Mom glanced at the wall clock. "Goodness! It's past seven-thirty already."

"The interview!" Nat wailed, dropped her tools, and hurried into the lounge. Everybody else scrambled after her.

The holoview wall cleared in full 3D as everyone found a seat or a place on the leather couch.

"*—cannot be condoned, and Commander Sutton will face disciplinary action.*"

Russell leaned forward and stared intently at Gibbs Gilmore. "*Mr. Minister, were you aware of Mr. Sutton's clandestine taskforce?*"

"*His terms of reference required him to investigate possible illegal activities by Lifeliner Help Center branches. His taskforce had no authority to pursue or detain lifeliners for experimental purposes.*"

"So he says!" Mark snorted.

The ABC anchor looked skeptical. "*You are saying that he acted on his own initiative?*"

"*The extent of his activities and those of his taskforce are under investigation by the Attorney-General.*"

"*Thank you for your time, Mr. Minister.*"

"*A pleasure, Rowena.*"

"He didn't look like he was getting any pleasure out of it," Natalie said.

The reporter turned toward the camera. "*Mr. Nash Bannon, a former IBM program manager, had the misfortune to be caught up in Mr. Sutton's taskforce. I recorded this interview with him earlier in the afternoon.*"

The picture switched to the G.S. & B boardroom. Nash sat at one end of a long conference table. Behind him, a ceiling-high shelf stood filled with green, red, and yellow legal volumes.

"My God. He's wearing a tie!" Mark chortled.

Nash turned and gave him the finger.

"Enough, boys," their dad growled.

"*Welcome to the 7.30 Report, Mr. Bannon.*"

"Thank you for having me, Rowena."

"People are primed to notice things that are different, surprising, or extreme. For those who don't understand, can you explain what it's like to be a lifeliner?"

In the holoview, Nash gave a small smile. *"In many ways, I am like everybody else. I have bills to pay, do my shopping, and not married, I also do the washing. The things that make me different arguably help me—"*

"Like your eidetic memory, increased strength, endurance, and intelligence?"

"Wow. The lady has been doing her homework," Natalie mused.

"They have helped me."

"What about the most controversial thing about lifeliners, Mr. Bannon? Your ability to draw energy from people."

Nash leaned forward and reached across the table to the reporter. *"Give me your hand, Miss Russell."*

The anchorwoman looked startled, then slowly held out her hand. Nash clasped it and held it for about ten seconds, then released her.

"Have you felt anything?"

"Why, no."

"I just jammed, taking a little of your bioelectromagnetic energy. There is nothing controversial about what I have done, but accepting that it is harmless would undermine alarmist propaganda."

Mom looked at Nash. "You actually did that?"

"Absolutely. It was the best way to try and defuse a fallacy."

In the holoview, looking a little flustered, Russell cleared her throat.

"Thank you for that demonstration," she said weakly.

Nash sat back and crossed his legs. *"Scientists cannot explain why lifeliners have to do that, but it appears to be an innocuous evolutionary byproduct."*

"Is it true that you could kill someone with that ability?"

"That's a hysterical myth, Rowena. I guess it might be possible to render

someone unconscious if you took too much, but there have not been any recorded incidents of this happening worldwide."

"Everyone has observed growing social unrest and protest marches against lifeliners. Why shouldn't an ordinary person on the street blame lifeliners for increased infertility, breakup of families, and economic problems?"

Nash sighed. *"It is unsettling to see placard-waving mobs demanding that lifeliners be exterminated, which amounts to racial cleansing. I have experienced two such protests directed against me, fueled by government misinformation in a deliberate campaign to blame lifeliners for failure of social and economic policies.*

"It is true that Western-style countries are experiencing accelerated sterility, which scientists attribute to our intense materialistic lifestyles. They also argue that this could have been one of many possible evolutionary triggers that gave rise to lifeliners. It is a tragedy when a couple finds they are infertile even after treatment, but it is also a calamity when they discover their children are lifeliners, a stigma placed on them by governments. It is much easier to blame lifeliners for personal and national economic problems than to come up with policies to address them."

"Mr. Bannon, despite stringent laws that prohibits discrimination on racial grounds, there is evidence that such discrimination is actively practiced against lifeliners in the private sector and by government bodies, which suggests tacit approval by political parties. Have you experienced any form of discrimination?"

"Having announced that I was a lifeliner, Rowena, IBM chose to dismiss me, saying my presence would be detrimental in their drive to attract and keep clients."

"I am sorry to hear that, Mr. Bannon. Are you going to take action against them?"

"I will be lodging a claim for wrongful dismissal with the Human Rights Commission."

"Have these experiences prejudiced you against normal people?"

Nash grinned. *"Not of people in general, far from it. We are all human beings. It is the policies of our government, and governments around the world, to exterminate lifeliners that is of concern."*

"Scientists claim that homo sapiens *as we know them will eventually*

be replaced by lifeliners, homo renata, *or newborns as some call you. Do you believe that lifeliners can coexist with normal people?"*

"I have been doing it for thirty-two years, Rowena, although not always comfortably. There has always been the fear of discovery, with possible repercussions for me and my family. As for lifeliners replacing people, I doubt that very much. Evolution takes the long view and works over thousands of years. We are all men facing challenging problems, which we can solve if we work together instead of being carried away by emotional propaganda."

"What does the future hold for you?"

"Being thrown out of a job, and the way things are going, I'm not likely to be offered one. I have to consider my options."

"Thank you for appearing on the program, Mr. Bannon."

"I welcomed the opportunity, Rowena."

The background faded and Miss Russell turned to the studio camera.

"With possible introduction of a PID tracking feature announced—"

"Computer, switch off," Dad ordered and the holoview faded into spooling colors.

"Not a bad show, twin," Mark murmured thoughtfully.

"The interview itself was much longer, around thirty minutes," Nash said, "but you can squeeze only so much into a ten-minute bite."

"What were the things taken out?" his dad asked.

"We talked about sterilization, Sutton using kids to trap lifeliners, the creeping restriction of rights and freedoms, but Garrett thought them too controversial to air this time around, which would make me appear as a political agitator. The focus of the interview was to demonstrate that I and lifeliners everywhere were like everybody else—"

"Almost," Natalie quipped with a smile.

"With a few added problems, agreed. He told me later the other issues would be pursued in an ongoing campaign."

"You appeared very calm during the interview," Mom said approvingly.

"You looked good," Nat agreed. "Very statesmanlike."

"Was that a hint, Nat?"

"It was."

"I agree with sis," Mark added. "You have a presence and you project authority, and you didn't inject emotion into the interview, which would have been very easy to do, and you answered Russell's questions directly."

"Garrett's coaching," Nash explained.

"In the future, you mustn't do that if you decide to become a politician."

"You mean, give an answer to a question that wasn't asked?" Nash said with a straight face, and everybody laughed.

"Damn right. That's how it's done, twin. What I think stole the interview was you jamming with Rowena."

"That was my idea. Garrett didn't seem too keen on it, but I figured a live demonstration on national TV would generate terrific impact."

"I am sure it did."

Nash gave a long sigh. "I have to untangle the mess I made for myself, but in the process, I also created a serious problem for all of you."

"We'll deal with it," his dad answered forcefully. "Nobody is coming to the door to arrest us. It hasn't come to that."

"Yet," Mark said with a heavy frown.

Mom cleared her throat and stood. "You have an opportunity, Nash, to make sure it doesn't happen, for us or anybody else, lifeliner or not. In the meantime, we still have dinner to finish."

* * *

High clouds smeared the last dawn stars with a red swathe. A bright orange bulge hugged the city's jagged skyline, heralding where the sun would rise. The silvery moon hung low in the sky, a chunk cut out of its side as it began to wane. Nothing stirred in the Domain Park, the air fanned by a warm northerly breeze. Even the bird chatter had a subdued undertone, accompanied by the ceaseless hiss of traffic along St. Kilda Road. A tram clanged its bell as it clattered across an intersection.

Nash slowed to a brisk walk as he approached Domain Road, his breathing deep and even. This morning, he did not see the tall girl with her swinging ponytail, but he left for his run rather late. One advantage of not having to go to work. Brisk calisthenics to round off his exercise program—sometimes he did his exercises first—a shower, a full breakfast of his homemade muesli, would set him up for lunch and his date with Cariana.

Yesterday's kaleidoscope of contrasting events still to settle into a coherent whole. The day ended more or less satisfactorily, but he needed to be sure about Cariana. With the emotional trauma of having the police hassle her, and time to look at things more objectively, despite what she told him yesterday, she might want to cool their relationship until things normalized a little, or even break it off. After all, they only had two real dates. Things were unlikely to settle down if he ran for office.

Usually, he never had problems falling asleep, but last night sleep eluded him into the small hours, and he understood why. He reached a major crossing point in his life that offered several turnings, each one irrevocably setting his future. He initially attempted to solve his problem in the same way he defined one of his work projects, by setting up a matrix of pros and cons for each option. Unfortunately, his methodology was only partially successful. The reason obvious even before he started. How does one assign a quantitative value to love, satisfaction, achievement, social accomplishment, making a difference in this crummy world? Impossible, hence his indecision which path to take. He read somewhere that one should never make an important commitment based on emotion, which left him in a quandary that could not be resolved logically. Human interaction that involved emotion could not be quantified, simple as that. Not at an individual level anyway.

Hands clasped behind his head, staring at a ceiling shrouded in blackness, only faintly visible from ambient street lighting, he found himself in a supersaturated situation that needed a single external input to crystalize. He must have resolved something, because sleep did eventually come, or perhaps he was too mentally exhausted to keep tilling the same ground.

As he walked, sunshine broke through the patchy cloud cover and the world became almost uplifting. More pedestrians filled the sidewalk, mostly office workers, judging by their attire, generally heading up the street; this portion of St. Kilda Road occupied by all types of companies. His tenement block loomed high and he visualized his breakfast. A car engine revved behind him and Nash instinctively turned his head to see what was going on.

He heard two sharp cracks and searing fire lanced across the top of his right bicep. Another crack and something slammed against his back that sent him sprawling to the sidewalk. A woman screamed. He smelled stinking rubber as a dark blue hatch accelerated past him. The passenger swiveled his handgun toward him and fired. Nash had no idea where the bullet went. As the car weaved through the traffic, he burned the image of the shooter into his mind.

His arm stung and blood oozed from the shallow wound. He was more concerned about the pressing weight on his back and inability to feel his legs. Was he shot in the spine? The thought of being a cripple the rest of his life left him horrified.

"Help me get her off him!" a strong masculine voice ordered, and the weight was gone. Someone knelt beside him.

"Were you hit anywhere else?" the same commanding voice demanded.

Nash grunted, rolled over, and sat up, vastly relieved. "Only my arm."

Wearing a dark gray suit and black tie, the man's obvious concern faded. He might have been in his late forties, but hard to tell. He reached with his hand and heaved Nash up.

"Thank you…"

His words died when he saw the woman on the pavement, a bright red spot coloring the back of her white shirt, her young face contorted with pain. He immediately knelt beside her and touched her neck. Her skin warm and pulse strong. Her eyelids fluttered and intense green eyes stared at him. She gasped, laboring for breath, then convulsed into a fit of coughing. Pink foam colored her mouth, which meant a lung shot. No telling how bad until the paramedics checked her out. It tore him up seeing her suffer, wishing he were in her place.

"What..." she managed to whisper after a moment.

"Lie still." Nash looked up at the executive type who helped him. "Please call an ambulance."

"Already done...and the police."

The commotion had gathered a crowd of curious onlookers. Hearing the word 'police', the sidewalk was suddenly empty. Those passing by gave him and the woman a cursory glance and hurried on their way, apparently not wanting entanglements in something messy, however momentarily diverting.

"Here..." The man held out his jacket.

Nash nodded and covered the wounded woman. She moaned and tried to rise, but he held her down. The sidewalk wasn't cold, but she should not be lying on it for too long.

"Don't move. The ambulance will be here in a moment."

"My bag..." she managed to gasp.

He looked around and saw a green handbag on the grassy nature strip, thrown there when she staggered against him. His helper immediately walked over and picked it up. Nash reached for the woman's right hand and held it. The gesture seemed to reassure her. He glanced at the weeping gash on his bicep and scowled. The five-centimeter groove stung, but he was lucky the bullet didn't go through bone. Cleaned and sealed, he would be all right. He was more worried about the young woman. Why did she have to get hurt because of him? It was all so senseless.

Rats!

He now had two bum shoulders, the left one still tender from yesterday's altercation. Cliff clearly couldn't take the hint and leave well enough alone. If they met again, Nash meant to do more than break bones.

The piercing sound of a wailing siren died as an ambulance pulled up. Two paramedics rushed to the back as the double door opened. A female medic stepped down and helped unload a gurney. After slapping on a pressure bandage on the entry hole, the three of them lifted the woman onto the gurney and wheeled her into the van.

"Her bag!" The executive hurried after them.

One of the medics emerged with a black satchel and stood beside Nash.

"Your arm, the only wound?"

Nash nodded.

The medic opened his satchel, took out a slim can, and sprayed the area.

"This will stop the bleeding and check any infection. It's also an anesthetic. I've got to run, but there is another ambulance van behind me. They'll take care of you."

Nash stared after the retreating medic, nonplussed by the cavalier treatment, understanding he wasn't a priority.

Siren wailing, the ambulance took off. The executive picked up his jacket off the sidewalk and sighed at the red stain on the inside lining. He glanced at Nash and scowled.

"You think the drycleaners can take this out?"

"Probably leave a hole trying," Nash quipped and held out his hand. "Thanks for your help."

"The guy who shot you, a grudge?" The man's grip dry and hard.

"He doesn't like lifeliners."

The man gave a faint smile. "Yeah, been there myself," he said softly, his dark eyes penetrating.

Nash took in the slim build, powerful physique, intelligent eyes, and nodded. A fellow traveler...

"A shitty way to start the morning."

"Especially for the young woman," the man agreed.

An ambulance pulled up, followed by a cop squad car. Two

medics got out and one of them gave Nash a quick examination.

"Your colleague sprayed it with an anesthetic," Nash explained.

"Any other injuries?"

"Nothing else."

"Sit down."

The medic cut away part of the bloody T-shirt and wiped the gash with alcohol. He reached into his bag and produced an instrument with a two-pronged clamp. He placed the fork end against the wound and the skin slowly closed. He then gradually moved the device along the wound, sealing it. Finished, he covered the gash with a large pad and cleaned the remaining blood off the arm.

"Don't remove the dressing for a week. The wound should be healed by then. Don't do anything strenuous that might pull the ends. If you do, see your GP right away."

"Thanks," Nash said and flexed his arm.

"I need permission to access your PID to record personal details."

"Fine."

Done, the medic glanced at his partner and they piled quickly into the ambulance. It sped off with a whine of electric motors.

Nash turned to look at the police officer waiting patiently and sighed.

"You have a singular interest in me, Sergeant?"

"When dispatch called and gave me the location, I thought it might be you, Mr. Bannon. What happened this time?"

"A drive-by shooting, and the shooter the assailant from yesterday, the one whose throat I caved in."

"Did you happen to see anything else?"

"The vehicle was a petrol engine dark blue Ford Focus hatch," Nash said and gave him the registration number. "How come he's allowed to prowl about?"

"He and his two accomplices were charged with assault and will appear in court on summons. There wasn't enough reason to

hold them on remand. This incident will put them away, though."
The sergeant stared at him and bit his lip. "How's the arm?"

"A shallow wound. I am more concerned about the woman."

"I heard. If it hadn't been for her…I've got to hang around until the forensics team gets here, but you, Mr. Bannon, need to take a ride to headquarters and make a statement. My partner will make sure nobody else takes potshots at you."

"I need to change my shirt."

"You can do that later." The cop turned to the executive quietly watching the proceedings. "You the witness? Might as well ride with Mr. Bannon. Once you're done, we'll take you wherever you want to go."

The man nodded and walked toward the squad car.

Nash felt grimy and in need of a shower, but it looked like he wasn't going to get one, or his breakfast. Definitely a shitty way to start the morning.

A dark blue sedan with a Nine News logo on its side pulled up to the curb and the police sergeant groaned.

"That's all I need."

Julia Candice stepped out, took in the scene and walked briskly toward Nash.

"Mr. Bannon, can you tell us what happened?"

"Nothing much to tell. I was shot by a member of the Humans Only League. I came off better than the young woman who took a bullet meant for me."

"Do you know her condition?"

"The ambulance just took her away. I can only hope she makes a full recovery."

"Does this latest incident have anything to do with the attacks made on you yesterday?"

"Yesterday was a case of harassment and intimidation. What happened here was attempted murder. This is not something we can tolerate, or pretend it isn't happening. Where does it stop, Miss Candice?"

The sergeant placed himself before the reporter. "You'll have to cut this short. Mr. Bannon needs to make a formal statement downtown."

Nash waved to Candice and climbed into the squad car. He belted up and the car surged into the traffic.

The executive beside him held out a business card.

Payne Ogelvy
General Manager, Integration Division
Telstra Corporation Ltd

Nash shook his head at the irony of finding himself with his former client.

"We have never met, Mr. Ogelvy, but we exchanged some emails."

"We did, Mr. Bannon, seeing how you were managing a major program of work for me. Amanda Fuller speaks highly of you, as does the Program Director."

"Zimsky is a tough manager, but we got along."

"Not according to Amanda."

Nash allowed himself a faint grin. "He and I had an occasional difference of opinion how to achieve our mutual objective. You must know that IBM canned me."

"I saw the *7.30 Report* last night. An interesting performance. What are your plans now?"

"I'll take them to the Human Rights Commission."

"And I expect you will win. It's grim what's going on out there."

"A dark face of humanity I pretended did not exist," Nash said softly, his thoughts churning. He had no reason to feel guilty over the woman, but he did. "I must apologize for the problem my dismissal has undoubtedly created for Telstra. I feel professionally responsible."

"Not your fault. IBM has generated a great deal of difficulty for us and we're also considering taking reparatory action." Ogelvy's lively eyes were searching. "Would you care to work for us, Mr. Bannon? You'd be a valuable asset, and I need someone to complete what you started. Telstra needs men of your caliber."

Nash stared at the man. Given his current situation, a terrific offer, but to step into his old job meant working with IBM again, although from the other side of the fence. Something he did not care for right now. He would be scraping at another raw wound.

"There might be an issue with my confidentiality agreement."

Ogelvy chuckled. "I'd get you a waiver. Telstra is a *very* important IBM customer. I don't think they would want to annoy us more than they already have."

"I appreciate the offer, more than you realize, but I cannot make a decision right now."

"Of course, I understand. Call me if you're prepared to consider it. One more thing. Telstra is a genuine equal opportunity employer."

"They know…about you?"

"They do, and I'm not the only lifeliner there."

Nash liked Ogelvy's quiet, yet intense manner, certain he was an effective, and probably demanding executive, demonstrated by the offer he made to fill a hole IBM had dug for him. How much that offer was made as a genuine gesture to help, or an opportunity to address a corporate problem, Nash didn't know. Probably a combination of both. An option he might consider if nothing else came up.

When they reached the Collins Street headquarters, a polite plainclothesman ushered Ogelvy away and bundled Nash into a nondescript room on the second floor, similar to the one he'd been in the first time, and told to wait. He hardly made himself comfortable when the door opened and he gave a mental groan.

"Inspector Worsley…"

"Mr. Bannon," the cop acknowledged crisply, pulled back a chair and sat down. "I must advise you that this room is monitored and our conversation recorded. Do you have any objection to being recorded?"

"I don't."

"Very well. Sergeant Bogan updated me on the incidents that transpired yesterday, namely the alleged—"

"Not so alleged from where I stood, Inspector."

"A figure of speech, Mr. Bannon, but I'll rephrase. An altercation yesterday morning in front of your apartment by a Humans Only League member, and an aborted attack on you yesterday afternoon in front of the same premises by three armed assailants belonging to the said organization. We obtained a copy of your building's security footage of both incidents, which corroborates the testimony you gave to Sergeant Bogan. You will be required to appear as a witness in any court proceedings. Do you have anything to add to your testimony that has not been divulged to Sergeant Bogan?"

"I can only speculate as to motive, a desire to exact revenge."

"I have examined the footage of the incidents and noted how you disposed of your assailants. Mind telling me where you picked up that sort of training?"

"A lot of practice, Inspector."

"I see. You may be called to elaborate on that in court."

"I understand."

The cop glanced at the arm patch. "I trust your wound is not serious?"

Nash blinked, not sure if the dober's concern was sincere, or merely being officially polite.

"A flesh wound. The medic told me I should be all right by next weekend."

"Glad to hear it. For your information, the second victim, the woman, was taken to The Alfred Hospital with a bullet through her right lung. I am told her injury is grave, but not life-threatening."

"Thank you for telling me. I feel bad that she happened to get caught up in this."

"Sergeant Bogan tells me you identified the shooter known as Cliff?"

"I saw him clearly as the getaway car sped off."

"And you also saw the registration plate?"

"You are aware that I am a lifeliner, Inspector?"

"I was briefed."

"Then you know why I can remember everything I see."

"Your eidetic memory, yes. You will probably be called to demonstrate that ability in court as well."

"Of course."

"I have no further reason to detain you, Mr. Bannon. You are free to go."

"That's it?" Nash glared at the cop. "I gave Sergeant Bogan all the details. There was no need to waste my time bringing me here."

"It may seem that way to you, Mr. Bannon, but the incidents you were involved in forms a chain of evidence that will be used in court to prosecute the perpetrators." Worsley cleared his throat, suddenly embarrassed. "This also gives me an opportunity to apologize for my behavior on Wednesday. I was out of line when I attempted to infringe on your rights. My apologies, sir."

Nash blanched at this attitude change. He stood and offered his hand.

"You were doing your job. No hard feelings. Perhaps one or two."

Worsley digested that, apparently not sure if Nash was joking, then broke into a grin and they shook hands.

"I'll arrange a squad car to take you home."

On the way to the door, Worsley paused. "I trust your friend Aleya is well?"

"You know...She's with her Aunty."

"The Department is buzzing about Commander Sutton and his taskforce. A shameful episode in Australian law enforcement."

"Makes me wonder what else is going on. Careful how you choose sides, Inspector."

Nash stepped out of the building into bright sunshine and noises from a city fully awake. An unmarked car waited at the bottom of the steps. Dressed in mufti, the driver immediately opened the back door. As Nash slid onto the seat, he wondered if the dobers were as nice to people under arrest, and decided not. Someone must have passed the word down to be extra polite to Mr. Bannon. He wondered why.

After crossing the Yarra, it was a relatively quick drive up Kings Way to the Domain Interchange despite the heavy traffic. His PID said it was only 9:16, but he felt as though he already had a full day.

He stared at the flowing cars and the occupants inside, faces intent as they concentrated on their driving, or relaxed as the car did the driving for them. Young, old, nicely dressed and some not so, all were trapped in their little world and apparently content to be like that, or perhaps couldn't do anything about it if they weren't. A few days ago, he also had his little bubble, happy to peer out, not letting anyone peer in, because outside that bubble, the world was cold and hard. It did not have to be, but unless he stepped out and tried to make others step out, those already outside would dictate where this river of people flowed. Right now, it was headed for a waterfall, and rocks lay at the bottom.

The squad car pulled up in front of his apartment block. Nash thanked the driver and strode quickly toward the entrance. He linked with the security system and the glass doors slid back. Eden saw him and came toward him.

"Mr. Bannon, are you all right? When I heard the shots—"

"I'm fine. A flesh wound."

"I called triple zero, but I couldn't leave my post to help."

"Don't worry about it."

"How's the woman?"

"Shot through the lung, but I'm told she'll be okay."

"That's something. Nasty business, this. After they took you away, Channel Ten and Seven media cars pulled up, followed by more cops. The reporters interviewed everyone on the scene, making a nuisance of themselves. Glad you're all right, sir."

In his apartment, Nash took a quick shower. The anesthetic

had worn off and his shoulder throbbed. Since both were sore, it all evened out.

He pulled on light black slacks and a black T-shirt, and started breakfast, ready to eat anything in sight.

"Sally, ABC news," he commanded as he poured himself some juice using his left hand.

The holoview wall rippled and the camera focused on Marina Lennon.

"—those just joining us, Prime Minister Atarah Readman announced a surprise double dissolution snap election to be held on Saturday, March 6, using Labor's failure to pass the controversial Superannuation amendment bill for the second time as the trigger. According to sources inside the Party Room, the election brought on by what amounted to a revolt from the back bench demanding a Cabinet reshuffle after revelation that Gibbs Gilmore, Minister for Home Affairs, orchestrated a sterilization program against life-liners. This gives the Liberal Party coalition thirty-five days to convince the voters that her administration should be returned to office."

Her suave partner stepped in with his deep radio announcer voice. Juice forgotten, Nash stared at the holoview.

"It is alleged the Minister also authorized formation of the Humans Only League as a propaganda tool to vilify lifeliners, and directed the CSIRO to conduct a research program to identify lifeliners using a routine blood test. At a Cabinet meeting last night, Mr. Gilmore tendered his resignation, accepted by the Prime Minister. Outside Parliament House, Mr. Gilmore stated that punitive lifeliner programs were sanctioned at the highest level of both major parties, which implicates the Prime Minister and the Labor opposition leader. Macey Gardner was not available for comment."

Marina picked up the commentary.

"Political analysts were astounded by the PM's announcement, which has left the country without a government in the middle of sensitive negotiations with our Pacific neighbors, aimed to curb China's expansion into the region where it could effectively control the ocean's shipping lanes, the U.S. having abandoned the region after allowing mainland China to absorb Taiwan in 2027, which also brought the oil and gas-rich Philippines into its economic and political sphere.

"We were told the Prime Minister will drive to the Presidential Lodge sometime this morning and advise President Ngarra to dissolve both Houses of the federal parliament—"

"Excuse me, Nash. You have a call from Chelsy Innes, CEO of Deloitte Consulting," Sally interrupted.

Deloitte? They were one of the top heavyweights in the consultancy industry, with a broad spectrum of activities other than IT. To get a call from the Australian CEO herself was highly unusual to say the least.

"Accept," he said and waited for the holoview to clear.

A handsome woman, perhaps in her forties, long face framed by short, totally white hair, smiled at him. Her cream shirt set a nice contrast with the somber business jacket. A single yellow pearl hung from a gold necklace.

"Thank you for taking my call, Mr. Bannon."

"Deloitte Consulting? I couldn't resist, Ms. Innes."

She laughed, a deep, resonant sound. "Please call me Chelsy."

"Thank you…Chelsy, and it's Nash."

"You had an interesting forty-eight hours, Nash, and not altogether pleasant. It is regrettable to see such events taking place…you have seen the announcement calling for a new election?"

"I just watched it."

"Perhaps things will change. Whether they do or not, business will continue, which is the reason for my call. I am aware of your dismissal by IBM and the circumstances surrounding it, which raised a few eyebrows. I believed they had a more progressive HR policy."

"So did I, Chelsy."

"Their loss is perhaps our gain. You have impressive qualifications and experience, Nash, which would be valuable to Deloitte. I am prepared to offer you a position where you will have an opportunity to apply and expand your skills. The posting will be to our Melbourne office, but you may be required to travel to Sydney and engage with our Asia-Pacific clients."

Taken aback, Nash blinked. This was totally out of the box, pleased to learn that not all corporations were coldhearted like CIS.

"I am flattered by your offer, Chelsy. If I may, isn't it somewhat unusual for a CEO to indulge in recruiting?"

"Somewhat, but when I see an unusual opportunity, I snap it up."

"Will you allow me some time to think about it?"

"Take all the time you need. If you decide to consider my offer, call me and we'll discuss specifics."

"Thank you. I appreciate your call, Ms. Innes."

"It was my pleasure, Nash, and I do hope you will accept."

The holoview image faded, replaced by spooling colors.

"Shall I resume the ABC news coverage?" Sally queried.

Deep in thought, Nash pulled at his chin. "No," he said softly and sipped his juice.

He linked his PID with the percolator and told it to reheat the coffee, then started on the vegetable patties. The cellphone gave a soft beep, indicating an incoming email. He opened the message list and clicked on the new item. Another offer, this time from Bain & Company, Francis Miller himself, Head of Australian Information Technology Practice based in Sydney. Nash recognized the high roller. Bain & Co was another prestigious industry hitter who demanded a lot from their people, but also paid a lot. That's what he heard on the industry network. Would he be interested in heading a major hardware/software integration project in Malaysia? The contract would run for two years. Most of the work would be done from the Bain Melbourne office via the VP link, but he would be required to spend some time in Kuala Lumpur.

Nash was gratified to receive three openings within two hours. Perhaps the world out there was not such a grim place after all. Did he want to step into harness right away? He would have a measure of financial security, but he wasn't doing too badly right now either. There was also his pending action against

IBM, which should generate a nice payout, but it wouldn't be anytime soon if IBM contested the Commission's decision. He did not believe they would, probably wary of further damage to their reputation. They still could, though, just to be a pain.

It might be interesting to handle a new program of work, but somewhat cool on the idea of finishing the Telstra project. A job meant that he would be in his comfortable shell again, and in a week, perhaps sooner, everybody would have forgotten about him, focused on the looming election. He and Cariana could rebuild their relationship without the glare of publicity and everything would be as before.

Nash bit his lip and frowned. No, things could never be the same. Too much had happened to both of them. To crawl back into his cocoon was to deny reality. The world might go to hell, but he wouldn't notice because he did not care.

But he did care, that was the point.

"Nash, Mr. Bartlett is calling."

"Accept call."

"Morning, my boy. I watched your interview last night. The ABC did a good job. I didn't like the idea of a jamming demonstration, but I must admit it was powerful imagery."

"It gave Miss Russell something to think about," Nash agreed.

"It certainly did. Have you seen the election announcement?"

"I watched it on ABC."

"The Prime Minister may have finessed us, Nash. Not that I'm saying she called the election solely because of Gibbs Gilmore, but it could have been a tipping factor. Lifeliners are a major social issue she and the Coalition must resolve, as does the Labor Party, for that matter. She wants to do it through erosion of individual rights, and that's a policy we cannot allow any party to implement. Today, it's lifeliners. Tomorrow, it could be Chinese and Asian immigration."

Nash laughed. "A nice campaign plug. You should be the one running for office, Garrett."

The elderly barrister sighed. "If I were twenty years younger,

I would, but this is a young man's game. Readman's announcement has severely cut our preparation window, which means we have to move immediately on everything. I hate to rush you, but I must know if you're coming on board, and I won't moralize if you decide not to run."

"The hell you won't!"

Garrett looked sad and old. "No, my boy. I won't. This is something that must come from your heart."

Time to step into the breeze, old son, or wall yourself in.

Nash didn't need new arguments to run. He debated enough of them with himself. He could return to his superficially content lifestyle and slam the door on the ugliness outside, which might work for a while. What if the government decided to follow President Mackay's lead and ignored the High Court when it didn't like its rulings? With people like Sutton in charge, he would end up sterilized and stripped of citizenship and dignity. It might even go further than that.

Take a cushy job and enjoy it for a few years, then watch as everything descended into darkness? The dreams he and Cariana might make shattered. And kids like Aleya? They wouldn't even have time to grow up.

With mild surprise, Nash realized the supersaturated situation he woke to this morning had crystalized, and the election announcement the external causal factor.

He felt sublimely calm as he looked Garrett in the eye.

"I'll run."

Garrett beamed with delight. "You'll regret it, but I promise you a fun ride."

Nash flinched. "That's not very reassuring."

"You'll find out. Seriously, you'll make a great candidate. You need to come to the party headquarters in Carlton Place as soon as possible and register your membership and candidacy. You'll also have to catch up on our policies and election tactics, and what we think will be the tactics of our opposition. We'll have a raft of single-issue parties contesting Senate seats, and each will be taking votes from us. We have strategies to marginalize them, which involves pounding the pulpit. That's where you and our other candidates come in."

"How many primary votes do I need to get elected?"

"In Victoria, the quota is around 439,000, but if we make preference deals, you won't need that many, perhaps 60,000."

"That's still a lot."

"We'll be competing for a seat with perhaps twenty other minor parties. Most don't have a hope of getting a candidate elected, but they can direct their preferences to us, and that's where we need to make deals. We'll also be relying on the fact that major party candidates get far more than the required quota. The excess is distributed to other candidates according to preferences, but Labor and the Coalition are not likely to direct their preferences to us as a first choice. It all depends how people number their voting tickets. Our chances of picking up a seat in a smaller state like Tasmania are much better. Too bad you're not living there. When can you come in?"

"I could be there by three."

Garrett scowled. "You want to finish reading a book, right?"

Nash grinned. "Something better. A lunch date with Cariana."

The lawyer waved a dismissive hand. "Have dinner instead. This is important."

"So is my relationship. I am prepared to commit myself 110 percent, but not if it ruins my personal life. Not a good PR image for the Lifeliner Party."

"Mmm. Dr. Lambert is also a victim, I guess, and something we could use in our campaign."

"Is that all this matters to you? Advantages and how to tear down an opponent?"

A cloud descended over Garrett's face. "That's right, Mr. Bannon. If you cannot accept this grim reality, don't get into the ring."

"I apologize. It's just—"

"This is serious business, with oblivion for the loser, but it doesn't have to be unethical. We'll run a clean campaign, but don't expect the same from your opposition. You'll see mud flying in all directions. We have to make damn sure that none sticks to us. Because of that, it's more important than ever that we complete thorough vetting of all our candidates from cradle up. One blemish could sink all of us."

"I suppose you'll be doing it with me?"

"You're on top of my list, my boy."

Nash laughed. "I'll give you whatever information you need, and you can call Dad if I don't have everything."

"Don't worry, we will." Garrett looked thoughtful. "*Do* you have any skeletons, Nash? It is better if this comes out now. Easier for everybody."

"Apart from concealing that I'm a lifeliner, my life is an open book. I have never been into drugs, prostitutes, and I don't have a drinking problem. There are no grounds where someone could blackmail me."

"Nice to know, but—"

"You're going to go through the process anyway."

"Of course. Nothing personal, you know."

"I understand completely," Nash said and scowled. Something didn't add up here. "You said that you'll run a clean campaign, but the other day, you told me that running a campaign means exploiting emotional fears. Whatever it takes, you said. How can this be clean or ethical?"

"It can be. We'll talk about it later."

Nash chewed his lip. "Excuse me while I get myself some coffee."

"What's the matter with your arm?" Garrett demanded when he saw Nash favoring his left hand.

"I got shot in the shoulder this morning."

"What happened?"

"A Humans Only League thug wanting to get even."

"You're okay?"

"Nothing serious. I'll fill you in later."

"This will generate great publicity for us, my boy."

"Is that all you can think about?" Nash snarled in outrage.

"I'm not being insensitive, but we don't throw away freebies. I've got to cut this short. When you get to the party headquarters, ask for Warren Kairns. He'll take care of you."

"Isn't he the Lifeliner Party national president?"

"And a top-drawer political operator. He ran the National's 2030 campaign, but quit halfway through."

"What soured his beer?"

"He didn't like their policies, or the Coalition's. By the way, he's not a lifeliner."

"Isn't that somewhat unusual?"

"We picked the best man for the job. The party has a number of people who aren't lifeliners. Welcome aboard, my boy."

The holoview cleared and Nash shrugged. It made sense the party would attract fellow travelers who wanted to voice the need for change, whether they were lifeliners or not. He realized he'd been standing all this time, breakfast forgotten.

* * *

Always crowded, especially during lunch hour when locals and tourists strove to find a table at one of the many restaurants along the Southbank promenade, it wasn't any different this time. Across the Yarra, the city towers clawed into a clear sky, wrapped in sounds of cars, trams, and milling people. An odd busker on the sidewalk tried his luck with a guitar or violin, hoping for a buck or two.

Nash hurried down broad steps that led to the promenade. A welcome cool breeze came off the river. Not oppressively hot, but surrounding buildings acted like radiators, reflecting bright sunshine. The pleasant weather gave everybody a chance to show off their particular taste in clothes. A couple of years ago, bell-bottom trousers were in vogue again, and some were atrocious; flapping sails as far as he was concerned. Teeners and the more adventurous oldies paraded them like placards of protest against the straitjacketed establishment. These days, stovepipes were coming back. He didn't like either, preferring a more normal cut always acceptable.

Skycars cluttered the skyline, seemingly buzzing over the city in random patterns. However, the fully automated level 5 drones were perfectly safe, with only one fatal crash since being introduced in 2026, due to a passenger attempting to take over the controls. Initially developed by Uber as an alternative to ground on-demand cabs, Virgin Air and Blue Origin were not far behind, operating their own variants.

Nash saw Cariana standing beside the railing looking at the city. Golden hair tied into a bun, she wore a dark green T-shirt and navy blue slacks. A beige leather bag hung on her left shoulder. She looked smart and attracted more than one glance from passersby, men and women.

He walked up to her and cleared his throat. "A penny for your thoughts."

She turned and flashed him a radiant smile. A necklace of blue zircon adorned her slim throat. She pushed up her shades and jammed them into her hair. He leaned forward and pecked her on the cheek.

"They're not worth that much," she said and brushed back a lock of hair.

"Must be worth something. I hope you haven't been waiting long."

"Just got here."

A cruise boat motored slowly upriver, the tourists inside snapping and filming everything with their phones. Nash hadn't seen a genuine camcorder since 2024, when they were largely replaced by sophisticated tablets and smartphones. Professionals and diehards still used them, though, but it was fading technology destined to vanish like DVDs and flash drives. Everything and everybody these days was stored in a worldwide encrypted data cloud.

She linked her arm with his and they slowly walked beneath a canopy of golden elms. Joggers, mostly wearing harsh colors, weaved between pedestrians. It looked good on the girls, but did nothing for the muscle pushers.

Nash paused and listened to a busker playing haunting strands on a pan flute, accompanied by soft background music coming from a speaker beside him. He linked his PID and transferred two dollars. The busker nodded without breaking his playing.

"How was your day?" Nash asked Cariana. "The dobers still after you?"

"I had a long session with a stern federal police detective, but nobody told me I was in any trouble. They were more interested in Sutton and his taskforce. I couldn't tell them much, except that he got some of my test subjects."

"What exactly did you do with them? I always wondered about that."

She shot him a mischievous look that made her almond eyes twinkle. "We didn't chop them up, Nash."

"I didn't mean—"

"Blood work, MRI scans doing mental tasks, endurance exercises, and general IQ tests. I spent a lot of my time analyzing gene sequence comparisons against normal human DNA controls. The test subjects were usually kept at Parkville for about four or five days, then released."

"After they were sterilized," Nash growled.

"From what I know now, that may have happened. Dr. Connell always told me that all lifeliners were volunteers and paid for their time even if they were inmates."

"Your work at Parkville—"

"They haven't shut me down, and we still want to unlock those gene switches, but the project will be totally under CSIRO control, and the subjects all genuine volunteers." She gave him an impish grin. "I can always use another one."

Nash laughed. "No, thanks. I don't have any desire to have my brain dissected."

She looked horrified. "We never did that!"

"As far as you know," he added darkly.

"I hate to say it, but I cannot dismiss the possibility," she acknowledged moodily. "It was never done at Parkville, but CSIRO has other facilities. I know they did it in the States where a lot of my data came from, but I buried that deep in my mind, not wanting to know. Gods, I really was twisted up."

Nash squeezed her hand. "Put it behind you, Cariana."

"The police wanted to interview Aleya, but I put my foot down. I didn't want her grilled by some insensitive gorilla. The AFP detective I mentioned? He actually smiled at that. He promised a nice lady would do the interview over a smoothie or ice cream. They weren't all like Sutton, he said."

"They probably want to know about her training and what she did on the street."

"I guess, but I didn't want her traumatized. She's had a rough couple of days." She gave him a searching look. "You've become quite attached to her, haven't you?"

"It was hard not to. She is quite a kid," he said. "I've become quite attached to you as well."

"After everything—"

"After everything," he said firmly. "There is a quality about you that shines without having to say the words. An aura that's a lure, and I have been hopelessly snared. Did I tell you that I love you?"

Her eyes sparkled. "You did, but I don't mind hearing it again."

Hand in hand, they walked in their little world without seeing anyone else. Nash liked having her close. He liked the way she occasionally brushed back a stray lock of hair, frowned when concentrating, and he liked her exuberant, carefree laugh. He liked her clear voice, a brook tumbling over smooth stones.

"And how was your day?" she asked, her voice coming from somewhere far away.

"Last night, I had dinner with my parents, and it went better than I expected. I thought I'd get reamed for revealing all, but they were actually very supportive."

"Sounds like a well-adjusted family."

"They are. I'm not saying there won't be consequences, but we'll handle it together."

"By the way, I saw the *7.30 Report*. You came across very statesmanlike."

"You know, Natalie said the same thing."

"Natalie?"

"My younger sister. The one my twin and I were mean to, remember?"

She laughed. "I remember. You made it up to her, didn't you?"

"As a matter of fact, I did. We're very close these days."

"So, now that you're out of a job, what's on the agenda? More golfing?"

"I doubt that I'll have much time. Getting elected will keep me pretty busy."

"You are actually running?"

"I'm giving it a go."

"What's happening to us, Nash? The world is going crazy, blaming lifeliners for everything…as I did."

"That's why I'm running for the Senate, my bright constellation."

"Constellation…that sounds nice," she said dreamily.

"Because you are my constellation, and I want you to shine for me always."

"My romantic prince…"

"Cariana, you understand that running for the Senate will turn a torch of publicity on me, not only because I'm running, but because I am a lifeliner, and you will be caught in that glare. It won't be comfortable. I won't blame you if you want to walk away."

She was silent as they walked. Then…

"I thought about it last night. About everything, but I want to be there when the days become dark, and they might."

"You have no idea. On your pretty head be it, but don't say I didn't warn you." He made light of her decision, but was also relieved. He should never have doubted her.

"Cube." She slapped him on the shoulder and he winced at a stab of pain. She immediately looked contrite.

"What's the matter?"

"Well...that's where I got shot this morning."

Color drained from her face. "Shot? What happened?"

"A Humans Only League thug looking for revenge waylaid me in front of my apartment when I came back from a run. We had an altercation yesterday on the way to my parents' place. I guess he wanted to get even."

"That's terrible! Have they caught him?"

"I don't know, but it shouldn't take them long, unless he disabled his PID. Even then, they'll get him eventually."

"You weren't badly hurt?"

"A flesh wound." He saw no purpose telling her about the young woman. She would probably hear it on the news anyway.

After a while, she turned and looked at him. "I was startled to hear Readman call an election."

"It caught everybody flatfooted, all right."

"Why call one now when the Coalition is down in the polls? They don't have to go until October."

"The lifeliner scandal has hit them hard, but they must have a strategy to deal with it, or they wouldn't have called one. Labor's polling numbers aren't good either."

"I wish I'd followed politics more," Cariana said. "I watch the newscasts and listen to commentators, but it's remote, not my business. It didn't bother me."

"That's the problem. Most people don't want to be bothered until it touches them in some personal way. Everybody has the right to vote, but people don't understand the power of that vote, content to drift."

"Electioneering already, Mr. Bannon?"

Nash chuckled. "I guess I am. Seriously, though. This may be a pivotal election and what might be our last chance to set some things right. If we squander it, we'll end up in a police state."

"You can't mean that!"

"I do mean it. If the Coalition wins and they manage to change the Constitution to allow fixed four-year terms for both Houses, I fear you and I won't have a future. And neither will any lifeliner in this country."

Cariana didn't say anything, but her somber look said it all. As well it might.

"But enough of this talk," Nash said. "I have a lunch treat for you."

He steered her past crowded tables filled with animated guests, loud conversation, laughter, and drinking. An attendant at the payment counter took them inside the more subdued en-closed section and showed them a reserved table tucked into a corner, the ceiling-high glass panels providing a panoramic view of the Yarra and the city, and protection from outside heat. She filled their glasses with water, handed them leather-bound menus, and strode quickly into La Asiago's dark interior.

Cariana sighed and fanned her face with her hand. "This is better," she said and sipped some water.

Not very hot outside, but Nash appreciated the air-condition-ing. He gave the menu a cursory glance, having already made his selection. He did not pick the same meal every time, but he had been here often enough to know what he liked. He glanced at the full tables along the promenade, the strolling, hurrying crush of people, swept his eyes at the city, then sat back and relaxed.

He used to go hiking in the bush using only a compass, map and protractor for navigation, his smartphone GPS locator as backup. Despite modern safety devices, hikers got lost every year, particularly those venturing into the desert interior, and some died, forgetting that the Aussie wilderness was always dangerous for the unprepared. Some of his trips were only for a day, but occasionally, he would camp overnight beside a meandering stream, a fire at his side, surrounded by bush sounds and smells. It allowed him to escape, if only for a while.

He hadn't done it for some time, but he was younger then, and the world more forgiving, or perhaps he didn't notice the ugliness. The truth, he admitted, was much harsher. He allowed himself to ignore the ugliness. A major drag.

"I can't believe the crowd around here," Cariana commented.

"It's a nice day and people are taking advantage of it," Nash said.

Their harried waitress weaved her way between the tables toward them, a tablet in hand.

"Ready to order?"

Nash nodded to Cariana.

"I'll have grilled calamari to start with, then the insalata vegane."

"Seared scallops and the insalatadi fagiolini with chicken," Nash said. "No cheese."

"Very good. Anything to drink?"

"Try the Cavalli Lambrusco," he suggested to Cariana. "It's a delicate, light Italian red."

She shrugged and Nash looked at the waitress. "Two glasses."

She flashed them a working smile and hurried off.

"Nash Bannon, Senator," Cariana mused with a grin. "When you do something, you certainly do it on a grand scale."

"Not a done deal yet, my sweet. I have to get elected first, by no means a certainty."

"You're running on the Lifeliner Party ticket?"

"They're the only ones who can fund a campaign, and this one promises to be a no holds barred slugfest."

"You have my vote," she promised, and her eyes glittered with amusement.

"How can I lose?"

She leaned forward and fiddled with her glass. "Seriously, if you do get elected, you'll be moving to Canberra?"

"I expect I'll be spending a lot of time there." He reached for her hand and squeezed. "It doesn't mean we can't be together."

"You in Canberra and me in Melbourne. Not very appealing."

"This is important to me, Cariana, but I'll drop it if it means losing you, which is the last thing I want. I already had job offers."

Her eyebrows rose. "You did? That was fast. In Melbourne?"

"We can be together all the time."

She sipped her water. "I know that running for the Senate is important to you, and I know why you want to do it. You're not in Canberra yet, and we have time to work it all out." She paused and licked her lips. "About Aleya—"

"Where you go, she goes."

She sighed and nodded. "Thank you. I'm not committing to anything, mind you, it's only—"

"The idea of an instant family might put me off?" he suggested gently.

"Something like that."

"She has wormed her way into my heart, just as you have. There is no way I could contemplate living without her, which I will probably regret more than once," he added dryly, and Cariana laughed.

"My cube prince." She played with her glass, then her enchanting eyes met his. "I could very easily fall in love with you, Nash Bannon, and I think I already have," she whispered.

Something warm and pleasurable spread through him. She was his for the asking, but not yet. Neither of them could allow to be swept into a hormonal haze that might lead to emotional disaster. Both must confront and deal with genuine practical problems his election would create, and the resulting strain on their relationship. That lay in an uncertain future, though, In the meantime, he could again love and have companionship, realizing he'd been starved of both for too long. Sally would understand and approve.

Nash squeezed her hand again. "I love you, Cariana Lambert."

They started into each other's eyes, lost in a world of magic and fantasy. The magic faded when the waitress cleared her throat, entrée dishes in hand.

Chapter Six

The cab whined to a stop beside the long four-story brick building and Nash linked his PID to pay the fare, his thoughts still on the pleasant lunch with Cariana. He looked forward to tomorrow night's dinner without Aleya underfoot. He hoped there would be some kissing, but he wasn't sure about the 'other' stuff, as the little imp put it. There would be time enough when Cariana wanted that level of intimacy.

He got out and watched the cab drive off. At the turn of the century, this part of Carlton used to be somewhat seedy, full of old townhouses, rundown hole-in-the-wall small enterprises, and car repair shops. Following the 2023 crash, developers moved in and turned the neighborhood into a tree-lined, fashionable business hub sprinkled with restaurants, a lot of them specializing in Asian cuisine, and dormitories for RMIT and Melbourne University students.

Nash gazed at rows of reflective glass separating the floors of what used to be a derelict warehouse, and ambled toward the entrance. Each step committed him further, but he did not hesitate. According to Garrett, the Lifeliner Party picked up the building cheap, the owners glad to offload a liability, a decision they probably came to regret later. After spending a considerable amount on renovation, the party set up its national headquarters and a Help Center, surplus floor space rented to offset maintenance costs.

As he approached the entrance, he saw a man in a blue coverall cleaning graffiti off the brickwork. Nash paused and nodded at the wall.

"Trouble?"

The man gave him a measured look. "A vandal sprayed anti-lifeliner slogans last night. Security got him," he muttered and resumed his scrubbing.

Nash nodded and waited for the heavy frosted glass doors to slide back. The brightly lit modern lobby held a round gray table flanked by three cloth chairs. A potted plant filled the corner. A young woman, features grave, gave him a blank look. The teener sitting in the chair beside her stared vacantly at the street. Nash figured they were probably visiting the Help Center or one of the resident businesses.

He strode to the security desk. "Nash Bannon to see Mr. Warren Kairns."

"The Lifeliner Party?" the burly guard asked and tapped a tablet keyboard.

"That's right," Nash said as his PID received a request to link with the security system. He granted permission.

"They are expecting you. Mr. Kairns is on the top floor, sir. I'll let them know you're coming."

"Thanks." Nash nodded and strode toward a bank of two elevators.

He wasn't surprised at the level of security. Given what the building represented, he expected it to be tight. As the election campaign ramped up, it would probably become a whole lot tighter. He half expected to see placard-waving agitators outside.

A soft *ting* announced arrival to the fourth floor and the polished steel doors slid back. A tall woman, he judged her to be in her mid-twenties, black hair cut short framing a smiling face, extended a slim arm. Dressed in a dark blue shirt and slacks, she looked elegant without being office formal.

"Mr. Bannon? I am Margot Jarvis, Mr. Kairns' executive assistant," she said in a friendly, crisp voice. "Call me Margi."

"Glad to meet you…Margi. And I'm Nash," he said and shook hands.

"When I get to know you better," she bantered. "Please follow me."

Weighing her up, he sensed a strong personality, someone efficient and an overachiever. He wondered if she was a lifeliner, not possible to tell by merely looking at someone.

The open plan floor, well-lit from front/back windows, was laid out in current vogue: desks arranged in no particular order without partitions, lots of tall plants, and two large open spaces with low coffee tables and comfortable lounge chairs, all occupied by mostly young men and women engaged in lively discussion.

Margot noted his scrutiny. "The election announcement caught us on the hop and we're busy trashing out our strategy and tactics. The strategy is straightforward enough—win as many seats as possible. It's the tactics how to get there that'll keep us awake at night…and you," she added with a grin.

"Sounds ominous."

"We are *very* glad to have you on board, Mr. Bannon. When you agreed to run, our chances of picking up one of the fourteen Victorian Senate seats improved immeasurably."

She stopped beside a white ceiling-high door, knocked and went in. There was no label to identify the occupant. Nash figured if someone had business here, they would know who was behind the door.

"Warren, Mr. Bannon is here."

Waist-to-ceiling glass panels covered the entire street-facing wall. The elderly man behind a plain gray executive desk stood and grinned broadly. Chunky, a fringe of white above the ears, shirt undone at the collar, Kairns projected authority and magnetism. Nash felt an immediate rapport with him. Of middle height, the man strode briskly from his desk and held out his hand.

"Glad to see you, Mr. Bannon."

"Just Nash."

"And I'm Warren, seeing how we're going to be working together, hopefully for a long time." He turned to Margot. "I'll bring him around once I'm done."

She nodded to Nash, and closed the door after her.

"Remarkable girl," Kairns gushed as he pulled back a visitor chair beside a square coffee table tucked into the corner. "Have a seat."

"Thank you." Nash sat down and crossed his legs. "Is she—"

"A lifeliner? She most definitely is, and I'd be lost without her. She's only twenty-six, but her energy and commitment is consuming." Kairns sat down and also crossed his legs. "Not everyone here is a lifeliner, though."

"Garrett told me."

"Like any organization, we pick talent and ability. Being a lifeliner doesn't automatically endow an individual with either."

"And you think I have those qualities?" Nash asked jokingly, and Kairns snorted.

"You wouldn't be here if we thought you didn't. Garrett and I talked about you a number of times. For a while there, we didn't think we'd be able to get you. Fortunately for us, events conspired against you."

"An interesting way of putting it," Nash said dryly, liking Warren's easy style.

"By the way, how's your arm?"

"Nothing strenuous for a week, but I'll be fine. Thanks for asking."

Kairns clicked his tongue. "Nasty business, and we can expect more of the same. Still, it makes good publicity."

"That's what Garrett said."

"And he's right. You were fortunate to have someone like him looking after you."

"I have always found him to be a good friend."

"Care for coffee or something?"

"Not at the moment, thanks."

Nash sensed the older man appraising him, but he didn't mind the scrutiny. He had done it himself when interviewing prospective employees. In many respects, this session was also a job interview, but far more serious.

"I don't have to go over your academic and professional qualifications, Nash. We've already checked. However, before the Lifeliner Party invests considerable time and resources to get you elected, I want to know why you want to run for the Senate."

A simple question that underpinned a multi-faceted dimension of complexity, social and political. Kairns undoubtedly knew what lifeliners faced under policies advocated by the major parties. Nash had experienced them firsthand. Senate seats would give lifeliners a national voice to remove, or at least blunt them. However, Kairns' question a pass/fail test that went beyond the obvious.

"I want to affect social change…for everybody," Nash said with quiet determination.

When interviewing, he preferred straightforward to the point answers that distilled the question. It showed that the candidate had thought things through beyond standard replies listed in job interview guides. He knew Kairns looked for the same decisiveness and clarity.

The older man pursed his lips and nodded. "Not bad. We could use that as our campaign slogan, 'Lifeliner Party, a voice for social change'."

"Isn't that the primary reason why anyone runs for office?"

Kairns shrugged. "As a young idealist, perhaps. Regrettably, that's not the main reason why people run, and I think you know it. It's power, Nash. Why else would they put up with long working days, a lot of travel for some, and endure broken families? Power gives them the means to enact some change, but the overriding factor for most parliamentarians is to hold onto that power once they gain a seat. Electioneering promises fade to a distant second when confronted with inflexible party policies and internal factions. Believe me, I know."

Harsh as it sounded, Nash understood and accepted the blunt reality. He studied the machinations of all parties and behind the scenes power struggles while presenting a smiling united front for public consumption. Everybody saw through the phony façade, but were still prepared to pretend it didn't exist, and reelected the same ineffective politicians in the hope the next round of promises would be kept, knowing all the time they wouldn't.

Nash had not walked into this building blindfolded. He had read up on the Lifeliner Party, its successes and failures, and the powerbrokers who ran it. Material publicly available anyway. The party had not descended into factional infighting, primarily because it was led by a strong, focused executive. The organization yet to grow to a point where state branches held significant authority, which often led to fractured loyalties and power jockeying…and loss of direction.

He also knew about Warren Kairns. A NSW Liberal Party numbers man, former chief of staff to a Coalition prime minister, and a two-time campaign manager for the Liberals and the Nationals. In 2030 the Lifeliner Party lured him from Canberra to run the organization and win seats. Kairns proved his worth with success in the Victorian and NSW parliaments. Satisfying as that was, and having raised the party's public profile, he sought federal representation for lifeliners, without which they would merely be an irritating and ineffective twitter.

"I know you do, Warren," Nash said bleakly. "But if that's all there was to it, you'd have remained in Canberra. You wanted more, not only for yourself and the people you helped elect, or you would never have soiled your hands with a small-time operation like the Lifeliner Party and what it represented."

Kairns' mouth twitched. "You don't pull your punches, do you?"

"I told you why I want to run, and it's not for personal power, prestige or ego. I am not that naïve to deny that a Senate seat won't give me a degree of power, but I see it as a tool. If I fail, if the party fails, we will all suffer at the hands of an emerging autocratic regime, whether under Labor or the Coalition, where the rule of law and the institutions that underpin it are ignored. I don't want to see that happen."

"It might, you know," Kairns mused, and uncrossed his legs. "Despite our best efforts, it still might."

"Perhaps, but I will know that I made a stand. If you're looking for a wheeler-dealer and a power manipulator, men prepared to sacrifice principles for expediency, I'm not going to waste my time here."

Kairns stood, strode to a bookshelf and extracted a bottle and two tumblers from a tall drawer. He sat down and poured them two fingers of Blue Label Johnnie Walker whiskey. He picked up a glass and handed it to Nash.

"I'm going to have trouble with you, Mr. Bannon, but our opposition will have even more. I want to welcome you as a Life-liner Party federal Senate candidate—if you pass our vetting process."

Nash took the tumbler and smiled. "Garrett told me I'll come to regret my decision," he said and took a sip of the fine liquor.

Kairns chuckled. "Mr. Bartlett's oblique sense of humor." He took a pull of whiskey and leaned back. "Seriously, Nash, I knew why you wanted to run. I wanted to see if you did. "

Nash didn't say anything for a few timeless moments. He turned his head and gazed at the white-clad building across the street. The smart glass threw back his image.

"For years, the holoview showed me riots against lifeliners the world over: stabbings, beatings, cases of active discrimination. I had my cushy job, a nice apartment, and a secure future, provided I didn't tell anyone what I was. All those nasty things happened to someone else. Remote and clinical, it didn't touch me. Intellectually, I knew things were getting worse, but I was safe behind my wall as long as no one looked my way.

"Even with Sutton, he went through the motions, a blind instrument the government used for its own ends. It wasn't entirely personal. You know what made it personal, Warren? Not that I got shot this morning, but yesterday when three Humans Only

League thugs were out to beat my brains to paste. Until then, I didn't believe such unreasoning hatred existed. And you know why they were allowed to do that? Not because they were twisted inside." He waved his arm at the window. "It's the uncaring silence out there. Wrapped in their little worlds and problems, the people didn't want to know…like I didn't want to know. Close my eyes and it'll go away. Never mind that I would be waking to a living nightmare." Nash took a pull of whiskey. "That's the thing, Warren. I want to wake up to a world where I can smile, laugh, and sing, knowing that nobody gives a shit if I am a lifeliner. It's a fool's dream, I know, but even if I can't laugh or sing, as long as I don't wake to a nightmare, I figure I'm ahead. All the lifeliners out there will be ahead."

Kairns palmed his chin and nodded slowly. "Everybody has many reasons why they run for office, many of them conflicting. Most of them worked a long time in the party machine before managing to overcome the gauntlet of internal backstabbing and preselection. Once elected, their outlook on the political process is often hopelessly jaded and the original reasons for running forgotten. Feed the constituents enough bull to get reelected, then claw for a ministerial position or the shadow front bench, making sure his colleague doesn't succeed in doing a character assassination number on him for that same posting. It can be exciting playing the game, but everybody reaches a point where they start to question themselves. Was the loss of personal integrity worth the gain? That's what happened to me, Nash. Playing their games, politicians everywhere have forgotten why they were elected. They forgot the people. I'm simplifying, of course, but you've seen the process at work yourself. It's amazing that anything actually gets done."

He took another sip, his eyes somewhere far away. "Garrett was right when he said you'll regret this, but someone has to step up and say it's enough. I know how the system works and I can manipulate it, but I don't have your vision and moral purpose. I've played the game too long. All I can do, all the party can do, is give you the best chance possible to see your vision realized, even when the deck is stacked against you. You and our other candidates have something in you I haven't seen for a while. Something I thought didn't exist anymore." He nodded, perhaps to himself, for memories past, then looked up, once again the executive.

"See me before you leave. I want to introduce you to the senior staff, including Curtis Sands. He's looking forward to meeting you. Right now, I'll hand you over to Margi's tender ministrations. You need to bone up on the party's policies, the mechanics of electioneering, conducting interviews, and handling your opposition. To speak with authority, you must be familiar with domestic and international politics and economics, federal and state relations, and have a working knowledge of every ministerial portfolio. It is particularly important that you understand the social issues relevant to each portfolio, because that's what matters to people. You probably have a good grounding on all those things already. We need to fill in the blanks. With your memory, that won't be a problem. First, we have to sign you up as a party member and register you as a candidate with the Electoral Office. A short campaign can be an advantage, provided we exploit available opportunities, and the government has given us several. Where there isn't an obvious opportunity—"

"You create one," Nash quipped wryly, and Kairns laughed.

"Damn right."

Nash uncrossed his legs and leaned forward. "I'm bothered about something, Warren."

"Let's have it."

"Garrett told me that campaigns are run on emotion by exposing people's fears and concerns, and then blame their problems on the opponent. If necessary, he said, you create that fear. I cannot reconcile that with what he told me about running a clean campaign."

"Nothing wrong with your eidetic memory, I see. He and I spoke about that this morning."

"How does this make the Lifeliner Party different from the others?"

"Garrett oversimplified, but he wasn't far off the mark either. This will be a dog-eat-dog fight, and you better accept this right now. More so because you're a lifeliner candidate with all the emotive baggage that comes with the label. However, we *will* be running a clean campaign, but that doesn't mean we cannot exploit or create favorable opportunities. When you're playing in a mud pit, you're bound to get your hands dirty." Kairns' eyes were hard and probing. "You don't look convinced."

Nash sighed. "Seeing how previous elections were run, I understand the need, but it's tough having my illusions shattered."

"We do what we must, but that doesn't mean we have to lose our honor along the way. Don't worry too much about it. You'll understand more once you finish your indoctrination."

"I hope so."

"You will."

"How do you want me to handle things with the media while I'm still in the public eye, probably not for long?"

"Margi will walk you through it. Basically, you toe the party line, but within those constraints, you are free to express your feelings and reasons for running. When you read our policies, you'll find they have much in common with your own objectives. We'll manage your public image, but you'll have to know your subject matter. You cannot afford to get tripped up by some wiseass reporter. That's instant death, but we'll teach you how to handle such questions, and believe me, they'll come your way."

"You'll be doing this with every candidate?"

"Everybody gets the same treatment. Dry runs will prove if we made the right choice. I'd rather have a single candidate who measures up, than a handful who aren't prepared. It takes one gaffe to taint an entire campaign and the party. We cannot allow that to happen."

"Garrett told me you will field a candidate in every state and the Capital Territory—"

"Four men and three women. Tamara Reed served two terms in the Queensland parliament and should be a great asset. Rodney Stevenson is a numbers man in our NSW branch—"

"Like you?" Nash asked with a grin, and Kairns chuckled.

"Nobody is like me. If elected, he'll be the Senate party Whip. The rest of you are all rookies. We simply don't have the financial resources to run in the Northern Territory, and they don't have a lifeliner problem…yet. The Electoral Commission will pay us around sixty cents for every primary vote we get, which will help cover some of our campaign costs, but that happens after the election, and doesn't help meet our up-front costs. The party gets donations like everybody else, but they are always less than what it costs to run a national campaign." Kairns cocked an eyebrow. "You'll be spending some of your time doing fundraisers."

Expected, Nash still winced, and Kairns chuckled. "No candidate I know of enjoys doing them, but it's one of the evils you guys have to put up with. There is one evil we won't have to face, though."

"Donation corruption," Nash said.

Prior to 2024, disclosure of donations made during campaigns were not required until after an election. Coupled with the complex interaction between state and federal donation laws, the opaque relationship between parties and a web of associated fundraising entities had obscured transparency. Bowing to public pressure, the Labor government of the day, with reluctant support from the Coalition, passed a law requiring disclosure of all donations above $5,000 regardless of when it is made, the information publicly accessible from the Electoral Commission website.

"The system is now more transparent, but party bean counters have to work harder for their money," Kairns agreed.

"Will I get to meet any of the other candidates?"

"Unlikely, unless one of them has a reason to come to Melbourne. You are a Victorian candidate, and Melbourne will be your primary beat. You'll be campaigning in regional cities, but

Melbourne holds the population and voters we need to capture."
Kairns rose and offered his hand. "Welcome to the team, Nash,
unless you want to change your mind. It's not too late, you
know."

Nash stood, grinned, and clasped the older man's hand. "I
want to run *before* it is too late."

Kairns lost his jovial look and nodded. "This is no ordinary
campaign, Nash. You obviously realize that. For what it's worth,
I offer you one piece of advice. When talking to reporters, show
passion and sincerity. Voters are sick of slick spin and will respond to someone young who isn't a product of a party machine."

"Thanks, Warren. I'll remember that."

Kairns nodded, strode to the door and jerked it open.
"Margi!"

Nash saw her disengage herself from a small group and hurry
toward the office.

"Take him away," Kairns growled, waited for Nash to walk
out, then shut the door with a flick of his wrist.

Margot gave him a speculative look. "Not ready to walk away
yet?"

"We'll see after you're done with me," Nash said wryly.

She laughed and extended an arm. "This way. You'll be spending the next two days reading. There is a lot of material to cover,
and it's laid out in a sequence you should follow. On Monday, be
here at seven. That's when we'll start doing media dry runs."

"Seven, eh?"

She paused before a door, her hand on the handle. "Mr. Bannon, until election day, this will be a 24/7 effort. Accept that now
and adjust your personal life accordingly." She noted his glum
expression and scrunched her nose. "It won't be that bad, but
you'll have an intense five weeks."

Nash wondered what Canberra would be like...if he got
elected.

"With your drive, Margi, I'm surprised that you're not running for office."

"I'm an organizer and gofer. I get things done and I like what I'm doing. Run for office? Maybe next time," she said firmly and walked into the room.

He could have been in a dentist's waiting room. A holoview wall cycled through spooling colors. Two soft beige couches fronted a rectangular glass-top coffee table. The low wall cabinet had all the gear for making coffee and tea.

"We call it 'The Room'," Margot explained with a grin. "Some call it 'The dungeon'. This is where we'll be doing most of the one-on-one dry runs. Crowd management and open air interviews are more fun, and we'll be doing them with one of my think groups outside." She walked to the cabinet, picked up some papers and held them to him. "Read and sign. We don't expect our candidates to be involved financially, but if you want to make a donation, we won't throw it back. I'll tell you later how to make one."

Nash scanned the documents, wondering what governments and organizations would do without forms. The Lifeliner Party membership and Electoral Office forms were already prefilled. He dashed off his signature and gave her the papers.

"Right, let's get started." She turned to the holoview. "Roger, link with Mr. Bannon."

Nash wondered about Roger as a computer name. Someone in her past like Sally? He received a request to his PID and authorized the link. The holoview immediately displayed a menu list of topics.

"You now have access to all orientation material. Access is available at any wall station through your PID, which means you can do this at home in a more conducive environment. Save your questions for Monday. As you go through the material, you'll find most of them answered anyway."

"I do have one question, Margi. Access to this building."

"Security has given you 24/7 access into the building and this floor."

"You trust me that much?"

She grinned. "Everything of importance is held in encrypted computer files on a need-to-know basis. To help you organize things, consider this campaign as one of your projects. Don't worry about appearance schedules. We'll manage those for you. Use the system to set up whatever personal files you need. Only you, Warren, Sands, and I will have access. I strongly suggest that you copy any emails, phone messages and conversations that relate to the campaign to our system."

"I have already been thinking along those lines."

Margot waved at the holoview. "Follow the initial sequence of topics as they are laid out. When you get to sections such as global politics, economics and such, use your discretion. Every section has links to additional material available from scholarly sources. Wikipedia is tremendously useful, but it is not always reliable or accurate. When you are interviewed, use statistics and quote resources without being pedantic."

"People don't like a pushy smartass."

Margot's expression did not change. "They don't. Always project a positive image and never descend into personalities. The media thrives on it at the expense of genuine policy discourse. It feeds viewer desire for the dramatic and the scandalous. However, when they get over their chuckles, they'll remember the strength or weakness of your message. If you cannot answer a question, deflect your ignorance by saying it is something you have to look into. Voters like honesty. Contrary to some opinion, they're not stupid. You try to snow them, they'll see through you right away, and that's electoral death. We'll have dry runs to make sure you get it."

"I get it already," Nash said quietly, sobered by the realization he was entering a totally new and alien world of public exposure. It looked so different watching it in the holoview.

"Intellectually perhaps, but you have to feel it inside, and you will once we get through with you."

Nash shook his head. "And here I was, thinking that all I had to do is front up to reporters and moan how life is tough for lifeliners."

Margot laughed. "Welcome to realpolitik...Nash."

He stripped off his jacket and mentally rolled up his sleeves. The amount of information he needed to absorb considerable, but not overwhelming. It would be a challenge for a normal person, but not for his eidetic memory. If he and Mark could wade through an abridged twelve-volume Encyclopedia Britannica, what Margot laid out for him wasn't at all daunting.

"Mr. Bartlett is calling," his PID announced.

Nash raised a finger. "Excuse me, Margi." She nodded as he dug out his cell.

"Hi, Garrett."

"I hope I'm not interrupting, but under the circumstances, I felt you would want to hear this."

"I'm in class doing homework," Nash quipped.

"With the formidable Miss Jarvis?"

"She's a hard taskmaster. What have you got?"

"G.S. & B. filed a defamation suit against Channel Seven. When they got the word, their chief legal weenie called. They're offering $200K in damages and a public retraction. It's a good deal and I recommend you take it. You've made your point, and a retraction will put other networks on notice."

"Agreed, and I accept. I must say, that was quick work."

"They didn't have a leg to stand on and knew it. I'm still waiting to hear from CIS, but I doubt they'll roll over this easily."

"Thanks for the update, Garrett."

The barrister grinned wickedly. "Thank me after you get my bill."

Nash smiled as he pocketed the smartphone.

"Defamation action?" Margot queried with a raised eyebrow.

"Yesterday, Seven broadcast a story that my arrest by Sutton was prompted on evidence from the Humans Only League that I and a group of lifeliners planned an attack on the Flinders Street station."

"The government didn't waste any time shifting the focus to you."

"A blunder that backfired badly."

"This is only the first salvo, Nash. Trust me. You'll be fielding other cannonballs."

During a coffee break, Nash appraised this capable woman.

"Tell me something, Margi. If you're loading every one of your candidates with this much information, why is it that the party holds only two seats in the Victorian Parliament?"

"Social inertia," she replied promptly, "and resource constraints. You may not think so, but we did well to secure two seats in the Upper House, and we almost got a Senate seat in the 2030 federal election, but Labor and the Coalition swapped preferences to keep us out."

"They might do the same thing this time around."

"That's why it's so important that we strike deals with the independents to take us over the line."

Around four-forty, she called it a day to allow everything to sink in, and stepped out. When she returned, she apologized, saying that Warren cannot see him. He was tied up in a meeting, but he would be available on Monday.

Head full of new data, Nash strode casually toward Swanston Street to catch a tram going up St. Kilda Road. For someone without a job, he found the day mentally exhausting and welcomed having a free evening and weekend, mindful of Margot's warning that getting elected would be a 24/7 effort. The prospect of long days didn't faze him. He actually found the challenge exciting, his logical mind already visualizing a spreadsheet of issues, risks, threats, and actions. As the campaign developed, so would his spreadsheet, but at least he had a working framework that reduced the next five weeks into something manageable. There was also Margot and the party machine to help him. This was doable, he decided confidently.

Getting elected was not entirely in his or the party's hands. A lot depended on what his opposition would do to discredit him and his message, which he was certain they would try, and what he could do to counter them. Nash found himself in a most curious situation, perhaps even amusing, but definitely ironic. After spending most of his life guarding his identity, he would now be proclaiming it.

The wry smile he wore attracted more than one passing glance.

Still high, the sun glared at the city, the air hot and heavy. With rush hour on—actually from three to six—cars crawled along clogged streets in the usual Friday afternoon tangle to escape for the weekend. Dark clouds bunched themselves on the western horizon, heralding a possible change. Melbourne needed a good downpour or two. Nash didn't worry about it, unable to do anything one way or another.

At the tram stop, he waited stoically with other commuters. When the practically empty tram rolled in—it would load up as it made its way through the CBD—he found a seat and asked his PID for a time check: 5:00 pm. He connected his cell to ABC in radio mode as the intro music finished.

"Welcome to the news summary on Friday, January 30, 2032. The headlines: President Ngarra formally dissolved both houses of Parliament following a visit by Prime Minister Atarah Readman, clearing the way for an election on March 6. A special program of Insiders *on Sunday at 9 am, will analyze the reasons for the snap election and likely outcome."*

Nash made a note to himself to watch it, and other political commentary segments, now that he was priming himself to engage with people. Margi would not need to tell him why this was necessary.

"The United States Supreme Court has declared President Mackay's executive order to reinstate the Lifeliner Act illegal. The Washington Post *and other leading publications criticized the President for ignoring the Constitution and the rule of law. The American Civil Liberties Union protesters are picketing the White House demanding withdrawal of the Act."*

Nash exhaled softly and shook his head, wishing the protesters luck. The declaration a symbolic gesture at best, as it had no effect if the Administration chose to ignore the ruling, unless the American Civil Liberties Union mounted an action in the circuit court to issue an arrest warrant against the President for contempt. Even if they managed to get one, the warrant would be unenforceable, as a U.S. marshal trying to serve it had no hope of getting past the president's protection detail.

"In a controversial decision backed by Germany, France, Italy, and Spain, the European Union Parliament in Brussels passed into law the Citizenship Act, requiring identification and registration of all lifeliners, resident or visitor, which has generated a major diplomatic rift with Great Britain, Denmark, Norway, and Sweden, who declared the law discriminatory and not binding. The Australian Foreign Affairs minister was not available for comment."

The announcement made Nash scowl. No travel for him to Europe, it seems. He had a grim suspicion that talks between Mackay and President Cheng Hung in May would have more than normalization of the Korean peninsula on their agenda. It appeared the world powers were uniting in a common front against lifeliners.

"Following illegal detention of Mr. Nash Bannon and Adam Gatt on Wednesday by Commander Lyle Sutton, the head of the Australian Federal Police tendered his resignation to Attorney-General Van Ross. At the arraignment hearing this afternoon, lawyers acting for Mr. Sutton moved for dismissal of all charges against their client, denied by the court. Bail was set at two hundred thousand dollars and promptly paid.

"Yesterday, Channel Seven aired a story alleging that Mr. Bannon and a group of lifeliners planned an attack on the Flinders Street station. G.S. & B. filed a defamation suit and the network apologized to Mr. Bannon and retracted the story with an offer of an undisclosed amount in damages.

"In a separate action, G.S. & B. filed a suit with the Human Rights and Equal Opportunity Commission against IBM for terminating Mr. Bannon's employment because he is a lifeliner."

Nash hoped IBM would choose to settle this promptly to avoid damaging media glare, but it would take a lot more than $200K to shut him up. What he didn't like was the idea of Sutton out on bail.

"In a startling development, the Lifeliner Party spokesperson announced that Mr. Bannon will be seeking election to the federal Senate. Restrictive legislation around the world poses a grave threat to minority groups everywhere, not only lifeliners, the spokesperson said. Mr. Bannon will add his voice to advocate social change and restrain Canberra's growing autocracy.

"Tomorrow's weather—"

Nash told his PID to cut the link. Kairns had not wasted any time seizing the moment. He did not blame him. Advocating social change required raising public awareness as a first step, not that they needed much raising. What they did need was a coherent bite-size clarification of all issues that emphasized genuine dangers for everybody inherent in autocratic rule. Time to wake the silent majority, because only their votes would bring him and other Lifeliner Party candidates over the line.

By the time the tram arrived at the Federation Square stop, there was practically standing room only, to the open dismay of those scrambling to board. A heavily pregnant young Asian woman lugging a bag looked around for a seat and stoically grasped a stanchion for support. Nash got up and touched her shoulder.

"Excuse me, there's an empty seat here."

She smiled faintly. "Where?"

Nash turned to point at his seat. The teenager who now sat there gazed vacantly out the window.

"That seat is taken," Nash told him mildly.

The youngster gave him an insolent stare. "Taken by me."

The passengers around him had become interested in the proceedings.

"That was my seat, and I wanted this lady to have it."

"Well, that's tough, 'cause I got it now."

"You don't want to do this the hard way, boy."

"Rack off, mother."

"Don't say I didn't warn you." Nash grabbed the kid's neck, squeezed the larynx, and dragged him into the aisle.

"Hey!" the youngster squealed, eyes bulging. "Let go!"

Nash turned to the lady and smiled. "Your seat."

The woman nodded self-consciously and eased herself down.

Nash looked at the youngster trying to free himself. "One peep out of you and I'll break it. Got it...mother?" To make sure the kid did get it, he squeezed a little harder. The kid gave a strangled croak and nodded. "I'll be right here in case you're tempted to change your mind," Nash grated and shoved him against the stanchion.

The kid gasped for breath and massaged his neck, glaring raw hate. One of the passengers grinned and began to clap slowly. Others cheered and picked up the clapping.

"Kids these days got no respect," someone muttered.

"I'll call the dobers on you," the youngster snarled.

Nash dug out his cell. "You can do it right now."

The kid mumbled something and hung his head.

As the tram clattered toward the Arts Center, Nash glanced at the park on the other side of the tracks. He spotted the naked statue of a Greek athlete in a hammer throw position, curious to see if the hammer would still be there. Vandals regularly cut off the ball and connecting rod, and the local council always replaced it. Glad to see the statue whole this time, wondering how long it would remain so.

The tram stopped at Bromby Street and Nash got off, but not before giving the youngster beside him a stern look. He hoped the kid would learn some manners from the experience, but his type rarely did. What bothered him, as the lady looked for a seat, nobody appeared eager to give up their own. Somewhere along the line, people have lost common courtesy. A symptom of social decay increasingly prevalent in large cities? Sociologists seemed to think so, attributing the behavior as another factor of modern high-density pressure living. So many millions squeezed into one place, yet individually alone, resenting intrusion of another person into the little spot they had carved out for themselves. It explained the regular Friday afternoon exodus into the countryside where they wouldn't have to see another person for a couple of days.

Nash liked the open outdoors, but he never had the urge to get away from the city, feeling content in his apartment. Mark was the same. Most lifeliners he spoke to, also felt comfortable living in the city. A genetic adaptation that enabled them to cope? Nash wasn't sure. He reminded himself to ask Cariana over dinner tomorrow night. She might know. The fact that she kept a house at Woodend was revealing, but he did not want to read too much into it.

A refreshing shower when he got home and a change of clothing made him feel immediately better. Although the tram was air-conditioned, the crush of people made the ride stifling and uncomfortable in the afternoon swelter. He mixed himself a bourbon and ginger ale with ice and took a long pull. Tall glass in hand, he rummaged through the fridge trying to decide what to have for dinner. He did not want to cook or go out. He decided to have a mixed salad with smoked salmon and chardonnay on the side.

At six, he watched world news on SBS. The commercial channels concentrated mostly on local events. At six-thirty, he switched to ABC's *The Beat*, a program that provided thoughtful commentary by guest speakers on the day's events without the annoying ads. A cancerous problem with all such shows, they were heavy on speculation by self-styled chair experts who often presented personal bias, sometimes making a big deal out of nothing. That's why he liked the *7.30 Report*. The program relied on interviews and shied away from injecting editorial slant.

By the time he washed up and fixed himself a straight bourbon, the seven o'clock news was just finishing. Rowena Russell looked cool and unflappable as she made the introduction.

"Tonight, we have the Prime Minister, Atarah Readman, and the Labor Party leader, Macey Gardner, to discuss some of the issues important to the electorate in the upcoming election." She turned to her guest. *"Prime Minister, welcome to the* 7.30 Report.*"*

Readman nodded and produced her stock restrained smile. At forty-nine, she still had her youthful looks, but her hazel eyes belonged to someone far older. Wearing a light gray business jacket with short sleeves, white shirt, she projected authority.

"Glad to be here, Rowena," she replied evenly in a deep voice.

"Minister Gibbs Gilmore stated that his activities were sanctioned at the highest level of the Liberal Party with Opposition support. Were they?"

Russell certainly didn't pull her questions, Nash mused.

"I had no knowledge that Mr. Gilmore authorized the Australian Federal Police to pursue lifeliners, or that he allegedly set up the Humans Only League. I certainly did not know that he initiated a policy to sterilize Australian citizens."

"You admit then, that lifeliners are citizens under law, and enjoy the same rights and privileges affirmed by the High Court?"

Realizing that she may have trapped herself, Readman cleared her throat.

"My priority, and the priority of my government, has always been focused on protecting Australian citizens from external and internal threats."

"Prime Minister, do you consider lifeliners an existential threat to our society?"

"Extremist elements consider them a threat, borne out of irrational fear and ignorance. My government has sought to discredit that fear through public education programs and measures designed to safeguard every citizen."

"Measures such as the Personal Identification Device tracking feature announced by Minister Neil Travers, designed to identify lifeliners?"

"The PID tracking feature has obvious social benefits, Rowena, and was not set up to track lifeliners or to maintain lifeliner registers, which would contravene the ruling by the High Court."

"Is it true that the Signals Directorate is collecting all electronic communication, private and commercial, which implies the government is able to decrypt such communication?"

"I cannot comment on the operation of our national security agencies."

"Your call for a snap election has caught everyone by surprise, especially since you did not have to run until October. What prompted you to change your mind, given that your personal approval rating has been falling for a

number of weeks?"

Readman allowed herself a small smile. *"There is only one poll that counts, Rowena, and that's on election day when every citizen casts his or her vote in a democratic process. I called an early election because the Labor Party and the Senate crossbench contrived to block the Superannuation Act, a vital social and economic initiative, purely for partisan reasons, even though they acknowledge the merit of that legislation to be in the national interest. I want to expose to the people their hypocritical stand and bankrupt policies. A firm government that enjoys a clear mandate will ensure this country's ongoing prosperity and security."*

"Will you be conducting a simultaneous referendum to change the Constitution to allow a fixed four-year term for both Houses?"

"History has repeatedly demonstrated the disruptive nature of the existing flexible three-year election cycle. A fixed term of office will enable the government of the day to implement its legislative program without being sidetracked having to plan for the next election."

"A fixed term will not guarantee passage of legislation without Senate support."

"The crossbench members have on occasions been a stumbling block, but they represent a segment of voters, and a responsible government must be cognizant of that voice. However, the crossbench has too often focused on single issues at the expense of broader national interests. In cooperation with my Coalition partners, I will urge the voters to tick 'YES', and I trust the Labor Party will join me, as they too recognize the disruptive nature of the three-year cycle."

"Prime Minister, you are aware that President Elliot Mackay has issued an executive order to reinstate the Lifeliner Act. Yesterday, the European Union passed a similar law. It is widely rumored that the meeting between the U.S. and China in May will discuss the possibility that China will also enact draconian measures against lifeliners. If elected, will the Coalition table an equivalent of the Lifeliner Act?"

"As I stated earlier, my government will always take appropriate measures to safeguard and protect our new republic."

"Right now, the Coalition holds seventy-six lower House seats, five short of an absolute majority. You were only able to form government with the

*support of the Australian Conservatives, which many people believe was be-
trayal of Liberal Party values. Do you anticipate a voter backlash unless you
commit not to entertain a similar alliance should you fail to secure a majority?"*

*"The Coalition has more in common with the Conservatives than we have
differences. That was why we entered into an alliance to keep Labor out of
office. Every party likes to govern in its own right. When the electorate sees
the value of our policies, the Coalition expects to win back those five seats."*

*"Isn't it true, Prime Minister, that this partnership has forced the gov-
ernment to promote oppressive measures that further curtail people's rights in
the name of national security? Legislation formulated by the Australian
Conservatives?"*

*"Rowena, every piece of legislation is formulated to benefit the Australian
people. As a partner, the Conservatives provided valuable input into that
process."*

"Thank you for appearing on the program, Prime Minister."

"Thank you for having me."

Nash took a sip of whiskey, deep in thought. Rowena Russell
had not been intimidated by interviewing the Prime Minister, going for the jugular with every question. Readman's responses
were concise and measured, but very revealing in what she did
not say, sometimes answering a question that had not been
asked…something Mark told him to cultivate.

*"My next guest is the Labor Party leader, Macey Gardner, former
ACTU president and Rhodes Scholar. Welcome to the program."*

*"I have always enjoyed our lively discussions, Rowena, and I anticipate
this one will enlighten the voters."*

At forty-four, a staunch republican, Gardner was young to
lead a major political party, but people who underestimated his
drive and ruthlessness paid the price of banishment for their mistake. Former boss of the infamous CFMEU, he reformed the
movement into an effective organization that focused on the
needs of its members, abandoning old-style militant standover
tactics with employers. A savage preselection battle six years ago
forced an elderly Labor MP to resign and Gardner entered the

federal parliament in a by-election.

"This will be your first election as leader of the parliamentary Labor Party. The latest Morgan Poll shows the party nine points behind the Coalition, 38 to 47. With these numbers, this may also be your last election as leader."

Gardner gave a faint smile. He projected a movie star image: tall, slim, an engaging debater, and popular with the electorate. The electorate did not question his charm, but outdated socialist policies forced on him by the party's National Executive. He fought hard to free the parliamentary wing from the smothering backroom left-leaning numbers men, but the party machine resisted moves that would dilute its authority, even when that cost them elections.

"As the Prime Minister commented a moment ago, there is only one poll that counts. The party faces a challenge, but we only need a swing of seven percent to win government. In the current social and economic climate, an achievable objective."

"Do you think it realistic that you can win thirteen seats?"

"The 2030 election was an anomaly that allowed the Coalition to secure what were traditionally Labor seats. In several cases by a margin of less than one percent. Given the broad dissatisfaction with the Coalition's performance, we expect to regain those seats."

"Can you elaborate on areas where you feel the Coalition has failed the electorate?"

"The Labor Party will always support legislation that safeguards national security, but not at the expense of eroding individual freedoms. Of particular concern were intrusive powers granted to the Department of Home Affairs."

"When the legislation was debated in 2031, the Labor Party voted to pass it."

Gardner raised a finger. *"With amendments that removed several odious segments."*

"When Minister Neil Travers announced the introduction of a PID tracking feature, you indicated the Labor Party would support the legislation. Legislation that would enable the police and intelligence agencies to track and

monitor the movement of every citizen, including lifeliners, which is widely accepted as being the real reason for its introduction."

"It can be interpreted that way, but our amendments guaranteed individual right of free movement with the ability to switch off the feature."

"Last week, the Victorian Premier, Raines Latham, gave the police power to interrogate PIDs without obtaining prior permission. He could not have done this without approval from the Labor National Executive and support of the federal wing. Is this something Labor wants to implement nationally?"

"The ability to interrogate a PID has obvious advantages in the fight against criminal elements in our society. However, I recognize that unfettered access can be seen as unwarranted violation of privacy. For that reason, Premier Latham has allowed individuals to partially block this function. If elected, we will table legislation to authorize access on a national basis."

"Why has the Labor Party resisted revealing its policy on lifeliners?"

"A detailed policy statement will be released shortly, but in summary, Labor views lifeliners as citizens under the 2027 UN reaffirmation of Human Rights, and the 2029 Curtis Sands High Court ruling. Nevertheless, the emergence of lifeliners has fractured the social fabric and we need to deal with the problem in a way that will maintain dignity and freedom for all."

"Does this dignity include sterilization, unlawful detention, and open discrimination?"

"Rowena, I was shocked by the revelation that the Australian Federal Police practiced forced sterilization of lifeliners. This is not only personally repugnant, but violates our laws and several international treaties to which Australia is a signatory."

"The practice might be personally repugnant, Mr. Gardner, but Mr. Gibbs Gilmore stated that this was approved by leaders of all major parties, which means you had knowledge of his program."

"Mr. Gilmore overstepped his authority and tried to shift the blame away from himself. The Labor Party would never condone such a measure against lifeliners or any other Australian citizen."

"That still doesn't answer my question."

"I can state categorically that I did not know the AFP was conducting a sterilization program."

"*Did you know that Mr. Gilmore authorized creation of the Humans Only League, whose sole purpose was to disseminate anti-lifeliner propaganda and harass anyone suspected of being a lifeliner?*"

"*Again, I deny any knowledge of this, and I resent the insinuation, Rowena.*"

"*There have been suggestions from some quarters that you yourself may be a lifeliner.*"

Instead of becoming annoyed, Gardner laughed. "*I heard the rumors. Does that mean every tall, slim man who exhibits some intelligence must be a lifeliner? I am surprised by the shallowness of your question.*"

"*Thank you for appearing on the program, Mr. Gardner.*"

"*Always a pleasure.*"

Russell faced the camera and smiled. "*Tune in to* Insiders *on Sunday at 9:00 am, for in-depth coverage—*"

"Sally, disconnect."

Nash sat back and rubbed his chin. Technically, both leaders have given a polished performance without actually saying anything of substance, pointing a finger at each other. It wasn't any wonder that people have switched off, tired of being patronized. Laying things on the line as Margi said will definitely not appeal to everyone, but sincerity and conviction was likely to get him more traction than trotting out alarmist slogans and hollow assurances. He understood that voters wanted politicians to voice and address issues touching them on a personal level, not promises impossible to keep. Politics had been run as a party game for too long. Kairns was right about that. Politicians only noticed voters when it came time to get reelected. Once safe in their seat, it was game on again. It came as no surprise that people rated politicians near the bottom of every trustworthiness list.

To win his Senate seat, Nash understood that he had to cultivate trust and do what he said without glossy spin varnish. Even if he didn't win, he needed to make an impression and get people thinking. His message must be relevant to everybody, simple as that.

Simple, right…

Rowena's insinuation that Gardner himself might be a lifeliner came out of nowhere. True or not, it would set some people wondering. Nash wondered himself...at the producer who set Rowena's script.

Speculation wasn't going to get him anywhere. He took a sip and sighed. Time for some homework.

"Sally, connect to Roger, Lifeliner Party."

"Connection established."

The holoview rippled and steadied to show his training menu.

"Welcome back, Mr. Bannon," the computer announced in a pleasant masculine voice.

"Thank you, Roger. Expand item one."

He had gone over each menu item with Margi, including individual sections and sub-sections, and had a working structural map he could visualize. Nevertheless, when Kairns said the party wanted to fill in blanks in his knowledge, he omitted to say they would use a tip truck to do it.

Focus and organization, old son.

He opened the text on the revised Australian Constitution and began to read.

* * *

Once Nash hit Calder freeway, the drive out of the city was easy. He set cruise control to 110, told the car to turn on FM 103.5, and relaxed to a nice classical piece. He could have taken an Uber skycab to Woodend, but he preferred using his car and a chance to see the countryside.

The suburban sprawl faded behind him and opened into gently rolling fields of native grass and scattered trees. There hadn't been any working farms here for decades. The face of agriculture had transformed from small holdings into corporate agribusinesses. Family farming had not totally disappeared, but to survive, many had banded together into computer-operated cooperatives. Small-time farmers who held on and kept going faded away when age caught up with them; their children not interested to work the land for a meager return.

From Gisborne, the freeway cut through native forest, two concrete ribbons that went all the way to Mildura on the Vic/NSW border and beyond. After sixteen minutes, he spied a large green board that indicated the Woodend turnoff and glanced at the digital clock. It took him fifty minutes to get here, which wasn't bad, but this was Saturday. He hated to think what it would be like during the week, glad he didn't have to endure it. Woodend had a high-speed train to Melbourne, but many people still chose to drive into the city. If they wanted to put up with the twice-daily crawl and scandalous parking expenses, they were welcome to it.

He took the off-ramp and drove toward the old part of Woodend. People seemed to live well here. Large plots, lots of trees everywhere, neat lawns, and broad frontages. Nash soaked in the easier pace of life and understood why Cariana liked the place. Her house one block from the center, a half-hectare lot with green colorbond fencing on the sides. The yellow stone, black-tiled cottage, a bed of mixed flowers along the front, revealed neatly mowed grass as he drove up the red gravel driveway, stones crunching under the tires. A pair of rainbow rosellas fluttered from a nearby white gum and settled on a wattle. Five minutes early, he figured Cariana wouldn't mind.

He stepped out of the car and took a deep breath of eucalyptus-scented air. The evening warm, but he felt freshness typical of country towns. Sleep would come easily here. On the broad veranda, a black cat lay curled near the front door. It deigned to look at him with green eyes, then resumed its meditation.

The heavy wooden door, varnished to a rich brown sheen, looked formidable. Not seeing a doorbell pad, he sent a query with his PID. He heard hurried footsteps and the door opened.

Cariana wore white slacks and a cream shirt with full-length sleeves. Her golden hair spilled down her back. She didn't wear any shoes, which made her appear shorter. Her cheek dimpled in a welcoming smile.

"I see you managed to get past Felix." She inclined her head at the cat.

"Yours?"

"My neighbor's, but he thinks he owns the place. I've got two magpies who patrol my backyard. They're the real owners."

"I would have thought there'd be fur and feathers everywhere."

"It's a live and let live arrangement. How do you like my retreat?"

"Seeing it, I know why you like coming here."

He looked deep into her almond eyes and kissed her, a gentle, sensuous caress that melted her lips. Her arms went around his neck and she pressed herself against him. He winced when his shoulder gave a protesting twinge and she immediately disengaged herself.

"Sorry. I forgot."

"It's okay." His arms went around her. "Shall we try that again?"

She leaned into his embrace. When they came up for air, he brushed her chin.

"You look radiant," he whispered tenderly.

"And you are a wolf," she declared softly and pulled back.

He opened his shopping bag and held out a flat package. "For you."

She raised an eyebrow. "What is it?"

"Teuscher, the finest Swiss chocolates in the world."

"Wow. Thank you." She flashed him a smile. "What else is in the bag?"

"A nice Barossa riesling. Crisp without being dry."

"That'll be useful. Come on in." She padded down a short corridor that opened into a dining/lounge room. Next to the cycling holoview wall stood an open fireplace. On his right lay a broad breakfast bench that separated a functional modern kitchen filled with warm cooking smells.

"There used to be a wall here," she explained as she checked a simmering pot, "but I had it taken down. Too confining. I like things open and airy."

"I noticed the large windows as I drove in," he said as he scanned the tastefully furnished lounge.

"The original ones did nothing for me. Too small. Care for a drink? I've got bourbon."

"Thanks. Make mine straight. You have floorboards everywhere?"

"Tasmanian oak."

"Don't tell me. Carpets don't do anything for you either," he said as he pulled back a breakfast stool and sat down.

"Boards are easy to clean and I think they look better than carpet."

She handed him his drink and pointed at the sofa. "Let's relax." She sank down and curled one leg under her.

He sat beside her and tasted the bourbon. "How is Aleya's slumber party?"

"I haven't heard from her, so it must be going well. And you?"

"Doing homework," he said and grinned at her puzzled expression. "I registered myself as a Senate candidate yesterday—"

"You told me you were going to do that."

"—and they've got me studying the art of character assassination. There is a lot of stuff to cover. I've been at it all day. Tomorrow will be more of the same."

"Not regretting your decision?"

"I don't mind being force-fed, and I expected something like this. I would have been surprised if they didn't have an orientation program. They are very organized and methodical how they do business. What about you?"

"Busy afternoon at The Alfred. Meetings mostly. Nobody gave me a hard time about my work at Parkville, something I appreciated. My research will go on, but with new protocols. Did I tell you Hardy resigned? Chopped off at the knees, more likely. He hasn't been charged with anything, but somebody had to wear the blame." Her eyes danced as she looked at him. "Did you watch the *7.30 Report* last night?"

"Russell did a number on the PM and Gardner. Neither said anything incriminating, but they're both polished media manipulators. More a sin of omission. It will get tougher as the campaign unravels."

"The idea that Gardner might be a lifeliner came out of nowhere."

"I must admit, he took it well," Nash said.

"Any possibility that it's true?"

"I doubt it, but it's got people talking."

"What about your campaign?"

Nash shrugged. "That's in the hands of the Lifeliner Party machine. I've got a serious, no-nonsense lady assigned as my minder. It's because of her that I'm doing homework."

"Poor you."

"Your sympathy is appreciated," he said dryly, and she chuckled.

Cariana rose and pointed at the heavy wooden table beside the window and curtsied. "Dinner is served, my lord."

Nash stood and bowed. "You are too gracious, my lady."

A magpie fluttered down onto the front lawn, raised its beak and let loose a clamoring warble. Felix pounced toward it and the magpie took flight with an indignant squawk.

"The front yard belongs to Felix," Cariana explained as she brought a steaming pot to the table. "They get even by mobbing him when he goes out back. Make yourself comfortable."

He pulled out a solid padded chair and eased himself down. A vase of assorted dry flowers at one end added a nice feminine touch. Cariana sat opposite him, picked up a cloth napkin and laid it across her lap. She nodded at the steaming pot.

"My own pumpkin soup recipe," she declared and pointed at a bowl of toasted croutons. "Add to taste."

He helped himself to the thick soup, added two spoons of croutons, and ground pepper over the lot.

"Don't forget the oil," she said and pointed at a small bottle.
"Oil?"

"Pumpkin oil. It enhances the flavor. Try it."

Willing to experiment, he poured a thin string of almost black oil over the soup, stirred it in, and gave it a cautious taste. The oil had a smoky aroma and a nutty flavor that reminded him of walnuts. He raised his eyebrows in appreciation.

"Excellent. I have to remember this when I make pumpkin soup."

She beamed as she loaded her bowl. "My neighbor introduced me to it. He's Greek. You can also add a bit to your salad. It makes a real difference."

"You learn new things every day," he murmured and dug into the delicious soup with vigor. "Where did you get the oil?" he asked after a pleasant silence. "I haven't seen it in any supermarket."

"They don't carry it. You have to go to one of the Italian specialty shops at the Vic Market for it. I'll give you a bottle."

He ladled himself another helping, marveling how well the soup and oil complemented each other. Finished, he dabbed his lips with the napkin and leaned back.

"That was terrific, thank you."

"I'm glad you liked it," Cariana said as she scooped out the remnants in her bowl. "I like to cook, but sometimes it's too much of a drag. Especially after a long day. You're lucky that you can work from home and have the time." She smiled and raised a finger. "Used to work, but you have more time now."

"Perhaps not with an election campaign to handle. I don't cook all the time either, but I find it helped me unwind and took my mind off work."

She regarded him with interest. "A novel approach to stress management."

"After a long stint at Parkville or the hospital, I can understand why you might not be bothered."

She stood, bowl in hand. "Done?" He nodded.

In the kitchen, he heard her open the oven and a pleasant baked odor filled the air. "Can I help?"

"You can get the wine and salad out of the fridge."

He retrieved a large glass bowl of mixed salad, stripped off the cling wrap, and placed it on the table. Getting out the riesling, he held up the bottle.

"Corker?"

"Bottom drawer," she said and pointed with her finger.

He opened the bottle and filled their glasses. She walked up, placed a black ceramic tray on the table and began carving the contents into generous squares. Finished, she sat down and turned a long wooden spatula toward him.

"Help yourself. It's lasagna with artificial mince. I figured you were not much into real meat."

"I enjoy it occasionally, but it doesn't form the bulk of my diet, and I like meat substitutes. These days, you can hardly tell the difference from the real thing."

"They've overcome early problems with texture and taste," Cariana agreed, "but real meat is complex and contains a range of nutrients not found in substitutes, but they're getting there."

Nash raised his glass. "To my shining constellation."

She touched her glass to his. "To my prince."

He stared into her eyes, totally captivated by this vibrant woman. Unpretentious, easy to talk to, a fun sense of humor, she made this cozy house complete. He felt totally comfortable and at ease being with her. Something of his hunger must have shown because she smiled faintly and took a sip.

"You're right. Crisp and not too dry."

He helped himself to a thick portion of lasagna and filled a small side bowl with salad smelling of pumpkin oil. The lasagna melted in his mouth, not at all chewy or overpowered with cheese.

After a few minutes, Cariana laid down her tools and looked at him. "I saw what the EU did. I couldn't believe it."

"They'll do the same thing here," Nash said soberly, "regardless of which party wins. All that talk about preserving people's security is window dressing. They're using lifeliners as a convenient vehicle to become more autocratic."

"You heard about increased attacks outside nightclubs? If this goes on, it won't be safe to go out."

"It's a worry, all right."

She waved a hand. "Let's not talk about it. Sorry I brought it up."

"Any new revelations with your research?" he asked, not minding a change of subject.

She shrugged. "The same old problem: identifying which switches have been turned on or off. We're looking at something we hardly understand, and some switches don't remain permanently open or closed. Comparison with normal human controls has helped us find a number of switches specific to lifeliners, but there are still a lot of unknowns. What makes my work even more complicated is that DNA changes are not uniform across all population groups. Add to that adjustments the body makes due to seasonal variations, and you've got a tangle of spaghetti. I've made some progress with a computer model that promises to unravel some of the mystery. What I need is a large data sample taken during the transition process into puberty when gene activity is at its peak. Unfortunately, such data is hard to come by. There is no way to tell which pubescent child will be a lifeliner, and there aren't too many lifeliner parents prepared to hand over their children for testing."

Nash's mouth twitched. "Understandable. Have you tested couples who are not lifeliners themselves, but have produced lifeliner children? Do you know which parent provides triggers that initiates the change?"

"Male or female, you mean? It's being looked into, but there is nothing definitive so far."

"It could also be hormonal, you know. From what I've read, it is still not clear how sperm and egg cells are coded. An embryo could be coded to be a lifeliner at conception, and puberty merely completes the transformation."

She bit her lip. "There have been a number of papers on this, and it's curious that you should bring it up. The whole thing needs more research. If lifeliners are a product of our technology, a hypothesis supported by a lot of indirect evidence, we already know that high-stress environments like cities produce different hormones when compared to population samples from rural settings. It's something I'm looking into myself."

"It sounds like this will keep you busy for a while," Nash said and patted his stomach. "That was good. Thank you."

She smiled. "You're welcome."

"If you can cook like this, Aleya must be pretty good herself."

"That little terror? She had to learn early to take care of herself. When Randal—that's my brother—and Sue died, I suddenly had a growing teen on my hands. My parents offered to look after her, as did Sue's, but I wanted her. It wasn't always easy juggling work and making sure she had the love and attention she needed. She's very bright and mature for her age. In many respects, she's more like a sixteen-year-old."

Nash nodded. "I could tell. Do you have her in a regular school?"

"She's at the Instram Institute. A regular school would bore her. Next year, she's doing year eleven high. Sometimes it's hard on her being so bright. Children her age are still very much children, and the older ones don't accept her as an equal because physically, she looks immature."

"And the education system doesn't cope well with gifted children. Mark and I had the same problem."

"I expect you did," she said thoughtfully and started gathering the dishes.

Nash got up and helped clear the table. He stacked the plates on the bench while Cariana fed the dishwasher. As she turned, she bumped into him and froze. Her cheeks flushed and her pointed tongue ran over her lips. She leaned into him and slowly wrapped her arms around his body. He brushed her yielding lips with his, then brought them down harder. Her mouth opened and their tongues danced as a tingle ran through his body. He squeezed her tight against him until she moaned. When she pulled back, tears glistened in her eyes.

"What's the matter, my sweet?"

"I'm happy that I haven't lost you," she murmured and rested her head against his chest.

He stroked her golden hair, content, wanting nothing more. After a moment, he pulled back.

"Let's do the rest of the dishes."

"Later." Eyes bright, she slid her hands under his T-shirt.

Her cool touch set him on fire and he embraced her, searching for her eager mouth, his own hands working their way up her shirt. She moaned and shivered, her lips roaming over his face in a frenzy of kisses. She tore off his T-shirt and her palms explored his broad chest.

"I always wanted a craggy man all to myself," she said with an impish smile.

He undid the buttons of her shirt and she shrugged it off. Her smile vanished, replaced with burning determination as she reached behind her back to undo the bra. He tugged at the straps and gently pulled down, then cupped her small, firm breasts and searched her eyes. She wanted him without reservation.

She led him through an open doorway into a spacious bedroom lit by the sun's dying fire and eased herself onto a large wood-frame bed. She stretched like a contented cat as he ripped off his clothing, her eyes drifting over his body. When she opened her arms, he sank into their welcoming embrace.

Their union intense and demanding, and he winced more than once as his shoulder protested her frenzied treatment. Seeing his discomfort, she had him lay on his back and straddled him, eyes screwed in ecstasy as his hands roamed over her body. She then spread herself across him and sighed with contentment.

Afterward, satiated and happy, stroking her back, he marveled at the texture of her smooth skin. When he stopped, she uttered a small growl deep in her throat and he resumed his caresses. He did not know how long they lay entwined without saying anything, but there was no need for words. Their souls had touched and the important things were said without words.

For the first time in a long while, Sally's face no longer hounded him, replaced by Cariana's radiant eyes. He still could not believe the wild abandon of her passion, and wondered whimsically how he would have coped with a whole shoulder. He'll have an opportunity to find out in due course, he told himself.

"Why are you smiling?" she purred softly, her fingernails marching across his chest.

"Just thinking how lucky I was having a bum arm. Do you always eat your men?"

"That's what they're for," she declared amiably. "Men are not the only ones who want just one thing, but women aren't supposed to admit it. Besides, you only had an intro, and I made allowances." She gently traced the outline of his shoulder patch.

He kissed the tip of her nose. "Thank you for sparing me."

"I had to leave something for next time." Her eyes turned dark and misty. "Like right now."

"I thought you were sparing me."

"You've been spared enough," she growled and her mouth clamped on his with demanding urgency.

Night had fallen a while back and Nash saw bright stars through a gauzy curtain stirred by a silent breeze. Cariana lay beside him, arm thrown across him, one leg entwined with his. Her breathing slow and even, face relaxed and serene. He pushed away a lock of stray hair and her eyes opened.

"You aren't sleeping," she murmured.

"I've been watching you."

"Not much to see in the dark," she mused.

"I've been watching you in my mind since the first moment I saw you. I thought my defenses were secure, but you walked right through them. There is something magical about you, Cariana, and I have fallen under your spell. My only fear is that I'll wake and you will be gone."

She touched his chin and her finger slid down his throat. "Who was Sally?"

He smiled into the night. Did she think his old flame was still a rival?

"A chance meeting—"

"Like ours?"

"We were on a tram attempting to jam off each other—"

"She was a lifeliner?"

"It started off innocently enough, if such things are ever innocent. We dated a few times and I thought we were building something permanent. I liked to think we were. Then they took her away…" There was no pain, only a memory of what they had and what might have been. Her ghost no longer haunted him.

"What happened?"

"In a fit of malice, her former boyfriend denounced her on Facebook. One night, three Humans Only League thugs beat her up in front of her apartment, then stabbed her to death."

"Oh, Nash. I'm so sorry."

"It's all right."

"When was that?"

"Two years ago, and I've been hiding ever since…until I met you."

"Your home computer—"

"I've been clinging to a memory, unwilling to let anyone else close, afraid that I might care and love again. Afraid that she too might be taken. You took away that fear, and I'm glad you set me free." He looked deep into her eyes. "No one will take you from me, not while I'm around."

She snuggled closer. "My last boyfriend was a doctor at The Alfred, a neurologist. We worked together on some of my research. Tall, ruggedly handsome—"

"Like me?" he retorted and she grinned.

"No one is like you. We had an occasional coffee and lunch at the canteen, had a couple of dates, nothing too involved. He wanted me, I could tell, and I was ready to give in, when over lunch one day, a radiologist I worked with clued me in about my would-be lover. I didn't believe him. I thought I was old enough to tell if someone scammed me, but it goes to show how hormones can screw up your judgment. Anyway, my boy broke a date with me, saying he had an operation that afternoon. These things happen and I didn't think anything of it. Except he didn't have an operation, at least not on a patient. I worked late that day and in the parking lot, I saw him."

"With someone else," Nash finished for her.

"I didn't know her, and I didn't care. The next morning we had a row and that ended things. He had the gall to tell me that I was stringing *him* along! Pig. There hadn't been anyone else after him, and I didn't want a relationship anyway. The Alfred and Parkville kept me too occupied to think about romance, and there was Aleya. Growing up, still getting over the loss of her parents, and rebellious. Then you came along…"

Her fingers marched across his chest.

"Was our meeting at Southbank really a random encounter?"

He chuckled. "You're still thinking I was hitting on you?"

"Well…"

"I wasn't, but when I saw you, I must admit my thoughts were not altogether noble."

She laughed softly. "You randy old thing. I always knew you were a wolf."

"I wasn't," he told her seriously. "But…"

"I'm not a lifeliner. You had every reason to be wary."

He pressed her close to him. "I'm glad our ghosts have left and we have each other now."

"For how long, Nash?"

"I don't know, my sweet, but we cannot give up simply because the odds seem stacked against us. I don't want to believe that people out there will allow things to slide into anarchy."

"They might."

He sighed. "You're right, but we're not there yet. Don't think about it."

"I can't help it."

"I know. No matter what happens, I'll be there to protect you, always."

"You're a hopeless romantic, my prince," she murmured and closed her eyes.

"And you're my morning star."

Slowly, she sank into sleep as he kept the demons at bay. At least for the night.

Nash woke to a magpie warble and a warm bundle snuggled against his back. Bright sunshine cast sharp shadows through the front yard. A car whispered by, another shadow. He turned on his back and gazed into the ceiling's white depths, his thoughts basking in the warmth of last night's searing lovemaking and intimate talk. Protected by comforting darkness, huddled in a tangled embrace, they lowered their guard. He appreciated that Cariana trusted him enough to open herself, knowing he would never hurt or shame her with her revelations. In a sense, an acceptance of him and what he was. Not a lifeliner, but a man she wanted to be with. A milestone in their relationship that marked a new beginning. In turn, he told her what it meant walking through life as a lifeliner, thankful to have understanding and loving parents, which helped him and Mark survive the perilous transition into growing teenagers. Underneath it all, there was fear of discovery, persecution, and later, possible professional ruin.

He did not know how long they talked as they lay entwined, body and spirit. A release for both of them, one that dispelled several veils that everyone wraps around themselves as protection against the sharp jabs of life. As he listened to Cariana's soft words that led him along the corridors of her mind, he felt an overwhelming desire to cherish this woman, never letting her down, always being there for her, making her safe. He hoped he was up to it.

When he swept away the romantic haze, though, real issues remained to be solved if they were to have a future. Both were independent, with lives that had direction and purpose not easily diverted. Yet, that was exactly what they would have to do if they wanted to be together. It wasn't sufficient to simply say they would face whatever came. That was wishful thinking and denial of reality. The future was not set, but often one was swept in a tide of events beyond control, which led to broken lives and shattered dreams.

Then again, he could be overanalyzing, and in the process denying himself happiness with a woman he loved. No life was secure. Any attempt to make it so meant walling himself from all human contact and intimacy—and he had already been there.

Her eyes fluttered and he smiled at her. "Morning, my bright star."

She blinked and lifted her head. "What time is it?"

"I have no idea. Does it matter?"

She sank back against the pillow. "I guess not," she purred, tracing the stubble on his chin with a delicate finger. "It's been a while since I woke with a man in my bed."

"Or his bed?" he teased her.

"Cube." She stretched and gave a contented sigh. "I think I'll keep you around for a while. Consider it a life science experiment."

"As long as I'm not poked or probed."

"Have you any complaints about my poking and probing so far?"

"The experiment is still to run its course," he said playfully.

Her laugh a ray of sunshine that lit her face with a soft glow and he allowed himself to sink into her captivating eyes, a whirlpool from which there was no escape. If this was entrapment, he did not want to be set free.

"Thank you for last night," she said tenderly and planted a kiss on his shoulder. "What's on the agenda for the day?"

"More homework, I'm afraid, and I've got to sit for a final tomorrow. Before then, though, we could have dinner."

"I can't, not tonight. I have to pick up Aleya, and there are chores I've been neglecting. Later, a drive back to the city. We could make it during the week if you like."

"I'd be happy to help with the chores."

"Your homework, remember?"

"Nothing that can't wait."

"Thanks, but I'm fine, and I don't mind. It helps me forget that I have to work tomorrow."

He didn't push it. She had a routine that worked for her. "I know what you mean. How about Tuesday at the Vue de Monde?"

"Wow, you know how to pick them." Her cheek dimpled in a mischievous grin. "Is this how you seduce innocent women?"

"That's how it's supposed to be done, wining and dining your date—"

"You're certainly dining me."

"Only because I want to show you off, my sweet, but I never subscribed to the practice of going to discos and dances," he told her soberly. "That might work for guys looking for one-night stands, but I've never been interested. I would rather have something more meaningful. I guess that makes me odd."

"No, it makes you honest and a man of character. Rare, as men spend a lot of their time pursuing one-night stands."

"And women don't?"

"Some do, but the good ones don't, and neither do good men." She wrapped an arm across his chest and snuggled closer. "I'm relieved to catch one of the good ones." After a moment, she sighed. "I need a hearty breakfast after our exhaustive encounters last night," she added wickedly as she threw back the cover and padded toward the bathroom.

He grinned as his eyes followed her retreating form, then locked his hands behind his head and listened to the warbling magpies.

Over breakfast, Nash kept staring at her, wanting to jump her there and then. She saw his hunger and gave a small smile.

With hardly any traffic along Calder Freeway, the drive into the city spent in thoughtful contemplation. Cariana's passionate kiss at the front door left a lingering, treasured memory, and a promise of more intimacy. He looked forward to exploring her complex facets, a voyage of mystery and discovery, one they had already started. He wondered if they would be able to finish it.

Stop with the pessimistic bits, old son.

Not wanting music, he connected to ABC's *Insiders*. When the heads-up view cleared in the center of the dome, he was surprised to see Gibbs Gilmore in the guest chair. With the car in level 3 autonomous mode, he watched the interview with only an occasional glance at the road.

"—claim the Prime Minister and the Opposition leader sanctioned the sterilization program?" the presenter demanded.

"This was a major ASIO and federal police operation, Wallace, which took manpower and considerable resources to set up. I could not have done it without approval of the National Security Committee. My understanding is that Mr. Gardner was appraised of the government's intentions."

"Was this initiative supported by the Attorney-General?"

"The Security Committee excluded Van Ross from the approval process of something that could be interpreted as inherently illegal."

"Aren't you breaking Cabinet discipline by divulging this information?"

"I would be if I were still a member of the Liberal Party. Last night, I resigned from the parliamentary wing with the intention of contesting a Senate seat in the March election as a member of the Australian Conservatives. My parliamentary colleagues and the media have vilified me for executing party policy on a matter of national security in an attempt to cover up an embarrassment. I supported the sterilization initiative as something that had to be done, but I resent being blamed for it."

"You can understand why people will consider your actions reprehensible."

"If governments everywhere don't take positive steps to address the lifeliner problem, people can expect social disintegration and widespread unrest as

human beings are slowly taken over by these mutants."

"Positive steps in the form of disinformation by the Humans Only League?"

"Contrary to some rumors, the federal government did not create them, but they did receive operational funding from my Department."

"Mr. Gilmore, viewers out there could interpret your revelations as pay-back against the government for destroying a promising political career. You must realize the negative impact this information will have on the Liberal Party Coalition."

"I simply wanted to set the record straight, Wallace. The voters can make up their own minds on polling day."

"Thank you for appearing on the program."

"Always a pleasure."

Nash told the car to switch off.

If he believed Gilmore, and he had no reason not to, the Co-alition's sterilization program had not only started, but actively supported by the Labor Party, which did not come as a total surprise. Gilmore's stark confirmation meant that whichever party secured the election, the pogrom would not only continue, but likely to intensify.

Were people prepared to accept this as a solution?

Unless a candidate belonged to one of the major parties, the way the system was structured, getting into the House of Representatives as an independent practically impossible, and the Lower House constituted the government. The only constraint on unchecked exercise of power was the Senate with its ability to block legislation. This worked if the Opposition of the day denied the government the necessary numbers to pass legislation. If as Gilmore revealed, the Labor Party and the Coalition professed to hold similar policies on lifeliners and colluded on certain initiatives, whichever party held government could do just about anything it wanted.

The rest of his drive into the city not as enjoyable as he anticipated when he started.

When he approached Bromby Street and saw the crowd, three

squad cars, and media vans in front of his apartment block, he wondered if he could stop the pessimistic bits. He slowed down and turned into the driveway. Two groups faced each other. The People First and Humans Only League placard-waving activists were separated from civil rights protesters by four grim cops determined not to allow the two to clash. Nash clamped his jaw when he saw his face plastered on two placards.

A dober blocked him and waved him to stop. Nash told the car to wind down part of the dome and waited.

"Your business here, sir?"

"I live here," Nash told him, eyeing the crowd. So far, those glancing at him did not recognize him, for which he was thankful, not relishing the prospect of being the focus of a possible brawl. He inclined his head at the cracked glass panel beside the entrance. "What happened there?"

"Some hothead threw a rock," the cop growled, then his eyes widened. "Wait a minute. You're—"

"Yeah, I know who I am," Nash snapped and connected with the building's security system. The wide parking lot door slowly wound up.

He eased the car forward, welcoming the protective embrace of the underground garage. The stark realization of what he was doing crashed through him and he jammed on the brakes. He was again walling himself in, denying reality, safe in his cocoon, the habit of eighteen years hard to break. He gazed at the two groups taunting each other, the embodiment of everything he wanted to change, and the reason he ran for public office. If he didn't face this now, he would be forever hiding behind a police cordon in the mistaken belief that he fought for everybody's rights. He reminded himself that foremost, freedom was a state of mind. People had forgotten this basic fact, allowing its erosion under the guise of protecting it.

He pursed his mouth, got out of the car, and strode toward the crowd.

The dober stepped in front of him. "Mr. Bannon, I wouldn't

do that."

"Get out of my way."

"We're trying to prevent a riot."

"There won't be any riot," Nash told him with more confidence than he felt.

He exhaled softly, not sure he was doing the right thing as he stepped into the clear space between the two groups. A hush fell as both sides eyed him.

"It's the lifeliner!" someone shouted. Predictably, this raised a ripple of restless murmuring.

"My name is Nash Bannon, and I am a lifeliner. If anyone here feels that I, and others like me, are responsible for whatever problems you might have, take your revenge on me. I won't resist."

Several Humans Only League agitators looked at each other, wanting somebody to take up the challenge. The cops were clearly nervous, expecting an outbreak of explosive violence. Channel Nine, Seven, and Ten reporters taped everything.

"You're an abomination!" a voice shouted, and others nodded.

"He's a man like you!" someone else countered.

Nash sensed a tipping point, both groups ready to tear into each other.

"I didn't ask to be born a lifeliner, but I was, and I've been hiding that fact all my life. Hiding from hate." He looked at a short man holding a People First poster.

"Why do *you* hate me?"

The man cleared his throat, uncomfortable being the center of attention. "Your kind wants to take over the world, and you're responsible for people being sterile."

"How are lifeliners responsible? Do you see them walking the streets spraying everybody, causing them to be sterile?"

A snicker ran through the crowd and some of the tension dissipated.

"I can hardly imagine the anguish a couple must feel when

they find one or both is sterile. Or suddenly discovering that their child is a lifeliner, but I'm not responsible for that. No one is. Lifeliner births are becoming the norm, but that doesn't mean the death of humanity. Children are humanity's future. If you condemn your lifeliner children, you are condemning your future."

"You talk posh, Mister, but words are cheap," the man with the poster snapped. "You twist things, but you cannot avoid the fact that lifeliners are the cause of crime and unemployment in our cities. You hide in your fancy pad, not giving a damn if someone like me loses his job to a robot in a fully automated factory. I'm forty-six with no hope of getting another job. How do I support my family?"

"He's right!"

"Filthy lifeliner!"

Nash stepped closer to the man. "I'm sorry that you lost your job. My words may not mean much to you, but I know how that feels. I also had a nice job that enabled me to live up there." He swept his arm at the building. "You were replaced by technology. I was fired because I am a lifeliner. Now that people know what I am, do I have a future?"

"So what? You're rich. Me, I got to go cap in hand to Centrelink begging for work."

"And you blame lifeliners for that? If you want to blame anyone, blame the government for not protecting workers. Instead, you're prepared to sit back and allow that same government to strip away your rights."

"What are you talking about?"

"Do you like the idea of a police officer walking up to you demanding to interrogate your PID on a whim? Do you want your every move tracked and all your conversations recorded, knowing there is nothing you can do about it? Is that the freedom you want for yourself and your children?"

"He's right," someone shouted. "I got slapped with a $500 fine for blocking a dober when he wanted to access my PID for no cause."

"Me too!"

Nash eyed the crowd. "I am a man like you. I have some differences, but is that justification for the government to sterilize me or for you to lynch me? Where does it stop? Do they sterilize the sick, the lame, kids with autism or cancer?" He held out his hand. "Who is prepared to touch me?"

"Everybody knows that you can kill with your touch!"

"That's blatant rumormongering to make it easier for you to hate me." He searched their faces. "Have all of you swallowed your own propaganda?"

A burly bruiser stepped forward and clasped Nash's hand. "I'm not afraid of you, lifeliner. Do your thing."

Nash looked into the man's eyes. "What do you feel?"

The man frowned. "Why, nothing."

"Nothing?"

"Your hand, of course."

"That's right. My hand. Nothing else. A human hand touching another human hand. You and I are different, living different lives with different problems, but underneath it all, we're both men. Born to struggle and provide something for ourselves and our children. We are destined to die, hoping that life will be easier for those we leave behind. If you want to blame me and other lifeliners because you may have gotten a shitty deal, you will be dooming yourself."

The man slowly looked down as though seeing his hand for the first time, then stared hard at Nash.

"I guess things aren't as simple as we've been told. I hear you're running for the Senate. Why?"

"Not because I'm a lifeliner, which started off being the reason. It's because I want to help stop whichever party gets elected from stealing our freedom. Not only my freedom, but yours as well." Nash pointed at a People First poster. "I'd change that to read 'People's Rights Party', if I were you. Your real enemies are in Canberra, not me."

The man nodded and glanced at his fellow protesters. "I'm done here," he growled and walked off. Another dropped his placard and followed him. Amid murmurings and sidewise glances at Nash, both groups slowly dispersed.

The cops looked at each other nonplussed, shook their heads, and made for their cars.

"You have my vote, Mr. Bannon!" a civil rights supporter shouted as he followed his group.

With the field clear, the media swarmed in.

"Mr. Bannon, will you be funding any portion of your campaign?" the Seven reporter demanded, his young face seasoned by hard experience.

"My campaign is funded and managed by the Lifeliner Party, but I will be proud to make a contribution."

"How many votes will you need to secure a seat?" an attractive brunette Ten reporter butted in.

"According to the Electoral Commission, Victoria has almost six point-six million registered voters divided across fourteen Senate seats. To win a seat outright, the quota is approximately 439 thousand primary votes. However, I don't expect to come even close to reaching that. I hope to secure preferences from other parties to substantially lower my threshold."

"What is meant by separation of powers?" the Nine reporter asked, and Nash smiled at the trick question designed to expose his possible lack of knowledge. He'd been warned to expect this, but not so soon.

"The doctrine of separation of powers divides the institutions of government into three branches: legislative, executive, and judicial, something I am sure you already know. In Australia, the distinction between the legislative and the executive are somewhat blurred, as the government of the day, in conjunction with the Senate, performs both roles. The state does not control the judiciary, which is an important cornerstone of our constitutional system."

"What about separation of church and state?"

"The Constitution is explicit on this point," Nash said. "Chapter 5, Section 116, states, *The government shall not make any law for establishing any religion, or for imposing any religious observance, or for prohibiting the free exercise of any religion, and no religious test shall be required as a qualification for any office or public trust in the republic.'* Although the federal government funds religious and public system schools, it does not promote or support any one religion. However, Australia is fundamentally a Christian society and the Catholic lobby does exert influence on our politicians."

"What are your religious leanings, Mr. Bannon?"

"Being religious does not automatically endow a person with spiritual righteousness. You only have to look at history to see the evils committed in the name of religion."

"That does not exactly answer my question."

Nash wasn't sure how to answer her. Someone could misconstrue whatever he said, but he would not pretend to be what he was not.

"Every person has an idealized image of what they think a politician should be, which makes my position impossible. I will not massage my answers to suit a particular audience. People can accept me for what I am or vote for someone else. As for my religious leanings, my faith is personal."

"You may be alienating an important segment of voters with that attitude."

"I want to be judged for what I stand and the policies of the Lifeliner Party, not whether I go to church or not."

The Seven reporter, figuring her opposite number had hounded enough time, raised her hand.

"Mr. Bannon, on the ABC *Insiders* program this morning, Mr. Gibbs Gilmore claimed that sterilization of lifeliners was authorized by the Prime Minister, with full knowledge of the opposition leader, Macey Gardner, something both of them repudiated on Friday's ABC *7.30 Report*. Care to comment?"

"I have no reason to question the veracity of Mr. Gilmore's claim. It is highly improbable that a program of that magnitude could be planned and executed without Cabinet knowledge and approval by the Prime Minister. Mr. Gardner's hollow denials merely confirms why the Labor Party has not produced a policy on lifeliners, because it is the same as the Coalition's. Both major parties seek to blame lifeliners for failed economic and social initiatives. I can only surmise the sterilization program was designed to demonstrate to voters that the government has solved the problem."

"If elected, what do you hope to achieve? After all, you will be merely one among several independents," the Ten reporter asked.

"The Lifeliner Party wants to expose lies promoted as truth by both major parties, and hopefully check erosion of our rights and freedoms pursued under the banner of national security." Nash smiled and lifted his arms. "Thank you for listening to me."

Cries of dismay and a flurry of questions followed him to the car.

He parked in his reserved spot and walked toward the elevator, buoyed by his encounter with the protesters. He hadn't won over everybody, and did not expect to, but if the media reported this faithfully, he hoped viewers would pause and reflect.

In his apartment, he filled himself a glass of juice and raised it in a salute.

"To our noble selves. There's damn few of us left."

Chapter Seven

Nash jerked awake from a vivid dream to the sound of breaking glass, car alarms going off, running footsteps, and the squeal of tires as a vehicle accelerated away. For a moment, he thought he still dreamed, the images clear in his mind. With a particularly pleasant episode, he could always recall and play it back…and often did. One of the quirks of having a garbage truck memory. He was still searching for that delete key to clean out some of the clutter. The noises outside, though, were not a dream. He muttered something uncharitable, jumped out of bed and padded to the balcony. Perhaps he could pick up the dream where it left off. He tried that a number of times, but it never worked. He leaned over the railing and looked down. Phil was walking up and down the sidewalk checking cracked domes and broken headlights.

Another case of wanton vandalism? Possible, but he didn't believe it. Admitting to being a lifeliner, he had become cynical of man's benevolent nature. A warm northerly breeze made the golden elms lining the boulevard whisper to each other. They had seen it all before.

Every resident had one reserved spot in the underground parking lot, but families had two, allocated on a first-come basis. Those who missed out had to leave their car outside under a special permit. Every now and then, hooligans damaged cars along the street, and this attack could be a coincidence, but Nash suspected a darker purpose. Make enough residents mad at him, and the body corporate might try to force him out. They could if he were a tenant, but he was an owner. The only option they had was to buy the unit from him if they thought it would restore peace.

He sat on enough body corporate meetings to know the regular members. On the whole, the committee operated along strict business guidelines with minimal friction, and the appointed manager watched expenses. Everybody got along. Would that continue once they found one of them was a lifeliner, and the reason for the protests, marches, and vandalism in front of their place? He was likely to find out at the next meeting.

Then again, he could be making a whole lot about nothing.

It *could* be a case of random vandalism.

Already up and wide awake, only 4:25 according to his PID, sleep far from his mind, he decided to work out a little and go for a run. The northerly wind had kept the night uncomfortable, and according to the wall weather station, still 22C outside. After a restrained bout of exercises—he had to watch his right shoulder—but feeling energized, he swallowed some juice and took the emergency stairs to the lobby. The night shift guard limped in. Three residents were already outside checking vehicle damage.

"Out for a run, Mr. Bannon?"

"The commotion outside woke me up, Phil."

"First, it's a smashed glass panel, and now this." The guard shook his head. "I don't know what's with kids these days. I blame the parents, you know."

Nash shrugged. It was complicated out there for the kids, and some parents simply didn't have time to provide the attention their children needed. Sometimes a kid simply fell into the wrong crowd and went bad. However, roaming the streets this early in the morning was a little unusual.

"I heard a car pull away."

"The security cameras got it, but it's probably stolen. I've called the dobers. You watch yourself out there, Mr. Bannon. Things are changing and I don't like it."

"I'll be careful, Phil. My regards to Betty."

"Thanks, Mr. Bannon. Enjoy your run."

Phil was an old-timer. Nash had known him ever since he moved into his apartment. An industrial accident crushed his left leg and they put Phil on a disability pension. Being a guard brought in additional income, but even with Betty's pay as a part-time VR programmer, raising twin girls was tough. Lack of job security, the latest social phobia and cause of much anxiety and youth unrest.

One early morning a month ago as Nash made to go out, Phil confided to him his secret fear that his girls would turn out to be lifeliners. Both would reach puberty next year. He didn't have anything against lifeliners, he hastened to add, but his girls deserved better from life than prejudice and persecution. Nash couldn't find anything wrong with that reasoning.

Outside, he saw his next-door neighbor checking the splintered dome of a red Mazda hatch.

"Sorry to see your son's car damaged, Leonard."

The small potbellied man paused and sighed. "It could have been worse. This will come up at the next body corporate meeting, Nash. Bet on it. Some of us have been advocating for more parking space, and this will help carry the argument. At least I hope it will. We've got space behind the building."

"No access for heavy machinery," Nash pointed out. "And I'm not sure the expense would be worth it, not for five parking spots, and most residents are fond of the backyard garden. They'll resist having it torn out."

"I don't mind trees and bushes either," Leonard countered, "but I also don't want cars busted up."

"Residents will resist any increase in body corporate fees to launch a major construction job. They're high enough already and I don't want them getting any higher. Neither do you. Cheaper to get more security."

"Yeah, there is always that. What we need is preventative security, not security after the fact," Leonard growled sourly.

Nash nodded. It was a valid point. He waved to him and began to jog toward the brightly lit city towers. A tram clattered by, empty. There wasn't much traffic, but it would build up quickly as people began a new working week. His muscles loose and comfortable, he picked up the pace and his body responded with relish. Not many joggers or power walkers about, but it was still early. He wondered what Cariana did for exercise. He would have to ask. Maybe they could arrange to do something together.

On the way back, he slowed as he approached Bromby Street and wiped sweat off his brow. A police sedan, its lights blinking, stood double-parked beside a damaged car. A cop was taking a statement from one of the residents under the watchful eye of a Seven reporter—vultures circling a carcass. They had to be monitoring police frequencies to be on the spot this quickly. Nash took the stairs to the third floor, looking forward to a relaxing shower.

Dressed and shaved, too early for breakfast, he told the percolator to start the water boiling.

"Sally, Channel Seven."

Normally, he started his mornings by listening to ABC for his news fix, but they didn't get going until six, which annoyed many viewers, including him. Tempted to switch to Al Jazeera's 5:30 world coverage, he wanted a slant on the local events first.

The holoview wall cleared, showing police cruisers and three fire brigade trucks next to a brick building. Coffee cup in hand, Nash blanched, recognizing the place.

"—lobby and the Help Center office were extensively damaged. Paramedics treated the injured security guard for head trauma at the site before taking him to the hospital. The building's fire suppression system contained the damage to the ground floor. The police have secured surveillance footage to identify the getaway vehicle and help apprehend the perpetrators. Reports coming in show that Lifeliner Help Centers in all capital cities were firebombed. We'll keep you updated as details become available."

Nash pulled at his chin. Every Help Center attacked? That stretched coincidence beyond the credible. Something murky was going on and he didn't like the vibes.

The camera switched to the presenter.

"Suspected vandals damaged several cars outside 401 St. Kilda Road, residence of Mr. Nash Bannon, a Senate candidate for the Lifeliner Party."

In the holoview, the picture panned over cars and a dober talking to Phil. *"On Friday, Mr. Bannon was shot in the shoulder in front of that building, the Humans Only League attacker still on the run. This morning's act could be coincidence, but it could also be an orchestrated campaign of intimidation.*

"Prime Minister Atarah Readman reacted angrily at the allegation made by former minister Gibbs Gilmore that she approved the lifeliner sterilization program, claiming it was mud raking of the worst kind. When asked how such a program could be set up without Cabinet knowledge, the Prime Minister scoffed at the suggestion that she had lost control over her departments. In the meantime, Van Ross, the federal Attorney-General, has extended his investigation to possible involvement by ASIO.

"In a communique to the European Parliament, Denmark, Norway, and Sweden, declared that they will not comply with the Citizenship Act, claiming it violates the longstanding Schengen agreement, which guarantees free and unrestricted travel between EU members. If Brussels enforces the Act, Scandinavian countries will implement strict visa and Customs inspections, and begin withdrawal proceedings from the EU. This development will further fracture what is already a shaky alliance.

"In the United States, the Secret Service prevented federal marshals from executing an arrest warrant against President Mackay for reinstating the Lifeliner Act. Under the Supreme Court declaration, employees of government agencies charged with administering the Act will be subject to arrest. The Democratic Party is urging the Republican-held Congress to overturn the executive order, citing abuse of power by the President. A number of Republican senators are extremely uncomfortable with the President's autocratic approach, and sources inside the House majority leader's office claim that Congress is discussing possible impeachment proceedings.

"Today's weather—"

Nash didn't have to hear today's weather. He already knew. It was going to be hot and steamy and grim.

"Sally, switch off."

The cream has hit the fan, old son.

He agreed, wondering who would get splattered, his appetite for more news gone. Now that he was in the public eye, he *needed* to keep abreast of everything, but right now, he'd had his dose of depression.

With the Lifeliner Party building damaged, should he keep his appointment? They said only the ground floor took a hit. He would go and take it from there. An election campaign didn't stop because of acts of arson.

He kept breakfast simple: muesli, a smoothie, and two soft-boiled eggs. When he washed up, it was 6:20, and high time for him to head off.

"Nash, you have a call from Aleya Lambert. Do you wish to accept connection?" Sally asked suddenly.

Something cold materialized in his chest and slid into his stomach. She wouldn't be calling this early unless something was badly wrong.

"Accept."

The holoview cleared and he froze when he saw her tear-streaked face.

"Aleya! What's the matter?"

"Nash, they've got Aunty!" she sobbed.

Her words were hammer blows. The thought of Cariana hurt churned his guts and tore him up inside. Awful scenarios flashed through his mind and made him tense up. He forced back the demons, replacing emotion with steely determination to remain calm and proactive, regardless how he might feel inside.

And right now, Aleya needed him to be strong. She also had demons to fight. She flinched, seeing something ugly in his expression.

"What's the matter? You're not mad at me for calling you?"

"No! Not at all. Just concerned. Who's got her?"

"Trent and Sutton. I didn't see them, but I recognized their voices. They must have overridden the security lock to get in. Trent wanted to know why I wasn't around, and Aunty told him I was away at a slumber party. Sutton said not to worry about it. They would get me later, but Trent searched the apartment anyway. I *was* going to a friend's place for the day and I had my room all made up. With nowhere to hide, I slipped under the bed. I was sure Trent would find me, but when he came in, he checked the wardrobe and walked out."

"Where are you?"

"Still at home. I didn't dare go out in case they watched the building. What am I going to do, Nash?"

"Did you call triple zero?"

"No, I wanted—"

"Don't. Did Sutton or Trent say why they wanted Cariana?" The only reason he could think of was to use her as a lever against him, but he had no idea what that could be.

"They just dragged her off. It was horrible." Aleya began to cry again.

"Stay put, I'll be right over. Ten minutes and I'll be there."

She sniffed and nodded. Nash cut the connection, ground his teeth, and smashed his fist against the breakfast counter. After taking a few deep breaths, he hurried for the door. Although tempted to run down the stairs to the parking level, he waited for the elevator. He wouldn't be any good to anybody if he tripped and broke a leg. Besides, the time for hurry was past. He needed to think things through and form an action plan.

The car surged toward the exit, the door barely clearing out of the way.

"Connect with Inspector Charles Worsley," he commanded.

After several agonizing seconds, the heads-up view cleared.

"Mr. Bannon, you keep strange hours for someone who is supposed to be unemployed."

"My apologies for disturbing you, Inspector, but I have an emergency. Dr. Cariana Lambert was kidnapped by Lyle Sutton and one of his associates."

The inspector immediately became serious. "How do you know this?"

"Her niece called me. She was there when it happened. I'm on my way to see her."

"I'll send a squad car. When you get there, Mr. Bannon, don't leave the apartment. I'll be over as soon as I can."

"Thank you, Inspector. Much appreciated."

"Tell me, Mr. Bannon, why would someone want to kidnap Dr. Lambert, and what's the connection?"

"The connection, Inspector, is that I am a lifeliner running for the Senate, and Dr. Lambert is someone important to me."

"I see. Sutton, eh?"

"I'll give you another connection—the coordinated firebombing of all Lifeliner Help Centers across the country. I might not be the only candidate singled out for this attention."

"An interesting observation," Worsley mused thoughtfully. "I need to make some calls." The heads-up view faded and Nash sighed.

Cariana!

As he drove through the dawn, he promised to find out if a lifeliner could actually kill someone by draining all his life-force. Despite efforts to keep his emotions under control, he could not help mulling over some of the nastier possibilities with this development. He wanted a normal life like everybody else, *damn it*!

If he wanted a normal life, he would have to carve it out for himself. No one was going to hand it to him giftwrapped.

Time for more proactive action.

He sent a brief message to Garrett—his lawyer's unique relationship with the federal Attorney-General might come in handy—and asked the car to connect with Margot Jarvis.

In the display, Margi ventured a drawn smile. "Mr. Bannon, I expect you heard the awful news?"

"I have, and this could get worse, but that's not why I'm calling. I have a problem of my own. Lyle Sutton has kidnapped Dr. Cariana Lambert and I'll be a little late coming in."

She looked stricken. "Oh no. I am so sorry to hear that, Nash. Is there anything we can do?"

"The police are in the loop. How's the building?"

"The Help Center is a mess, but other ground floor offices

301

have only minor water and smoke damage. We're still in business."

"I'm glad to hear it. Have you heard from Mr. Kairns?"

She frowned. "Why, no. I've been trying to get hold of him, but his cell doesn't answer."

"Margi, I suggest you run a check on all candidates. I think something big is going down and they could be in some danger. If you need any kind of help, call Inspector Charles Worsley."

"You mean they could be kidnapped?"

"They or family members. If Sutton is involved, it won't be anything subtle."

She pursed her lips, then nodded. "An organized assault against the party? Keep in touch, okay? And take care."

"You too," Nash said and cut contact.

He felt a rush of affection for Margot. She kept her head and didn't descend into emotional hysterics. Cool girl, that. People reflect the organization they work for. If she was a typical Lifeliner Party example, he looked forward to being one of them. With the situation handled on several fronts, he immediately felt better. It remained to be seen how successful those efforts would turn out.

He found an empty spot near The Fawkner Residences building and parked, then raced toward the entrance. He told the security system to contact Aleya Lambert and waited. The lock cycled almost immediately and the door panels slid back. He ran toward the elevator past a startled guard and skidded to a stop.

The ride to the sixth floor seemed to take forever, and he kept clenching and unclenching his fists. He hurried down the corridor, stopped before Cariana's apartment, and asked his PID to request entry. The door opened and a small bundle crashed into his embrace.

"Oh, Nash. I was so scared, afraid that Trent would come back."

He hugged the trembling girl and kissed the top of her head, figuring she wouldn't mind a display of affection right now.

"It's okay. I'm here," he whispered tenderly and patted her back. "We'll handle it."

She clung to him and sniffed. After a moment, she pulled back and the corner of her mouth lifted in a small smile. He rose and closed the door.

"You're the only one I felt I could call," she said, fighting to regain composure.

"I'm glad you did."

"Nash, what's happening here? Why did they take her? If it's because of me and what I did for Trent, I'll never forgive myself."

"I doubt that this has anything to do with you. I'm only guessing, but I think it's more to do with me."

"You?"

"I and Mr. Gatt are the reason why Sutton lost his job, and he might be trying to get even."

"I don't understand."

Before he could answer, his cell went off. He dug it out of his pocket and glanced at the caller ID—Unknown.

"Nash Bannon."

The image cleared to show a familiar face framed by silver hair around the temples. In the background, heavy red drapes covered a wide window.

"Mr. Bannon, I am so pleased to hear from you."

"Sutton! What have you done with Dr. Lambert?"

"The lovely doctor is unharmed and will remain un-harmed...provided you do your part."

"Which is?"

"At nine o'clock, you will renounce to the networks your Senate candidacy and the Lifeliner Party. Not too much to ask, is it?"

Nash understood what Sutton was doing. He wasn't interested in him directly, regardless of any emotional pain Nash might suffer from the experience. That would be a bonus. He wanted to destroy the Lifeliner Party movement, or the ones who pulled his strings did.

"And if I don't?"

Sutton sighed and shook his head. "Ah, so negative this early in the morning. I could have gone after you, Mr. Bannon, but doing it this way, my argument carries more weight."

"If you harm her—"

"Harm her? Whatever gave you that idea? She'll merely get an injection, that's all. Then we'll get the kid. If that doesn't convince you, we'll be paying your brother a visit. Messy business, but easily avoided with a little cooperation."

Nash felt himself go pale, certain the vile man would do exactly what he said. "You would sterilize them?"

"Such a harsh word. Consider it preventative inoculation. Parkville was a minor setback, a miscalculation on my part, which merely slowed me down. I'm still prosecuting my war."

"You firebombed the Help Centers?"

"I always knew you were smart. Under different circumstances, I wouldn't mind having you on my team."

"You cannot hope to get away with this."

"I already have," Sutton said and laughed. "If you want to call the police, go ahead. It won't change a thing. Don't consider yourself anything special, Mr. Bannon. We're giving all Lifeliner Party candidates equal attention. This is bigger than you can imagine, and I am untouchable."

Untouchable? Who exactly was Sutton, and who were the people behind him? An operation this size was beyond the capability of a handful of lifeliner haters.

"The Prime Minister has her hand over you?"

"Readman? She's nothing, a pawn, but enough of this. You will do what I say or Dr. Lambert takes the fall for you, and you needn't bother denying your relationship with her. I know all about it."

"You're a bastard," Nash hissed.

"No, Mr. Bannon. I'm a patriot, paying a small price of honor for humanity's sake. So, what'll it be?"

"I want to see her."

"Proof of life, eh? Very well."

The hologram view shifted to show Cariana bound to a chair, her back to a kitchen done in brown cabinets and large beige floor tiles.

"Nash! Don't do it!"

"Cariana!"

Sutton's smirking face reappeared. "That was touching. Rare to see true love in action."

"If I agree, how do I know you'll let her go?"

"I'm not interested in sadistic infliction of pain, Mr. Bannon. It's always counterproductive, and I have a broader objective in mind. Remember, nine o'clock." The image faded and Nash ground his teeth with impotent anger.

He could not forget the sterilized children at the safe house. Regardless of what Sutton said, Nash was certain Cariana would suffer the same fate…as might the others. The problem he faced was how to stop this from happening.

Aleya searched his face, her expression serious. "I heard what he said. Would he actually sterilize Aunty to get even with you?"

"He might, but he's not just after me. This is about lifeliners in general."

Her eyes misted and she sniffed. "Why are some people so mean?"

He sighed and stroked her shoulder. "I don't know, honey."

"What do we do now?"

He bit his lip and searched Aleya's face. This might be a shot in the dark, but one worth pursuing.

"Tell me something. The safe houses you've been in. Did any of them have an old-fashioned kitchen with beige floor tiles?"

She shook her head. "I've never seen one like that. Why?"

"Because that's where Sutton is holding Cariana. Never mind. We'll find her," he said with more assurance than he felt and rubbed his hands. "Have you had breakfast?"

Her face lit up. "I was about to make some when we were interrupted."

"In that case, that's job one. We'll put on our worry hat later."

She looked up and inclined her head at the door. "A dober wants to get in."

Nash stood. "Okay, let him."

The door opened and a uniformed cop touched the tip of his visored cap. "Mr. Bannon?"

"That's right."

"I am Senior Constable Jake Maloney. I'll be standing guard outside until Inspector Worsley gets here. My partner is downstairs."

"Thank you, officer."

The cop nodded and withdrew.

Aleya switched on the holoview and became domestic, operating the kitchen like a pro. She refused help, insisting that he sit down and watch the news. It was all grim stuff: robbery of a 7-Eleven store near the Southern Cross station, a teenager crashed his dad's car after a speed rampage through the neighborhood, a pedestrian killed in a hit-and-run, JB Hi-Fi released a software plugin that deactivated the link between the PID's modules—

Nash sat up to listen.

"—on and off at will, guaranteed to defeat attempts to track your PID. The plugin is available for download from your holoview wall for $25, and is certified virus and malware free. The JB Hi-Fi website has already received more than 120,000 hits. A spokesperson for the federal Department of Social Services labeled the plugin a scam, stating that individuals already had that ability. JB Hi-Fi countered by saying that blocking access was not the same as deactivating the PID's communications module.

"A report just in from the Lifeliner Party Melbourne headquarters claims that the party president, Warren Kairns, and three Senate candidates were kidnapped by a rogue cell inside the Australian Federal Police demanding dissolution of the party. Failure to comply would result in unspecified action against the kidnapped.

"Recapping the main points—"

"Computer, switch off," Nash grated, deep in thought. He'd had enough politics to last him the day, which was an odd thing to think, seeing how his days would be absorbed with nothing but politics. Was he doing the right thing running for the Senate? Perhaps being gloomy over Cariana, but the image of her tied up, frightened, not knowing what Sutton might do, sent his blood fizzing with suppressed rage.

The holoview dissolved into a cascade of pooling colors.

Aleya held out a mug of coffee for him. "That was about Aunty, wasn't it?"

"And others," he said and took a sip.

"Was it wise to leak the story?" Her solemn dark eyes regarded him without blinking.

An intelligent question from someone more grownup than she looked.

"I'm not sure, honey. It might generate public sympathy and prod the government to help find them."

"It could also cause the kidnappers to do something bad."

"It might. In these cases, it's sometimes hard to know the right thing to do."

Aleya bit her lip, then her face broke into a smile. "Next time you operate the holoview, call it 'Missy'."

"Missy?"

"Better than calling it Computer. Aunty can sometimes be too clinical. Besides, I think it likes being called Missy."

He smiled and nodded. "Okay, Missy it is. Will I get into trouble with Cariana over this?"

"She'll probably call you a cube."

Nash laughed, picturing Cariana doing just that.

Aleya scooped out her vegetable omelet onto a plate and sat next to him, a purple smoothie on the bench already fatally damaged. She glanced at him, then began demolishing the omelet with undisguised appetite.

With a fork halfway to her mouth, she paused. "Inspector Worsley is outside."

Nash nodded, stood and strode toward the door. "Let him in."

Looking somewhat harried, Worsley walked in, broke into an

absent grin, and extended his hand. "Mr. Bannon, have you heard?"

"About the kidnappings? I heard," Nash said and shook hands, then inclined his head toward the kitchen. "Care for some coffee or something?"

"Thanks, but I can't stay long. Your Lifeliner Party has lit a roaring fire and I'm a piece of kindling. Never mind, it's done and we'll have to deal with it." Worsley turned to Aleya. "And this, I presume, is the young lady we've been hearing so much about lately? How are you, Aleya?"

"I'm fine, thank you," she said reservedly, apparently not sure how to take the dober.

He sensed this and lifted his palm. "I'm one of the good guys here." He looked at Nash. "All the networks are carrying the news, Mr. Bannon—"

"Just Nash, okay?"

"Fine…Nash. But it's not three kidnappings. It's eight, if you include Mr. Kairns, three Senate candidates and family members. You have been caught up in what looks like a major retaliatory operation, and Dr. Lambert is merely one piece in a much larger picture."

"Sutton made that altogether clear."

"What exactly did Sutton tell you?"

"Do you have a recorder?"

Worsley dug out his cell. "Go."

Nash repeated every word of his conversation. When he stopped, Worsley pocketed the cell and sighed.

"I've spoken to the Commissioner, and by now, I dare say every state Premier is also in the loop. If the Prime Minister isn't, I'm sure she'll be shortly. My cut on this? The government wouldn't mind seeing the Lifeliner Party in disarray, but this is something they cannot dismiss or drag their heels on. Disregarding the political dimension, this is a criminal case and will be treated as such."

"Any ideas how to break this?" Nash asked.

"Sutton is a skilled operative. I've read his file. He'll know all the tricks to avoid apprehension."

"When we talked, he said he was untouchable."

"An interesting remark, including the one about Readman. Our Mr. Sutton may be more than he appears. Powerful enough to mount an operation across all states, and equally unconcerned about the Prime Minister."

Nash dug into his memory. "When Sutton was stopped at Essendon Airport the other day, who made the arrest?"

"Victoria police, but they were tipped off by the AFP. Why do you ask?"

"For someone supposedly skilled in counterintelligence as you say, he was caught very easily. He was either sloppy, which seems out of character, or we're missing a contributing factor."

"Such as?"

"I believe the Signals Directorate can track a PID that's been switched off, something he would have done as step one."

Worsley stared. "That's not—"

"Supposed to be possible," Nash finished for him. "I know, but I think the Signals Directorate did just that. If I'm right, you have the means to find him and the victims."

"If what you say is true, the implication for law enforcement—"

"I don't care about that, Inspector. You can dissect the ramifications later."

Worsley cleared his throat. "You're right, of course. My apologies. It's almost seven, which leaves us two hours to find him, provided your allegation about the Signals Directorate capability is true. This has to go to the Commissioner, you know."

"They might deny it."

Worsley shrugged. "Then they deny it, but I have a feeling they'll cooperate—if what you say is true. In the meantime, we'll be checking every safe house the federal police have in the city."

"Sutton could have gone someplace else after our conversation. He knows lifeliners and our ability to remember everything we hear and see. He'll anticipate your search."

"It's worth a shot anyway. Until this is over, I would like you to remain here. I'll have uniformed men check everyone who attempts to enter the building. Sutton may have Dr. Lambert, but you and this young lady here could still be targets."

Nash shook his head. "I've got work to do at the Lifeliner Party headquarters, and I would prefer spending my time there."

"It's against my better judgment, but…okay. I'll take you there, but no wandering around. Deal?"

Nash grinned and extended his hand. "Deal."

They shook hands and Worsley sniffed the air. "I could use that coffee now, if I may."

Aleya looked anxiously at Nash and cleared her throat. "Does this mean I'll have to stay here?"

He turned to her. "No, of course not. You're coming with me. Get your pack."

She beamed at him and ran to her room.

Nash kicked himself for being insensitive. He was so engrossed with Worsley, he forgot about the most important person in the room. Probably not understanding everything, Aleya naturally thought she faced confinement in the apartment, a virtual prisoner. No wonder she looked worried. She might be smart and mature for her age, but she was still to fully develop emotionally.

* * *

A police cruiser on either side of the party headquarters building blocked access to the site and kept the curious at bay. Nothing attracted onlookers more than the macabre sight of fire and mangled metal. Speedways also dragged in their share of vultures. They weren't interested in cars going around in circles. What they wanted to see were vehicles smashing themselves to bits, parts flying everywhere, sirens wailing. Man's innate thirst for blood spectacles?

Worsley drove up and one of the dobers waved him through. A red fire brigade truck stood parked beside the entrance. Two firemen were winding in a long hose. The street and sidewalk glistened with water dribbling from inside the building. An entire section of glass wall beside the entrance gaped into a black interior, probably smashed in by firefighters needing to gain quick entry. Three dobers huddled together talking.

Nash got out and surveyed the damage with interest. He thanked Worsley for the ride and picked his way toward the open doorway. A work gang inside were already clearing away rubbish. He wrinkled his nose at the sharp burnt stink lingering in the air and led Aleya toward the elevators. Margot waited for them upstairs.

"Margi, I want you to meet Aleya. I'm told she is a little terror, so be warned."

Margot smiled warmly at Aleya and extended her hand. "I'm sure it's not true. You're just not being appreciated, right?"

Her face serious, Aleya nodded. "Right," she said and they solemnly shook hands. "My Aunty thinks I misbehave sometimes, but Nash doesn't." She looked at him. "Do you?"

He frowned, pretending to think it over. "Well…"

Aleya snorted. "I knew it! He always sides with Aunty."

Margot chuckled and wrapped a protective arm around the little girl's shoulder. "Come. I'll introduce you to someone who'll look after you." She gave Nash a conspiratorial wink and led Aleya away.

When she returned, she took him to The Room. Nash poured himself coffee and offered some to Margot, but she declined.

"Aleya is adorable," she gushed. "Mr. Bartlett told Warren and me how you two met. I think it's priceless."

"She certainly played her role to perfection," Nash agreed ruefully.

"How did she come to be in Dr. Lambert's custody?"

"Her parents were killed in a car accident by a drunken lifeliner."

Margot winced. "That's terrible, poor thing. I'm sorry about Dr. Lambert. I hope she'll be all right. What are you going to do?"

"Sutton demanded that I denounce the Lifeliner Party or he'll have her sterilized."

Her eyes grew round. "He wouldn't!"

"I'm afraid he would. It's not only me. You were told about the other kidnappings?"

She nodded. "The government cannot hope to get away with this."

"It might not be the government at all, Margi. From what Sutton told me, I think he is part of a much larger movement to eradicate lifeliners."

"I cannot believe this is happening, Nash. People aren't that cruel."

"What did you tell me the other day, welcome to realpolitik? Uncertainty and fear leads to hate. Governments know this and use it to promote their propaganda."

"Unfortunately, everything you said is true, and much of our campaign is based on countering that mindset."

"I know. I've been studying your indoctrination material."

She gave him a speculative smile. "I liked the impromptu interview you did yesterday morning. All the networks carried it. You handled it well, but you shouldn't take such risks. You could have been hurt if things got out of hand."

Nash shrugged. "I couldn't hide forever, and I had to face the mob sooner or later. I'm sure there will be more of the same as the campaign develops, but I think I managed to cast some uncertainty of my own."

Margot frowned. "When do you have to make your announcement?"

"Nine o'clock."

"That doesn't leave much time for the authorities to find Dr. Lambert and the others."

Glum, Nash nodded. "I know, but there is nothing else I can

do."

"There is. Do what Sutton wants."

"You think I haven't thought about it? I can hardly imagine what Cariana is going through right now. What is eating me up, Sutton will probably sterilize her regardless of what I do just to get back at me. Even if I do what he asks and she is unharmed, I'll be left with the realization that I walked away from something important for purely personal convenience."

"The party would survive, Nash, and the cause is not worth sacrificing Dr. Lambert."

He winced at the stab of helplessness that lanced through his chest. Could he sacrifice her for a movement that might not make any difference anyway? If he got her back, they would have their lives, but for how long? If he and others like him remained silent in the face of injustice, then he deserved what might come. Life, fortune, and honor. Wasn't that the price once paid?

"My sacrifice might not be the only one."

Her mouth curved down and her eyes glistened with raw emotion. "I'm so sorry, Nash," she whispered brokenly. "I never thought—"

"That's the problem, Margi. Everybody thinks this is purely a political fight, but it's much more. It is a fight for lifeliner survival in this country. I'm being melodramatic, but if the Suttons of this world are not stopped now, there is no hole large enough for us to crawl into and pretend everything is all right."

"That was well said, Mr. Bannon," a quiet voice said from the doorway.

Nash turned in surprise to see a distinguished figure, not having heard the door open.

Margot gasped and scrambled to her feet. "Nash, meet Curtis Sands, the party's national campaign manager."

Sands closed the door, smiled, and offered his hand. "I've been looking forward to meeting you," he said, his voice deep and resonant.

After reading so much about him, Nash felt slightly unnerved meeting a man who had done so much to influence laws on lifeliners. Not a tall individual, black hair slicked back, face lined with determination, hazel eyes shining with intelligence, Sands projected an aura of intensity and total commitment Nash found refreshing. This man appeared prepared to do whatever was necessary for the party.

He stood and they shook hands. "I am honored to meet you, Mr. Sands."

"Just Curtis, okay? Warren planned an introduction on Friday, but things got in the way." Sands pulled out a chair and sat down. "Normally, this is where I trot out my packaged welcome aboard spiel. Right now, though, we have a crisis of identity to deal with. You know by now that you're not the only candidate who's been targeted by Sutton's operation. I also had the dubious pleasure of talking to him. He wants more than have the Lifeliner Party denounced. He wants it disbanded. I believe him. I already received calls from wives and candidates begging me to do whatever it takes to get their loved ones released."

"Sutton asked you to make a public announcement?"

"Also at nine. I think it was timed to allow all capital city viewers to tune in."

"Have you heard from the other three candidates?"

"Two resignations: South Australia and Tasmania, but we have replacements in mind. Our ACT candidate is hoping she'll get her husband back."

"Has Sutton released the hostages following the resignations?"

"Not yet."

"He's waiting to see what you will do," Nash said.

"Or he has already acted and we haven't heard."

"He's applying maximum pressure, wanting to get us rattled." Sands gave a sour grin. "He hasn't done a bad job."

Nash pursed his mouth. "I'll make my announcement."

Sands and Margot exchanged glances. "You're doing the right thing."

"You got me wrong, Curtis. I'm not resigning or denouncing the party. I'll be denouncing Sutton and the faceless men behind him. People out there need to know what is going on."

Margot's eyes grew huge and her hand covered her mouth. After a moment of intense silence, Sands nodded.

"Are you sure you want to do this?"

"After what I said when you came in, this is hardly a time for second thoughts."

"Very well. I've already called the networks. They've been bugging me for an announcement." Sands stood and gave Nash a curious stare. "You know what might happen if the authorities fail to find the hostages in time?"

"Sutton could carry out his threat. I know. Have you heard from Warren?"

"He told me to spit in Sutton's eye."

Nash could clearly picture the crusty man doing just that. "How did Sutton take it?"

"He laughed."

"There is your answer, Curtis. Sutton told me he is fighting a war, and in war, you use whatever means you have to win. His words. I believe the hostages are doomed, regardless of what any of us do."

"I considered that possibility myself. If he and his backers intend to destroy the Lifeliner Party, this is merely the first salvo. We can debate this endlessly, but right now, I better get those reporters here or we'll miss our nine o'clock deadline. You'll make your announcement first."

When Sands left, Margot got up, fixed him a fresh cup of coffee and made one for herself. She sat down, took a sip and held the cup between her hands.

"What do you think of him?"

"I never expected to see a legend," Nash said. "He appears driven."

"He can be pretty intense sometimes," Margot agreed, "but

he's very much down to earth. These kidnappings, it's simply awful. When I joined the party, they told me I'd be organizing interviews, fundraisers, speeches, and grooming candidates. So far, it's been like that, but I never imagined in my darkest nightmares that we'd be facing something like this."

"This is not campaigning, Margi, but a program of species cleansing," Nash said softly. "All these years, I've been looking the other way, pretending it wasn't really happening."

She searched his face. "What if Sutton carries out his threat?"

Nash felt his face go hard. "If he does and I get my hands on him, I'll kill him."

His PID announced a call from Inspector Worsley. Nash dug out the smartphone and placed it on the table.

"What have you got, Inspector?"

"Hopefully something positive. The Signals Directorate did not openly admit they had the ability to track a PID that's been switched off, but they didn't deny it either. Police forces in all states are waiting to hear from them."

"That's encouraging, even if not definitive," Nash said.

"Has Sutton called you?"

"I doubt he will, especially after he sees my announcement, which gives you forty-three minutes to find Dr. Lambert."

Worsley scowled. "That's cutting it fine, Mr. Bannon."

"If the police Commissioner has any influence with the Signals Directorate, I would ask them to expedite their cooperation."

"Everything possible is being done," Worsley said and cut contact.

"This doesn't sound hopeful, Nash," Margot commented.

"Forty-odd minutes to locate Sutton and the hostages and marshal police to various state locations? Two hours wouldn't be enough. No, it doesn't sound hopeful. I have one more shot I can try, though."

Nash directed his PID to connect with Garrett Bartlett. The hologram cleared to show someone who aged years since last time they talked.

"I was about to call you, my boy," Garrett said in a tired voice. "Hell of a mess, this. I did get your message and I spoke to Van Ross. He built a fire under the Signals Directorate, but intelligence agencies are jealous of their secrets and reluctant to reveal them, especially to a politician who might be gone tomorrow."

Nash felt the weight around his heart grow heavier and, for the first time, he contemplated a real possibility of losing Cariana. He sympathized with others whose loved ones were taken, but they were remote, just words in a conversation. They did not touch him personally.

"It's hopeless, then."

"I wouldn't say that. Like any bureaucracy, they had to be persuaded using language they understood. Van threatened them with immediate personnel and budget cuts, and organizational restructuring if they failed to cooperate. I think they got the message. I hope it's in time to do some good."

"That's one secret I will reveal at my earliest opportunity."

Garrett frowned. "That might not be wise. There are security considerations."

"What considerations? When PIDs were introduced, the government guaranteed everybody total privacy."

"And you believed them? Well, do what you think you must. What are you going to do about Sutton?"

"I'm making a network announcement at nine to denounce him and his backers."

"I am sure you understand the implication."

"I understand all too well."

"If I hadn't dragged you into this—"

"Don't sweat it, Garrett. Sutton is not just after me."

"Thanks, my boy. Let me know what happens, okay?"

"Watch the nine o'clock news," Nash said and cut contact. He took a sip of coffee and smiled at Margot. "I came here for some training. It occurs to me that a good way to start would be a dry run of my announcement."

She returned his smile and spread her arms. "Might as well make myself useful."

It did not take long to go over what he wanted to say. Margot told him there might be questions afterword, reporters rarely satisfied with a bare statement. She tossed a few questions at him, but his heart wasn't in it.

Rats!

At 8:50, she went out to check if the media scrum had arrived. ABC, Nine, and Seven crews were in the boardroom, she told him, standing in the doorway.

One more thing left to be done.

"Can you give me a minute with Aleya?" he asked.

She nodded without saying anything. There wasn't anything to be said.

Aleya came in looking chipper. Margot glanced at him and closed the door after her.

Nash swiveled his chair and pointed at a spot on the floor in front of him. "Come here."

The envelope of radiance surrounding her changed to concern as she slowly walked toward him. He took her small hands in his and swallowed hard, not expecting this to be so difficult.

"Aleya, you know I love Cariana very much."

She crunched her nose. "I gathered that. What are all those reporters doing here?"

"I have to talk to them." He gently squeezed her hands. "What I have to say might cause Sutton to hurt your Aunty. I don't want that to happen, but I may not be able to stop him."

"Because you're not resigning as a Senate candidate? I heard what he would do if you didn't. You're afraid I might hate you if she gets hurt?"

Nash had always been amazed by her intelligence and speed of thought, and proud. More so now than ever.

"That's it."

"I will never hate you, Nash. No matter what happens."

He hugged her and patted her back. "Thanks. That means a

318

great deal to me."

His cell went off and he told his PID to accept the call.

"We found them, Nash!" Worsley gushed. "All of them. Dr. Lambert and Mr. Kairns are at the same location, but—"

"You won't reach them in time," Nash finished for him, feeling unbearably weary.

"I don't know about the interstate operations, but Sutton's mine. A house not far from the Lifeliner Party headquarters, as a matter of fact."

"Sirens wailing and lights blazing?" Nash blurted out, and immediately lifted his hand. "I apologize, Inspector. That was tactless."

"An understandable reaction. Don't worry about it. Can you delay your announcement by ten minutes?"

Nash checked his PID: 8:56.

"A couple of minutes at most while the stations make their intro. Sutton will know if I'm stalling."

Worsley sighed. "Well, do what you can," he said and cut contact.

Nash stood and pocketed his cell. He took Aleya's hand and made for the door.

"I hope the dobers get there in time," she said.

"Me too, honey. Let's go."

Her eyes grew round. "You want me there with you? In front of cameras and stuff?"

"Definitely. You need to hear what I have to say."

Margot waited outside and bundled them unceremoniously into the boardroom. Nash stood beside Sands and faced the reporters.

"We're all ready for you, Mr. Bannon," the Nine reporter announced, looking cool and composed. "You'll have to wait three minutes for top of the hour station lead-ins." She glanced at Aleya enjoying the attention, and smiled.

Well, that gave Worsley six minutes, Nash reflected.

"Will you take questions?" the Seven reporter asked.

"After my announcement," he told the tall, slim woman dressed in a gray business suit. Short black hair framed her pleasant round face.

Now that he faced his moment, Nash found it hard to wait as time seemed to slow down.

"Forty-five seconds," the Nine reporter said, her hand on her ear transceiver.

As the seconds wound down, she raised her right hand, then pointed an index finger at him.

This is it, old son. Don't blow it.

"My name is Nash Bannon, and I am a Senate candidate for the Lifeliner Party. Earlier this morning, Lifeliner Help Centers in every capital city were firebombed in a coordinated attack. At the same time, Lyle Sutton, a suspended Federal Police officer, and his men carried out a series of kidnappings. Three Lifeliner Party Senate candidates and family members, including the party's national president, Warren Kairns. Among the kidnapped was Dr. Cariana Lambert, a woman I happen to love. Standing beside me is her niece, Aleya.

"Sutton's demands are simple. All the candidates must resign and denounce the Lifeliner Party, or every hostage would be sterilized, perhaps even killed." Nash paused, and straightened. "I am here to announce that I will not resign, regardless of any personal tragedy this decision may cost me, and I am painfully aware what this announcement might mean for the hostages. Instead of denouncing the Lifeliner Party, I denounce Sutton and the faceless men behind this vile plot.

"A philosopher once said, 'The only thing necessary for the triumph of evil is for good men to do nothing.' I am making my stand, not for lifeliners, but for every person in this country. If we sit back and allow Sutton or any government to blatantly strip away our rights for which past generations have fought for, we will wake up tomorrow without any rights. Aleya and children everywhere will grow up without knowing what it is to be free. Is this the heritage we want them to have? Is this what we want for ourselves?" Nash looked at each reporter in turn and nodded. "Thank you for your time."

The Nine reporter immediately raised her hand. "Mr. Bannon, what is being done to rescue the hostages?"

Nash thought about that one for a second. Sutton undoubtedly watched, and would know his gambit had failed. Before acting, he may need to consult with his interstate teams first, unless they already had their orders. If he did not know about the Signals Directorate capability, it would not be wise to tell him. Every second Nash gave the dobers might make a huge difference for the hostages.

"I understand that police forces in every state are mounting a coordinated operation to free them."

"How do they know where they are held?" the Seven reporter demanded.

"I don't have that information."

"Do you believe Lyle Sutton's operation had government backing?" the ABC reporter interjected.

"Government and the Opposition, according to the former minister Gibbs Gilmore," Nash said. "On Sunday's *Insiders* program, he said, and I quote, 'This was a major ASIO and federal police operation. It could not have been done without approval of the National Security Committee. My understanding is that Mr. Gardner was appraised of the government's intentions.'"

"The Prime Minister categorically denied that allegation," she countered.

"All governments lie," Nash said and lifted his arm. "One more question only."

The Nine reporter stepped toward him. "Some will allege the kidnappings never happened, and the Lifeliner Party firebombed its own Help Centers to garner public sympathy for lifeliners."

The comment raised a stir among everybody. Nash stared hard at the reporter.

"I expected honest coverage from Channel Nine, not gutter journalism. I'm disappointed that you chose to sensationalize what is a grave event."

The reporter had the grace to blush as she stepped back. Her colleagues looked at her with disdain.

Nash's cell went off. He dug it out of his pocket and offered a small smile. "Excuse me. I have a call from Inspector Worsley." He directed his PID to accept.

Worsley looked harried and Nash felt a flutter of apprehension.

"Mr. Bannon, the raid on Sutton's safe house was successful, inasmuch that we got him and his accomplice."

"The hostages?"

"Mr. Kairns was shot, but is expected to pull through." Worsley cleared his throat and Nash steeled himself for bad news. "Dr. Lambert was injected with an unknown substance, presumably a chemosterilant. Tests will determine the exact nature of the substance."

Aleya reached for Nash's hand and quietly sobbed.

"Where is she now?" Nash demanded, his voice cold, devoid of feeling.

"We're moving her and Mr. Kairns to The Alfred. They have the necessary testing facilities."

"Please send a squad car to pick me up at the Lifeliner Party headquarters," Nash ordered harshly.

Worsley nodded. "I expected you would want that. It's already on the way."

"Any word on the other hostages?"

"I am still waiting for a full report."

Nash swallowed a hard lump that suddenly blocked his throat. "Thank you, Inspector." He switched off and glared at the Nine reporter with contempt. "Do you still think this was staged?" He turned to the Seven reporter. "You asked me how the police knew where the hostages were held. I did not deliberately mislead you, but I was not free to answer, fearing Sutton might take immediate action.

"Everything the government told us about personal PID privacy is a sham. The Australian Signals Directorate has the capability to track a person's PID even when switched off. That's how the hostages were found. The PID Tracking Feature legislation Neil Travers wanted to introduce would merely serve to legitimize an existing capability. Now, if you will excuse me."

He looked down at Aleya and led her toward the door as thick silence blanketed the room. Margot followed in his wake. Outside, cheeks wet, she hugged him.

"I don't know what to say," she choked against his chest.

"You just did," he told her tenderly. When she let go, he stroked Aleya's head and attempted a small smile. "Shall we go?"

She sniffed, put on a brave face, and nodded.

Side by side, they walked toward the elevator.

Downstairs, workmen were stripping away wall and ceiling cladding, which made an untidy pile in the middle of the floor. Nash picked his way among the debris and breathed easier when he stepped out. The dober standing beside the police car straightened and opened the back door. Nash waited for Aleya to clamber in, then slid in beside her.

Cariana sterilized...

There had to be some way to reverse the condition. He knew very little about the subject, but what he did know was not encouraging. He looked out the dome and the city was suddenly alien. Cold permeated from every building, and people scurrying about were objects of hate. He hated their indifference, apathy, and self-absorbed existence. The world around them could go to hell as long as it did not touch them personally. Wake up, go to work, come home, sleep, wake up...Mice on an endless, pointless, treadmill. Collectively, they held so much raw power in their hands to change everything, if only they could be made to care a little about what was happening around them. Most of them cared only about their little corner of life, hoping it hadn't crumbled away when they got home. One day when everything was rubble, it would be too late.

Nash hoped it wasn't already too late.

It did not help knowing that only a few days ago, he was exactly like them.

They crossed the Yarra and sped up St. Kilda Road. Gazing at the park sliding by, Nash was gratified to see the Olympic hammer thrower still had his hammer.

Aleya tugged at his arm. "What are you thinking about?"

Absorbed in his personal misery, he had forgotten about her.

"Hoping your Aunty will be all right."

"If Sutton had her sterilized, that means she cannot have children, right?"

"That's about the size of it."

"Can't the doctors do something about it?"

"We'll find out when we get to the hospital, but I hope there are things they can do."

She looked at him with large, dark eyes. "Even if they cannot help her, you'll still love her?"

He touched her shoulder and nodded. "I will always love her, no matter what."

"You're saying that now—"

"Aleya, when you love someone, it doesn't matter what happens to them. Right now, if I could make her whole, I would gladly have myself sterilized."

She digested that for a moment. "I sort of understand—"

He smiled at her. "Wait until you're in love. Then you'll understand."

In sickness and in health, for richer for poorer...

The car turned onto Commercial Road and did a U-turn in front of The Alfred Hospital.

"End of the line," the dober up front announced cheerfully.

"Thank you, officer," Nash said and climbed out.

Overhead, a sky ambulance was coming down for a landing. Autonomous cabs were pulling in and out from the taxi rank. Aleya in tow, he made his way up the flight of steps that led to the main entrance.

People filled the large lobby, hurrying from one connecting corridor to another. He gave his details at the Admissions desk and waited for the attendant to consult her computer. She looked up and smiled mechanically.

"Room 314 in this wing. Take the elevator behind you."

The third floor had a faint antiseptic smell and felt cold. Nash wondered why hospitals had to be this cold. A secret plan to keep patients longer when they caught pneumonia, no doubt.

Nash stopped at the wide doorway of room 314 and peered inside, his heart doing a little overtime. Four beds filled the sterile interior, two on either side of the room. A white plastic curtain hid the bed beside the window. Next to it, an elderly woman, her silver hair spilled across the pillow, lay motionless. He saw Cariana sitting up in the opposite window bed. Red tubes connected her wrists to a machine beside her. She spotted him and waved.

"Nash! Am I glad to see you."

"Aunty!" Aleya squealed and rushed in. Cariana helped her climb the bed and they hugged.

"Little terror. What have you been up to, eh?"

"Nothing. Honest. Isn't that right, Nash?"

"She's been an angel," he said and walked slowly toward the bed. Cariana fixed her eyes on him and her lower lip began to quiver. He took her in his arms and squeezed hard, not minding the twinge from his shoulder.

"It's okay," he whispered tenderly. "You're safe. That's all that counts."

She sniffed and dabbed at her eyes. "But—"

"No buts. We'll deal with it." He lifted her chin and kissed her.

Aleya squirmed and made a face. "Guys, do you have to?"

Cariana ruffled her hair. "Nobody said you have to watch."

"What's the red stuff?" Aleya pointed at the tubes.

"Blood. They're giving me a transfusion. It's only the first one. One more to go, but that won't be until tomorrow. Trent hadn't managed to give me a full shot and the doctors want to flush out

325

as much of the chemosterilant from my system as possible before my body absorbs it. It takes a while for the stuff to work, and because they got me early, they're hopeful the effect will be minimal."

Aleya looked at her. "Does that mean you won't be sterile?"

"They're not sure, my darling. I'll have to do some follow-up tests. It won't interfere with my work since I'll be here anyway."

"You'll be able to come home?"

"Tomorrow," Cariana said and turned to Nash. "I saw your announcement."

He gathered her hands. "Cariana—"

"You don't have to explain anything. I understand. I really do. What about the others?"

Nash rubbed her hands. "I don't know. Has Sutton mistreated you in any way?"

"They bundled me into a car and Trent sprayed something in my face. I woke up tied to a chair in a rundown kitchen."

"I saw that when I spoke to you. How were you freed?"

"We were watching your announcement and I could see Sutton getting angry. The lounge window suddenly shattered and a canister popped open. Sutton yelled 'Gas' and immediately shot another man tied up in the lounge. I felt Trent's injection, then everything went blank." She smiled and looked at Aleya. "I'm glad they didn't get you, my little terror."

Aleya squirmed with pleasure. "Nash looked after me."

He cleared his throat. "How long before you know—"

"The initial test results should be in by tomorrow night," Cariana said. "Fortunately for me, the syringe Trent used still half full when they found me." She reached up and brushed his cheek. "This must have been harrowing for you."

"Not as harrowing as it was for you, my bright constellation," he said in a tight voice. "That you can still smile after what they did to you…"

Her face clouded and some light in her eyes faded. "What if the tests show I'm sterile?"

He stroked her hand. "Even if that happens, there must be something they can do. Genotherapy or stem cell repair." He stared deep into her magical eyes. "No matter what, Cariana, I will never leave you. Never."

Despite her brave smile, a fat tear rolled down her cheek.

"Cube," she murmured and drew him to her.

Chapter Eight

"This election is not only to regain your freedom and privacy, which Labor and the Coalition are determined to steal from you. It is a fight for the rights that underpin that freedom. Rights which successive governments have already taken from you!"

Wild cheering broke from the modest crowd on the steps of the Victorian Parliament. Lifeliner Party banners and placards added color. Grim police held a cordon on the sidewalk to keep prowling Humans Only League and People First Party agitators from disrupting the rally. That did not prevent both sides from hurling invectives at each other. Media crews taped everything for immediate transmission and evening news segments.

Nash surveyed the crowd and pointed a finger at them. "Have you lost your job because you're a lifeliner? Do you like it when a dober stops you on the street and demands that he interrogate your PID because he felt like it? Do you like the idea of a $500 spot fine if you tried to block him? I don't want Centrelink forcing me every twelve months to update my photo, and if you don't, you are fined, and your benefits suspended until you comply. Every phone call you make right now is recorded. Everything you do on the Internet is recorded. Everything you buy is recorded. Big Brother isn't just coming. He is already here! I say enough! If you feel your privacy is being unjustly invaded, don't simply moan. Do something about it. Your vote matters, and you *can* change things."

More cheering spurred him on and he felt an electric tingle of excitement race through him. He never imagined that campaigning could be this exhilarating. He'd been run ragged since the launch on Tuesday, but standing before these people gave him a boost. He raised his arms.

"Canberra wants to legalize a PID tracking feature, supposedly to help you in an emergency, something that has already been made available to our intelligence agencies. At first glance, a noble objective, but they have a darker objective in mind. Readman and Gardner want nothing else than total control over your every movement and thought! Everywhere you go and everything you do will be monitored and analyzed for some sinister purpose. You won't be able to see a footy or cricket match without your motives being questioned. I don't want to see that happen to anyone, lifeliner or not. A government's singular responsibility is to protect its citizens and the country, but that does not mean looking suspiciously over your shoulder at everything you do! If you want to keep your privacy and freedom, vote for the Lifeliner Party! A party that is your voice for change! Raise that voice!"

The crowd went wild.

"Bannon! Bannon!"

Nash felt sweat run down his neck. The hot sun beat down from a clear sky and burned where it touched. Right then, he would have loved a cold beer.

"The government is calling for a referendum to introduce a fixed four-year term for both Houses. Ordinarily, I would support such an initiative. We are all tired having an election called whenever the government of the day feels it can beat the opposition. This hardly leaves any time for policymaking and getting things done. A four-year term would fix that, yes. But not right now! Voting 'Yes' will give the government unchecked power to further strip away your rights under the guise of protecting them. As a lifeliner, I won't have *any* rights! If you vote 'Yes', your freedom will be restricted even further. Is that the legacy you want for your children? Vote 'Yes' and you will be voting for autocracy, not democracy! Vote 'No' and vote for freedom!"

As the crowd cheered, Nash waved at them and strode toward the welcoming shade cast by the towering colonnades.

Margot beamed at him and clapped. Curtis Sands nodded as they shook hands.

"That was well done," he said solemnly. "You carried them."

"I didn't much like the looks from the prowling Humans Only League thugs," Nash growled.

"The cops kept them in check, but they did us a favor by being here."

Nash raised an eyebrow. "Oh? In what way?"

"You spoke about rights and freedoms, not sticking entirely to the script, but your spontaneity had conviction. The protesters represent the grim face of our opponents, and I think everybody here got the point. If the government organized the agitators, they overplayed their hand. The passersby would have seen the anti-lifeliner slogans and People First brown shirts. I hope it made them wonder at the shape of the next government they elect."

"I'm not comfortable having them around every time we have a rally somewhere."

Sands shrugged. "It's the price we pay for exposure. We cannot control who shows up. I wouldn't worry too much, though. Right now, we need to differentiate ourselves from the major party candidates and the extreme fringe, especially since we're not fully geared up with fliers, email drops, and ads. If we can get the guy on the street equating the People First Party with Labor and the Coalition, we're halfway there."

Nash wasn't sure he liked the tactic, but he understood the rationale, Garrett's maxim loud in his mind. *You run on emotion by exposing people's fears and concerns, regardless how irrational, and blame it on the other guy.*

Sands scowled at him. "Wipe that holier-than-thou look off your face, Nash. This isn't kindergarten squabbling. You rip out your opponent's heart, or by damn, he'll do it to you. Now, ready to face the networks?"

Nash raised a hand in surrender. "I'm still green when it

comes to campaigning, Curtis. You'll have to give me time to adjust, but you're running me into the ground! Two breakfast appearances, three radio shows, a lunchtime rally, and now more interviews?"

"That's how the game's played," Sands said without showing any sympathy.

"Your schedule doesn't leave me any room to breathe! At this pace, I won't last the distance."

"You'll live. You have a radio show with Triple R at 2:30 and a Sky News plug at four," Sands bore on remorselessly. "Don't forget the fundraiser at the Hawthorn Town Hall tomorrow."

"Even if I could, I'm sure you'll remind me," Nash said dryly and Sands chuckled.

"Now you know why I never ran for office again."

"Is there time for lunch anywhere in this?"

"We'll squeeze something in before your Triple R."

Nash sneered. "It's not an afterthought, is it?"

Margot laughed and patted his shoulder. The patch had come off yesterday and the scar hardly showed. Everybody in his family healed quickly. On a swimming outing when sixteen, he and Mark were fooling around at the local pool. Nash slipped on wet tiling and gashed his right thigh. Lots of blood and screaming from the girls, and the wound required nine stitches, but he had them out within three days. Now, he could not even tell where he'd been hurt.

"You're doing well, Nash. People respond to you, and you don't couch your message with spin. That's refreshing. More importantly, you are starting to draw in more normals than lifeliners, and that's significant. We need to syphon off voters from the major parties if we're to win seats."

Sands frowned. "I would still like to hold the Geelong rally on Saturday—"

"Nothing doing, Curtis!" Nash shook his head. "No weekend campaigning."

"The first ten days—"

"Are important to establish visibility and profile. I know, you keep telling me, but I think I had enough visibility after being shot and Cariana kidnapped. I'll go this far. I'm prepared to do Geelong on Sunday afternoon and Ballarat on Monday."

Sands glanced at Margot and sighed. "Three days on the campaign trail and he wants weekends off."

She smiled and raised her arms in surrender.

By the time he finished the Sky News interview, Nash had about as much campaigning as he could take. Emotionally and physically drained, the exhilaration he felt earlier had faded to dull weariness. Four more weeks? He didn't have a packed schedule every day, Margot told him, but he should not expect much letup until polling day. Her observation failed to cheer him up. At least he did not have to worry about the organizational side of campaigning.

The party had found a replacement candidate for South Australia and, according to Sands, she was on board, provided she passed the grueling vetting process, made much harder by the fact that she wasn't a lifeliner. Wary of a plant by one of the major parties, the organization didn't take any chances. If accepted, she would make a tremendous publicity asset. A non-lifeliner on a Lifeliner Party ticket...it would draw them in.

Nash had read Paula McNeil's resume, a former ABC political journalist, and liked the positive image she projected, but he would only start to follow her closely once she began to run. He had enough homework viewing and absorbing what the other candidates were doing. Somebody else's blooper could derail his own campaign.

He started to appreciate the level of responsibility Sands, Margot, and the party administrative staff carried to coordinate and manage the overall national operation. State branches did a lot of the grunt work, which helped, but policy and tactics came from Melbourne. He didn't envy them their job.

Then stop moaning about yours, old son.

The summer sun still high, Nash was grateful for the cab's

soothing air-conditioning. Surrounded by the polarized plastic dome, he had an excellent view of everything around him. The Flinders Street hub swarmed with people getting off trams, surging toward the station to catch that train home, or waiting to board a tram out of the city. As always, enough individuals were scrambling across the tracks to give the tram computer a nervous breakdown and clang its bell in alarm. Trams were nose to tail during the afternoon rush, but missing a train meant waiting in the heat on a platform crowded with commuters who wanted to be out of there. Having a city apartment did have its advantages.

Although heavy, the traffic moved smoothly up St. Kilda Road. A low bank of fluffy clouds hung in the south, heralding a welcomed cool change and rain during the night. Tomorrow, though, would be hot again; 34C the man said. Hot or cold, Nash didn't worry about it. He never wasted energy on things he could not influence.

His PID told him he had a call from his father. He dug out the cell and waited for the hologram image to appear.

"Hi, Dad. What's up?"

His father smiled, and Nash marveled at his old man's youthful looks. Genes, as he quipped once to Cariana.

"Checking how you're doing. From what I see in the news, they're keeping you busy."

"I'm glad tomorrow is Friday," Nash said, "and I'll have the weekend to myself…almost. They've got me booked for a rally in Geelong on Sunday afternoon."

"The party is getting good reviews from commentators, and your polling numbers are climbing."

"It's still early in the game, Dad, but I *am* encouraged by the public response so far. Our Western Australian candidate isn't doing well and Sands is flying up there on Monday to shake the party tree."

"Not everybody can cut it. How's Kairns?"

"He's a tough old bird and he'll pull through. Fortunately, there were no postoperative complications. I'm on my way to

The Alfred to see him."

"And Cariana?"

The cab walls closed around Nash and the world became darker.

"They managed to get most of the chemosterilant out of her system, but she has a damaged left ovary. They're hoping stem cell therapy will repair it, but the ovary is a complicated organ. No way to tell if any of her eggs were damaged. We'll have to wait and see. Rodney Stevenson, our NSW candidate, wasn't so lucky; his testes are completely fried. Tamara Reed, the QLD candidate, is also totally sterile, but both are sticking with the campaign. Unless they do something dumb, they stand a good chance of getting elected. Fortunately for the other hostages, the dobers got to them in time."

His dad sighed and shook his head. "Nasty business. I hope they nail Sutton to the wall."

"I wanted to see him, but they wouldn't let me near him."

"Killing such vermin isn't worth ruining your life, son," Dad said gently.

"I'll never know, will I? What about you? Has QANTAS decided to keep you?"

"There were the usual office rumors about letting me go, but the CEO can read the public opinion tealeaves as well as anybody. As a matter of fact, they're advertising for pilots, lifeliners welcome."

"Well, what do you know? Perhaps there is hope for us yet."

"I wouldn't celebrate too soon, son. Whoever is behind Sutton won't be giving up because one operation went sour."

"It's a grim scenario, Dad, but I have to agree. I talked to Mark yesterday, and it looks like his job is secure—"

"For the time being. The bureaucrats are probably waiting to see who'll be in government in March before doing anything. Firing him now would give the Coalition publicity they don't want. Readman's polling numbers have taken a dive."

"From what I've seen of Labor's policies, there isn't much to pick between them."

"Like you said, it's still early. The reason I called, if you and Cariana don't have anything arranged for tomorrow evening, we'd like to have you over for dinner. It's about time we met the girl."

"I'd love to, Dad, but I promised Nat—"

"Didn't I tell you?" his father frowned and gave a sheepish smile. "No, I guess I didn't. Nat said if it's okay with you, she's happy to come with Shaun and the kids. By the way, you must bring Aleya. We're all dying to see her."

"Mom's going to be run off her feet cooking for everybody."

"It'll be a barbeque in the backyard. Your mother will do the salads and enjoy a culinary treat, courtesy of your old man."

Nash laughed. His dad's barby events were legendary, and his cooking philosophy simple. Once it stopped bleeding, it was okay to eat.

"If Cariana agrees, we'll be there, and thanks. I'll let you know this evening."

"Take care, son."

"A hug for Mom, okay?"

"I'll give her more than that!" His dad laughed and cut contact.

Nash pocketed the cell, leaned back against the upholstery and smiled. Nothing fazed his old man. He dealt with problems as they came and didn't worry too much about the future. Nash figured that some of that attitude must have rubbed off on him, because he also never worried too much about the what-ifs. Planning was one thing, but he did not indulge in pathological fingernail gnawing.

He told the PID to connect with Cariana. Her hologram image flickered into life and he reached with his hand to touch her, wishing the image were real. She had to be hurting inside, and he wanted badly to take away her pain and doubts.

"I'm on my way over to see Warren. When I'm done, we'll meet at the Admissions desk. I'll call you. Suits?"

"Fine. I'm looking forward to a break, but it'll have to be a short one. I'm running a computer model and I want to see how it comes out."

"Well, if it's something *important*…"

"Cube." She laughed and her face became radiant. "I may have done it, Nash!"

"Done what?"

"Found one of the hormonal switching triggers that comes into play at onset of pubescence."

"Say, that's great. Writing a paper on it?"

"As soon as I get confirmation from my model. This is *exciting*!"

"I can see that. You're positively glowing."

Her left cheek dimpled. "Call me when you're done with Warren and I'll tell you all about it."

"Deal. See you soon."

Her bubbling enthusiasm, personal problem momentarily forgotten, made him happy.

Tuesday had been a rough day…for both of them. Margi had lined up a breakfast show appearance, two radio interviews, and a walkabout through the CBD with two of her assistants, glad-handing and chatting to people and reporters. He had to build visibility, she told him, and accept the slog of ground roots campaigning.

Cariana called him late in the afternoon, clearly upset. Her tests were in, the news not all good. Feeling lousy and angry that this happened, he tried to soothe her, but not something he could do over the phone. He told his two minders the day was over and took a cab to The Alfred, simmering with impatience as the car crawled through the traffic.

She waited for him at the Admissions desk wearing a white lab coat. A working day for her, but he suspected it was only to keep her distracted; trying not to think about the tests, nevertheless dreading what might come. When she saw him, her features broke and tears of misery slid down her cheeks. He embraced her and held her tight, whispering calming words, wishing he could make her smile again. He led her into the coffee shop and waited for her to settle down.

"The egg was damaged. They'll do more tests over the next three ovulation cycles, but…" Her eyes glistened as she searched his face.

"You're afraid that you might not have a healthy baby?"

She nodded and dabbed at her eyes with a tissue.

He reached for her hands and squeezed. "There are things they can do."

"I know, but even after treatment, there will be a residual risk factor."

"Don't shatter yourself emotionally over a remote possibility—"

"Not so remote."

"My sweet, I cannot imagine what you must be going through, but no matter what happens, we'll work it out, okay?" He reached with a finger and stroked her cheek. "We still have dinner tonight at the Vue de Monde, or have you forgotten?"

"Nash, I don't feel like going out. Not tonight."

"And miss seeing Melbourne's night lights? I'll drag you there if I have to."

She managed a small smile and sniffed.

Understandably moody when he picked her up, she perked up as they strolled hand in hand along the crowded lower Collins Street toward the Rialto Tower. The air had a soft, intimate quality, and the sun did not burn as it slowly settled for the evening, painting the sky with a yellow and orange brush.

Cariana didn't say much, apparently content to have his reassuring presence near her, and he did not intrude into her thoughts with shallow banalities. She accepted that he would not leave her, and he liked to think the realization helped give her strength in some small way.

When they rode the empty elevator to the revolving restaurant, she turned her almond eyes on him and smiled faintly.

"Thank you," she whispered, and his heart lifted.

When dusk fell and the city cloaked itself with light, so did Cariana's face.

They talked about inconsequential things, happy to enjoy each other's company, pushing back the shadows for a time. It developed into a very pleasant evening for both of them.

Two days ago, but it seemed like a lifetime.

Nash watched the cars flow around him, memories playing in his mind. He made her forget, even if only for a little while, and he treasured her rewarding smile when he dropped her off.

The cab stopped at The Alfred taxi rank and he made his way inside. On the fifth floor, he missed a turn and had to double back, all wards looking the same. He spotted Warren's private room, knocked and went in.

"Anybody home?"

Warren's face broke into a broad smile. "Nash! This is a pleasant surprise. Come on in and pull up a chair."

White and sterile, the room not exactly the Hilton, but it looked comfortable. Nash recognized the Channel Ten presenter as the holoview wall died, replaced by pooling colors.

"Just watching the news," Warren explained as he propped himself higher again the pillows. "Not much else to do around here, and Margot won't let me connect with Roger. Damned cheek, I say."

Nash smiled as he eased himself into a chair. "She doesn't want you stressed."

"Stressed? I get stressed when I don't know what's going on!"

"How's the old body?"

"The surgeon tells me I'll live. I suppose he ought to know. At least I hope he does."

"Any pain?"

"I'm a little sore despite being doped up, but it could have been worse. No peritonitis and the sutures should be absorbed in a couple of weeks."

"How long before you're up and about?"

"Another four days or so, they tell me, and then it's on crutches! Bah! At least I'll start having decent food. They've got me on this liquid mush, which doesn't taste bad, but you cannot get your teeth into it." Warren gave Nash a speculative gaze. "You wouldn't happen to have a Big Mac on you or something?"

Nash laughed, glad to see the older man in good spirits.

"Next time," he said, and Warren hooted with delight.

"I'll hold you to it." His face became serious. "Thanks for coming to see me, Nash. I mean it."

"Sorry I couldn't do it earlier," Nash told him. "You weren't in any shape for visitors on Tuesday, and they had me running around all day yesterday."

"Don't worry about it. I know what campaigning is like."

"I also came to see Cariana."

"How is she?"

Nash shrugged. "Fine physically, all things considered. It will take a while to sort herself out emotionally. The prospect of being partially sterile or producing a defective baby down the track is eating at her."

"You're not running out on her, are you?" Warren demanded sternly.

"Not a chance."

"Good. Going to marry the girl?"

Nash found himself in a cauldron of mixed emotions. He wouldn't mind taking the next step, but it was one of those future things, and she did say she didn't want to rush it. She might be even more reluctant to pursue a relationship with the problem she faced now. Did she look for an excuse to push him away—like he pushed her away—sparing him possible pain for not being able to have a family?

Another supersaturated situation?

"We've only been dating for about two months. She's not ready."

"Piffle! Women are never ready. You have to drag them into it, and sometimes they do the dragging," he added with a grin. "I

339

proposed to my second wife a week after I met her. After fourteen years, we're still together. We had our bumps and potholes, but we worked through them. You only have to know two things about a woman. Do you love her and does she love you? If you can tick both boxes, you can stop at GO and collect your two hundred. You kids overanalyze things too much." Warren smirked. "Caught you flatfooted for a minute, eh?"

Nash returned the smile. "You have an unusual way of looking at things."

"Balls! When you get to be my age, you learn to cut through the crap, that's all." Warren sighed, shifted slightly and grunted. "Those damned stitches. I feel like I'm in a straightjacket. We're running our most important campaign ever and I'm stuck here."

"That doesn't seem to have hampered your style," Nash told him.

Warren cocked an eyebrow. "Margi ratted on me?"

"You know Margi. She never gossips."

"Ah, it's that bastard Sands, then. He could have been the party president if he wanted to, but he prefers to jerk my strings."

Nash grinned. "You know everything there is to know about campaigning. He'd be a fool not to take advantage of that, even if you're in a hospital bed."

"I suppose." Warren waved at the holoview. "They should let me connect with Roger!" he growled irritably. "From what I've seen, the campaign is doing okay and I like how you've been handling yourself, Nash. You have intensity and a good delivery style. The crowds respond to you and your interviews are polished."

"Margi's coaching. I must admit, public speaking has given me a buzz a few times."

"It should, and passion comes across. People see it and respond. It sticks in their head, which is important when they compare you with the opposition. I saw the Sky News clip you did this afternoon. It was good, but you're being too nice to Readman and Gardner. Get stuck into them and expose their bankrupt policies! You haven't descended into personalities, and don't. Voters don't like it. As the campaign wears on, you'll be tempted to make promises. Again, don't. Even if we manage to get a couple of Senate seats, we may not be in a position to do much unless the crossbench sides with us, but we *can* voice voter concerns."

"That might not be enough," Nash said quietly.

The older man sighed and nodded. "I know, but we're getting ahead of ourselves. Let's get you elected first." He winced again as he shifted, suddenly looking tired.

Warren tried to project a chipper image, but he had a serious injury and needed rest and quiet without worrying about campaigning. Nash stood.

"You take it easy and don't break anything inside. I'll be seeing you."

"Thanks again for dropping by." Warren smiled, his eyes alive with fire. "I wish to God I was out there with you."

"You will be. We still have four weeks to go. Sands has things under control."

"I'll hand out the congratulations when I see our candidates elected," Warren mused. "Don't forget the Big Mac!"

Nash smiled, waved to him and walked out.

In the elevator, flanked by two bulky ladies and a woman driving a double pram, Nash looked forward to having Warren's firm hand back in charge, even if from a wheelchair or with crutches.

In the lobby, he called Cariana and waited for her to come down. Her lab coat did not hide her radiant face as she hurried confidently toward him. Without saying anything, she wrapped her arms around his neck and glued her lips to his. Not very professional behavior, but no one seemed to mind, judging by smiles from several men and indulgent glances from the ladies.

She disengaged herself after a satisfying moment, curled her arm through his, and steered him toward the coffee shop. They snagged an empty little corner table facing the street and Nash went to the counter to get their drinks. Cariana downed her mineral water as if she'd been out in the desert. After demolishing half the bottle, she looked up and raised her eyebrows.

"What?"

"A little thirsty, are we?"

She smiled sheepishly. "It's that damn computer model. I've been tweaking it since last week. It's finally starting to produce decent data and I'm keen to see the latest run."

"You do your own programming?"

"Some of it, but I've got a master's candidate doing the hackwork for me."

"What exactly are you doing?"

She sipped more water. "At eleven or twelve, the brain releases a hormone that starts the onset of puberty. When it reaches the pituitary, the gland produces two other hormones that begin to transform the body. The pituitary also releases prolactin, primarily known for its role in mammals to produce milk, but the hormone is essential for some 300 other processes, many poorly understood. One of the main production regulators of prolactin is dopamine, which is produced by the hypothalamus, responsible for controlling a range of metabolic processes. Remember our discussion about energy management?"

Nash furrowed his head in concentration. "In lifeliners, prolactin switches on the synthesis of pyruvate into leucine and valine?"

"It certainly does! Remove the pituitary and a lifeliner ends up with a normal liver."

"Wait a minute. This means the ability to synthesize pyruvate is coded at conception, not by your gene switchboard at onset of puberty." Nash stared at her, then lifted a finger. "Ah, dopamine."

"You should have been a geneticist." Cariana beamed at him. "The brain has a number of distinct dopamine pathways. The most understood is the role it plays in reward-motivated behavior. What is less understood are environmental factors that influence production of dopamine. Somehow, at conception, dopamine is responsible for switching on a number of genes that produce a lifeliner baby."

"What about changes triggered during puberty?"

"That's where the hypothalamus rears its head. I'm hoping the model will confirm my hypothesis. I told you organic chemistry is complicated."

Nash finished his mineral water and sat back. "Not complicated at all. Couples make love when they have a mortgage they cannot serve, credit they cannot repay, jobs taken over by robots, stress they cannot cope with, the hypothalamus kicks in and you end up with a lifeliner."

"You're being facetious, but you could be more right than you know," Cariana said. "The problem is finding out how it does it."

"It doesn't sound like you'll be getting to the bottom of it anytime soon."

"I'm not the only researcher working on this." She examined his face. "You haven't asked me the obvious question."

"No, I haven't, because I already know the answer. There was only one way to obtain the body of knowledge you've been working with…living tissue."

She gave a sour smile. "And I'm guilty by association."

"It's a complicated ethical dilemma, Cariana, and I wasn't moralizing. Knowledge has its own inertia, regardless how it's obtained."

For a second, she had a distracted look common to people consulting their PID.

"I'd love to chat some more, Nash, but you'll have to excuse me. I've got to get back to my lab."

He nodded. "I understand. About our outing tomorrow night. A change of plans."

"Oh? You're booked for an interview or something?"

He smiled. "No interviews."

"By the way, I've seen coverage of your Parliament rally. You're a good public speaker."

"I must admit I'm enjoying it, but the pace is killing me. I never figured it would be this intense."

"Four more weeks, you'll live."

"Your sympathy for my suffering is appreciated," he told her wryly, and Cariana laughed.

"I'll express my sympathy more fully this weekend. You're still okay for Woodend on Saturday?"

"I wouldn't miss it. I'll drop by around ten, and we're off to Daylesford."

"I'll pack a picnic hamper. So, what's the change in plan for tomorrow?"

"My old man has invited us for a barbeque. Nat and her brood will be there. They're all keen to see you and Aleya. I'll call it off if it makes you uncomfortable."

"I'd love to meet your family, but…"

"But what?"

"After what happened—"

"You have nothing to worry about, my sweet. Trust me. Nat is already talking like you're her sister."

"Well, if you think it's all right…"

"My family is different. You'll like them. I'll pick you up at six."

"Okay." She reached for her bottle and drained it. "Thanks for dropping by, Nash. It was nice of you to do that." She stood, gave him a quick kiss on the mouth, fluttered her fingers at him and walked out.

He sat in the noisy little café, empty bottle between his hands, and gazed at Fawkner Park across the street. Two trams passed each other and clanked their bells. Traffic already heavy as people headed for the suburbs. Patchy clouds smeared the sky with gray, heralding the change.

He was pleased to see Cariana chipper and making progress with her research. Once they cracked the lifeliner genome, what then? Another tool to identify and track lifeliners? Man's insatiable thirst for knowledge opened unimaginable opportunities, but knowledge was also a sword without compassion. A knife was a useful tool around the kitchen, but it can also kill. It wasn't the knife's fault. It takes a twisted mind to turn a tool into a weapon.

There was no getting around man's duality. Savages in suits.

A woman with two boys in tow walked in and searched anxiously for a free table. Nash got up and waved to her. She thanked him and smiled as he walked past her. Outside, he climbed into a cab and told it to take him to Federation Square. He needed to buy something.

* * *

Nash drove up the driveway, stopped beside the veranda and got out. Although warm, the air felt fresh and alive, and he breathed deeply. Felix deigned to give him a brief look without lifting his head off his paws and went back to dozing. How carefree can life get!

The front door flew open and Aleya swarmed over him.

"Nash! You're here!"

He gave her a tight hug and allowed her to drag him into the house.

"My last free weekend before going back to school," she declared without enthusiasm and pouted.

"You don't like your school?"

"It's not bad, I suppose," she conceded reluctantly. "But holidays are better. Aunty! We have a visitor!"

In the kitchen, Cariana placed a red checkered towel over the woven hamper, looked up, and smiled.

"Hi there. We're almost ready." She glanced at Aleya. "Aren't we, little terror?"

Aleya rolled her eyes. "Do you have to call me that?"

"I do, because you are a little terror."

Aleya turned imploringly to Nash. "Make her stop calling me that, can you?"

Nash chuckled and nodded. "I'll see what I can do." He

pointed at Cariana's outfit. "Looking good, my sweet."

Blue jeans and a black T-shirt suited her and highlighted her fine figure. Golden hair tied into a ponytail, her face shone with health.

"You're not bad yourself."

He wore jeans and a short-sleeve shirt, but with a reversed color combination.

She pursed her lips and looked searchingly around the kitchen. "Nothing left behind…All set."

Aleya came out with her signature red backpack and headed for the main door. Nash picked up the hamper and followed. Felix did not even bother opening his eyes. Nash slid the hamper and two empty ten-liter plastic water containers into the trunk and doors banged as everyone got into the car.

Once on the tree-lined arterial, he set speed at 100 and re-laxed. Rolling fields fell away behind them as the car ate up the kilometers. Sunlight flickered at them between the passing gums.

Aleya leaned forward and propped her arms on the back of Nash's seat. "What's the program?"

Cariana scowled. "Aleya!"

"Just asking."

Nash glanced at her image displayed on the dome. "I thought we'd do some horse-riding at Boomerang Ranch—"

"Cool!"

"After that, we'll stop at Jubilee Lake for a picnic lunch and some canoeing. Then, if you're still feeling energetic, we can stroll through the Mill Markets and maybe pick up some trinkets."

"Can we go swimming?"

"At the lake."

"Cool. I had a great time at your parents' place yesterday, and I like Adriana."

Nash smiled. "She has taken a shine to you as well."

"Can I see her again sometime? They could all come to Woodend. Can they, Aunty?"

"We'll see, my darling." Cariana turned to Nash. "Your parents are remarkable people, and I was quite taken in by Natalie. A new oilfield in Bass Strait? That's quite a find."

"I have always been proud of Nat," Nash said.

"That's not what she told me. You and Mark played some horrible pranks on her."

"You're right, we did, but as she got older, both of us started to appreciate how much fun it was having her around."

"She has a soft spot for you. She has never forgotten what you did for her at Jubilee Lake."

"Did she tell you how she drove a nail through my runner?"

"She did what?"

"I spiked my heel and hobbled around for two days. Mom was worried I'd get tetanus despite getting a shot a while back."

Cariana laughed. "Ah, not such an innocent little girl after all. I'll have to ask her to fill me in on everything."

"We all played pranks on each other," Nash admitted.

"I think your mother is a darling. She has intensity and determination, but there is also steel behind her kind face."

"That's my Mom. Mark and I gave her a hard time as teenagers, but she kept us in check."

"You didn't turn out too badly," she said softly and rested her hand on his thigh.

"Oh, that is so touching," Aleya said, hand across her heart, pretending to swoon.

Cariana glared at her. "One more remark like that and you'll be eating breadcrumbs!"

"Nash will feed me, won't you?"

"I don't know. If I take sides, I could also end up eating breadcrumbs."

Aleya snorted in disgust. "Nobody cares about me."

Nash glanced at Cariana and chuckled.

Wound up, Aleya chattered about her friends and going back to school. Despite her disclaimer that she didn't like school much, she admitted that some subjects were challenging, and teachers allowed them scope to pursue studies outside the loosely defined curriculum.

"Next year, I'm going to finish high school and apply to go to a university," she declared with determination.

University at fourteen? With bright kids around her, Nash did not see any reason why she couldn't.

After thirty minutes of easy country driving, they hit leafy Daylesford. From a sleepy little town tucked against the hills, it had expanded into a trendy tourist attraction, popular even during winter months. The main street crawled with cars, and people enjoyed a warm day in a relaxed atmosphere absent in the impersonal city. Nash drove through and took the road that led to the Boomerang Ranch.

They got there in time to join a small group preparing to ride out. Nash was surprised when Aleya told him shyly that she had never seen a real live horse close up before. He showed her how to make friends with her mount, all saddled up and ready to go. She reached up to touch its muzzle and gasped in surprise.

"It's so soft!"

The horse snorted and nuzzled her shoulder.

More confident, she stroked its neck.

Watching her, Nash felt that kids these days were losing a vital link with nature. Not only with animals, but the outdoors in general. He recalled a holoview clip he saw three years ago of children at the Melbourne Easter Show. There were the usual rides, amusement stalls, food courts, and animal pens. A young woman led her little girl to a duck enclosure. The kid stared in fascination at the white ducks and clutches of yellow ducklings. She crouched and stared at the little creatures. When several of them padded toward her, she shrank back in alarm, clung to her mother and began to cry.

He was not surprised to learn that many kids thought that milk, eggs, fruit, and meat were grown on supermarket shelves. Impersonal, sterile suburbs and cities, that's where children grew up these days, not knowing the joy and freedom of running in meadows, exploring the bush, climbing trees, and getting dirty. The last part might not be all that exciting if it resulted in a massaged posterior.

The academics pontificated learnedly and wrote papers, but those papers had done nothing to reassure the little girl that ducklings were friendly and fun to be with.

After an hour of meandering along bush tracks, a stop at a small lake for drinks, some exhilarating galloping, feeling a little saddle sore, they returned to the parking lot. Aleya pranced among the horses, touching and stroking them, her face radiant with joy. On the way to Jubilee Lake, she insisted that they had to do this again, and soon.

Although somewhat crowded, the Lake's grounds weren't packed with weekenders, and Nash managed to find a small wooden bench beneath a towering white gum where they could have lunch. Cariana unpacked the hamper, which caused a scramble for chicken drumsticks, coleslaw, juice, and crusty bread, with Aleya providing most of the excitement.

Bright sunshine, clear skies, a whispering breeze stirring the leaves, the smell of eucalyptus in the air, all contributed to a healthy appetite. Having satisfied her immediate needs, Aleya scampered off to feed bread to wandering peacocks strutting their plumage.

Kids chased each other in the open playground. One little boy pointed a bright orange toy gun at his running friend and shouted, "You're dead, lifeliner! You're dead!" The other kid skidded to a stop, clutched his chest, and crumpled to the ground. The kid with the gun danced triumphantly around his fallen foe.

Along the glistening lake waters, picnickers enjoyed their snacks, or simply sprawled on the grass soaking in the rays. A few canoes dotted the lake and several couples sat side by side on small pedal boats.

Watching one pair, more interested in gazing at each other than where the boat was taking them, prompted Nash into action. He did not expect this to happen so soon, but after talking

349

to Kairns on Thursday, he saw no reason why he should not make the commitment now.

Cariana sipped some juice, placed the plastic cup on the bench with a sigh, and leaned against the tree trunk.

"Ah, this is grand. If we bottled this air and sold it back in the city, we'd make a fortune."

"After a day here, life has a different slant, all right," he agreed and dug into his trouser pocket. He held out a small red velvet jewel box and opened it. A clear blue sapphire ring rested on a bed of white satin.

"Cariana…"

She turned, saw the ring, and her eyes grew huge.

"Oh my," she whispered.

He reached for her hand and stroked her fingers.

"I love you, my bright constellation, and I want you to shine for me always. Will you do that for me, my sweet? Will you marry me?"

She blushed, then something faded in her face. When she looked at him, instead of seeing joy, sadness had taken the glitter out of her eyes.

"My prince…under different circumstances, I would love to be your constellation, but it cannot be. I cannot shine for you."

Nash had anticipated this, but her words still squeezed his heart. Instead of making her happy, his proposal had turned into rejection. Because he was a lifeliner? No, there had to be something else.

"Because you might be sterile?" He brought her hand to his lips and kissed it. "I love you, my Cariana, and I will always love you, no matter what. You have filled something in me that has been empty for too long. I don't want you to take it away now. Nothing I do would matter anymore. Whatever shadows may hang over us, we'll work through them. I want you to stand beside me, Cariana. Always."

A tear slid down her cheek and she bit her lower lip. "Oh, Nash. I don't know. I don't want to disappoint you."

"Disappoint me? I feared that I would disappoint *you*!" He took the ring and slipped it on her finger. "For all time if you will have me," he told her gently, searching her eyes, bright with emotion.

She looked at the ring for a long time, then gave him a radiant smile.

"I will shine for you, my prince." She leaned across the bench and wrapped her arms around his neck. The kiss lingering and sweet, a promise of love shared.

He cupped her face between his hands and they touched foreheads. After a moment, at peace, he pulled back and wiped her wet cheek. She grasped his hand and held it tight.

"For all time," she said.

Aleya ran toward them, saw something in their faces, and skidded to a stop.

"What's going on?"

Smiling, Cariana showed her the ring.

Aleya gaped. "Wow. Does this mean—"

"It does, my little terror."

"Cool!" She suddenly froze. "You guys will want to be alone now and you won't want me around anymore, right?"

Nash's heart tore seeing her like that. Did she think they would abandon her?

"Come."

Hesitating, she slowly walked toward him. He took her small hands in his.

"Remember how you wished I could be your dad? I can be now if you still want to."

She blinked. "You mean it?"

"I would love to be your dad, Aleya."

Her eyes lit with inner fire and she threw herself at him. "Oh, Nash, I so much wanted this."

He held her and stroked her hair.

Cariana sniffed and smiled at him. "Thank you, my shining prince."

Aleya pulled back. "Dad…I like the sound of that." She crunched her nose. "Wait a minute. How can you be my dad? Aunty isn't my mother."

"We'll adopt you," Nash told her and watched as she worked that out. "Once I do that, I'll be able to call you little terror."

She beamed at him. "You can call me anything you like…Dad. Wow, wait till I tell my friends. This is so awesome."

They spent most of the afternoon on water and in it. Nash and Cariana rented a pedal boat and drifted lazily across the lake. Aleya powered her canoe around them, taunting them to a race, which she won easily. He could not believe her energy, supplemented by an occasional raid on the hamper.

Cariana's hand in his, he allowed the boat to meander over the placid water where it liked. They didn't talk a lot, both getting used to the leap in their relationship. Nash liked the idea of having Cariana as his wife, but it also left him nonplussed that his carefree bachelor life had ended. Having someone else share his space would take some adjustment, but he felt ready to make the change. He wondered how he would cope with a precocious twelve-year-old. Cariana seemed to have managed okay, but probably glad to share the load.

They did settle one important question—two really: No wedding until after the election, which made perfect sense. If he did not get elected, he would fall back on one of the job offers. The other question was having Cariana and Aleya move in with him right away. He would not mind that at all, but Cariana firmly vetoed the idea, and she was right. He needed to concentrate on his campaign.

It would be a hard, lonely four weeks.

By four, Aleya finally admitted that she'd had enough. A stroll through the Mill Markets? She declined politely and Nash suppressed a smile. After a detour to Hepburn Springs for mineral water, they headed home, not surprised to find Aleya dozing on the back seat.

When they arrived, Felix wasn't anywhere to be seen. Aleya

scrambled out of the car, raced into the garage for her bike and tore down the street to a friend's place, 'To share the news' she shouted over her shoulder. That left Nash and Cariana on the back veranda sharing a mellow shiraz. The two magpie property owners patrolled the backyard, pecking at the lawn in search of worms and insects. Everything still and silent, which Nash found soothing and relaxing. Even in the quiet of his apartment, city noises were an ever-present background blanket.

"We'll definitely have to keep this retreat," he told Cariana.

"I would love to, but I don't think I can afford the mortgage repayments."

"How much do you have left on it?"

He saw her hesitate until she realized there were no more secrets between them. Nash appreciated that it cut both ways.

"Around 240 thousand," she finally said. "But—"

"But nothing. You know what they say, 'What is mine is mine, and what is yours is mine'," he quipped, and she laughed.

"Cube. Seriously, Nash, I couldn't—"

"My sweet, why pay the bank interest when we can invest the money more profitably somewhere else? Besides, what is mine *is* now yours."

She looked at him. "Are you wealthy? It will take a lot to keep me in diamonds and champagne."

"Diamonds are overrated, and Australia makes better sparkling wine." He told her about his Channel Seven settlement and IBM claim. "So you see, we can afford to get rid of your mortgage."

She shook her head. "I'm still getting my head around what it means having you as a partner."

"I would show you what it means, my sweet, but I don't want Aleya barging in on us."

She threw a cashew at him. "Randy old goat. Although I wouldn't mind it at all." She sipped her wine and smiled seductively. "You can spend the night, you know."

"Talk about being put in the path of temptation." He sighed

and shook his head. "I'd love to, but—"

"If you're worried what Aleya might think, she already asked me if we did 'other stuff' last weekend."

"What did you tell her?"

"The truth. We love each other and that was another way to express our love. She is very mature for her age."

"I know." He spent a timeless moment going over every part of Cariana's face, allowing himself to sink into her magical eyes.

"Why are you staring at me like that?" she asked over the rim of her glass.

"I want to remember you like this, my constellation," he said softly.

"I thought you couldn't forget anything."

"I can't, but it's not every day I get a chance to be with the most wondrous woman in the world."

"You're making it awfully difficult to keep my hands off you, my prince," she whispered.

"Aleya, remember?"

They both laughed.

The evening became soft and dreamy as the sun sank and began to color the sky. Nash was content to remain in this little hideaway, removed from city crowds and sounds where politics was just another word and people weren't bothered. Idyllic as this retreat appeared, it was an escape, a place where reality could be forgotten for a time, a diverting illusion. Illusion or not, it helped recharge the soul for the morrow.

Dinner a noisy affair, with Aleya insisting on chopping carrots, parsnip and a piece of turnip for the vegetable soup, as nobody was keen on a heavy meal. Nash made a cold chicken salad, surprising the girls when he added cashews and little chopped apple squares to the mix. A dash of pumpkin oil finished the gourmet dish.

A cup of freshly ground coffee and a small slice of Aleya's rhubarb pie—he *had* to try it—finished the evening. Reluctant to go, he could not hide himself, pretending that Woodend was his whole world, which would be very easy to do.

On the front porch, Aleya gave him a fierce hug, eyes shining.

"Can I come and stay with you sometimes? I won't be any trouble. Promise."

"Sure thing. I'll arrange something with your Aunty."

"Once you guys are married and you adopt me, she'll be my mother, right?"

"That's the deal."

"Mother…I like the sound of that."

"I'm sure she likes it as well."

Nash squeezed her until she gasped in protest, then turned to Cariana. She flowed into his arms and kissed him. A brief, tender touch, but there was no need for more. It said everything that needed saying.

They waved as he drove out.

You've done it now for sure, old son.

He gave a contented sigh and nodded. He certainly had.

Wearing a faint smile, he told the car to connect with Dad.

* * *

With instant communication, campaigning no longer involved candidates walking down streets and shops making letterbox drops. A component still done by volunteers, but today, it was direct PID messaging, holoview plugs, blogging, and online promotions. A party with deep pockets could afford to swamp social media outlets, which sometimes turned counterproductive. People disliked being hammered with tired election slogans, shallow promises, finger pointing, and badmouthing the opponent. They wanted solid policies from parties, and more importantly, they wanted a candidate to represent and fight for issues that affected their lives above any party allegiance. A tough ask, as party machines funded candidates, and they expected loyalty. Calls were regularly made for the government to fund elections, which would eliminate problems associated with influence exerted by powerful lobby interests, but Labor and the Coalition never warmed to the idea, understandably enough.

Crossbench senators can introduce private members' bills, but the government usually voted them down. What senators *can* do was force amendments to tabled bills that were favorable to their constituents. If the government of the day wanted a critical piece of legislation passed and they didn't hold a Senate majority, which was usually the case, they had to agree to amendments or see the bill vetoed. This horse-trading not always in the national interest. Governments on both sides of the aisle hated having to bargain with the Senate crossbench, but they represented a significant fraction of Australian voters and the government was obliged to heed their voice. Moreover, voters these days were not bashful about tossing out a senator or even a minister who failed to listen to the electorate.

In Geelong, Nash found himself electioneering on two fronts. The obvious one was to gain acceptance not only as a lifeliner, but as an ordinary person with the same problems faced by everyone else, and in many respects, graver problems because he was a lifeliner. The other front was to identify himself and the Lifeliner Party as the social conscience, protesting against creeping government autocracy. That part was easier to handle and he had plenty of ammunition.

'Make things personal to the voter on the street and you will get there', Sands pounded into Nash every day. From what he saw in the holoview, the Coalition was running a tried old tactic, trumpeting the usual slogans about increasing support for education, health, law enforcement, and national security, and blaming lifeliners for everything not working. They were hard pressed to explain why they failed to address those issues years ago. The public had little appetite for increased defense spending to guard against nonexistent threats. The age of standing armies and set-piece battles were relegated to history and entertaining action movies. Wars were now fought in boardrooms and stock exchanges, with cyber experts as the foot soldiers.

Labor's 'we-can-do-better' strategy convinced only the die-hard party faithful.

Margot picked him up at his apartment and, with two assistants, she took the Princess Freeway to Geelong. The air-con provided soothing relief against a warm summer day in the low thirties. It took forty-five minutes to reach the satellite city nestled around Corio Bay and grab a light lunch before his one o'clock interview at the local 3CAT radio station. His host a wily old bird and didn't go out of his way to make Nash's life charming. Sensation and controversy brought audiences and helped ratings.

"Mr. Bannon, you keep telling listeners that you are like anybody else, but you're not, and some fear that difference. How do you counter that?"

"As a lifeliner, I am more like you than the differences that set me apart. I eat, sleep, go to work—at least I used to until I lost my job—pay bills, do my shopping, watch movies, listen to music, and concerned at what Atarah Readman and her Coalition have done to this country, as I am sure your listeners are also concerned."

"Good point, but people out there still worry that their children will be lifeliners—if they can have children at all."

"They have reason to worry, not because their children might be lifeliners, but because Raines Latham and Readman are blaming lifeliners for loss of jobs, poor economic decisions, hate crime, and growing right-wing extremism. Children are our future, to be loved, nurtured and cherished, not feared and ostracized."

"What about the accelerating rate of infertility sweeping the Western world, and couples finding that even having lifeliner children isn't possible?"

"That's a personal tragedy, but lifeliners are not responsible for the rise in infertility. That might be scant comfort to those affected, but your listeners should not be swayed by alarmist government propaganda."

"The Vatican claims that lifeliners don't have a soul, and you should be stoned where you stand."

"I would suggest the Vatican doesn't have a soul. Instead of extending their hand in fellowship to every human being regardless of race, they divide people under a bankrupt dogma. Over the centuries, they abused children placed in their care, and betrayed our trust. Those crimes are unforgivable, but the Vatican continues to perpetrate these crimes under a façade of denial, protecting pedophile priests and paying off parents to keep them silent. It should look hard at itself before declaring that lifeliners don't have souls."

"Do you believe in God, Mr. Bannon?"

"I believe in moral principles advocated by all religions, and I try to live by them. If there is a God, I like to think He would look favorably on me as a human being, even if flawed around the edges."

"Why should the people of Geelong support you?"

"As a senator, I'll raise their concerns and try to address things Geelong might lack. More frequent services on your fast rail link to Melbourne. A badly needed upgrade to the University Hospital. New primary schools and expanded employment in the Australian aerospace industry. Things are not bad everywhere. Geelong's unemployment is four point-two percent, and youth unemployment even lower. I will not pretend that technological change has not hit some people hard, but that is a failure of government policy. If elected, I will try and ameliorate the effects of bad policies.

"People have a right to be afraid of losing their jobs and homes, but they're even more afraid of marauding Humans Only League and People First Party thugs spreading fear and molesting anyone they suspect of being a lifeliner. People are afraid of Canberra's growing intrusion into their lives, recording everything they do and say. They are afraid when they see their rights taken away by Readman and Gardner in the belief that they cannot do anything about it.

"They are wrong! They can do something about it. All of us can. If elected, I and the Lifeliner Party will be Geelong's voice in Canberra, saying, 'No more'. This country fought wars to establish a free society where multiculturalism welcomes everyone, and everybody is free to say and do whatever they want, provided it does not harm someone else. Readman and the Coalition are taking away our freedom, and I want mine back. If your listeners want their freedom back, vote for the Lifeliner Party."

"Trevor Riddock, the Liberal Party member for Corio, accuses lifeliners of organizing youth gangs to engage in clashes with far-right groups such as the Humans Only League, proving, he claims, that lifeliners represent a genuine threat to social order, and validates measures taken by the government to identify and control radical lifeliner elements."

"Radical lifeliner elements? When I see Humans Only League and People First Party agitators openly marching through our streets, vandalizing property, and attacking citizens in a campaign of intimidation, I find it difficult to accept Mr. Riddock's accusation that lifeliners are a social threat.

"Lifeliners are people who want to live a normal life like everyone else. They want to feel secure and raise children in the hope they will have a prosperous future. If your listeners are looking for a social threat, Atarah Readman and her government are that threat, promoting fear, uncertainty, and unrest, by blaming lifeliners for the failure of her policies."

"Thank you for your candid responses, Mr. Bannon."

"Always a pleasure."

"This is 95.5 3CAT K-Rock on your FM dial. We'll be back after this announcement."

The radio host pressed a glowing pad on his console and smiled. "Not bad for someone who is not a politician, Mr. Bannon. If you're in Geelong again, I wouldn't mind another interview. I have lots more questions for you."

Nash shook hands and grinned. "Four weeks to go, and I will definitely be in Geelong again."

"Good luck with your campaign."

Outside the studio, Margot beamed at him. "He's right. It was a good performance."

"Thanks, Margi. I was stymied for a second when he asked me if I believed in God."

"You answered that well, but there is no right answer when it comes to religion. No matter what you say, somebody out there will be offended. We'll just have to wear it."

Nash looked around. "Where are our two helpers?"

"Handing out fliers along the beachfront. We'll catch up with them later, but first, the Town Hall rally. Curtis said there is a sizeable crowd waiting for you, and the mood is favorable."

The script for the rally simple. Sands would roll out the party's platform, and Nash would provide the personal angle.

"Right, let's do it."

It only took a few minutes to drive to the stately gray building next to Johnstone Park that invoked images of colonial days and horse-drawn carriages. Curtis Sands was speaking to a gathering of perhaps three hundred people. A squad of cops spoiled the festive mood somewhat as they kept a wary eye on a small group of People First Party activists waving placards. Three reporters hovered in the background recording everything.

Sands made the introduction and handed the mike to Nash.

"My name is Nash Bannon and I am a lifeliner."

This produced some laughter and waving of little Lifeliner Party flags. The People First agitators began to chant.

"Down with lifeliners…Down with lifeliners…Down with lifeliners. People first…People first."

The dobers moved in and pushed them back. Nash pointed at the protesters.

"There is your reason why I'm running for the Senate, and why the Lifeliner Party wants your support. Those protesters seek to tear down everything you have fought for, everything our fathers have fought for. They want to take away your rights and freedom, replacing it with silence and unquestioning obedience.

They want to rule your lives in the same way Prime Minister At-arah Readman rules us and how Macey Gardner and his Labor Party want to rule us. Step up and tell them, 'No more'!"

Some people cheered and Nash saw several nodding agreement.

"The Humans Only League may or may not be the government's puppet, but they reflect government policy to control and dictate what you can and cannot do. They reflect Labor's policy. When it comes to curtailing your rights and my rights, Labor and the Opposition represent a united front. What they're taking from you is clandestine erosion of our freedom. You complain to each other, but you are putting up with it, not realizing that tomorrow, you might not be allowed to complain at all. What they're taking from me and other lifeliners is not merely our rights, but our lives! The government wants nothing less than eradication of all lifeliners, and their sterilization program is merely the first step. I say, no more!"

This time, the crowd burst into more enthusiastic cheering. Buoyed, Nash raised his arms.

"The government wanted to sterilize me simply because I'm a lifeliner. Tomorrow, it might be you! This will happen if you remain silent. Remain silent and our streets will also become silent. Do you want this for yourself? Do you want this for your children? Stand up to Labor and the Coalition! Stand up for your rights and vote Lifeliner Party, a voice for social change!"

"Bannon! Bannon! Bannon!"

"I don't know how many among you are lifeliners, and I'm not asking that you identify yourselves, but consider this. If we lived in a truly democratic and free society, we would not fear to say, 'I am a lifeliner'. We would not fear anything! But fear is exactly what Readman and Gardner are promoting. Fear that somehow lifeliners are the cause of all your problems. Fear that we're a social cancer to be cut out. What *they* fear is that you will see through their deception and say to them, 'Enough'!"

Wild cheering broke out and it took a few moments to die

down.

"The federal police kidnapped several Lifeliner Party candidates and members of our families. They sterilized some of them not to silence the Party, but to destroy it! This is the free society Readman and Labor want for you. Tell them no!"

It took longer to settle the enthusiastic crowd.

"Your vote counts and should be cast wisely," Nash shouted. "If you don't know who to vote for, you can certainly tell whom to vote against! Scrutinize your current representative. How long has he held his seat and what has he done for you? Have you ever written to him or called and never received a response? That means he did not care about you and what you had to say, simple as that. If you only see him when it's election time, ditch the bugger!"

They surged up the steps, waving banners and flags. Nash shook hands and received more than one hearty slap on the back with words of encouragement. Nash felt an electric excitement and rising hope that it might be possible to stem the tide of government autocracy. He might also be deluding himself, carried away by the moment and a receptive crowd. He would find out in four weeks' time.

People slowly drifted away and the reporters moved in. Nash put on a friendly face and answered questions without elaboration, knowing that whatever the networks might air would be cut down to thirty-second bites, which said a lot about what they thought people could absorb. According to Margot, he needed to exploit holoview chat shows and radio interviews as platforms of choice to put the party's message across. Nevertheless, thirty seconds of exposure better than no exposure at all.

Two volunteers packed up banners, flags, and posters, and helped clean up some of the rubbish left by the crowd.

"Geelong is small-time compared to Melbourne," Sands told Nash, "but it is an important segment of voters we want to capture and should not be underestimated. We'll be here again, but today was an opportunity for people to see you and start differentiating with the sitting member. That's why I kept this rally deliberately short. Next time around will be more intense."

"I thought it went well," Nash said.

"It did, but we're looking to draw in crowds of two thousand or more, not a mere handful. Don't worry about it. That's my department." Sands turned to Margot. "Turn him loose."

"My two aides are already working the promenade."

"Good. I won't be in Ballarat with you guys. I've got to see what's going on in Perth, but I'll be back on deck on Tuesday." With a smile and a wave, Sands walked briskly toward his car.

Margot turned to Nash. "Time to mix with more people. How are you holding up?"

"Ready to eat them," Nash said, and she laughed.

They found the two girls on the Eastern Beach Road promenade that ran along the beachfront, standing between two large posters with Nash's face plastered over them, handing out leaflets to passersby strolling along the waterfront. Corio Bay merged with a sharp horizon and yachts played the calm water.

After two hours of handshakes and chatting with those more interested, Margot and Nash shifted themselves farther up the beachfront. Nash was pleasantly surprised to find that most people were friendly, not at all bothered that he was a lifeliner. An elderly couple from San Francisco stopped to talk. Americans did not like what President Mackay and his administration were doing. People were nervous, and lifeliners dared not reveal themselves, everybody watching over their shoulder for something bad to happen. Mackay pressured two Supreme Court justices to resign, and nominated far-right conservatives as replacements to stack the court. Congress was still to conduct confirmation hearings, and the tourist told Nash that he hoped both would be rejected. His advice, don't come to America.

Nash did not give much credence to the many conspiracy theories advocated by self-styled panickers of all persuasions, but the conversation with the Americans left him wondering if an international cabal operated to identify and eventually destroy all lifeliners, Sutton's claim that he was untouchable nagging at the back of his mind.

He wondered what Sutton, out on bail, was doing these days. Probably nothing good as far as lifeliners were concerned.

About to pack up for the day, a Channel Nine reporter snagged him into an impromptu interview. The media always attracts attention, and a small crowd gathered around Nash to hear him speak. It was valuable free advertising, provided he didn't make some gaffe.

"Mr. Bannon, reading your manifesto, the Lifeliner Party appears to be centrist, with no evident left or right leanings. How can voters judge what you stand for?"

Nash smiled at the young reporter, a light breeze stirring her long auburn hair. "Very easily. The Lifeliner Party has no affiliation with any faction or special interest group. Our policies are clear. We will seek to repeal draconian laws that unjustly limit people's rights, and we will attempt to block any legislation that attempts to curtail existing rights. We will focus on all legislation that targets lifeliners. We have a right to live in a free society, as do our children."

"If the government of the day doesn't hold a Senate majority, will the Lifeliner Party block supply if it finds itself holding the balance of power?"

"We will treat every piece of legislation on its merits. We recognize that an elected government has a mandate from the people to govern, and blocking supply would be a last measure to prevent a government enacting laws that contravene Lifeliner Party policies and do not serve the interests of the broader community."

"Does that mean you would be prepared to make deals?"

"We would negotiate with the government of the day regardless of its political leanings, provided the outcome does not compromise our policies. The people who vote for us expect the Lifeliner Party to adhere to its platform. Should we betray that trust, we would be no better than Labor and the Coalition."

"Thank you, Mr. Nash."

With the sun hovering above a mercury sea, the assistants packed up and Margot drove them to the Bay City Motel three blocks from the beach where they would spend the night. Comfortable if not fancy, it provided a clean bed. In the morning, a short drive to Ballarat for more interviews, pumping hands, and pounding the main street. Then back to Melbourne for more drumbeating. Over dinner, Margot sympathized when she saw his dejected expression. This 'Friends, Romans, countrymen, lend me your ears' stuff not as easy as the play made it out.

If nothing else, the frenetic pace ensured that he got his quota of fresh air and exercise.

He would rather have those with Cariana in Woodend.

Ah, rats.

* * *

From a sunny, warm Ballarat, Melbourne's jagged towers reached toward an overhang of dark clouds that looked happy to stay there. The car hummed softly and Nash stared absently at the stream of traffic flowing toward the city, his thoughts a rumble of images in no particular order. Flashbacks of yesterday's rally, the excursion through Ballarat, which he felt generated positive interest, his engagement to Cariana, and the overflowing support from his family at the news. Two of his best friends offered their hearty congratulations.

A riot in the city dampened his spirits somewhat.

Margot told him about it as they prepared to leave Ballarat. A group of People First Party agitators chanting anti-lifeliner slogans, some wearing brown shirts with stylized swastika armbands, marched up the Bourke Street pedestrian mall toward Parliament, blocking trams both ways. Police followed the group, but things got out of hand when bystanders started to shout at them to take their banners and placards and buzz off, accompanied by taunts and catcalls.

One People First protester punched a pedestrian in the face, and those looking on let him have it. The dobers moved in to break up the resulting melee, but not before several store windows were smashed and a number of people injured. The cops broke up the march and arrested some People First agitators.

According to Margot, a similar march by a gang of Humans Only League protesters at the Sydney Town Hall disrupted traffic and broke windows before the cops hauled them away. A few protesters ran off, pursued by outraged bystanders. There were reports of injuries, none serious.

Disturbed by the news, Nash took solace from the troubling events to reflect that ordinary people were taking notice, not afraid to confront the agitators. If the protesters were put on the defensive, reluctant to march openly, they could be relegated to the impotent far-right fringe. Before that happened, it may cost some blood and broken bones, but if the person on the street wasn't prepared to speak out against this form of intimidation, liberty would be lost for all. History was replete with examples of dictatorships rising because people did not want to be involved.

Sands was right. The fight must be made personal to overcome the inertia of social indifference.

Margot drove directly to the party headquarters to catch up on some administration, which gave Nash an opportunity to grab a tuna salad at a nearby restaurant crowded with RMIT university students. He expected to be recognized, but instead of being stared at and avoided, they were eager to talk to him. Two youths glared at him and walked out. Young, educated, their minds unfettered by bigotry and prejudice, the students expressed lively interest in the federal election, debated heatedly the pros and cons of major party policies, and expressed sympathy for lifeliners, not liking what Europe and America were doing, and fearful it might happen in Australia.

A tall, skinny Asian, dressed neatly in casual gear, handed Nash a card. The youngster was the vice-president of the RMIT Student Union, and left Nash with an invitation to come and speak at the campus.

"I think it's a great idea," Margot gushed later.

"We're not going to change the mindset of those who are already prejudiced against lifeliners," Nash told her. "We can make our message personal, but ordinary families are a fraction of the population. An important and large fraction, granted, but there are over 400 thousand local graduate and undergraduate students in Victoria, not counting international ones, and one-and-a-half million Australia-wide, and they're all voters. From what I experienced now, most of them are on our side, Margi."

"One-and-a-half million votes we hardly have to fight for," Margi mused, her eyes bright.

"At least they won't be prejudiced. Talk it over with Kairns and Sands. I want to visit every major university in the city, and we should ask our volunteers to start dropping fliers at each one of them, including bars and clubs they frequented. I suggest all party branches should look at doing the same thing."

"Let me leave a message with Roger for both of them."

"You're letting Warren access Roger?"

"He threatened to fire me if I didn't."

Towing two volunteers armed with placards and fliers, Margot and Nash walked to Swanston Street and took a tram to Bourke Street where the mall started. Closed to cars, they could stroll up and down without being run over, an occasional tram notwithstanding. Their presence on the tram caused more than one curious, bemused glance, and several passengers gave them friendly waves.

At the corner of Bourke and Swanston, Nash chatted with passersby, glad-handing some, a flier ready in his hand. Many people hurried by with a brief glance, which was normal. He got a few hostile looks, but no one stopped to abuse him, Margot, or the two volunteers.

By four-thirty, with the afternoon crush well under way, Nash held a last stand at Federation Square. Seagulls fluttered about looking for tidbits, and squawked in a scramble of wings when someone threw them a morsel. Channel Nine and ABC reporters asked some questions and took shots without engaging in lengthy interviews. He was amused to see a Liberal Party candidate for the Lower House holding a rally on the Flinders Street station steps. The Square and station approaches were busy, natural focus points to extract maximum exposure.

At five, Margot told him they should pack up. At this hour, people were more interested in getting home, not politicking. They would return around seven when the city switched on its evening attractions and they could expect a more receptive audience.

Two pedestrians were hurrying past Nash when a deafening blast ripped the air. One of them was hurled back, and the other crashed into him. The impact sent him flailing and he landed hard against the pavement. Searing pain slashed across his chest, and his right leg burned with fire. His ears rang. Gradually, he could hear screams and running feet. As he stared up at the gray clouds, they appeared to swim, becoming surreal. He had difficulty breathing with a body pressing him down. A sharp chemical stink lingered in the air, mixed with the rank odor of blood and ripped entrails.

He grunted and pushed the body off him. He looked at the man who saved him and swallowed hard. The front of the body torn and raw, and he gagged. Bits of metal protruded from gaping wounds and oozing guts. He turned and saw Margot sprawled just out of reach and blanched.

"Margi!"

He crawled to her. Blood seeped from a wound on her left side, and she had cuts on her legs, right arm, and a gash on the cheek. He cradled her head in his lap and brushed away a strand of hair. Her eyes fluttered and she winced.

"My side," she gasped, and Nash smiled with relief.

"It doesn't look too bad. Lie still."

"Nash…you're bloody all over."

He looked at the gaping wound across his chest, wishing he hadn't. He looked like a slab of sliced beef.

"A flesh wound."

"What happened?"

"Someone set off a bomb as we walked by."

He lifted his head and scrutinized the carnage around him. Three men and two women lay unmoving, blood splattered all over the pavement. The wounded wandered in a daze, appearing only vaguely conscious of their injuries. Some huddled on the sidewalk, moaning, clutching themselves, sobbing.

This was horror unleashed, and for what? It did not make any sense. Rage, frustration, and helplessness swept through him. He wanted to physically maim whoever did this. Make him suffer all the agonies those around him were suffering.

He heard approaching sirens and saw a dober push back the morbidly curious. A cop leaned over him.

"Are you all right?"

Nash glared at him. "Do I look all right, you idiot!" Bloody, in shock, he found the question absurdly ridiculous.

"Hang in there. We've got ambulances coming."

His chest wound began to sting abominably and he winced. An awful lot of blood had soaked his shirt and pants.

"Margi…"

He blinked hard as his vision began to fade. It deepened into blackness and his head hit the pavement.

Like coming up for air in a swimming pool, Nash slowly stirred from dark nothingness. Bright light shone into his eyes and he squinted. A plastic tube snaked from a drip bottle to his arm. A pink tube ran from his chest to a bag beside the bed. The air smelled of antiseptic. He turned his head and gazed stupidly at a familiar face. The face grinned at him.

"Awake at last."

"Warren?" Nash managed to croak.

"Who did you expect? The Prime Minister?"

Nash pulled himself up and gasped as his chest sent out waves of cutting pain.

"Take it easy there," Kairns warned him, "or you'll pull the stitches."

Nash slowly dragged himself up and leaned against the bed frame with only minor protests from his chest and leg. Opposite him, Margot smiled and fluttered her fingers, her right cheek covered by a bandage.

"Good morning. Feeling better?"

His mind clearing fast, Nash turned to Kairns. "You arranged to have all of us together?"

Kairns glanced at Margot. "No detail escapes that sharp brain."

Margot laughed, winced, and held her side. "I lost part of my kidney, but it'll grow back with stem cell therapy. Otherwise, I am much luckier than some, and that includes you."

Nash prodded the thick bandage around his upper torso. "I remember a little blood—"

"A little blood? I'm told you lost a bucketful, but it's only a deep gash. A piece of shrapnel made a hole in your leg, but nothing's broken."

"And you?"

"Me? Just superficial cuts. Looks worse than it is. The man who fell on you saved us both. He took a lot of the blast, as did the man next to him."

Nash turned to Kairns. "What's the count?"

"According to reports, five dead, three critical, and sixteen with various degrees of injury. Two of them were children. They're saying a remote-controlled device planted in a trash can caused the resulting debris to inflict most of the carnage. You were targeted, you know that."

The images came with a rush and Nash felt a wave of anger wash through him. That someone could do something like this to innocent people wasn't just political intimidation, it was barbarism. He was targeted, all right, but it went further than that. Whoever planned this wanted to create terror by association. Support lifeliners and the next blast might kill or maim *you*.

A short individual in a white lab coat, silver hair balding on top, stethoscope around his neck, walked in and beamed.

"I am glad to see you awake, Mr. Bannon." He checked the drip and drainage tube. "Hardly any color. That's good. We'll have that out tomorrow."

"My chest—" Nash began.

"A nineteen-centimeter contusion across both pectoral muscles. Fortunately for you, the sternum is intact and no broken ribs. You have a nice collection of sutures and you'll have a scar for the girls to admire. You were lucky."

"So I'm told. How long before I'm up and about?"

"I'll check on you tomorrow before I can tell you that. If things look good, I might let you go on Thursday. That will not be permission to resume campaigning, Mr. Bannon," the doctor told him sternly, finger raised in warning. "Right, I'll arrange a light meal for you, and I'll see you in the morning."

Lab coat swirling around his legs, he walked out. The door closed after him with a solid click.

Nash checked his PID, 9:20 pm, and looked at Margot. "He ignored you completely."

"He was here half an hour ago to check on me."

A knock and the door opened.

Nash beamed and tried to lift one arm, ignoring a spasm of pain that shot across his chest. "Cariana!"

She smiled and hurried to his side. He embraced her and gave her a quick kiss. Aleya pushed past her and her dark eyes regarded him with concern.

"We were all worried about you, weren't we, Aunty?"

"We certainly were. You don't know what went through my head when Doctor Young called."

"Only a flesh wound, my sweet. I'll be my normal self in a

couple of days."

"That's not what Dr. Young tells me."

"I'll surprise you. Cariana, meet Warren Kairns, the Lifeliner Party national president. The other walking wounded is Margot Jarvis, my minder."

"I'm pleased to see you both," Cariana said and nodded to them.

"A pleasure, Dr. Lambert," Margot said with a smile.

"Likewise, Doctor," Kairns growled.

Cariana turned to Nash. "I saw the news clips. It looked ghastly. All those deaths."

"That will not make me stop," Nash declared firmly.

She gave him a speculative stare. "No, I don't suppose it will. You don't know?"

"Know what?"

"There have been other attacks, Nash," Kairns said, face grim. "During a rally in Sydney, a bomb took off Stevenson's right leg, poor bastard, and he's out of it. In Brisbane, Tamara Reed was wounded, but she should be all right in a week or so."

Wild thoughts rampaged through Nash. First sterilized, and now this.

"They showed it on the news," Aleya confirmed. "It looked awful."

"Stop this talk," Cariana scolded them. "It's depressing."

Kairns looked nonplussed as he glanced at Nash. "Is she always like that?"

"A strong willed lady, take it from me," Nash said easily.

"Cube." Cariana gave him a playful smack on the arm. "You wanted a break from campaigning, and now you've got it. So don't complain."

"I didn't want my break to be in a hospital!" Nash reached for her hand and squeezed. "But I'm glad you came to see me."

"It's a short walk from the apartment. I'll drop in tomorrow. Since I work here, it won't be any trouble. Just get well, that's all I want."

A nurse came in bearing a covered metal tray. "Your dinner, Mr. Bannon."

"Thank you."

She checked the drip bottle, patted his shoulder, and walked out.

Cariana brushed his lips with her fingers and glanced at Aleya. "Say good night to Nash."

"Good night to Nash," Aleya said promptly.

He chuckled and ruffled her hair. "Good night, sweetie."

When they left, Kairns gave him an approving smile. "I saw the ring. Congratulations."

"Too bad," Margot moaned. "I wanted to snag him."

Nash laughed. "First come, and all that."

"She is lovely," Margot added. "I hope the stem cell therapy works."

"Me too."

He placed the tray on his lap and uncovered it. He did not much care for the pile of green peas, a dollop of mashed potatoes, and an anemic slice of undefined meat. The fruit juice and tub of yogurt looked more promising.

"Now you know why I want to get out of here," Kairns growled sourly. "Makes me wonder why I bother paying private insurance. Gold class, no less!"

"Write to your senator," Nash told him and started on the yogurt.

"You've got a sadistic sense of humor, Mr. Bannon."

Another knock on the door and Natalie peered in.

"Nat!" Nash gushed and put the tray on the side table. "Mom, Dad, good to see you."

Nat beamed and gave him a gentle hug and a kiss on the cheek. Mom followed with another hug and kiss. Nash introduced his fellow invalids.

"You don't look that bad, son," his dad said.

"The news clips said you'd been hurt pretty badly," Nat added. "As the evening wore on, the extent of your injuries grew worse."

"Goes to show that you cannot believe the media," Nash told her, wearing a broad grin. "As it is, I got off lightly, sis."

"They showed all those poor people in Federation Square. Positively horrid," his mother said and shuddered.

"Planning to quit?" Dad demanded sternly.

"Only if I don't get elected."

"That's my boy."

After ten minutes or so of general chatter, they left, wishing him well.

"Your mother is beautiful," Margot gushed.

"Nat takes after her. A good thing too."

Nash finished his yogurt and sank back against the pillows. His chest throbbed, but not badly enough to require medication.

"I don't know about you guys, but I'm ready to turn in," Kairns declared.

Nash merely grunted. Margot already had her eyes closed.

A hell of a day, he decided.

Chapter Nine

"Another beer, twin?" Mark asked and held out a stubby. Nash took the icy bottle and nodded. "Thanks."

"Shaun?"

"I'm fine," Natalie's husband replied, holding up his glass.

"Dad?"

Bent over the sizzling barbecue, his father used long tongs to turn over sausages, steaks, and chicken pieces. Onions, potato wedges, and assorted vegetables were browning on a side plate.

"I still have some left in mine."

"You guys are easy to please," Mark snorted and cocked his head at Nash. "How does it feel facing your first election?"

"Excited, nervous, and relieved to have the damn campaign behind me. The last two weeks were a grueling grind. I felt more than once that only a masochist would put himself through this. Garrett told me I would regret it. I thought he was kidding."

It had been mentally and physically exhausting, but Nash saw a side of politics most people were not aware of. The holoview clips showed candidates parading down streets, pumping hands, and cuddling smelly babies, but people did not see the back room operators who enabled all that to happen. While Labor and the Coalition slugged at each other, the Lifeliner Party quietly lobbied the small parties for preference deals. Most of them knew they had no hope of securing a senate seat, but if the Lifeliner Party were prepared to push some of their policies, they were happy to swap preferences. Nash did not know what Kairns and Sands did behind closed doors to secure those deals, and Margot told him it was better that way. Nash did not insist.

Win or lose, it was over. He looked forward to a few days when he did not have to think about politics.

"Garrett also told me that things out there would get worse," Nash said, looking glum. "I didn't want to believe him, but I cannot ignore what's been happening."

Mark took a pull of beer. "You're talking about those home invasions?"

On February 16, a surge in home attacks by Humans Only League and People First Party gangs, some of them causing serious injuries and property damage, began in all capital cities. There was no apparent pattern or reason why those homes were singled out—until several victims identified themselves as lifeliners. When the story broke, every victim turned out to be a lifeliner. What puzzled the authorities, how did the gangs know which house or apartment to attack? The explosive ABC *Four Corners* exposé on Monday told everybody how they knew. Two key public servants in the federal Department of Human Services were compromised, forcing them to divulge access codes to a national lifeliner register, something the High Court specifically ruled the government could not maintain. The register by no means complete or current, but it held enough information for the gangs to conduct a program of systematic assaults.

"A national campaign of intimidation is not something the Humans Only League and People First agitators could mount," Nash said. "Such an operation takes planning, organization, coordination, and information. Somebody was pulling the strings here, Mark."

"The government, ASIO, the federal police? It could have been anybody, twin. Leave it, okay? We're supposed to be enjoying ourselves."

"You're right," Nash said, but he couldn't stop thinking about it.

Quiet and still, the warm evening silence broken by Aleya and Nat's kids chasing each other around the yard. Nash glanced into the dining room. His mom, Cariana, and Nat were setting the table chatting. He often wondered what women talked about when alone. Perhaps it was better not to know.

Mark sniffed at the aromas coming off the barby. "I could get used to having someone cook for me."

"Get married," Dad told him. "That'll solve your cooking problems."

"It will solve Nash's problem," Mark quipped.

Next Saturday, he would be married. It hardly seemed real.

With the election campaign in full swing, he and Cariana agreed not to have an engagement party. Instead, they settled on an early wedding date. An engagement and wedding all in one. Nash did not mind at all, although Mom and Cariana's parents were slightly miffed. The decision to get married made, there was no logical reason to have a prolonged engagement period. Try and explain that to his mom.

He got a chance to meet Cariana's parents two weeks ago over dinner at the Box Seafood Restaurant. Her old man was a professor of medicine at Monash University, and her mom wrote Regency romance, having published nine novels, which went to prove that it is impossible to tell what a person does by looking at them. At fifty-four, Lambert senior hardly looked the professor type. Of average height, brown hair combed straight back, lively dark eyes, he had a warm conversational style that put Nash at ease. Mrs. Lambert, trim in a gray cardigan and black slacks, blond hair cut short, a strikingly pretty woman. An older version of Cariana. The Lamberts were charming and friendly, and intensely interested in Nash's experience as a politician and lifeliner. With a mischievous glance at Cariana, Mrs. Lambert said that his life gave her an idea for a book, which caused her daughter to groan and roll her eyes.

Last Sunday, Dad and Mom had the Lamberts over for dinner. Mom told him later the encounter was a resounding success. Nash was pleased, not liking the idea of inter-family tension hanging over his marriage. He was prepared to take some time off campaigning to organize the wedding, but both parents insisted they had things in hand. A modest affair, please, he and

Cariana told them. When approached, Nash's closest friend delighted to act as best man.

"I heard you settled with CIS," Mark said. "It was all over the news on Thursday."

"Pressure from New York corporate. They made a public apology and offered to reinstate me, but I told Garrett to stuff them."

"How much did you sting them for?"

"Three million."

"Three mil?" His brother whistled. "Nice going, twin."

"Garrett figured the Equal Opportunity Commission would probably give me five, but IBM might appeal and I wouldn't see anything for a couple of years. The bad publicity cost them far more than my settlement. Two Melbourne execs got the block over this, not that I'm about to burst into tears."

Mark laughed and raised his stubby in a salute.

"Don't tell Cariana," Nash said. "I want to surprise her."

"She'll be surprised, all right, and delighted."

Natalie slid open the back door glass panel and poked out her head. "Labor is ahead by four seats!" she shouted and closed the panel.

"The Liberals never expected to hold those marginal seats they won from Labor last time," his father announced comfortably. "I think they could have if the party machine supported their candidates."

"Their loss is our gain, Dad," Nash mused.

Online voting produced quick results, and the last three federal elections went smoothly despite dire warnings from doomsayers that results would be rigged, or the computer system compromised. This election was somewhat more complicated, as it involved choosing the Lower House, a full Senate, and deciding a referendum question, but his dad was right. It should be all over by eight.

"Okay, guys. The sizzle is ready. Cart it in," Dad declared and started filling trays.

Nash strode to the house and opened the glass panel. "Nat, we're good to go."

"Right, I'll sort out the kids."

"I'll give you a hand," Cariana said and grabbed small bowls of mixed salad and baked potato slices.

Nash made himself useful helping carry heaped trays into the house.

Aleya and Sandra led the charge to the table laid out for them outside, not interested mixing it with the oldies and their boring talk, as she put it. Nat and Cariana made sure they had plenty of everything.

The usual banter accompanied the meal, interrupted by an occasional yell or scream from outside. Although much older than the others, Aleya did not seem to mind playing with them, dropping her usual reserve.

Nash glanced at the holoview where four ABC commentators pontificated pompously on the emerging voting pattern. A clear trend had firmed as the computer announced Lower House results.

"The Liberals are getting hammered," Nash observed. "Five seats down already. The Nationals seem to be holding their own, as are the Greens. It also looks like the Australian Conservatives might pick up an extra seat."

"We're heading for a hung parliament," Dad declared. "Just watch."

A glass of shiraz in hand, Nash looked sharply at his old man. His father had an uncanny eye for patterns and trends, and Nash did not dismiss his prediction outright.

"What happens if there is a hung parliament?" Cariana asked. "Who forms the government?"

"The Prime Minister will go to President Ngarra and ask to form a minority government."

"But if Labor and the Coalition have the same number of seats, the President could ask the Opposition to form government. Couldn't he?"

"He can, but under strict precedent, he is obliged to ask Readman to form a coalition government."

"Wouldn't that be inherently unstable?"

"It sure would, my sweet. Readman would have to go cap in hand to the Greens for support if Labor opposed a bill, and the Greens would exact a price for that support."

"The referendum question is likely to go through," Mark observed. "Sixty-four percent of counted votes have given it a thumbs up. It looks like the people value a four-year term more than the dangers it represents."

Nash scowled. "Disappointing, but not altogether unexpected. Both major parties supported the change and ran a persuasive campaign."

"What about the Senate, dear?" his mom queried.

"It's looking good for the Lifeliner Party, Mom," Nash said. "We got a seat in Tasmania and the Australian Capital Territory. The computer is predicting a probable in South Australia, but it's not a done deal yet. All the primary votes are counted, but it takes a little longer to allocate the preferences."

"You seem to be doing well, twin," Mark said, pointing at the holoview. "Queensland and Western Australia are shaky."

"With those numbers, I think we'll take Queensland, but WA has always been shaky for us," Nash said wryly. "Our candidate there hasn't been pulling his weight."

"Why didn't you replace him?" Nat asked.

"It wouldn't have looked good for the party, and we didn't have a suitable replacement anyway."

"But I have seen senators resign or retire, and the party replaced them," his mom said.

"That's for sitting senators, Mom," Mark explained.

Their mother waved a dismissive hand. "I never could understand these things."

Nash laughed and patted her shoulder. "That's okay, Mom. You're not the only one."

At 7:35 pm, the computer announced the final tally. In the

Lower House, Labor had 78 seats, and the Coalition 66, with the Greens four. The Australian Conservatives picked up seats and held twelve.

"You were right, Dad," Nash said. "We have a hung parliament if the Coalition brings in the Conservatives."

In the Senate, Tamara Reed got in for Queensland, as did Paula McNeil for South Australia.

"You made it, twin! You're in!" Mark gushed and slapped Nash on the back. "Five seats! Wow."

Wild cheering broke out and Nash felt a lump of emotion in his throat. He had given his all during the campaign, but deep down, he never expected to make it, with everything stacked against him. Having actually won his seat, he felt somewhat unnerved and daunted by a challenge he might not be able to meet. He would also have to live in Canberra, at least part of the time. The entire thing outrageously surreal.

You want to wall yourself in again, old son?

Screw them all! He got his seat, and by damn, he would rub every one of those Canberra weenies noses in it.

His father stood and lifted his glass. "A toast to Senator-elect, Nash Bannon! Well done, son."

Glasses were raised and drained and everybody clapped madly. Beaming, Cariana wrapped an arm around him and gave him a lingering kiss, to hoots of delight and pounding of the table.

"I'm so proud of you, my prince," she whispered, eyes brimming with happy tears.

He brushed away a lock of stray hair that ventured across her forehead. "I couldn't have done it without you, my bright constellation."

Nat cocked an eyebrow. "Prince? Constellation? Wow, you two got it bad."

Nash turned to Shaun, who had kept a low profile during the evening. "And you two don't?"

"We certainly do, as she'll find out later," he growled, and

Mark laughed with delight.

Nat threw a piece of bread at her husband. "You'll pay for that."

"Happily."

This generated more merriment.

Nash stood and looked at each of them in turn. "Thanks for your support, everyone. It meant a great deal having you stand by me. Right now, though, much as I would love to hang around and celebrate, I need to go to the party headquarters and thank all those hardworking volunteers who helped get me and others over the line." He turned to Cariana and held out his hand. "Come with me."

A radiant smile lit her face as she took his hand and stood.

Nat scowled at Shaun and jabbed him in the ribs. "You're looking at real love there, you insensitive lug."

Shaun grabbed Nat and squeezed her, reducing her to helpless squeals.

"Let me go, you beast!"

"Not before you say you love me."

"Never!"

Shaun squeezed harder.

"Ouch! Okay!"

"Okay, what?"

"I love you."

"I didn't hear that."

"I said I love you."

He bent over her and kissed her. The kiss went for longer than strict protocol required, but no one seemed to mind.

Cariana looked at Nash. "I think we better get out of here before you decide to squeeze me."

"Later, my sweet," Nash murmured and Dad roared approval.

She opened the sliding panel and stuck out her head. "Aleya! We're going!"

"Aw, Aunty! Do I have to? I'm having so much fun here."

"I can take her home with me, Cariana," Natalie called out.

"You and Nash can pick her up in the morning and have breakfast with us. Right, Shaun?"

"Absolutely. Let the kids enjoy themselves."

"She's not set for a sleepover," Cariana protested.

"We'll drop by your place and she can pick up stuff," Nat said. Cariana looked at Nash, who shrugged. "She'll be fine."

"Well…You can stay, little terror. You'll spend the night at Aunty Natalie's place. I'll pick you up in the morning."

"Awesome!"

Nash said his goodbyes, escorted out by his dad.

"Don't forget lunch tomorrow," his father said and turned to Cariana. "It will be nice to see your parents again."

The car whispered as it headed downtown along Punt Road behind Fawkner Park. Not the most direct route, but Nash could not drive through the Swanston Street pedestrian mall to get to Carlton Place. This late in the evening, the traffic flowed smoothly. Melbourne's lit towers clawed toward a black sky.

Cariana touched his shoulder. "You're quiet. Anything the matter?"

"It's the election."

"What about it? I thought you'd be pleased. By all accounts the Lifeliner Party did better than anyone expected."

"I'm pleased, but also worried."

"Why?"

"Between them, the Coalition lost thirteen Lower House seats, and the Australian Conservatives picked up two and now hold twelve."

"So?"

"Don't you get it? To form government the Coalition will have to bring in the Conservatives, and they're the force behind the anti-lifeliner campaign. Readman must dance to their tune or she's out."

"There is still the Senate to block any anti-lifeliner legislation, and she might not be such a reluctant dancer as you might think."

"I know. I feel I'm missing something."

"Take off your political hat, Senator Bannon. The world is not going to cave in if you stop worrying for a while."

He smiled and stroked her hand. "You're right, and I am spoiling what should be a personal triumph." He cleared his throat. "There is something we need to settle. We've put it on the backburner, but now that I'm elected—"

"CSIRO is based in Canberra, Nash, and they offered me a posting. I can resume my research with minimal interruption, and the Dean of the Australian National University Medical School is delighted to have me on the faculty."

Nash stared at her, then hastily turned his head to watch the road. "You did all this without talking to me?"

"You were busy, and you don't know how to play the academic system."

"What about Aleya?"

"The Instram Institute has a school at ANU. She'll like Canberra, although it gets pretty cold over there during winter. I thought we'd rent something and lease our apartments and my Woodend place. I don't really want to sell it."

Nash felt her eyes on him.

"If you have another option…" she ventured.

"What you have done is fine, Cariana. More than fine. It's perfect, but we should keep one of the apartments and your Woodend place. Parliament doesn't sit all the time."

"When do you have to be in Canberra?"

"The new parliament is being sworn in on the twenty-second. Since this was a double dissolution election, I'll have to take up my seat right away. However, Parliament doesn't sit in April, which will give us time to organize ourselves and get away for a week."

"A break sounds nice, but I don't want to leave Aleya by herself."

"Nat will look after her, and the kids will love having her around, and she'll be able to attend classes at Instram."

"I don't know…"

"We'll sort it out, my sweet."

After crossing the Yarra, the drive along Exhibition Street a tunnel through wonderland. Lit by colored lights, the elms on either side of the street and the median strip glowed yellow, orange and red, mirrored off plate glass windows and their smoky interiors. A popular part of town with numerous bars and restaurants, the sidewalks teemed with mostly young people. Their animated carefree faces reflected satisfied lives, or perhaps they didn't want to spoil their Saturday night with grim reality.

Nash was being morbid and knew it.

When he attempted to turn into Carlton Place, two police cruisers blocked the entrance. A uniformed dober lifted his arm, palm open. Nash stopped and told the car to wind down part of the dome.

"Road closed to traffic, sir," the cop announced briskly.

"I'm visiting the Lifeliner Party headquarters," Nash told him.

The cop blinked, his face momentarily blank as he consulted his PID. "You may go, Mr. Bannon, and congratulations on your election."

"Thank you, officer. Why the roadblock?"

"There was some trouble earlier in the afternoon. People First Party prowlers picking fights with anyone trying to get in here."

Nash pursed his lips and sighed. He wound up the dome panel and slowly drove up the street. A paddy wagon stood outside the headquarters entrance. People living in tenement blocks and going to restaurants along the street would not be happy with the security blanket.

Nash parked and got out. Cariana at his side, he strode toward the entrance. Two dobers stood guard and he had to endure another PID identification before they would let him in.

The security guard looked up from his desk and waved. "Evening, Mr. Bannon. I heard you got elected. Congratulations."

"Thanks, Archie." Nash hooked a thumb at the dobers outside. "They're making sure you could nap in peace?"

The guard chuckled. "We had protesters marching up and down all morning, and there were some fights later. It's been quiet since the cops mopped them up."

Nash walked toward the elevators, the ground floor showing no sign of damage.

Upstairs, he blinked at the sound of merriment and loud conversation that swept over him. Laughter, waving of hands and glasses, the victory celebration in full swing. Margot spotted him, beamed, and hurried toward him.

"Nash! Glad you could make it. Congratulations!" She hugged him and kissed him on both cheeks.

Cariana looked on bemused. Seeing her expression, Margot laughed.

"Don't worry, Dr. Lambert, he's safe. Come on."

She grabbed Nash's hand and dragged him through the crowd. Kairns and Bartlett, beer glasses in hand, stood toe to toe in animated discussion. Sands watched them with tolerant amusement.

"Our man has arrived," Margot announced.

Garrett smiled broadly and slapped Nash on the back, none too gently. "Well done, my boy! I always knew you could do it."

"Same goes for me," Kairns declared, pumping Nash's hand. "I'm still getting over my shock that we managed to win five seats. It doesn't seem real."

"I know the feeling," Nash said, somewhat overwhelmed by the genuine warmth of his reception. "I couldn't have done it without you guys."

"Your idea to lobby university students nothing short of brilliant."

Adam Gatt pushed through the crowd. "Good work, buddy."

Nash shook hands and they embraced.

Margot raised her arms. "Quiet, everybody! Quiet! Let's hear it for Senator-elect, Nash Bannon!"

Wild cheering broke out amid congratulatory whistles. When the clapping stopped, Nash smiled at them.

"Your tireless efforts pounding the streets handing out fliers, standing at my side at rallies, helped me make it. I owe it all to you and Margi. Without her patient tutoring and guidance, I would not be here tonight."

Everyone clapped and Margot blushed.

"I also want to thank Warren and Curtis, whose behind the scenes work helped all of us get elected. I would like to know how they did it, but I was told better not to know."

This generated lusty laughter and several coarse remarks, all taken in good humor.

"When Garrett hijacked me to run, he told me I would regret it. I never have, but there were moments during the campaign where I would have gladly punched out his lights."

Catcalls and jeers for the lawyer, who shrugged and raised his glass.

"On a serious note, I want to thank my fiancé, who suffered grievously because she chose to stand by me." Nash turned, took Cariana's hands and brought them to his lips. Her eyes glittered with emotion. On impulse, he gathered her in his arms and kissed her.

Everyone cheered and hooted support.

"Love you," he whispered. She smiled and sniffed.

"I'm glad I got you before Margi could sink her claws into you. I heard about aggressive lifeliner women."

Kairns tapped Nash on the shoulder and shoved a tumbler into his hand. "You can have him later, Dr. Lambert. Right now, he's ours."

"How's the old body, Warren?" Nash demanded.

Kairns patted his stomach. "Almost back to normal, but I've got to watch my alcohol intake. Irritates the insides, so I'm told." He turned and dropped his arm across the shoulders of a tall, youthful looking man wearing navy blue slacks and dark green shirt. "By the way, I want you to meet Chad Everett, our Victorian state member. Wilson, our other member, couldn't make it tonight. Bastard."

"I heard a lot about you, Chad," Nash said as they shook hands. "It's a pleasure to meet you."

"You have made somewhat of a name for yourself, Nash," Everett said with a faint smile and nodded to Cariana. "Dr. Lambert…"

"What are your immediate plans, Nash?" Garrett asked over the rim of his glass.

"Getting married next weekend is job one."

Garrett laughed. "Take it from me, you'll never regret it."

"Unlike my campaign?"

"You said that you didn't regret it."

"I'm a politician. I lied."

Garrett snorted.

"Just kidding. My dad is looking forward to meeting Warren and Curtis at the reception."

Hearing his name, Kairns turned. "What are you two conspiring?"

"Talking about Nash's wedding, you old fool," Garrett retorted.

"Never mind that. See me on Monday, Nash, and we'll talk about getting you settled into the Senate. I know a few people in Parliamentary Services. They'll set you up with an office and everything you need when you get there. We'll provide the staff. You'll get an email telling you when to report for orientation, probably late in April. If this were a normal election, you wouldn't have to take up your seat until July 1."

"I have read up on what to expect, but a lot of it is confusing," Nash admitted and took a sip from his tumbler.

"They give you the *Pocket Guide to Senate Procedures* and the *Standing Orders* booklet, and you are on your own. It can be tough for a new parliamentarian, but I'll clue you in on everything you need to know."

"That would be appreciated."

"Stop talking politics, you two," Sands admonished. "We're supposed to be celebrating."

"We are," Kairns retorted, "but the world keeps turning and we got to turn with it or get left behind."

Sands glanced at Nash. "You heard about Sutton?"

"That he disappeared? I heard."

"Never showed up for his pre-trial hearing. There is a warrant out for him, but he seems to have dropped off the planet. He could have been given a new communications interface module for his PID. It's a favorite gambit by the intelligence community when they want to give someone a new identity."

"You think he was behind the lifeliner attacks?"

"It has his organizational signature."

"Who's talking politics now?" Kairns demanded. "Mingle, Nash. It will please the youngsters."

Nash took Cariana's hand and smiled. "The man said mingle. So, let's mingle."

* * *

"I do," Cariana said, her voice crisp and firm, eyes radiant with joy.

The civil celebrant smiled benignly. "I now pronounce you man and wife. You may kiss the bride."

Her arms went around his neck and held him tight. Heart beating a little faster than normal, he kissed her tenderly and, after a timeless moment, pulled back, immensely content.

His best man whistled approval and Natalie clapped enthusiastically. His mom beamed at him, sniffed and dabbed at her moist eyes. Everybody cheered and clapped, and Nash ducked as a rain of rice fell around him. Aleya gave him a thumbs up. He picked her up and squeezed until she cried out in protest, her small fists beating against his chest. Their official videographer started making noises to get the formal shots out of the way.

Cariana at his side, gorgeous in her white gown and small tiara of white carnations, Nash had a protective arm around her waist. The look of glowing happiness she gave him filled him with quiet satisfaction. They would make this work, no matter what.

Towering trees in the Treasury Gardens provided welcomed shade, although not overly hot. Nothing stirred, not even the birds, and the hum of traffic hardly noticeable. Some of the guests started to drift away for the reception and an early start on snacks and drinks.

It all seemed to have happened such a long time ago, not just days.

Hands clasped behind his head, Nash tried to make out the ceiling hidden by the night's veil. Faint light seeping in from the street lingered around the heavy drapes. In the tranquil darkness, he replayed the wedding, the boisterous reception, their over-night stay at the Melbourne Airport Parkroyal hotel—no mis-chief as both were exhausted—the morning flight to Cairns and drive to a Port Douglas seashore resort.

Two lazy days walking along the beach hand in hand, swim-ming, snorkeling among the reefs, gentle and sometimes frenzied lovemaking—he was glad all his injuries had healed—and lying on white sands with the hiss of surf whispering in the back-ground, made an idyllic start to their honeymoon. They took a day trip to Atherton Tablelands waterfalls, followed by a 7.5 kil-ometer Skyrail ride over the Barron National Park rainforest to a sleepy little Kuranda village where they strolled through the sin-gle main street, pausing to peek into the many curio shops, totally oblivious to the throng of tourists around them.

They took a half-day trip to Green Island coral paradise by a fast catamaran ferry, where they found a secluded little beach empty of life and enjoyed a couple of hours of tranquility, pre-tending they were castaways. The ocean stretched to touch a sharp horizon where a bank of fluffy gray clouds climbed into a deep blue sky. Gentle waves lapped the hard, wet sand as they searched for shells and pieces of pumice. The fantasy ended and they had to board the ferry for the return trip.

Cariana was loving, passionate, carefree, full of laughter and glee, and she made him complete. They would wake in the middle of the night, hands exploring each other, saying nothing, content to be together as one. They talked softly, laying bare their secret thoughts, desires, fears, and hopes, avoiding current politics and social strife, not wishing to tarnish the enchanting days. Simply having her beside him, knowing she was totally his in the same way that he belonged to her, left him fulfilled in a way he did not believe possible. He wished their idyllic days of magic would never end, but they had to. Reality returned as they took a flight to Canberra where a new life awaited them. They may have left the tropical wonders behind, but it made them richer inside.

Cariana stirred, mumbled something and wrapped a protective arm around his chest, pressing closer against him. He stroked the silky smoothness of her shoulder and arm. Women did not have skin like men. They had something mysterious and compelling that begged to be caressed. Nash loved her cool, sensuous touch, which filled him with tenderness and the need to protect and cherish her, never letting go.

After a while, he closed his eyes.

When he woke, the drapes were pulled back and sunshine streamed into the room. He turned, smiled at Cariana, and kissed the tip of her nose.

"Good morning, Mrs. Bannon."

"My, aren't we formal today."

"Because it is a formal day. It's the day when your loving husband is sworn in as a federal senator."

"That might be, but if you don't want to miss getting sworn in, it might be an idea to get out of this bed."

"What time is it?"

"Just passed six."

"Mmm. I'd rather stay in bed."

"So would I, but you're an important man now and cannot do what you want anymore."

"In that case…" He swung out his legs and slid his feet into slippers. "A quick shower and the bathroom is yours, unless you need your back soaped?"

"You've been soaping it enough…and other things." She smiled wickedly and waved him off. "Go! My flight isn't until ten, which means I can stay in bed a little longer."

"Not fair. I cannot talk you into staying for the opening ceremony?"

"You have to attend. I don't. Besides, it's boring."

"You're right, it will be boring, but seeing you in the public gallery would make it less boring."

"We talked about this already, Nash. You'll be busy with your party colleagues and I'll be twiddling my thumbs. I have work of my own, you know, and there is Aleya. Anyway, you'll be home on Friday."

Nash sighed. "With four lonely nights in between." He gave her a hopeful look. "Last chance."

She threw a pillow at him.

He did not mind that she was going back to Melbourne, although it would have been nice having her with him. He consoled himself that they would have the whole of April together. Her transfer from The Alfred to ANU done, and Aleya enrolled with the Instram Institute, Nash had laid down a holding deposit on a two-bedroom apartment in Acton, virtually a three-minute drive or leisurely walk to ANU. His would be a slightly longer drive across the Molonglo River to Capital Hill, but not much longer. He initially considered leasing two cars for their use while in Canberra, but after doing the math, it was cheaper to buy new ones outright. Not a question of money, he could afford to lease, but simple economics. Why throw away good money when he did not have to.

At eight, not wanting to leave Cariana after a week of enchanting ecstasy, he hugged her tight and said goodbye. She put on a brave face, but he could see she fought to control her emotions. After being inseparable for a week, it was hard to walk away. He had to clear his own throat a couple of times as he took the elevator to the lobby.

She is not a captive bird, old son.

No, she wasn't, he told himself. They might be married and living together, but they were still two individuals with goals to pursue and a need to soar free. A sure way to drive his marriage against rocks was to become possessive.

Outside, the autonomous cab waited.

When he and Cariana flew in yesterday afternoon, they did not have much time to play tourist. Once they settled in, she told him, and she was right. There would be plenty of time to explore this city. Looking at the surrounds as the cab headed for Parliament House, Canberra a contrast to Melbourne's skyscrapers and suburban sprawl. The Capital Territory had developed fast, but the city planners made sure the small suburbs retained an open countryside feel. Designed from ground up, they had not wasted a singular opportunity to get it right.

The cab took the inside run of Parliament Drive and dropped him off at the Senate side of the building. Nash spent a moment gazing at the imposing stone structure that symbolized Australia. The white colonnades loomed huge, protecting a cathedral-like entrance. Visitors sprinkled the immaculately kept grounds, taping everything in sight with smart tablets and phones. Nash turned and gazed at Canberra spread before him.

As he stood there, a shiver ran through him. A shiver of excitement and a touch of doubt. Now that he was actually here, he was not certain he could discharge his responsibilities. Kairns had briefed him in detail how to navigate through the tortuous Senate and House procedures, the tactics and deals ministers would employ to push through legislation, the acerbic debates he could expect from adults who often behaved like spoiled brats. Nash did not have to have that part explained; he had seen enough of their antics during Question Time.

Just another program of work, old son.

He took a deep breath, strode into the spacious foyer, and headed for the senate members' suites, his footsteps echoing in the marble hall. The security system interrogated his PID at a portal and he was admitted entry. Senators and House members had their offices on the ground and first floor, depending on rank and seniority. As a new member, Nash was assigned a ground floor office, which he did not mind at all. He was here, that was all that mattered. With the building's layout memorized from the introductory material sent to him, he had no trouble reaching his hole-in-the-wall. Another security check and he was in.

He was surprised to find the plain office quite spacious, holding three modern workstations. A potted plant and a framed picture here and there would do wonders for it.

A young Asian man looked up from the large computer display on his desk and hastily rose. Not tall, in his late twenties, black hair trimmed back in severe military style, formal in suit and tie, he had the serious face of someone dedicated to his work.

"Senator Bannon? I am Tony Hong, your strategic and tactical advisor. You have two other staffers, but they won't be on board until the May sitting. We don't expect much to happen in the way of business this week anyway. Routine administration bills only. You have been tapped for several committees, but we'll go into that later."

Nash smiled and shook hands. "Glad to have you, Tony. Between the two of us, I will need all the advising I can get."

Tony nodded politely. "This is my first time in Canberra, sir, but I spent three years working for a NSW Liberal Party MP before joining the Lifeliner Party, and I have detailed understanding of all parliamentary procedures."

"Are you a lifeliner?"

"No, sir. I trust this will not prejudice my commitment."

"Not at all, Tony, and you don't have to call me 'sir', at least not in private. Do your job and see to it that I don't put my foot in it, and we'll get along."

"Works for me. Senator Reed requested that you see her at your convenience. Her office is on the left next to this one. Here, let me take your jacket. I'll leave it in your private office," he said, hooking a thumb at a door beside his desk.

"I thought this's all there is."

Tony managed a small smile. "No, sir."

"Any trouble here with protesters?"

"By the People First Party and the Humans Only League? I was told there was some, but the dobers kept them off the grounds."

Nash fronted at Reed's office and waited for security to clear his PID. Inside, a plump brunette, frizzed hair framing an attractive round face, stood and grinned, revealing a gap in her top teeth. Dressed in a maroon shirt and black slacks, she could not have been more than 155 centimeters tall.

"Senator Bannon, Mrs. Reed is expecting you. Please come in."

The office was identical to his own, needing a feminine touch to make it presentable. The young woman opened the door to the inner office and peered in.

"Senator Bannon is here."

"Don't just stand there, let him in," a strong voice ordered, and Nash suppressed a smile.

He read Tamara Reed's resume and followed her campaign closely. A seasoned Queensland politician, she had a record of intimidating those who stood in her way. He figured it must have been tough keeping her lifeliner identity secret, and she may have compensated by being somewhat abrasive. Sterilized at the hands of Sutton's men, he hoped the incident had not embittered her.

A tall woman, mature and sure of herself, her short hair extenuated a long face, and her small, dark eyes did not waver as they scrutinized him. He hoped they would not have to cross swords.

"I have looked forward to meeting you, Nash." Her handshake firm and dry. "Please, make yourself comfortable."

He pulled back a chair, sat down and crossed his legs. "Likewise, Tamara." He swept his eyes around the utilitarian office painted soft green. Apart from a steel cabinet, chairs, and her desk, the stark interior also needed decoration.

Reed noted his look and gave a small smile. "I know. It needs something, but I cannot do everything on my first day." She leaned forward. "How does it feel to be in Canberra?" she asked.

"I'm still coming to terms with the fact that I am actually a senator."

She gave a pleasant laugh. "I know how you feel. Believe me, the novelty will wear off quickly. It did with me when I first went into politics. It's a good thing Parliament isn't sitting in April. It will give all of us time to settle in. You will meet the other three party members before the opening ceremony, but once we're sworn in and the Senate rises, I'd like to have a short meeting. I think Atarah Readman is cooking something."

"Oh? What have you heard?"

"Last night, I ran into Holt Ryner, the Greens—"

"I know who he is."

Reed smiled. "I am sure you do. He said the government will be tabling the Superannuation amendment bill again."

"She used that as a trigger to call a double dissolution," Nash said. "What makes her think it will pass this time around? She doesn't have the numbers. Are the Greens going to support it?"

"Ryner said they won't. Not without several changes."

"So, why is the PM pushing it?"

"That, Senator Bannon, is the million-dollar question. Ryner said he tried to sound off a number of Labor and Coalition House members, but no one is saying anything. The meeting this afternoon is to work out our position should the bill pass the House."

"The only way it can pass the House is if the Greens support it, and you said Ryner won't do that."

Reed gave him a hard look. "It *can* pass if Labor has struck a deal with the government, which seems likely, or Readman would never table it, knowing it wouldn't get past the first reading. What's your position on the bill?"

"I think it has merit, and I was surprised when Labor knocked it back last October."

"That's how the rest of us feel as well. We'll see what happens tomorrow. I'll see you in the Senate chamber at ten, Nash. I hope that together, we can make a difference for lifeliners."

"We'll give it a good shot," he said and stood. "I'm glad we have someone with your experience at the helm, Tamara."

She chuckled. "Canberra isn't Queensland, but I appreciate your vote of confidence. We'll talk more this afternoon."

Around ten, Nash took the elevator to the first floor where he joined a throng of senators and House reps making for the Senate chamber. The reps gathered in a large group waiting to be summoned. Beside the doorway, Tamara Reed chatted with the other three Lifeliner Party members. She saw him and smiled.

"Nash! Glad you could join us. Let me introduce you to the others." She turned to the thin individual beside her. "Meet Frank Mercer, former Air Force wing commander and our ACT member. He shoots down anyone who gets in his sights."

Mercer chuckled and extended his hand. "Only those who piss me off," he said with a broad grin. "I did a character assassination on a superior officer, which landed me in politics."

Nash liked the man on sight, and suspected the team had a rebel in their midst. Then again, they were all rebels or they would not be here.

"Your campaign has left more than one burning body in your jet wash," he observed as they shook hands.

"We all had a few scrapes."

"Swap stories later," Reed said and turned to a slim woman whose penetrating gray eyes indicated that she had seen life in the raw. Being a reporter tended to do that.

"From South Australia, Paula McNeil, former ABC political journalist who had the bad habit of unearthing things others preferred buried."

Nash smiled warmly at the only non-lifeliner among them. "Welcome to this august gathering, Paula...I think."

She returned his smile. "Thanks, Nash. It's been a bumpy ride just to get here."

"I know what you mean."

"And lastly, Viola Spencer, Associate Professor of Civil Engineering at the University of Tasmania. We are lucky to have her."

Spencer's mahogany hair spilled in pleasing waves across narrow shoulders. She had a youthful face and deep green eyes that did not look away. Everything about her exuded drive and determination, which Nash figured summed up all of them.

"I am pleased to meet you, Viola."

"I look forward to working with you, Nash," she replied in a husky contralto.

Reed rubbed her hands. "Right. We better get inside."

Nash waited for the others to amble in. He stopped at the entrance and swept his eyes around the chamber. He saw holoview shots, but they did not prepare him for the emotional impact he felt. At the far end was the Senate president's dais and padded chair. In front of it was a table where the Clerk and Deputy Clerk presided over the business agenda and proceedings minutes. On the left were four rows of pew-like benches where government senators sat. On the right sat the Opposition. Facing them were the crossbench seats. Public gallery seating stood arrayed on three sides above the chamber.

The place buzzed with conversation. Old timers chatted amiably among themselves, while the freshly caught looked somewhat dazed. Nash sympathized. He noted the blood-red carpet and allowed himself a humorless grin. The color scheme might be appropriate, seeing what went on here.

Since 2008, the opening of a new parliament began with a Welcome to Country ceremony performed by a local Aboriginal group. In 2025 when Australia declared itself a republic on the death of Queen Elizabeth II three years earlier—nobody fancied having King Charles as their monarch—the Senate and the House of Representatives agreed to amend the standing orders and removed it. The electorate had grown weary catering to Aboriginal groups because they happened to occupy the country for the last fifty thousand years. Everyone was a citizen, whether Aboriginal, settler, or immigrant, and enjoyed equal standing. Of course, not everybody agreed with the decision to abolish the ceremonial and the acknowledgment it represented, but it was interesting that no one moved to have it reinstated.

At 10:30, the Chief Justice of the High Court took the Senate president's chair in his capacity as Deputy in absence of an elected president, and the Clerk read the Proclamation, instructing the Usher of the Black Rod, decked out in a black tux and a flared white cravat, to request the presence of all House reps in the chamber. With everybody gathered, the Clerk read out President Ngarra's authorization for the Chief Justice to declare the 4th parliament of the republic open. The House reps retired to their own chamber where they would be sworn in and a presiding Speaker elected from the government ranks.

With the Senate chamber a lot roomier after 160 House members had left, the Chief Justice administered the oath or affirmation to the 85 senators. When his turn came, Nash felt a prickle of exhilaration ripple down his back. He found the opening ceremonial anachronistic and boring, but it did provide a sense of history and stability. Nevertheless, when he made his affirmation and the Chief Justice congratulated him, he felt a wave of emotion at the realization that he now represented a significant block of Victorian voters, and was expected to stand up for their interests and concerns.

He took his seat and swept his eyes at government and Opposition members. For seasoned members, it was business as usual. Toe the party line and play the game, as Kairns remarked in his cynical way, giving lip service to the people who put them there. Nash made a solemn promise to himself not to ever forget the people who supported him, even if that meant going against Lifeliner Party policies.

Once all the members were sworn in, the government members elected the Senate President, who immediately suspended the session until 3:30, when President Ngarra would present the government's legislative agenda. With immediate business out of the way, everybody headed for the member's bar.

* * *

"We are totally and absolutely screwed!" Frank Mercer declared vehemently. "I'd give anything to get my hands on Readman right now, and I would do more than merely jam."

"You'll have to stand in line," Reed replied with a mirthless grin.

"There must be something we can do!" Viola Spencer said, looking imploringly at Reed, who shook her head in resignation.

"I'm afraid not. Between them, Labor and the Coalition have an absolute majority in both chambers, and can pass whatever legislation they want. Before we declared ourselves a republic, the Commonwealth Governor-General had to provide royal assent before a piece of legislation became law. Under the new Constitution, President Ngarra was relieved of that symbolic, but important, ceremonial."

Nash was still getting over his shock at how quickly everything had unraveled. Yesterday, he and his colleagues felt euphoric and optimistic, promising to exact toll from the government if Readman attempted to introduce legislation detrimental to lifeliners. This morning, he had an initial taste of Senate workings, voting on routine administrative bills that passed without amendment. Not the most exciting stuff usually shown in the holoview. The horrible news came after the chamber adjourned for lunch.

What nobody believed could happen, did happen. Labor had sided with the Coalition.

Normally, a minister who wants to introduce a portfolio bill provided written notice to the Clerk of the House for the bill to be listed in the Notice Paper for the next sitting. On the following day, the minister introduces the bill, known as the first reading, and the bill is made available to both chambers and the general public. The minister then usually moves a motion to read the bill a second time, where he explains the purpose, general principles, and effect of the bill. Procedure then called for the bill to be debated, where members discussed the substance of the bill clause by clause, whether it should be accepted, opposed, or changed.

With the Superannuation amendment bill, despite objections from the Greens, Labor and Coalition members moved a motion to bypass the debate and second reading, and passed the bill unopposed. What made the bill so hideous was the attached rider. With a few changes to make it relevant to the Australian political landscape, it was the American Lifeliner Act in its original despicable form. Mandatory registration of lifeliners, PID tagging, storing DNA records, franchise right revoked, forced sterilization, and job dismissal without appeal, were some of its more onerous clauses.

"This can't be happening," Viola Spencer groaned, chocking back a sob. "There *must* be something we can do."

"Very little," Reed said softly. "When the bill comes before the Senate, the government Whip will move a motion to suspend standing orders. If Labor supports the motion, there won't be any debate and the bill will be passed without a call for a division. If it passes the Senate, it will become law with immediate effect."

"That's why Labor opposed the Superannuation bill last October," Nash snarled savagely. "Gardner cooked a deal with Readman. When Labor failed to pass the bill a second time, it gave her a double dissolution trigger."

Mercer spread his arms. "I don't get it. If Labor and the Coalition wanted to pass this bill, they already had the numbers. Why call an election?"

Nash gave him a humorless smile. "Simple. Gardner wanted a shot at becoming the Prime Minister or no deal."

"I hate to say it, but I think Nash is right," Reed said.

"If this bill becomes law, we'll lose our seats," Mercer added, looking glum. "Except for you, Paula. You're not a lifeliner."

"Aren't bills supposed to be scrutinized by various committees before proceeding to the second and third reading?" McNeil demanded.

"Not if the government suspends standing orders," Nash told her. "This doesn't happen often, as the Opposition of the day rarely sides with the government."

"Then we *are* screwed, as Frank said."

"Perhaps not," Nash mused.

"I think I know what you have in mind, but go ahead and tell us," Reed prompted.

"When the bill passes, we petition President Ngarra to dismiss the government. Section 64 of the Constitution gives him that authority. He can dismiss individual ministers, including the Prime Minister, when he or she has lost the confidence of the Parliament or acted unlawfully, which is certainly the case here."

"Individual ministers, but not the whole government, and Readman has not lost the confidence of the Parliament," Reed pointed out.

Nash shrugged. "It is open to interpretation, I agree, but if the President is prepared to act, public pressure will force her to yield. The question, of course, will he act or watch our country sink into darkness?"

"The last time government faced dismissal happened was in 1975 when Governor-General Sir John Kerr colluded with the Liberal Party to boot out Gough Whitlam," Reed said. "Ngarra is a Rhodes Scholar with a PhD in astrophysics, and nobody's fool, but he serves at the pleasure of the Prime Minister. All she needs is a majority vote in both Houses and he's gone."

"Then she missed a bet by not replacing him with a puppet before calling a double dissolution," Nash retorted. "His position may be ceremonial, but his reserve powers derive from the Constitution and a very real."

"If he is prepared to use them," Reed said.

"The Superannuation bill rider is not just an attack on lifeliners," Nash shot back. "It is an attack against the very institutions that underpin our social fabric. If we allow the government to pull this off, we'll have a virtual autocracy."

"Somewhat extreme, but I agree," Mercer declared. "What's more, I think the Greens and most of the crossbench will support us. Not all, as some of them don't love lifeliners, you know."

"Readman probably anticipated that we would make this move," Spencer said.

"So what?" Mercer snapped. "Short of arresting us, she cannot stop us from seeing the President."

"Why not make an appeal to the High Court?" Spencer pushed further, looking at each of them in turn.

"We will, and the Court will more than likely strike down the Act, but it takes time for them to deliberate and make a ruling," McNeil said. "In the meantime, we'll have chaos on the streets."

"Readman must have known the Court would reverse her before she concocted this deal with Labor," Nash reflected. "Which means she doesn't care."

"She is prepared to ignore the Court," Spencer said in wonder. "What if the states follow suit and ignore *their* courts?"

"Our worst nightmares will come true," Nash declared, shuddering at the awful consequences. This couldn't be happening.

Spencer raised her hand. "Wait a minute. Even if the President dismisses the government, the Act is still law until the High Court strikes it down…if it strikes it down."

Nash gave her a hard stare. "If the President dismisses Readman, it will be a brave dober, business, or individual, who will take any action under it."

Reed lifted her arms. "We're shooting in the dark here. Let's wait and see what happens when the bill comes before the Senate. Some Labor senators may have a conscience and vote it down."

"You've been smoking pot, Tamara," Mercer growled, which generated several half-hearted chuckles.

"Labor won't vote it down," Nash declared. "If any of them had a conscience, this would have leaked during the campaign."

"Not if they kept the deal within a tight group in both parties," McNeil said.

"Hold it!" Reed commanded. "We can hash this into mush. I say, let's wait and see what happens before we get all worked up. We can't do much until then anyway."

Nash shook his head. "I disagree. I suggest you have a quiet talk with Holt Ryner and the other crossbench members and get their position."

Spencer nodded. "He's right. We have to know where they stand."

Reed nodded. "Okay, I'll talk to him. If necessary, we'll do this alone."

"What the government is doing violates a number of treaties to which Australia is a signatory," Spencer lamented.

"The United States and the European Union are also signatories," Mercer said. "That did not stop them from passing a discriminatory law."

"We'll pick this up later," Reed said. "Right now, you guys better return to the chamber."

In the corridor, Mercer pulled Nash back. "What do you make of all this?"

Nash stared hard at his colleague. "It's a bloody disaster. I would never have believed it possible that Labor and the Coalition were capable of something like this. I can accept it from the Conservatives, but I thought Gardner and Readman were more rational. They must hate us bad."

"I remember what Gibbs Gilmore said," Mercer mused. "*If governments everywhere don't take positive steps to address the lifeliner problem, people can expect social disintegration and widespread unrest as human beings are slowly taken over by these mutants.* I guess our government has listened, but they'll get their social disintegration sooner than expected."

Nash stopped in his tracks. "Gilmore won his seat by joining the Conservatives camp. His resignation from the Liberal Party when the Sutton scandal broke could have been clever misdirection."

Mercer chewed his lower lip. "You have a devious way of looking at things, Nash."

"I think it is time we all better start being devious, Frank."

"That would mean turning into one of them. I don't think I could stoop that low."

"We don't have to become like them. We have to sharpen our tactics."

When Reed joined them in the chamber, she leaned toward Nash and whispered, "I spoke to Ryner. He said to wait."

"That helps." Nash made a derisive snort.

Ah, rats!

When the sitting resumed, it was quick and brutal.

The Senate President called the chamber to order and the government Whip immediately moved a motion to suspend standing orders. The Coalition and Labor majority passed the motion despite calls of protest from the crossbench. The Whip then introduced the bill amending the Superannuation Act and moved that it be passed without debate or change. In a last ditch effort to refer the bill to the Scrutiny of Bills Committee, Reed called for a division, supported by Ryner and two other crossbench members. This was voted down and the bill went through amid protests of outrage from Holt Ryner and Tamara Reed.

Senators were able to make a submission to the Senate president for an urgency motion on matters of public importance. However, the lodgment must be made no later than 12:30 pm on the sitting day. The government neatly sidestepped that provision by passing the Superannuation bill in the House at 12:00 when the Senate adjourned for lunch.

The Senate president banged his gavel, suspending the day's proceedings, and that was that. Looking pleased with themselves as they filed out, several Labor and Coalition members cast smirks of satisfaction at the Lifeliner Party seats.

As he watched them go, Nash realized that under strict interpretation of the Act, apart from Paula McNeil, he was no longer a senator. The Lifeliner Party stood decimated, the campaign against it planned, organized, and executed with masterly craftsmanship. Nothing stood in Readman's way now, except a questionable public conscience.

One day, that was all it took to bring parliamentary democracy to its knees. He slowly turned and gazed deep into Reed's dark eyes, reflecting his own helplessness and despair. He could clearly picture rioting, open conflict between lifeliners and normals, a breakdown of civil order, even martial law. It made for a grim scenario. Unless, of course, the ordinary person on the street simply took it in stride and didn't say anything, accepting the inevitable. Serves the lifeliners right, he might say. They were the cause of all his problems and the government had finally acted decisively to protect the welfare of its citizens.

Readman and Gardner must have considered the impact of the Act before ramming it through. They probably figured that any initial social disruption would blow over and they could gradually clamp down even more.

Social inertia and public apathy a high hurdle to overcome.

He and Mark had a lot to discuss this evening over dinner.

Reed touched his shoulder and gathered the others with a glance. "Let's talk to Ryner. Security could eject us at any moment."

When they fronted up at the Greens leader's office, his secretary told them that Ryner and most of the crossbench were in the common meeting room.

It could have been any tastefully furnished boardroom. A long polished table, high-backed wooden chairs with leather seats, beige carpet, and walls without extraneous decorations. Nash nodded to the Greens leader. Of middle height, going on the heavy side, he nevertheless projected power and determination. In Canberra's cauldron, you cooked your opponent or got cooked. There was no middle ground. Only four Greens members were present, and six of the ten independent crossbench. Nash glanced at Mercer, who shrugged. Abhorrent legislation or not, some members were not shedding any tears for lifeliners.

"Ah, Senator Reed! I expected you'd show up," Ryner gushed as he strode toward Tamara to shake her hand. "You know everybody here," he said, making it a statement, aware of her eidetic memory.

"I wish it were under different circumstances, Holt," Reed

said and nodded to the others in the room.

"So do I, Tamara. So do I. Not everybody is here, for which I apologize, but—"

"No need for explanations. I understand perfectly. You've had more experience dealing with problematic legislation. What action do you have in mind?"

"Same as yours. The first thing we need to do is make a submission to the High Court to strike down the rider part of the Act, but as you pointed out, there is a real possibility the Prime Minister might ignore the ruling, and I concur with your assessment. To prevent that from happening, we petition President Ngarra to dismiss the government under Section 64."

"How do we see him?" Nash demanded.

"I'll ring his Chief of Staff and arrange an audience. Under strict precedence, he is obliged to see any member of Parliament, which you're not. Technically, you're no longer even citizens. It's only been a couple of hours, but the bill has already stirred up a lot of public reaction. People First Party and the Humans Only League are celebrating, but the media are vehemently critical of Readman and Gardner. Civil rights groups have vowed to challenge the legislation. I am sure the President will be watching his holoview and is bound to reflect on what he sees."

The door flew open and four uniformed Australian Federal Police officers barged in. The sergeant in charge paused as he consulted his PID, then strode toward Tamara Reed.

"Ma'am, I must ask you and your lifeliner colleagues to come with us."

Nash and Reed exchanged glances. Readman had not wasted any time getting rid of them.

She glared at the cop. "Are we under arrest?"

"No, ma'am, but you no longer have any official business in this building."

Ryner touched her arm. "Wait for us at the entrance. We'll pick you up at 3:40."

The cops escorted Nash and the others to the ground floor

and left them in the foyer, dazed by the speed of events. Viola Spencer looked imploringly at Reed, trying gamely to keep from crying. Tamara embraced her and spoke soothingly. Nash and Mercer looked at each other, seeing chaos.

Shortly before 4:00 pm, a convoy of four cars drove through the main gate of the Presidential Lodge. At six, President Ngarra made a national broadcast. Nash, his senate colleagues, Ryner and his Greens, with most of the crossbench, gathered at a local restaurant and watched the preliminary ABC commentary.

Chocolate brown rather than black, Ngarra had finely molded features, a departure from the normal flat nose, heavy lips, and prominent eyebrow ridge. His thick bush of white hair gave him an air of dignity. Dressed in a navy blue suit and yellow tie, he could have been an ordinary executive, but he was not ordinary at all, Nash reflected, remembering vividly the meeting with the elderly statesman. The man had dignity and charisma that hung on him like a cloak. Fifty thousand years of ancient culture were reflected in his penetrating black eyes. Nash had not been impressed by many men, but he felt awed and humbled to stand in this man's presence.

The President showed that he could be friendly and charming, and quickly put everybody at ease, dispensing with formality and protocol. He listened to Reed and Ryner without interruption, nodding several times as he considered their arguments. When the meeting ended, he said he would make a national address at six.

Marina Lennon, the ABC presenter, introduced the president and Nash found that his hands were sweaty. His life, the life of every lifeliner in the country, and the lives of ordinary people, for that matter, would be affected by what Ngarra said.

"My fellow Australians, it is a sad day that I must address you as President of this noble land, settled by my ancestors for thousands of years and, more recently, by people from all corners of the world. I have watched this country grow and its citizens prosper, seeing a bright future for themselves and their children. Not everyone has been fortunate enough to enjoy the fruits of this country's prosperity as technology took away jobs and closed industries. But we have coped with adversity before, natural and man-made, and rose up to take advantage of new opportunities. I trust that we shall overcome the march of unfeeling technology and pause to reflect on the impact our creative genius had on us.

"Regrettably, a shadow threatens to destroy what we have collectively achieved. It is a shadow of intolerance, bigotry, and racism. It is a failure to embrace those who are different from the rest of us into the collective family of man. I have suffered under such discrimination and intolerance. Many of you who settled here and do not share a white ancestry have also been subject to racial prejudice. Australia prides itself for being a progressive multicultural society, but in many ways, this is government conditioning which hides a darker disturbing truth. Their propaganda has recently been focused on a new and potentially wonderful segment of not only our society, but societies around the world. I am, of course, referring to lifeliners. Why do people hate them? Because they are different from the rest of us? We're all different. Mankind is an amalgamation of races and cultures, each unique, and all of them have contributed to what makes us human.

"Nature can sometimes be cruel to those who fail to meet the evolutionary challenge. We see those failures around us when species disappear, sometimes through man's thoughtlessness. It is a tragedy, but new life always emerges, better able to cope and thrive. That is now happening with the human race. Nature has decreed that the only way to survive the accelerating pace of our technology and intensely stressful modern lifestyle, a new type of human is needed. These new humans are lifeliners. It is an individual tragedy to find yourself sterile, but we cannot blame lifeliners for an act of nature. They did not choose to be born a lifeliner, in the same way I had no choice being born an Aboriginal. I had to grow up in a world that did not always accept me, my culture, and my people. Lifeliners are now subjected to the same intolerance. Unreasoning fear and prejudice is sweeping the world in an organized campaign of hatred against lifeliners and their children, who represent our future and survival as a species. Yet we are seeking to destroy them. We're seeking to destroy our very future.

"I have seen what hatred and bigotry has done to us. I have seen what the United States, the European Union, and repressive regimes around the world have done. The stripping away of our rights enacted by governments not done to protect us from lifeliners. This was merely a convenient screen to introduce authoritarian rule. Many of you have experienced the impact of these draconian laws, but you were reluctant to voice your protest, hoping they would not affect you. Today, the Coalition government, led by Prime Minister Atarah Readman, has taken an unprecedented step in its fight against lifeliners. The law passed earlier this afternoon has stripped away all rights and privileges from lifeliners, which the rest of us take for granted. This not only violates implicit human rights enshrined in our Constitution and treaties to which Australia is a signatory, it is a program of species cleansing.

"Everyone has the right to live with dignity and hold their head high, irrespective of who they are, and no government can be permitted to take that away. It is therefore with a heavy heart that I announce the dissolution of the Senate and the House of Representatives, and dismiss the Readman administration with immediate effect. I call for new elections be held on Saturday, April 17. Until then, I will be asking the opposition leader, the Honorable Macey Gardner, to form a caretaker government." Ngarra gave a faint smile and nodded. "Elect your representatives wisely. I wish you all good night and a brighter future."

His image slowly faded and returned to the studio desk. Somewhat shell-shocked, Marina Lennon smiled bravely. "Stay tuned for our special *The Beat* program where we will have a panel of political commentators—"

Nash did not care what *The Beat* had to say. He locked eyes with Tamara Reed and raised his arms, fists clenched.

"Yes!"

A smile lit her face as she stepped into his embrace and they hugged. The room broke into cheering and slapping of backs. When he untangled himself, he turned to Ryner and pumped his hand.

"Thank you, Senator. You came through for us."

"I did it for everybody," Ryner growled. "I wonder, though, how much real difference a new election will make. I hope Readman, Gardner, and the Coalition's rump get the chop, but the factional party machines are still there. Real change won't happen until rank and file members make themselves heard and remove the entrenched numbers men. Party branches are still run too much like private fiefdoms."

Nash was about to point out that the Greens ran an autocratic party, but refrained. He did not want to start a fight with someone who could be useful in the future.

"This is a start, Holt, and a wakeup call," Reed told him. "Neither party will be tempted to repeat what was done today. Why so gloomy?"

"Because, my dear Tamara, this has only won lifeliners a reprieve. Despite President Ngarra's stirring words calling for unity and understanding; bigotry, racism, and intolerance will continue. You cannot change human nature by striking down illegal legislation."

"Perhaps not, but you can do it through education to stem the tide of apathy, and a willingness by individuals on the street to stand up to intimidation," Reed insisted. "If those who care remain silent, then we have already walked through the gates of chaos, and I refuse to believe that. People out there *do* care; otherwise, I and my colleagues would not have been elected."

"All I'm saying, Senator, the war is far from over."

"It might not be over, but we have shown that it can be won," Tamara said and gave him a lopsided grin. "And it's ex-senator."

Ryner laughed, appreciating the joke.

* * *

Aleya leaned against the steel railing and threw pebbles into the wall of water tumbling eight meters into a rugged gorge below. A mist of fine spray hung above the rocks where the fall dashed itself with a muted roar. Tall trees bordered the gorge, providing cool relief from the sun, and filled the air with an intoxicating eucalyptus smell.

Nash could hear children scampering around the small picnic grounds, yelling as they played their games. A young couple, hand in hand, strolled past him heading down a gravel path to the foot of the fall. In the deep pool beyond the crashing water, swimmers enjoyed a refreshing dip.

He breathed deeply of the scented air mixed with smells of cooking from several barbecues, and turned to Cariana. Her golden hair fluttered in the breeze thrown up by the waterfall. She looked at him and her cheek dimpled as she smiled a small, secretive smile.

"Okay, we're alone now," Nash said. "What's the big secret? I know you're hiding something from me. You've been wearing that smug look all day."

"I got my tests…and everything looks good."

The radiant glow that lit her face flooded him with warmth and relief. He knew she secretly fretted that stem cell therapy would fail, but her bubbling joy made her look like a teenager. He gathered her in his arms and held her for several seconds, saying nothing. When he pulled back, he swept a lock of hair that strayed across her cheek.

"I'm happy for you, my sweet. I really am, but you could have told me this last night."

"You were campaigning and got back late. When we were in bed, I felt you wanted to unwind and not think about anything."

She was right. It had been a tough day. A very short campaign, Margot had his schedule packed from morning to night, sometimes with evening chat shows and local hall rallies. He thought he had it tough the first time.

"I think your logic has a few holes in it."

She playfully slapped his shoulder. "Cube. You know what this means?"

"That we can have little terrors of our own?"

She searched his face. "You don't want to?"

He cupped her face between his hands. "As many as you can stand. We need to work up a solid lifeliner majority."

She laughed. "You're hopeless, did you know that?"

He arched his eyebrows. "Hopeless? For your information, lady, I was once a federal senator, albeit for only two days. Doesn't that count for anything?"

"It does, and you will be a senator again. Hopefully for more than just two days."

"If I can believe the polls, Labor and the Coalition parties, including the Conservatives, are facing a wipeout."

"Looks like it," Nash Agreed. "Readman holds her seat by a margin of fourteen percent, supposedly unassailable. Yet the swing away from her is already eleven percent. Polls don't always reflect true voter intent, but the numbers suggested that several of her ministers and shadow cabinet frontbenchers who managed to retain their endorsement, might be ousted."

Cariana frowned. "Gardner's safe Labor seat is looking equally shaky."

Nash cocked an eyebrow at her. "Taking an interest in politics these days?"

She smiled at him. "Keeping an eye on how my man is doing. Seriously, though. It can be fascinating in a grim sort of way."

"It's grim, all right. A significant number of sitting politicians on both sides were disendorsed by the rank and file, replaced by candidates I hope will be more progressive."

"If they get elected."

"There is that. Anyway, we'll find out next Saturday. The federal political landscape may be changing, but that doesn't mean that everybody suddenly likes lifeliners. Protest marches and attacks are still happening, but what Readman attempted to do with her radical legislation has alarmed voters."

"She certainly alarmed me."

"She violated the basic tenet that everyone deserved a fair go. People don't like being treated like brainless sheep."

Mindful of the upcoming November election, Premier Raines Latham appeared to have gotten the message as well. Yesterday morning, he tabled legislation to repeal the controversial PID interrogation act, denying the police power to link with someone's PID on a whim. In an unprecedented show of unity, the bill passed both houses without opposition. There were undoubtedly those who wanted to oppose the bill, but were smart enough to recognize which way the political wind was blowing. People would remember those who voted against the bill.

"Our political landscape is not the only one that's changing," she added.

"The U.S. Congress forcing President Elliott Mackay to rescind the Lifeliner Act?"

"That has to be good, no?"

"Definitely."

"According to holoview reports, the European Court of Justice appears ready to strike down the Citizenship Act."

"Only after threats of withdrawal from the European Union by Scandinavian countries, and massive rallies in Paris and Berlin."

"Is it possible that we're looking for gradual return to sanity?"

"I hope so, my sweet, but I'm not prepared to celebrate just yet. Still, the dark clouds of doom may be breaking up, if only a little."

"It's a start," she said softly.

He took Cariana's hand in his. "Care for a little walk?"

"I don't mind," she said and tugged at Aleya's hand. "Come on. We're going for a stroll."

"Down there?" She pointed at the pool below.

"Down there, and you can have a swim."
"Cool!"

About the Author

Stefan Vučak has written twenty-one novels, which include eight SF books in the Shadow Gods Saga. His *Cry of Eagles* won the coveted Readers' Favorite silver medal award, and his *All the Evils* was the prestigious Eric Hoffer contest finalist and Readers' Favorite silver medal winner. *Strike for Honor* won the gold medal.

Stefan leveraged a successful career in the Information Technology industry, which took him to the Middle East working on cellphone systems. Writing has been a road of discovery, helping him broaden his horizons. He also spends time as an editor and book reviewer. Stefan lives in Melbourne, Australia.

To learn more about Stefan, visit his:
Website: www.stefanvucak.com
Facebook: www.facebook.com/StefanVucakAuthor
Twitter: @stefanvucak

More Books by Stefan Vučak

https://www.stefanvucak.com/Books/

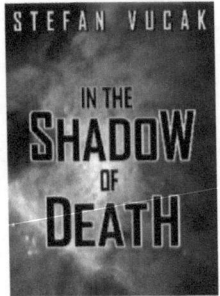
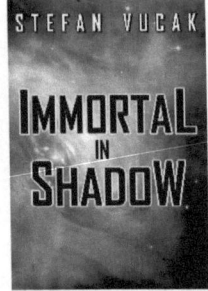